AMBUSH ON LUCAZEC

Luke started across the open ground toward the ruined ring dwelling at the foot of the highest of the enclosing hills. But he was not even halfway there when a scream froze him. He whirled, his cape sweeping outward, and a blaster bolt burned past him, so close that he could smell the heat.

He rolled away from the heat, came out of the roll with a forward flip that carried him five meters away from where he had stood, and ended the flip searching for his attacker, his lightsaber in his right hand. There were two men near Akanah, who was huddled on her knees with an arm raised as though she had just fended off a blow.

"Akanah!" he cried, and charged toward them.

The next blaster bolt was dead on target, but Luke deflected it neatly skyward with his lightsaber. . . .

The Sensational *Star Wars* Series published by
Bantam Books and available from all good bookshops

The *Empire* Trilogy by Timothy Zahn
**The Heir to the Empire • Dark Force Rising
The Last Command**

The *Jedi Academy* Trilogy by Kevin J. Anderson
**Jedi Search • Dark Apprentice
Champions of the Force**

The Truce at Bakura
by Kathy Tyers

The Courtship of Princess Leia
by Dave Wolverton

The *Corellian* Trilogy by Roger MacBride Allen
**Ambush at Corellia • Assault at Selonia
Showdown at Centerpoint**

The *Cantina* Trilogy edited by Kevin J. Anderson
**Tales from the Mos Eisley Cantina
Tales from Jabba's Palace • The Bounty Hunters***

Crystal Star
by Vonda McIntyre

The *X-Wing* Series by Michael Stackpole
Rogue Squadron • Wedge's Gamble*
The Krytos Trap* • Rogues Unbound*

Children of the Jedi
by Barbara Hambly

and in hardcover

The Illustrated Star Wars Universe
by Kevin J. Anderson & Ralph McQuarrie

Darksaber
by Kevin J. Anderson

* Forthcoming

The Black Fleet Crisis
Book One

♦

Before
the
Storm

♦

Michael P. Kube-McDowell

BANTAM BOOKS
NEW YORK TORONTO LONDON SYDNEY AUCKLAND

BEFORE THE STORM
A BANTAM BOOK : 0 553 50431 2

First publication in Great Britain

PRINTING HISTORY
Bantam edition published 1996

Condition of Sale

Bantam Books are published by Transworld Publishers Ltd,
61–63 Uxbridge Road, London W5 5SA,
in Australia by Transworld Publishers (Australia) Pty Ltd,
15–25 Helles Avenue, Moorebank, NSW 2170,
and in New Zealand by Transworld Publishers (NZ) Ltd,
3 William Pickering Drive, Albany, Auckland.

Printed and bound in Great Britain by
Cox & Wyman Ltd, Reading, Berkshire

In memory of my grandfather,
Dayton Percival Deich, 1896–1975,
who believed in a universe of wonders
beyond this Earth.

And for my children,
Matthew Tyndall, born 1983,
and Amanda Kathryn, born 1995.
May their lives be joyful journeys
through their own universe of wonders.

Author's Note

◆

Three people stand out above all others in deserving my gratitude and appreciation, though my poor words are hardly the equal of their gifts to me. Those three are Gwendolyn Zak, my best friend, SO, and POSSLQ, for her unwavering love, patience, support, and faith; Tom Dupree, my editor, for believing in me and giving me a chance; and Russ Galen, my agent, for going out on a limb and trusting me not to saw it off behind him. This book would not exist without them and their contributions.

I also want to thank Gwen, Matt, and Arlyn, for being such helpful ("Didn't you blow up this ship in the last chapter?") and encouraging ("All right—where's the rest of it? What? Go write more!") first readers. Sue Rostoni at Lucasfilm saw to it that I had all the references and resources I asked for, and then applied her extensive knowledge of the Star Wars universe to keep me from violating the historical record as often as I tried to. Fellow SW novelists Vonda McIntyre, Roger MacBride Allen, and Kevin J. Anderson generously shared their insights and their maps of the minefields. Also pitching in with SW trivia and general encouragement were Rich Mason, Timothy O'Brien, Matt Hart, Skip Shayotovich, and the rest of the Star Wars fan communities on GEnie and CompuServe.

The writing of *Before the Storm* bracketed a long-awaited move and the even longer-awaited birth of a daughter. Generous gifts of time and perspiration from Rod and Marion Zak, Tracy Holland, Greg Cronau, Arlyn Wilson, Mary Ellen Wessels, Faye Wessels, Mike Thelan, Roberta Kennedy, and other friends and family members allowed us to survive those transitions and me to keep working.

Finally, I'd like to thank George Lucas, for his blessing to tell this story in his wonderful universe—which I first visited nearly twenty years ago in a theater in Mishawaka, Indiana. If someone had told me then that someday I'd have a chance to add a few chapters to the life stories of Luke, Han, Leia, and their friends and enemies, I'd have just laughed.

As it is, I'm still smiling.

—*Michael P. Kube-McDowell*
September 12, 1995
Okemos, Michigan

Before the Storm

Prologue

♦

Eight months after the Battle of Endor

The Empire's orbiting repair yard at N'zoth, code-named Black 15, was of standard Imperial design, with nine great shipways arrayed in a square. On the morning of the retreat from N'zoth, all nine slips were occupied by Imperial warships.

Under most circumstances, nine Star Destroyers together would have been an intimidating sight to any who might come under their guns.

But on the morning of the retreat from N'zoth, only one of the nine was ready for space.

That was the sorry assessment of Jian Paret, commander of the Imperial garrison at N'zoth, as he looked out on the yards from his command center. The orders he had received hours ago were still playing before his eyes:

You are ordered to evacuate the planetary garrison to the last man, at best possible speed, using any and all ships that are spaceworthy. Destroy the repair yard and any and all remaining assets before withdrawing from the system.

Paret's assessment was shared by Nil Spaar, master of the Yevethan underground, as he rode the work shuttle up from the surface with the first commando team. The orders he had given hours ago were still ringing in his ears:

"Notify all teams that an Imperial evacuation has been ordered. Execute the primary plan without delay. It is our day for retribution. Our blood is in those vessels, and they will be ours. May each of us honor the name of the Yevetha today."

Nine ships.

Nine prizes.

The most badly damaged, *Redoubtable,* had taken terrible punishment in the retreat from Endor. The others ranged from old medium cruisers being upgraded and recommissioned, to the *EX-F,* a weapons and propulsion test bed built on a Dreadnaught hull.

The key to them all was the massive Star Destroyer *Intimidator,* moored at one of the open slips. Spaceworthy but completely unblooded, it had been sent to Black 15 from the Core for finish work, to free up a *Super*-class shipway at the command's home shipbuilding yard.

There was more than enough room aboard it for the garrison, and more than enough firepower aboard to destroy the yard and the hulls within. Paret transferred his command to the bridge of the *Intimidator* within an hour of receiving his orders.

But *Intimidator* could not leave the yard as quickly as Paret would have liked. He had only one-third of a standard crew aboard, a single watch—too few hands to quickly ready a ship of that size to fly free.

Moreover, nine of every ten workers on Black 15 were Yevetha. Paret despised the gaudy-faced skeletons. He would have liked to seal the ship in the interest of security, or to draft additional work details in the interest of speed. But either act would prematurely alert the Yevetha that the occupation force was leaving N'zoth, threatening the withdrawal from the surface.

All Paret would do was call a surprise departure drill and wait out its lengthy checks and countdowns, letting the normal work details continue until the troop transports and the governor's shuttle had lifted off and were en route. Then, and only then, could his crew close the hatches, cut the moorings, and turn its back on N'zoth.

Nil Spaar knew of Commander Paret's dilemma. He knew all that Paret knew, and much more. For more than five years he had worked to position allies of the underground throughout the conscript work-force. Nothing of importance happened without Nil Spaar's swiftly hearing of it. And he had taken the information he had collected and woven it into an elegant scheme.

He had put an end to the rash of minor "mistakes" and "accidents," demanding that those who worked for the Empire show diligence and strive for excellence—while learning everything they could about the ships and their operation. He had seen to it that the Yevetha made themselves indispensable to the Black Fleet's yard bosses and earned the trust of its commanders.

It was that trust which had allowed the work slow-down in the months since the Battle of Endor to go on unquestioned. It was that trust which had given his Yevetha the run of both the yard and the ships moored in the slips.

And it was the patient and calculating exploitation of that trust which had brought Nil Spaar and those who followed him to this moment.

He knew that he no longer need fear the *Harridan*, the *Victory*-class Star Destroyer that had been protecting the yard and patrolling the system. The *Harridan* had been ordered to the front three weeks ago, joining the Imperial force fighting a losing rear-guard action at Notak.

He knew that Paret could not seal the *Intimidator* against his men, even by ordering a battle-stations lockdown. More than a dozen external hatches in Sections 17 and 21 had been rigged by Yevetha technicians to report that they were secured when they were not, and to report that they were closed when they were not.

He knew that even if *Intimidator* got free of the slip in which it was moored, it would not have a chance to escape or turn its guns on the abandoned vessels. The packages of explosives concealed inside *Intimidator*'s hull would break it open like an egg the moment its shields went up and blocked the signal that was safing the bombs.

As the work shuttle neared the receiving dock, Nil Spaar felt no fear, no apprehension. Everything that could be done had been done, and there was a joyful inevitability about the fighting to come. He had no doubt what the outcome would be.

Nil Spaar and the first commando team entered *Intimidator* through the hatches in Section 17, while his second, Dar Bille, and the backup team entered through Section 21.

There was no talking. None was necessary. Every member of both teams knew the layout of the ship as well as any Imperial crewman. They moved through it like ghosts, down corridors closed or cleared by friends on work details, through crawlways and up access ladders that appeared on no construction blueprint. In minutes they had reached the bridge—without ever being challenged, or drawing a weapon, or firing a shot.

But they entered the bridge with weapons drawn, knowing exactly which stations would be occupied, where the guard station was, who could sound a shipwide alarm. Nil Spaar shouted out no warnings, made no theatrical announcement, demanded no surrender. He simply walked briskly across the deck toward the executive officer, raised his blaster, and burned the officer's face away.

As he did, the rest of the team fanned out behind him, each to his own assigned target. Six of *Intimidator*'s bridge crew were struck down in the first seconds, sitting at their stations, because of the power that rested at their fingertips. The others, including Commander Paret, quickly ended up facedown on the floor, hands bound behind them.

Taking the ship was not difficult. Timing the raid to avoid retribution had always been the challenge.

"Signal from the governor's shuttle," called out a Yevetha commando, slipping into the seat at the communications station. "The transports are leaving the surface. No trouble reported."

Nil Spaar nodded approvingly. "Acknowledge the signal. Advise the crew that we're moving out to pick up the garrison. Notify the yard that *Intimidator* is leaving."

Like a cluster of insects returning to the hive, the fleet of Imperial transports rose from N'zoth toward the great dagger-shaped Star Destroyer. More than twenty thousand citizens of the Empire were crammed into the insect fleet—soldiers and bureaucrats, technicians and families.

"Open all hangars," said Nil Spaar.

Their destination in sight, the transports slowed and began to align themselves on approach vectors.

"Activate all autotargeting batteries," said Nil Spaar.

There was a collective gasp from the prisoners on the bridge, who were watching the same display screens as the Yevetha commandos who now occupied their stations.

"You're all cowards," Commander Paret called out to the invaders, his voice bitter with contempt and anger. "A real soldier would never do this. There's no honor in killing the defenseless."

Nil Spaar ignored him. "Lock on targets."

"You vicious, pathetic fool. You've already won. How can you justify this?"

"Fire," said Nil Spaar.

The deck plates barely vibrated as the gun batteries erupted and the approaching transports disappeared in balls of fire and fragments. It did not take long. None escaped. Moments later the communications station began to scream with shocked and panicked inquiries from all over the ship. There had been many witnesses to the carnage.

Nil Spaar turned away from the tracking display and crossed the bridge to where Commander Paret lay on the decking. Grabbing the Imperial officer by the hair, he dragged Paret out of line and rolled him over roughly with his booted foot. Seizing the front of Paret's tunic with one hand, Nil Spaar lifted him half off the deck. For a long moment he loomed over the officer, looking like a tall, vengeful demon with his cold, black, widely set eyes, the white slash down his nasal ridge, and the deep scarlet-splashed ridges that furrowed his cheeks and chin.

Then, hissing, the Yevetha made a fist with his free hand and cocked it back. A sharp, curving dew-claw emerged from the swelling at his wrist.

"You are vermin," Nil Spaar said coldly, and slashed the claw across the Imperial captain's throat.

Nil Spaar held on through the commander's death throes, then dropped the body carelessly to the floor. Turning, he looked down into the pit at the commando who had taken over the communications station.

"Tell the crew that they are the prisoners of the Yevetha Protectorate and His Glory the viceroy," said Nil Spaar, wiping his claw on the trouser leg of his victim. "Tell them that beginning today, their lives depend on their being useful to us. And then I wish to speak to the viceroy, and tell him of our triumph."

Chapter 1

◆

Twelve years later

In the pristine silence of space, the Fifth Battle Group of the New Republic Defense Fleet blossomed over the planet Bessimir like a beautiful, deadly flower.

The formation of capital ships sprang into view with startling suddenness, trailing fire-white wakes of twisted space and bristling with weapons. Angular Star Destroyers guarded fat-hulled fleet carriers, while the assault cruisers, their mirror finishes gleaming, took the point.

A halo of smaller ships appeared at the same time. The fighters among them quickly deployed in a spherical defensive screen. As the Star Destroyers firmed up their formation, their flight decks quickly spawned scores of additional fighters.

At the same time, the carriers and cruisers began to disgorge the bombers, transports, and gunboats they had ferried to the battle. There was no reason to risk the loss of one fully loaded—a lesson the Republic had learned in pain. At Orinda, the commander of the fleet carrier *Endurance* had kept his pilots waiting in the launch bays, to protect the smaller craft from Imperial fire as long as possible. They were still there when *Endurance* took the brunt of a Super Star Destroyer attack and vanished in a ball of metal fire.

Before long more than two hundred warships, large and small, were bearing down on Bessimir and its twin moons. But the terrible, restless power of the armada could be heard and felt only by the ships' crews. The silence of the approach was broken only on the fleet comm channels, which had crackled to life in the first moments with encoded bursts of noise and cryptic ship-to-ship chatter.

At the center of the formation of great vessels was the flagship of the Fifth Battle Group, the fleet carrier *Intrepid*. She was so new from the yards at Hakassi that her corridors still reeked of sealing compound and cleaning solvent. Her huge realspace thruster engines still sang with the high-pitched squeal that the engine crews called "the baby's cry."

It would take more than a year for the mingled scents of the crew to displace the chemical smells from the first impressions of visitors. But after a hundred more hours under way, her engines' vibrations would drop two octaves, to the reassuring thrum of a seasoned thruster bank.

On *Intrepid*'s bridge, a tall Dornean in general's uniform paced along an arc of command stations equipped with large monitors. His eye-folds were swollen and fanned by an unconscious Dornean defensive reflex, and his leathery face was flushed purple by concern. Before the deployment was even a minute old, Etahn A'baht's first command had been bloodied.

The fleet tender *Ahazi* had overshot its jump, coming out of hyperspace too close to Bessimir and too late for its crew to recover from the error. Etahn A'baht watched the bright flare of light in the upper atmosphere from *Intrepid*'s forward viewstation, knowing that it meant six young men were dead.

But there was no time to linger over the loss. The monitors were flashing images from dozens of scanners on ships and spy satellites at a frenzied pace. Reports from the battle management section changed moment to moment, almost as quickly as the master battle clock counted up the tenths and hundredths.

The assault plan was too intricate and tightly scheduled for a few deaths to stop it. Battle management quickly assigned a reserve fleet tender to *Ahazi*'s section. *May your spirits fly to the zenith and your bodies rest peacefully in the depths,* General A'baht thought, recalling an old Dornean sailors' blessing for the dead. Then he turned away and studied the order of battle and tactical plan. There would be time to mourn later.

"Penetration phase complete," sang out a lieutenant at one of the consoles. "Deployment complete. Assault leader is approaching wave-off failsafe and requests final authorization."

"Penetration complete, copy," echoed A'baht. "Deployment complete, copy. All stations, call off."

"Battle management, go."

"Combat intelligence, go."

"Tactical, go."

"Communications, go."

"Fleet ops, go."

"Flight ops, go."

"Ground ops, go."

"I read the call board as clear," General A'baht said in a strong, confident voice. "Failsafe authorization is go, combat rules are green—repeat, go green."

"Authorization is go green, copy," acknowledged the lieutenant, turning a key on his console. "Assault leader, the word is go—you are clear to proceed. All weapons are live, and the target is hot."

Almost at once, a trio of assault cruisers and their complement of K-wing bombers broke away and surged ahead of the primary formation. Their new course would take them looping under the planet's south pole en route to their targets—the primary spacefighter base and planetary defense batteries located on the alpha moon, which was still over the horizon from the armada's jumppoint.

Pairs of speedy A-wing fighters flashed out of formation and fanned out to intercept and destroy the planet's lightly armed sensor and communications satellites. The A-wings fired the first shots of the assault on Bessimir, and did so with unerring accuracy, transforming their targets into sparkling clouds of metal and plasteel.

The A-wings also drew the first opposing fire. Several ion-cannon batteries on the surface opened up in a vain attempt to protect their high-orbiting eyes. Moments after the ground batteries revealed their location, gunners on the lead Republic assault cruisers had them targeted.

High-powered lasers on the cruisers painted the batteries, blinding ground sensors and testing for counterpunch fire from secondary sites. When there was none, the great pulse cannon mounted aboard the Star Destroyers methodically turned the ground batteries into smoking black craters. The only casualty for the Republic was an A-wing from Blackfire Flight, which picked up a sleeper mine on the right wing while making its pass against a recon satellite.

On the far side of Bessimir, the cruiser detachment approached the alpha moon on a high-speed collision course. As drone fighters appeared from concealed launch chutes on the surface, the big ships fanned out three abreast and began releasing clusters of penetration bombs.

Tall as a man and tipped by a reinforced spike, the black-cased bombs sped down toward the fighter base as the cruisers veered off. The drone fighters rising from the moon veered off as well. Moments later a dozen antiship batteries on the surface surrendered their camouflage, opening fire on the infalling bombs.

But the penetration bombs—propelled only by inertia, and with their casings as dark and nearly as cold as space itself—did not offer much of a target. Most fell through the defensive barrage unmolested. Two seconds before impact, small thrusters in the tail of each bomb fired, slamming them into the surface at even greater speed and driving them twice their length into the barren ground.

A moment later, with the dust of impact still rising, the bombs exploded as one. The flash and flame were swallowed by the moon's face. But the terrible concussion propagated downward and outward through the rock. It shattered reinforced walls like matchsticks, and collapsed underground chambers like eggshells. Great plumes of gray dust shot out of the launch chutes, and the ground itself subsided over what had been the main hangar.

At the moment the bombs exploded, Esege Tuketu was flying lead in an eighteen-ship formation following the cruisers toward the alpha moon. "Sweet mother of chaos," he breathed, awestruck by the sight. For just a moment, he took his hands off the controls of his K-wing and lowered his forehead against his crossed wrists—the Narvath gesture of surrender to the fire that consumes all.

From the second seat of Tuketu's bomber came an equally heartfelt and respectful "Wow!" voiced by his weapons technician. "And I don't care what they say," he added. "I felt that one."

"Seemed like I did, too, Skids," said Tuketu.

"No one had a better seat for it than we did, that's for sure."

They watched carefully ahead with eyes as well as passive scanners. No more fighters emerged from the hidden base. The antiship batteries were still.

But the drone fighters already launched fought on, even though deprived of their controllers. Following internal combat protocols, they flung themselves against the largest targets, the cruisers. Agile but lightly armed, the drones did not last long. The cruisers batted them down like so many insects.

"Good shooting!" Tuketu exclaimed. None of the other crews in the formation heard him. The attack force was following blackout protocols—including strict comm silence, despite the close formation and the critical timing of what lay ahead.

"This is going to work," the weapons tech said hopefully. "Isn't it?"

"It has to," said Tuketu, thinking about what lay ahead.

Only one real threat to the fleet remained—the great hypervelocity gun on the far side of the gravity-locked moon. Like a swift-footed sentry making its rounds, the alpha moon would soon revolve around Bessimir to a point where the HV gun would have its pick of targets in the fleet.

According to the New Republic's surveillance droids, the gun emplacement was both ray-shielded and particle-shielded. Moreover, with the weapon's power plants and shield generator buried deep in the rock, it could easily survive the sort of assault that had destroyed the fighter base. If Etahn A'baht's capital ships had to slug it out with the alpha moon's big gun, the Fifth Battle Group would surely lose several ships in the process. The key to avoiding that outcome lay with Tuketu's eighteen bombers.

"Coming up on the break," said Skids, glancing at the mission clock and then at the broken surface of the alpha moon, rushing toward them.

"I'm on top of it," said Tuketu.

"You'd better be," was the nervous reply. "My mama's counting on me doing more with my life than making a hole in the ground someplace where they already got enough holes in the ground."

"Break in ten," said Tuketu. "Signaling the others. Break in five." A collision alarm began to sound in the cockpit. The moon's surface seemed terribly close. "Break!"

The entire spaceship shuddered as the emergency deceleration thrusters roared and the nose of the K-wing swung up toward the horizon. Tuketu and Skids were slammed back into their flight couches as the moon rotated dizzily under them. Breathing came hard throughout the long moments of the pullout.

When the ship stopped shaking and it was possible to breathe again, Tuketu's ship was skimming the surface of the alpha moon with only two other bombers nestled in behind. The K-wings had scattered in six groups, each taking a different compass heading to the target. With luck, they would meet again over the aperture of the electromagnetic gun.

"Pardon me, but has anyone seen my wits?" Skids said in a squeaky voice. "I had them right here just a moment ago—"

Tuketu laughed. "That *was* fun, wasn't it?"

"Fun?" Skids shook his head. "Fun like having a rancor sit on your lap is fun. Sir, I am afraid I must relieve you of command, effective immediately, on the grounds that you are clearly insane. Please surrender the controls and come along quietly."

Smiling, Tuketu reached overhead and adjusted the trim thrusters. "We were a little late getting to the first ground check. I'm taking us up a couple of points. Check back there and make sure the others stay with us."

"Copy, Tuke," Skids said, twisting his head first to the left, then to the right. "By the jewel of Haarkan, you put that much ordnance on a K, and you get one mean-looking, chip-on-a-shoulder, fixing-for-trouble star kitty."

"Let's hope we don't need all of it," Tuketu said soberly, almost to himself.

According to reports Fleet Intelligence had provided to the Fifth's planners, Bessimir's hypervelocity gun fired at a rate of 120 slugs per minute, though rarely for more than ten seconds at a time. To avoid deflecting the superaccelerated projectiles, the particle shield protecting the gun was synchronized with the firing controller. The shield would open for each outbound slug when the gun was fired, while the ray shielding would remain in place throughout, protecting the emplacement from any long-range counterfire.

Open, close, open, close, like the winking eye of a shutter, like a tempting carnival game. Time the opening correctly and win the prize. That was why two of the three K-wings in each flight were configured as penetrators, carrying no energy weapons at all—just ordinary slug cannon and an extraordinary number of fléchette missiles. If even one round, one explosive splinter, could slip through and find its target—

But to have even that slim chance, they had to get very close—and something had to coax the gunners into firing.

That something was the New Republic Star Destroyer *Resolve*. Specially outfitted with multiple shields into which were poured the full power of her engines, she came out of hyperspace nearly dead center in the gun's field of fire. The K-wings were approaching the perimeter of the shield zone, hiding in the clutter, hugging every contour of the surface as they closed in.

A'baht watched nervously, his shoulder spines rippling. A few moments longer, and the approaching bombers would be spotted, the threat analyzed. "Fire," he whispered. "Come on—take the bait."

Esege Tuketu, watching his penetrators race toward the red line on his battle display, tensed himself for the high-G abort maneuver he expected them to have to execute.

A heartbeat stretched out to a lifetime.

On impulse, Tuketu thumbed his comm switch and broke comm silence. "Red Leader to Red Two, Red Three, stay on the tower, stay on it!"

"What are you doing?" Skids demanded.

Tuketu shook his head. "We have to get the game in before it rains."

Red Three suddenly broke right, away from its target, trying to escape the invisible wall that lay ahead. But Red Two flew past the wave-off point and opened fire. Streams of silver missiles flashed from under its wings toward the stubby shield tower in their sights.

"Sorry, Tuke, too late, going around," Red Three called.

At the same moment, the big gun roared, belching a staccato stream of slugs toward the *Resolve*.

Red Two broke left and up, its cannon tracking the shield tower and firing nonstop.

"Come on, come on, come on," Tuketu said under his breath. "Make a hole for us."

The leading edge of Red Two's salvo reached the shield boundary as the gun was still firing. Most shattered without exploding, crushed like insects hurled against a cockpit canopy. A few exploded against nothingness, their triggers overwhelmed by a surging induction current as the particle shield cycled on and off. But two fléchette missiles slipped through. The hemispheric dome of the shield tower disappeared in a small but brilliant explosion that left the metal remnants burning.

"How did you know?" Skids said wonderingly.

Tuketu shook his head. "I didn't," he said, pushing the throttles forward. Ahead lay the aperture of the big gun.

Like a frantic animal fighting for its life, the hypergun fired on the *Resolve* without pause from the moment the particle shield vanished. The big cruiser wasn't nimble enough to evade the barrage pattern thrown at it from the alpha moon, and Commander Syub Snunb wondered if it was tough enough to withstand the hits it was taking. Shells crashed against its invisible shields with such force that the ship itself shuddered and shook.

"Red Flight is inside the perimeter," a lieutenant sang out.

Steadying himself against a bulkhead, Snunb acknowledged the report with a nod. "Then we've done our job. Keep tracking the incoming fire," he said. "Navigator, turn and show them our heels. Keep us on an escape heading. If they give us any kind of break at all, drop the auxiliary shields and jump us out of here."

"Yes, Commander."

Just then the outermost shield buckled under a salvo of shells, the impacts sucking the field strength from the protective bubble faster than the shield generators could restore it. An alarm sounded on the bridge as the shaking abruptly got worse.

"The D shield is down. The generators are slagged!"

Snunb shook his head. "I must remember to tell General A'baht that I do not much like being the bait tied outside the predator's lair. How much longer?"

His first officer pointed to the tactical display. "Tuketu should be over the target in another few seconds."

Another alarm sounded on the bridge of the *Resolve*. "I hope we have another few seconds to give him."

The aperture of the hypergun was glowing brilliantly in the infrared on Tuketu's targeting computer. "Let's finish this on the first pass."

"Arming Number One," Skids sang out. "Arming Number Two. Taking attitude control, now."

Tuketu lifted his hands from the stick and throttle. "All yours."

The nose of the K-wing lifted skyward, and the bomber began to climb. "Range—mark. Number One away. Number Two away. Let's not hang around, Tuke."

As the lob bombs began to trace a clean, elegant ballistic arc, up and over the top of a gravitational hill, Tuketu hauled the nose of the bomber back and around to the left so sharply that he felt momentarily dizzy. While the broad bottom of the ship was facing the target, there was a dull roaring sound, a brilliant flash that cast long shadows on the surface, and a neck-snapping vertical translation, as though some mighty hand had shoved the K-wing from below.

"Too soon, too soon!" Skids cried in alarm. "Not ours."

At that moment Black One flashed by overhead, and the comm speaker crackled to life with gleeful exultations. "Scratch one big gun," drawled Black Leader. "My stars, that was a big splash. She was still firin' when we bracketed her—we must have jammed up a couple of shells in the barrel. Did you see it, Red Leader?"

"Negative, Black Leader." The landscape lit up again with a double flash that was a pale echo of the first. "Sounds like you didn't leave much for us, Hodo," Tuketu said with a grin.

"That'll teach you not to dawdle—sir."

"This is Green Leader," said a new voice. "I've made a verification pass and I confirm target destroyed."

"This is the *Resolve*. We concur with Green Leader, target destroyed. Thank you, boys."

"Copy, Green Leader. Copy, *Resolve*," said Tuketu, turning his ship skyward, toward where the cruisers waited for them. "All ships, form up with me. We have a rendezvous to keep."

Standing at a podium and wearing the uniform of the Joint Defense Operations Staff rather than the Mon Calamari battle dress in which he had earned his fame, Admiral Ackbar gestured with a large hand toward the display screen on his right.

"With the Fleet firmly in control of local space, it is now relatively safe for the gunships to begin opening a corridor to the surface," Ackbar said, looking out at the small, select audience. "The tactics echo those used against the hypergun—to expose well-armored vessels to enemy fire in order to locate and destroy the defensive emplacements in the target sector. In this case, as you can see, the counterfire is coming from the heavy batteries of the vessels in orbit."

The monitors in the conference hall at the New Republic Defense Force's headquarters on Coruscant showed much the same images as those on *Intrepid*'s bridge, though lagging some seconds behind.

The signals were being relayed across fifteen parsecs by hyperspace transponder, then reviewed by military censors to make sure that what appeared on the displays was appropriate to the clearances of the audience in the hall. That afternoon, little censorship was needed. The audience included all eight members of the Senate's Council on the Common Defense, half a dozen senior Fleet officers, and Princess Leia Organa Solo, president of the Senate and commander-in-chief of the New Republic's defense forces.

Ackbar went on, "The curvature of a planetary body limits the effectiveness of fixed emplacements with line-of-sight weapons. Destruction of only a few such emplacements creates a breach in the planetary defenses, and a corridor from space to the surface. You see here that the Fleet is close to opening such a corridor. The threat at this point would be from atmospheric fighters or ground-to-air missiles launched from over the horizon. But Bessimir has no such defenses. When the breach is fully opened, the invasion will begin."

"Admiral Ackbar—a question," Senator Tolik Yar called out. "How realistic a test is this for the Fleet? Is this anything more than a scripted performance?"

"It is as realistic as possible," said Ackbar. "This is an operational readiness exercise, not a simulation. It is true that the Fleet is opposed only by battle drones and computer sims. But I can assure you that the defense team takes pride and pleasure in constructing a difficult problem for the Fleet tacticians."

"Admiral Ackbar," said Senator Cion Marook, rising from his seat and allowing the great, heavily veined air sacs on his back to fully inflate. "This has been a most impressive demonstration so far. But on behalf of my colleagues, and those we represent, I must wonder why command of the new task force was given to such a newcomer."

"Senator, General Etahn A'baht is hardly a hatchling—he is easily twice my age, and I suspect he is senior to you as well."

Marook bristled. "I did not say he was young, Senator, I said he was a newcomer. The commanders of the other fleets are all veterans of the Rebellion—

leaders who, like yourself, earned honor in the great battles at Yavin, Hoth, and Endor."

Ackbar acknowledged the compliment with a nod.

"But this Dornean has worn our uniform for less than two standard years. The Fifth Fleet was authorized in no small part on your personal testimony and assurances, and built at great expense to the New Republic. I would be much happier if it were you on the bridge of the *Intrepid* and General A'baht were here waving a pointer in front of us."

"But you ought not be, Senator," Ackbar said sharply. "Though it was not part of the Rebel Alliance, Dornea has its own heroes from the fight against the Empire. General A'baht has a long and exemplary record as a fleet commander with the Dornean Navy. We are fortunate to be able to call upon his services."

"The entire Dornean Navy numbers barely eighty vessels," Senator Marook said with a grand gesture of contempt.

Standing by the back wall of the conference room, Princess Leia rolled her eyes and shook her head. It was wholly predictable that the complainant was Marook. Hrasskis society was built around a strict notion of succession by seniority, and the highest social value was waiting one's turn. After five years in the Senate, he still had not embraced the notion of basing appointments on merit.

"And yet, the Dornean Navy successfully defended Dornea's independence throughout the reign of Palpatine, against Imperial forces several times as large," said Princess Leia, intervening in the hope of cutting the argument short. "Come now, Senator Marook—surely this is an inappropriate time to argue over command assignments. Let's move on."

Admiral Ackbar held up his broad hand. "Princess Leia, if you please—there is no better time to put this to rest. I have heard rumors of discontent in the Council for weeks, but this is the first time anyone has voiced such sentiments in my hearing. I would like the chance to explain to Senator Marook exactly why he is so terribly wrong."

Even offered in his measured tones, such a direct rebuke was out of character for Admiral Ackbar, and told Leia how angry her Calamari friend was. "Very well, Admiral," she said, nodding and settling into a seat to listen.

Given the floor, Ackbar proceeded to ignore Senator Marook completely, addressing himself to the rest of the gathering. "You must understand that the problems of invading a planetary body from space, or defending one against an invasion, are quite different from the problems of destroying a planet, or blockading one, or laying siege to one."

Ackbar moved out from behind the podium. "And it is a set of problems with which we have had very little experience. The veterans of the Alliance, whom Senator Marook so kindly praised, know all the secrets of fighting as an insurgent force—the roles of stealth, of mobility, of hit-and-run tactics, of disrupting the enemy's lines of supply and communication.

"But a commando force cannot defend a homeworld, a system, a sector. A commando force cannot tie up its assets waiting to be attacked. A commando force cannot carry out an invasion. You should remind yourself that at no time in its history did the Alliance enjoy the resources to fight a conventional war. And the one time we were forced by circumstance to do so, at Hoth, we suffered a terrible defeat.

"That is why Etahn A'baht was selected to command the Fifth Fleet. He brings to that bridge all the hard-won expertise of the Dornea, an expertise which I cannot match. And it is his tactical plan which we are testing at Bessimir," Ackbar said, pointing at the screens behind him.

"Unlike my colleague from the Hrasskis, I do not question the qualifications of General A'baht. I am more concerned about the sharp end of the knife than I am with who wields it," said Senator Tig Peramis, rising from his seat near the door. "Admiral Ackbar, I have questions concerning the conditions of the test."

Leia's attention immediately perked up. Senator Peramis was the newest member of the Council on the Common Defense, representing the worlds of the Seventh Security Zone, including his own, Walalla. So far he had been a quiet member, diligently studying the Council records that his new level of clearance opened to his eyes, asking many thoughtful questions, and expressing few opinions.

"Proceed," said Admiral Ackbar, making a sweeping gesture.

"You chose to send the Fifth Fleet against a target which lacks a planetary shield. Why is that?"

"Senator, it is not possible to assault a planet which enjoys the protection of a planetary shield until that shield has been disabled. We would learn nothing about our new tactics from such an exercise. And there are far more worlds like Bessimir than there are worlds with the wealth and technology to sustain a planetwide shield."

"But, Admiral, did you not warn the Council that it was exactly those well-armed worlds which the New Republic lacked the capacity to confront? And did you not promise the Council that if we built the Fifth Fleet, even the strongest of the old Imperial worlds would not be able to threaten us with impunity?"

Ackbar nodded gravely. "I believe that we are keeping that promise, Senator Peramis. The defense of Bessimir was designed in accord with our existing threat profiles. Operation Hammerblow represents a likely scenario for the use of the Fifth Fleet."

"What, to overwhelm an underdefended world?"

"Senator, I did not say—"

"This is exactly the point that concerns me. An army fights as it trains," said Senator Peramis. "Did you build the Fifth Fleet to protect us against a strategic threat, or to strengthen Coruscant? Does the danger you saw lie outside our borders, or within them?"

He turned and pointed an accusing finger in Leia's direction. "Exactly who are you preparing to invade?"

Ackbar blinked, rendered wordless by surprise. The other officers in the room scowled and bristled. The other members of the Council were taken aback—by Peramis's intimations themselves, or, like Senator Marook, by his temerity in speaking out of turn.

"I can only think that if you had been here when the votes were taken, Senator Peramis, you would not ask such questions," Leia said sharply, moving to the front of the room with a purposeful stride and a swirl of robes. "You unfairly malign Admiral Ackbar's honor."

"I do not malign him in the slightest. I am sure Admiral Ackbar is faithful in his duties and loyal to his superiors," Peramis said, looking purposefully at Leia.

"How dare you!" bellowed Senator Tolik Yar as he leaped to his feet. "If you do not withdraw your words, I will knock you down myself."

Leia sent a small, tight smile in the direction of her champion but waved off his assistance. "Senator Peramis, the Fifth Fleet was built to protect the New Republic, and for no other reason. We have no territorial aspirations, no hunger for conquest. How could we, with ten new applications for membership arriving every day? On the honor of the House of Organa, I give my word—the Fifth Fleet will never be used to invade a member world, or to coerce its will, or subdue its legitimate ambitions."

Even before he spoke, it was clear that Peramis was unimpressed. "What weight shall I give a vow made on the honor of an extinct family—a family you have no blood claim with?"

Tolik Yar's face flushed, and his hand moved toward the ceremonial dagger he wore on his breastplate. But the hand of the officer standing beside him stayed the impulse. "Wait," General Antilles said softly. "Give him a little more rope."

Senator Peramis swept his gaze across the room

and found that every face was turned toward him. "I am sorry to spoil the festive moment, and waste the expensive pyrotechnics thoughtfully arranged for us by Admiral Ackbar and General A'baht. I am sorry to raise Senator Yar's blood pressure, and to offend Senator Marook's well-honed sense of propriety. But I cannot be silent.

"What I've learned in the months since I took my Council oath, what I've heard and seen today, alarms me profoundly. If I could, I would speak of this in the well of the Senate, before the eyes of the entire Republic. You have not bought security—you have built the machinery of oppression, and are about to hand it over to the progeny of the most brutal oppressor in history's memory.

"I am deeply, unalterably opposed to arming the New Republic against its own members—"

"You are mistaken—" Admiral Ackbar began.

"That is what you've done!" Senator Peramis said angrily. "The Fifth Fleet is a weapon of conquest and tyranny, nothing less and nothing more. And once a weapon is forged, it tantalizes, and tempts, and transfixes, until someone finds a reason to use it. You've given the son of Darth Vader a glittering temptation to follow his father's path. You've given the daughter of Darth Vader a gift-wrapped invitation to secure her power by force of arms.

"And yet you sit here smiling and nodding and swallowing the fiction that all of it is for your protection. I am ashamed for you—ashamed." Senator Peramis shook his head vigorously, as though to clear it of unwelcome thoughts, then stalked out of the conference room.

Leia quickly turned her head away, struggling to control her expression, and to conceal the struggle. The stunned silence was broken by embarrassed coughing and the squirming, shuffling sounds of officers and Council members shifting uncomfortably in their seats.

"Chairman! Chairman Behn-kihl-nahm!" Senator

Tolik Yar exclaimed, finding his voice at last. "I want him reprimanded! I want him brought before the Review! This is intolerable. The Seventh must send someone else to represent it. Intolerable, do you hear?"

"We all hear, Senator Yar," Behn-kihl-nahm said in his most silken, soothing voice as he moved toward Leia. "President Organa, allow me to apologize for Senator Peramis's regrettable lapse—"

Tolik Yar snorted. "Why not apologize for the Emperor's regrettable lapses as well? It would mean about as much."

Behn-kihl-nahm ignored the comment. "You may remember, Princess Leia, that the hand of the Empire fell heavily on Walalla. Tig Peramis remembers all too well. He was only a boy, watching his world conquered, his people's spirit destroyed. The memories fill him with a passion which inspires his diligence but betrays his good sense. I will speak with him. I am sure he already regrets his intemperate words."

Behn-kihl-nahm's exit was the cue for the room to empty. The others nearly fell over each other in their eagerness to excuse themselves, the ritual etiquette of salutes, congratulations, and good wishes so rushed that it took on the flavor of farce. Almost before she knew it, Leia was alone with Admiral Ackbar.

As she lifted a weary face to Ackbar's sympathetic gaze, she attempted a wry smile. "I thought that went well—didn't you?"

Just then, an image of General A'baht appeared on the primary display screen. "Etahn A'baht, reporting to Fleet Ops, Coruscant, with copy to president of the Senate," the image said. "Live-fire exercise Hammerblow satisfactorily concluded. Detailed report on casualties, deficiencies, and the performance of individual commands to follow. Recommend that the Fifth Defense Task Force be considered operational this date." Then the display went dark.

Ackbar nodded, and clasped Leia's shoulder with one large hand in a friendly and comforting gesture. "Well enough, Madame President," he said. "Better to face bitter words than to face more fighting and dying. I think we have all had enough of that for a lifetime."

She stared out the doorway through which Peramis had exited. "How could he be so foolish?" she asked plaintively. "After Palpatine, Hethrir, Durga, Daala, Thrawn—one after another, with hardly enough time in between to heal the wounds and patch the hulls—how could he think we love war so much?"

"I have found that most foolishness begins with fear," said Ackbar.

"I'm not accustomed to being feared." Leia shook her head. "Especially for no reason. It makes me angry."

Ackbar grunted sympathetically. "I intend to go to my quarters and bite the head off a frozen ormachek. I suggest you go home and find something ugly to smash."

Leia laughed tiredly and patted Ackbar's hand. "I just may do that. You know, I think we still have that Calamari blessing pot you gave Han and me at our wedding—"

Chapter 2

◆

A hot, humid, breeze blew across the crown of Temple Atun, the steepest of the ruined temples of the Massassi on Yavin 4. Luke Skywalker turned his face into the wind and looked out over the vibrant jungle that stretched unbroken to the horizon. The enormous orange disk of the gas giant Yavin dominated the sky, hanging just above the edge of the world as its fourth moon turned toward night.

Even after five years, Luke found it a compelling, nearly overwhelming sight. He had grown up on Tatooine, where the only stars in the night were pale speckles of white on a black canvas, and where the terrible daytime heat came from two disks he could easily block from view simply by raising his hand. *This, I will miss,* he thought.

For months Luke had been using Temple Atun as his sanctuary. Unlike the Great Temple, which had been given new life as the home of the Jedi praexeum, Atun had been left as it had been found, its mechanisms inert, its passageways dark. Its outer chambers had been looted, but a trap made of two great sliding stones had long ago sealed off the upper chambers. The trap still held the crushed bodies of the would-be thieves who had tripped it.

Something tickled Luke's consciousness at the

hazy fringe of awareness. He closed his eyes and lowered his inner shields long enough to search the temple, reading the currents of the Force as they flowed around and beneath him.

There was life everywhere, for the creatures of Yavin 4 had long ago claimed what the Massassi had abandoned. Collapsed stairways limited most vermin to the lower levels. But stonebats had made nests in tiny ventilation shafts all over the temple's face, and Luke shared the eyrie with purple-winged kitehawks, which soared into the sky each evening to search the jungle's upper canopy for prey.

There was an unfamiliar presence, too—but not an unexpected one. Streen was coming, as Luke had asked.

Luke had given Streen no instructions except to meet him at the top of Temple Atun, thereby turning the keeping of the appointment into a final test, and the temple into a puzzle and potential horror-house. Concealing himself by exerting no will at all on the currents of the Force, Luke marked his protégé's progress. Even as an apprentice, Streen had distinguished himself by his maturity. That quality was evident in his purposeful ascent of the tower. He moved lightly through the rookeries, surefootedly through the dark passages.

The last fifty meters of the trip to the crown required a dizzying fingertips-and-toes climb up the steep, crumbling sunset face of Temple Atun. As Streen neared the top, Luke nudged the kitehawks into the air with a thought. They passed over Streen's head like beclawed shadows, crying and beating the air with their wings. But Streen did not startle. Holding very still, he made himself invisible against the crumbling stone until the kitehawks wheeled away, then finished his climb.

"I'm pleased," Luke said, opening his eyes as Streen joined him. "You've confirmed me in my choice. Come, sit, and face the east with me."

Streen complied wordlessly. The curve of Yavin

was just touching the line of the horizon, forming the geometry of the symbol found everywhere on the Massassi ruins.

"Have you made any progress in your reading of the Books of Massassi?" asked Luke quietly.

He was referring to a collection of tablets unearthed from a collapsed underground chamber found two years earlier in the jungle nearby. The tablets were written in the dense, arcane symbology of the Sith, but not by a Sith consciousness. The Books were silent on their authorship, but Luke believed they were the creation of a single Massassi, a life work of essays in history and faith. A minority view held that they were the original sacred texts of the Massassi, an ancient oral tradition recorded by educated slaves.

"I thought I would have finished by now, but I've only reached the sixteenth Book," Streen said. "Reading them is more tiring than I expected. It seems to be a thing that cannot be hurried."

"And what have you learned about what the sight before us meant to those who built this place?"

"That Yavin was both a beautiful and a terrible god to the Massassi," said Streen. "It lifted their eyes to the heavens, but made their hearts small and fearful."

"Go on."

Streen gestured toward the horizon. "If I have understood what I have read, the Massassi measured themselves against this all-dominating presence and found themselves wanting. They stood at the pinnacle of life on a fecund world, and yet felt themselves and their attainments to be nothing. And that paradox colored their entire history."

"Yes," said Luke. "They failed to learn the lesson of humility. The grander their works, the more they ached for the power that still seemed so far out of reach. They gathered these stones for the Sith in a vain effort to touch the face of their god. And they pursued the dark power of the Sith in a vain effort to become like gods themselves."

"It was a kind of madness."

"A glimpse of the truth can bring on madness," Luke said softly.

"What truth is that?"

"Look around us," Luke said, spreading his hands. "The Massassi are gone, their works crumbling, battered by war, violated by trespassers. But Yavin still rules over their world."

"Yes. Yes, I see."

"Streen, I am leaving in the morning," Luke said quietly. "I am no longer needed here. It is time for someone else to take over the Academy. I've chosen you."

Those words succeeded in startling Streen in a way the kitehawks had failed to. "Leaving? I don't understand," he said, turning toward Luke.

"Once the Force was to me like a whispered voice on the wind," Luke said, standing and looking back toward the Great Temple. "Obi-Wan taught me to hear it, and Yoda to understand it. I trained myself to hear it no matter where I was. And in my turn I taught others to hear and understand. But I have not been hearing that voice well of late, though my hearing is more acute than ever. There is too much noise. There is too much I must screen out. There are too many questions, too many demands. Everyone seems to be shouting at me. It's painful, and tiring."

He turned back to Streen. "I can no longer do this work. And the work I have to do cannot be done here."

"Then it's time for you to leave," Streen said, rising to his feet. "Past time, I think, now that I understand why you've been pulling away from us. And I will not ask where you are going."

"Thank you," Luke said. "Do you accept the burden I have offered you?"

"Yes," said Streen, offering his open hand. "I accept it. I free you in good conscience from your duties. I will carry this weight now." The two men clasped hands firmly and meaningfully. Then Streen smiled. "Though I don't feel ready."

"Good," said Luke, answering Streen's smile and releasing his hand. "That feeling will help ensure your diligence."

"Will you tell the apprentices, or shall I?"

"I'll tell them. They'll expect it. And I want them to know you have my confidence. Come, let it be done."

Taking two long, swift steps, Luke launched himself from the crown of Temple Atun into the warm, empty air, just as the kitehawks did. He tumbled, then extended his limbs as though his robes were wings. Falling, he meditated on fear for long seconds, then made himself in his mind a creature of the air. Making his body as light as his heart, he touched down so softly near the base of the temple that the grasses barely protested. Streen took longer to arrive, descending the sun-bronzed face of the temple as though rappelling with an invisible rope.

"I hope that wasn't my last test," Streen said breathlessly as he joined Luke.

"No," Luke said. "Just something I wanted to do one more time before I left."

Later, in the small hours of night, a solitary E-wing fighter made an arrow of light across the sky, climbing from the island of ruins in the dark sea of jungle toward the stars. Only one pair of eyes saw it go—Streen's. He was seated atop the Great Temple, meditating, and the light and sound caused him to look up.

"Good-bye, my teacher," he said softly as the ion trail faded. "May the Force be with you on your journey."

In some ways Jacen Solo was like any seven-year-old boy. He liked building houses from a deck of sabacc cards, driving toy speeders through mud puddles, and playing with model spacecraft. The only problem, as Han saw it, was that Jacen wanted to do all of those things with his mind rather than his hands.

So far, the ability to levitate even small objects had

eluded Jacen. The E-wing and TIE fighter that dueled in the air above his bed were suspended by threads, not by thoughts. But knowing that it was possible was motivation enough for Han's elder son. Like a parent enduring the first year of a child's clarinet lessons, Han had learned how to keep the sound of small disasters, failed experiments, and the occasional display of impatience in the next room from making his blood pressure spike. And, unlike Leia, he had no trouble with the noise and chaos that are a child at play.

But Han had a harder time with the realization that Jacen was becoming, well, a bit pudgy. Han remembered childhood as long days of rough-and-tumble play, as a time when he had a lean, strong body that never tired for long. Not so for Jacen. Though the children had the run of the grounds, Han never saw his elder son come in from the courtyard having run himself to a sweaty exhaustion, or emerge from the gardens as dirty and happy as a worm. And Han worried over it.

Still harder to accept was seeing Jacen always playing alone, with no friends outside the family and less interest all the time in playing with Jaina or Anakin. Han blamed the lack of friends on himself and Leia. The children had been whisked from one place to another, sent away with bodyguards and hidden away with nannies, all in the name of protecting them. In the process, they had been "protected" from having anything remotely like a normal childhood. And for all that, they had still been kidnapped by Hethrir, and nearly lost.

There was nothing to be done about it now except to try not to compound the mistake. On the first night the family was reunited, with Leia crying tears of relief as they held each other, Han had silently vowed never to leave the children without the care and protection of a parent again.

There was no disentangling Leia from the business of the government, but Han saw his own position differently. On their return to Coruscant, he had tried to resign his commission. Admiral Ackbar had pointed out that he would lose his security clearances and Class 1 pass, and Leia would lose his counsel and companionship on sensitive matters.

"Finding you indispensable to the defense of the New Republic, I must refuse your resignation," Ackbar said.

"Now, just a blasted moment—"

"However, I also find that your current assignment does not make the best use of your experience and abilities," Ackbar went on. "Effective immediately, I order you placed on detached duty, assigned to the president of the Senate as liaison for domestic defense. You are to assist her in whatever way she sees fit. Do you understand?" If the big-eyed Calamarian had been capable of a wink, he would have sent a sly one in Han's direction at that moment.

So Han's days were now spent at the president's residence, which he shared with Leia, trying to make up for lost time. But he was discovering that children made the *Millennium Falcon*'s hyperdrive look dependable and predictable by comparison. Little Anakin was Han's loyal ally, but the twins tested him early and often. They had their own ideas about the proper order of things, and their place in it.

"But, Dad, Winter let us—"

"But, Dad, Chewie always—"

"But, Dad, Threepio never—"

Sentences beginning with those constructions were banned from the household by the end of the first month. "It's not fair!" followed soon thereafter. With Leia backing up his edicts down the line (discreetly negotiating her dissents with him in private), all three children eventually acknowledged Dad as boss of the house.

But he worried about the day he thought must inevitably come—the day a disagreement would turn into a fight he would lose. Raising Jedi children, he decided, was like raising Ralltiir tigers—cute as they were when young and much as they might love you, they still grew long, deadly claws. Han would never forget the afternoon Anakin had an hourlong, Force-assisted tantrum. Every object in the playroom was shoved or thrown against the wall, leaving the youngster alone in the middle of a bare floor, kicking his heels and pounding his fists.

One mercy was that all the three children were basically good-hearted. Another was that playing with the Force seemed to make them sleep longer and more deeply. Unfortunately, Anakin and Jacen both had their mother's stubbornness—neither could be readily compelled to do anything they didn't want to. And Jaina and Jacen both had a streak of irrepressible mischief, which Leia blamed on Han—both could be regularly counted on to do something you didn't want them to.

They had established a new family ritual that seemed to please everyone: When Leia came home, they would all climb into the vortex pool in the garden and spend half an hour or more being carried around by its currents. The kids could play—Anakin had suddenly begun to love the water so much that Ackbar proudly called him "my little fish"—or just cling to Mom and Dad, while for Leia and Han it was therapy, a sigh of relief at the end of a long day.

Then, while the children were off with the valet droid, dressing for dinner, Han and Leia retreated to their own bedroom for what they jokingly called the "the daily briefing." It was as much a part of the ritual as the pool—a chance for them to rail, complain, or simply entertain while swapping stories about their day.

That evening Leia threw herself on the bed and hugged a pillow to her chest. "What news from the front, General?" she asked.

Han let himself drop into a Kesslerite lounging chair that faced the foot of the bed. It quickly softened and conformed to his body shape, leaving him feeling as though he were still floating in the vortex. "I don't know what to do about Jacen," he said. "This morning I tried to interest him in some friendly bolo-ball with Dad. He turned me down."

"Well—he's not very good at it, and kids want their parents to be proud of them," said Leia, rolling over and staring at the ceiling. "Maybe he's embarrassed to play with you, since you're so much better than him."

"He's not very good at it because he never practices. There's no reason he couldn't be good at it. But he said it was a stupid game."

Leia was diplomatically silent.

"So I said, 'Okay, you pick,'" Han continued. "'Do you want to go skate in the velocidrome, play wallball in the courtyard, what?' He says, 'No, thank you, Dad.' I told him he had to start doing something physical, strengthen his body. Or I'd have to assign him a few laps around the inner fence with the sentry droid every day."

"What did he say to that?"

"He said, 'Why do I have to be strong? Someday I'll be able to go anywhere I want, or get anything I want, just by thinking about it—like Uncle Luke.'" Han shook his head. "He doesn't seem to have noticed that Uncle Luke doesn't look a bit like Jabba the Hutt."

"Neither does Jacen!" Leia said defensively.

"Give him time."

"You're exaggerating."

"I hope," Han said, though his tone was skeptical. "But I'd be glad to see Luke remind Jacen about the physical side of Jedi training—you know, all that stuff he used to bore us with about the body being the instrument of the mind, not just its vessel?"

Leia rolled over again and propped herself up on her elbows, her expression suddenly earnest. "Han, have you heard anything from Luke?"

"What? No, not for a while." He frowned while he thought. "Not for a long time. Why?"

"I heard from Tionne on Yavin Four today. Luke's disappeared."

"Disappeared?"

"Gone off somewhere. He turned over the Academy to Streen."

"He's done that before."

"From what Tionne said, this time was different—it sounded like he wasn't ever coming back."

"Hmm," said Han. "Highly mysterious, I agree. I can't think of a single reason why he might not want to put himself on a deserted island in the middle of the big Nowhere with a gaggle of Force adepts."

Leia threw a pillow at him, which he neatly parried. "I just wish I knew where he was," she said. "With neither of us having heard from him in months, and no word before he left—"

"You're worried about him?"

"A little. And if he's not going to be at the Academy, we could surely use his help here. I tried sending a message to the hyperspace comm in his fighter, but it's not receiving. If it still exists."

"When did he leave?"

"Days ago. Can we do anything from here to find him?"

Han snorted. "A Jedi Master who knows everything there is to know about New Republic geography and technology? Not unless he wants to be found. You've got a better chance of finding him yourself, with your latent whatsis and that twin thing you two seem to have."

Leia looked vaguely uncomfortable. "I wondered if I could quietly ask Admiral Ackbar to list Luke's E-wing as missing."

"You could do that," Han said, "but you couldn't do it quietly. It'd take about two hours for the whole fleet to be buzzing with 'Luke Skywalker has vanished!' Face it, Leia, anything involving Luke is news. Which might be exactly why he slipped out the back door. What does Streen say?"

"Streen says there's nothing he can tell us. But I got the impression he was protecting Luke."

"Protecting Luke's privacy, maybe?"

"Maybe," Leia said. "I suppose you're going to tell me I should *respect* his privacy, and stop worrying about it?"

"It's an idea," Han said. "He's a Jedi Master—and he's out there in the best fighter we have, thanks to Admiral Ackbar. If anyone can take care of himself, my buddy Luke can."

Leia flopped on her back on the bed. "Funny, when I think that thought, it comes out, 'If anyone can manage to find trouble, Luke can.' "

"That," said Han, "is the difference between a friend and a sister."

"I suppose," Leia said, sighing. "Speaking of sisters—did anything else happen today?"

"Well, let's see," Han said, crossing his arms over his chest and gazing at the ceiling. "After lunch, Jaina got tired of being ignored by Jacen again and started sabotaging his practice. They ended up in a fight that went on so long it made them both sick to their stomachs. . . ."

As soon as Luke shut down the engines, he could hear the wind howling outside. It rocked the E-wing on its skids and pelted its surface with freezing salt spray ripped from the crests of the waves breaking near the beach.

"Keep the stabilizers on," Luke told R7-T1 as he unbuckled his harness.

The astromech droid chirped in response, and the words RECOMMEND WING DE-ICERS ON flashed on the cockpit monitor.

"Fine, keep the wing de-icers on, too."

R7-T1 purred. PLEASE CONFIRM NEGATIVE RESPONSE TO CORUSCANT TRAFFIC CONTROL.

"Yes, I'm sure I don't want you to notify traffic control of our arrival. Not a peep out of you—not even so much as a time synchronization check." He reached forward and released the cockpit latch, and the seamless bubble tilted up on concealed hinges.

Damp, bitterly cold air poured in with the sound of the surf. "I'll be back when I've found the hangar."

The beach was barely thirty meters wide, squeezed between an angry-looking greenish sea and a rocky cliff half again that high. Just beyond the breakers, sculpted spires of the same reddish-black rock jutted up from the water. Smaller chunks of rock were scattered through the surf and all along the beach, half buried in the coarse brown sand. Overhead, a thick gray mat of clouds churned as the wind drove it briskly along.

Oblivious to the cold and the wind, Luke walked slowly south along the rocky beach. He held one hand out in front of him, palm down, sweeping it methodically back and forth through the air, looking almost like a blind man feeling his way through an unfamiliar room.

Luke had not gone far when he stopped and looked up at the top of the cliff for a long moment, then out at the twin spires of rock. Dropping his chin to his chest and closing his eyes, he turned through two full circles, then looked back up at the cliff edge.

"Yes," he said, the wind stealing the word from his lips. "Yes, it is here."

He sat down on the sand, cross-legged and straight-backed, and brought his hands together in his lap, fingertip to fingertip. Concentrating on a picture in his mind, Luke dipped his awareness deeply into the flow of the Force beneath him. With eyes that looked inward, he found what he was seeking, like flaws in a near-perfect crystal. He extended his will.

The sand around him stirred. The rocks shuddered, shifted, then began to rise from the sea and the sand as though sifted from them by an invisible screen. Swirling through the air as they sought their place, the stones took shape as broken wall and shattered foundation, as arch and gate and dome—the ruins of Darth Vader's fortress retreat. It hung in the air around and above Luke as it had once stood atop the cliff, a dark-faced and forbidding edifice.

There was no record in Imperial City's files to say whether his father had ever occupied the fortress, though it had clearly been built for him in accord with his instructions. It had been empty when it was destroyed by a B-wing's blasters, in the days after the New Republic reclaimed Coruscant.

Was this where Vader plotted his conquests in the Emperor's service? Was this where he had come to rejuvenate after a battle? Had there been celebrations here, self-indulgent pleasures or cruelties? Luke listened for the echoes of the old evils, and could not be certain. But that did not matter to his plans. As he had redeemed and reclaimed his father, he would redeem and reclaim his father's house.

Now the stones swirled again in the air, joined by others plucked from the sea and stripped from the face of the cliff. Now broken edge fused against broken edge, and the dark faces of the rock lightened as their mineral structure was reshuffled. Now heavy rock walls and floors thinned to an airy elegance as if they were clay in a potter's press. Now a tower stretched skyward until it rose above the edge of the cliff.

When it was done, the last gap closed, the last rock transformed, the structure securely perched just above the sand on pillars of stone extending down to the bedrock, Luke brought the E-wing down the beach and nestled it in the chamber he had made for it. It was not a door that closed over the opening, though, but a solid wall that closed out not only the wind and the cold, but the world.

"Shut down all systems," Luke told R7-T1. "Then place yourself in standby mode, I won't be needing you for a while."

The last task was to inspect his retreat from the perspective of any outsiders whose gaze might fall upon it. All was as he had planned. From the sky, it appeared as part of the beach. From the sea, as part of the cliffs. From the beach, as part of the sky. From the cliffs, as part of the sea. It was not a trick of camouflage, but a simple matter of allowing the essences of its substance to be seen. The retreat was of the sea, and the rock, and the sand, and the sky, in harmony with them rather than imposed on them.

The last test was to climb the tower and inspect the view. But when he looked to the east, he found his view blocked by the lowering clouds. So he waited, shrugging off time as easily as he shrugged off the cold. He waited until the wind finally blew the storm away, until he could see the snow-capped Menarai Mountains ruling over the jewel of the Core, outlined against the sky by the light from the yellow-faced inner moon.

"May this sight remind me always that the few stones I've gathered will not last," he said softly. "And may the memory of Anakin Skywalker remind me always that surrender is more powerful than will."

Then he descended at last into his retreat, sealing the opening behind him.

Leia sat bolt upright in the darkness. "He's here."

"What?" Han said sleepily.

"He's here—on Coruscant."

"Who's here?"

"Luke. I felt his mind touch mine."

"Great. Invite him to dinner," Han said with a yawn.

"You don't understand," she said impatiently. "I was sleeping, or thought I was. I was dreaming that Luke was looking down at me. Then I realized I was awake. We looked at each other for a moment, and then he disappeared—as though he'd drawn a curtain."

"Sounds like dreaming to me."

"No," she said, shaking her head. "You were right, Han—he's hiding. He doesn't want to be found."

Han pulled a pillow over his head. "Let him hide, then. I could sleep at night."

"I just want to know why. I don't understand

what's happening." *And I need to know that he's there if I need him,* she thought.

"He'll tell us when he's ready," Han said, drawing Leia down into the comforting circle of his arms. "Sleep, my princess. Mornings always come too soon."

Chapter 3

◆

The broad, curving viewpanes of the staff conference room, high in the restored remnant of the Imperial Palace, looked out toward the oldest and busiest of the three spaceports serving Imperial City.

For safety and security reasons, neither the landing nor the launch patterns brought ships anywhere near the rebuilt administrative complex. But it was still possible to watch their comings and goings, and—for the sharp-eyed—to identify familiar types and even individual vessels. On more than one occasion Leia had come to the conference room to watch the *Millennium Falcon* leave on a mission or watch impatiently for its return.

Rarely, though, did any of the activity at Eastport actually demand the attention of those in the staff conference room. Only the largest ships, the occasional crash landing and explosion, or a full-power launch abort could be heard through the transparisteel. So when the viewpanes began to hum in sympathy with the sound beating on them from outside, both Leia and Ackbar glanced up from their work to see why.

They saw a bright spherical shape three times the size of an ordinary transport descending toward the spaceport. Three much smaller escorts circled it like planets around a star. At the bottom of the spherical vessel, waves of atmospheric distortion rolled out of scalloped depressions in its hull.

"I believe that ship is using Aradian pulse-lifters, undampered," said Ackbar. "Remarkable. Look how slow and steady the descent is. I shall have to have a closer look at that vessel."

"It appears the Duskhan delegation is finally here," Leia said. "I guess they don't put their spaceports in family neighborhoods over in the Koornacht Cluster."

"Are you not going to go greet Ambassador Spaar?"

"First Administrator Engh is there, with a protocol droid," Leia said.

"I see," said Ackbar. "Sending a message?"

"Only that they have to understand that *President* isn't a ceremonial title," Leia said. "But I'm not singling them out. I'm slighting everyone from now on. There are just too many ambassadorial missions arriving each week. I was spending half my day waiting in arrival lounges." Her face wrinkled with annoyance. "Especially when someone postpones his landing three times, and always at the last minute."

As she spoke she quietly refolded the blue triangle of Walallan vellum which a courier had placed in front of her a few moment before, and set it aside.

The act did not escape Ackbar's notice, since only one of his eyes was trained on the window. "Is that the letter from Senator Peramis?"

Leia nodded.

"And?"

"It's pretty humble," she said.

"Excellent."

She nodded again. "I wish I had Behn-kihl-nahm's gift. He almost never leaves thumb bruises on the throats of his vict— of the people he's persuading."

"You must find out where he buys his gloves," said Ackbar. The Duskhan transport was on the ground now, and the escorts were disappearing one after another into a landing bay near the top of the sphere. "Do you have meetings scheduled with Nil Spaar?"

"In ten days."

"That long? You should allow the First to handle some of the smaller worlds on your schedule. Not merely meeting their delegations—the entire admission process."

"Showing them that they're going to be second-class members of the New Republic? I don't think so."

"There must be a way to shift some of the weight you're carrying to other shoulders."

"I'll take suggestions," she said. "But Nil Spaar asked for the delay. He's never been to Coruscant before. He said he wants to explore a bit before negotiations occupy him."

"I see," said Ackbar. "Perhaps he's the one sending a message."

"I'm not sure," Leia said. She reached out and pulled a datapad across the tabletop toward her. "Well, Admiral—now that it's operational, what shall we do with the Fifth Fleet?"

"A trickier question than I thought it would be," admitted Ackbar. "Tig Peramis has shown us what we can expect if there is even the appearance of gunboat diplomacy."

Leia frowned. "I don't want us afraid to show the flag where it might help cooler heads prevail."

"Then I would like to send the new fleet into the Seventh Security Zone," said Ackbar. "I know of several worlds which would welcome even a short visit from a New Republic ship. And I can think of at least five pins on the trouble map where a legitimate government has asked for our help, on matters where even Senator Peramis can't object if we intervene."

"Give me an example."

"There was a new one this morning," Ackbar said, folding his hands. "The Right Earl of Qalita Prime is appealing for help in dealing with pirate raiders. Six ships have been attacked within a month, four of them successfully. The cargo syndicates are threatening to stop supplying the planet."

"Good. Very good! Go ahead and put together a patrol itinerary for the Fifth Fleet," said Leia. "Make sure it's heavy on tea parties and rescuing lost children. If there's anyone else in the Seventh Security Zone who thinks the way Senator Peramis does, I want his fears put to rest."

"I can have an itinerary ready before the end of the day."

They talked for several minutes more, discussing the deployment of the rest of the New Republic's spacegoing forces. The Second Fleet had been on patrol the longest without home leave and shipyard services, while the First Fleet had been enjoying the perks of serving as Coruscant's defense force for nearly as long. On Ackbar's recommendation, Leia agreed to recall the Second Fleet and to send the First Fleet to replace it along the crucial border patrol routes the crews called Thunder Alley.

"It should have been done sooner," said Ackbar, "but we have had too few pieces to move about the board. I have limited myself to rotating individual vessels back to the yards, out of fear some enemy would take advantage. But if we hold the Fifth Fleet here a few days longer, we can make the exchange without leaving either the capital or the frontier unprotected."

"Do you think there's an enemy still out there?" Leia asked. "Someone with both the means and the will to take on the entire New Republic? I find myself much more worried about our stability than our security."

"You have that luxury—I do not," Ackbar said. "And remember that Admiral Daala is still alive, and has the resources of hundreds, perhaps thousands, of Core worlds to draw upon. She can only grow stronger as time passes, and may well have spies in Imperial City."

At that moment Leia's comlink chirped. "Leia?" It was Tolik Yar. "You're needed here at the Senate. There's a problem with Y'taa petition."

Leia stood up from the table. "I'm on my way." She turned toward Ackbar and said, "We can take up the rest this afternoon, when you have an itinerary for me to approve." Then she smiled. "You may find that some of the information you need is over at Eastport."

"I am almost certain of it," Ackbar said gravely.

Leia's bodyguards fell in beside her as she left the room. The guard changed four times a day, but somehow they all seemed the same—tall, broad-shouldered, alert-eyed, and silent. Leia had nicknamed them the Sniffer and the Shooter.

The former was plugged into a backpack full of electrical and chemical sensors. It was his job to make sure no bomb, poison, pathogen, radiation, or microdroid harmed her. He preceded her around corners, through doors, and into closed spaces.

The latter wore combat armor, a personal shield, and a SoroSuub blaster rifle with backpack generator. Since Leia refused to wear a personal shield, it was his job to place himself between her and any would-be assassin, shield her, and strike down her attackers.

Han had gotten the chief of security to order the protection and had won a reluctant promise from Leia to accept it.

But Leia had never adjusted to the guards' presence, which seemed ever more unnecessary. And, paradoxically, she found that the presence of her personal guards didn't make her feel safer—just the opposite, since they were a constant reminder that someone might want to kill her.

So she had learned to pretend they weren't there, even when they shared a liftcar, a scooter, or a slidewalk with her. She didn't want to learn their real names or to become friendly with them—her promise didn't extend that far. She wanted them to be furniture.

The only time she acknowledged their presence was when the Sniffer silently signaled an alarm. Then she would let the Shooter guide her to whatever shel-

tered spot he chose, and would wait there until the
Sniffer satisfied himself that there was no threat. It
happened often enough that it no longer startled her,
but infrequently enough that it was only a minor annoyance. ·

Still, Leia never expected it to happen while she
was walking along the Memorial Corridor, just outside
the walls of the Senate chamber.

One moment she was striding briskly past the
holo statuary of the heroes of the Rebellion, robes flying, her mind sorting through what she knew about the
Y'taa. Then, in an eyeblink, the Sniffer sharply raised
his hands and the Shooter pushed Leia sideways into
one of the niches where the pillar between it and the
next offered cover.

Her heart was suddenly racing, and her thoughts
raced with it. Unreasoning fear brought back the memory of Tig Peramis, livid with anger, looking at her as
Vader's daughter instead of as a royal child of Alderaan. Was he angry enough to kill? Had Tolik Yar been
tricked into betraying her? How horrible to be forced
to be afraid *here*, on the doorstep of the New Republic's most famous symbol of freedom, the first structure
to be rebuilt after Imperial factions turned Imperial
City into a battle zone.

Then, just as suddenly, it was over. "Clear," the
Shooter said in his emotionless voice, moving aside to
allow Leia to emerge from the niche. Frowning crossly,
Leia hurried after the Sniffer and demanded to know
what had prompted the alarm.

"I detected a new energy field at the entrance to
the Senate Hall," the Sniffer said, pointing. "It became
active as we approached."

Still frowning, Leia strode a few dozen steps farther down the corridor, then stopped short and
laughed despite herself. Hanging over the ornate double doors of the Senate chamber was a large holosign.
On appearance alone, the sign belonged in a factory,
beside the entry to the work floor. The text it displayed
cemented that impression. It read:

882 DAYS WITHOUT
A SHOT FIRED IN ANGER
Remember,
Peace Is No Accident

Wearing a smile that was broad enough to touch her eyes, Leia looked left and right for the perpetrators of the joke. "All right, 'fess up," she called out. "Whose handiwork is this?"

Tolik Yar emerged from the shadow of a pillar to Leia's left and showed a toothy, self-satisfied grin. "If it works for broken toes, bumped heads, and burned fingers, why not for higher stakes as well?"

"I like it," Leia confessed. "But isn't it a bit—undignified? Behn-kihl-nahm will never let it stay."

"Behn-kihl-nahm helped arrange for it to be installed," said Tolik Yar. "And as for dignity—any senator more concerned with dignity than outcomes desperately needs to be reminded why we're here. Wouldn't you agree?"

"You are a gem, Tolik Yar," she said, surprising him with a hug. She turned back and looked up at the sign. "I do agree. And I think we should have a little celebration when that number reaches a thousand."

"I'll let it be known. In the meantime, good news—the problem with the Y'taa has unexpectedly been resolved. My apologies for interrupting your day." He bowed deeply and backed away.

"Scamp," she said. Her smile lasted all the way back to her desk.

The shipyard boss beamed broadly as he led Han Solo and Chewbacca into the hangar where a gleaming *Millennium Falcon* rested on its skids. "You're going to be very happy, very happy," he said, rubbing his palms together. "I only let my best mechanics touch her."

"No droids," Han said in a warning tone, surveying the ship's exterior. "You better not have used any droids. Droids don't understand creative engineering."

"No droids," the yard boss said reassuringly. "It
was all hand work. Which is why the rebuild took so
long, of course. The crew chief used to work on
Corellian freighters at Toprawa. Stock, of course, nothing like what you have here. But at least he knows the
model well enough to spot your modifications."

Chewbacca stopped under one of the ship's
forward-pointing mandibles and looked up at the
equipment-studded hull plates. Pointing at one of the
lower deflector emitters, he turned his head toward
Han and loosed a plaintive howl.

"What?" asked the yard boss, his gaze quickly settling on the Wookiee's point of concern. "Oh, yes, we
realigned all the emitters. You were getting interference
nodes to port and starboard—left her vulnerable to a
side attack."

"You promised you wouldn't change anything,"
Han said threateningly.

"I promised we'd put her right, and that's what
we did," the yard boss said, leading the way to the
boarding ramp. "First we took her apart down to
the frame, then we took the frame apart—we have
holos, you'll have to see how twisted some of the ribs
and stringers were. Structurally, she's about fifteen percent new."

Han walked right past the boarding ramp, continuing to circle the ship as though doing a preflight
check. "Yeah, well, she's had a few bumps. Never
failed me in the clutch, though."

Chewbacca voiced his agreement in a defiant gut-
tural growl.

Frowning, the yard boss came back down the
ramp and fell in behind them. "Well, that's a small miracle, considering what we found under the access panels. How you serviced her systems the way she was, I'll
never know. When we built her back up, all the cables
were properly tagged and bundled, all the mechanicals
shock-mounted, all the electricals grounded and pulse-
shielded—"

"I knew I should have been keeping an eye on

you," Han said. "Probably added a couple of tons to her displacement—"

"She's three hundred kilos lighter."

"I would have done it all myself, you know. But there just isn't time anymore."

Chewie grunted expressively.

"Yeah, I couldn't stand to see her all in pieces, either," Han agreed. "Not with someone else's hands in her guts. Autopsies and rebuilds—don't want to be around either one." He paused, looking up at the drive matrix. "Say, is that a Seinar Systems augmentor?"

"It is."

"Well, I'll be a—" His expression softened to wonder. "We tried for years to get one of those on the black market. Remember, Chewie? But every time we got a lead on one, it turned out to be pre-Imperial junk, or something pulled out of the wreck of a TIE fighter, with the scorch marks painted over. How did you—"

The yard boss smiled. "Don't ask, General."

Chewbacca yawned a comment under his breath, and Han answered with a crooked smile. "Yeah, I guess there're a few advantages to wearing a braid." He cocked his head at the yard boss. "So are there any more surprises?"

"A few," the yard boss said, reclaiming the role of tour guide. "We replaced your missing escape pods. Upgraded the tractor beam generator to a Mark Seven, and the hyperdrive motivator to a Series Four-oh-one—"

"Holy mother of meteors."

"—Replaced all the sensor lenses. Duplicated an original YT-1300 battery regulator from Corellian specs—"

"That was probably a mistake."

"—Recarpeted the holds and crew quarters. Fixed the sticky latch on the Number Two storage locker. Recharged the sanitizer in the refresher." He smiled. "Want to take her for a spin?"

Gesturing with one furry hand, Chewbacca registered his vote.

"Yeah, all that history gone. It won't be the same *Falcon* without the creaks and the shakes," Han said.

"No, it won't," said the yard boss. "She'll be about twenty percent faster, ten percent more efficient, and a hundred percent more reliable."

"Keys in the ignition?"

The yard boss nodded. "The security system's been reinitialized for you—just enter new authorization codes."

Han looked at Chewbacca. "I think Leia can get by without us for a little longer. Let's wring her out a little."

"Have fun," the yard boss said, his self-satisfied smile restored to full brightness. "You're already cleared for orbit."

Waving their ID cards at the scanners, Han and Chewbacca entered the grounds of the presidential residence in full stride and in the middle of a full-blown argument.

"I know, I know, she's perfect," Han said. "I *know*, we couldn't have gotten her into that kind of shape in a year of weekends. So what? I hate perfect."

Chewbacca shook his head and uttered a long, whining growl that bespoke his frustration.

"I am *not* being unreasonable. How can you say that?" Han demanded, raising his hands in disgust. "Weren't you paying attention? Were you even listening while we were landing?"

Jerking his head back sharply, Chewbacca grunted a sharp retort.

"That's right—hardly a sound. She's as tight as a new boot," Han said, stopping and turning on his friend. "Listen, buddy, I *hate* new boots. I like my boots covered with scuffs, worn just this side of falling apart, with room for my toes and a little roll in the heels. All those noises they took out, that's how I used to know when I was pushing her. How am I gonna know how hard we're hit next time we're in a scrap?"

Chewbacca shook his head and growled his disgust.

"I thought *you'd* understand," Han said plaintively. "Chewie, they replaced the cushions on the acceleration couches." His tone was rich with indignation. "Don't they understand why people keep old furniture around the house? That's not my *Falcon*. It feels like I'm sitting in somebody's else's ship. I tell you, I'm gonna have to take a whole day to go around with a wrench and start loosening things—"

Somewhere in the middle of Han's tirade, Chewbacca stopped listening to him. He stood straighter and cocked his head while attending to a sound from farther away. Finally he grabbed Han by the shoulder and gave him a little shake to interrupt him.

"*Arroora,*" the Wookiee said chidingly.

"What?" Han said, twisting around to look toward the gardens. "I didn't hear her."

Together they hurried down the walk toward Leia's voice. They found her on the back lawn, tailor-sitting on the grass with a datapad in her lap. Nearby, all three children lay side by side on their backs, with eyes either closed or staring blankly upward. "I thought you'd be back long before this," Leia said, with a hint of impatience in her voice. "I had to postpone an appointment with Senator Noimm."

Han looked down, embarrassed. "Sorry, honey," he said, sitting beside her and reaching for her hand. "There were problems at the yard."

"And I'll bet you caused most of 'em," she said, leaning over to kiss his cheek. "Right, Chewie?"

The bronze-furred Wookiee looked away, shifted his weight from one foot to the other, and scratched his head distractedly.

"It's okay, Chewie," Han said. "I'll rat on myself, so you don't have to." He nodded toward the children, who had neither moved nor made a sound since he and

Chewbacca had arrived. "What did you do to them, kill them?"

Jaina giggled at that, spoiling the effect.

"It's an exercise," Leia said.

"What, to see who can levitate the longest?"

"Bite your tongue," said Leia sharply. "They're working on feeling the Force flowing through the grass, through each separate plant, without disturbing the flow. It's one of the Jedi disciplines of moving lightly, leaving no sign."

Chewbacca growled.

"Don't look at me, Chewie," said Han, lying back in the grass. "The best discipline I know is the sentence 'Wait till your mother gets home.' "

Leia smiled and poked him with a forefinger. "I feel like I hardly know enough myself to be their teacher," she said with a sigh, "but I have to do what I can." More loudly she added, "All right, children, that's enough."

One after another, Jacen, Jaina, and Anakin sat up. Jacen plucked a blade of grass and started trying to whistle through it, drawing a glare from his sister and a look of injured surprise from his younger brother.

"Tell me what you learned," Leia said.

Jaina looked toward her parents. "The grass doesn't mind being walked on, but it does feel it."

"Everything that's alive can feel what happens to it," said Leia. "That's an important truth to remember. Anakin? Jacen? What about you?"

Anakin laced his fingers behind his neck as a pillow. "I don't know if I learned something or made it up."

"Tell us."

"Well—I was looking at the clouds. And I thought I could feel the grass looking at them, too. Like they were wondering if it was going to rain."

"I'm sure the grass is aware of the weather," Leia said. "But wondering is something conscious beings are blessed with."

"Or cursed," said Han.

"I learned that the grass thinks Jaina smells bad," Jacen said impishly, giving his twin a push and rolling away from her. "Can we go in the pool, Mother?"

"All right," she said, accepting that the exercise was over. Three small bodies scrambled up from the grass and ran fleet-footedly toward the courtyard and the vortex pool.

"I can go watch them," Han said, sitting up.

"Stay. They'll be all right," Leia said, shielding her eyes. "Chewie, you look even taller than usual from down here. I hope your mate is bigger than me. Did you have as hard a time as my dear husband did, letting someone else work on his jalopy?"

Chewbacca crouched down, sitting on his heels with an easy balance that reminded Han that his friend came from an arboreal planet. Lifting his face to the sky, he growled proudly.

"Oh, right, fine, you're the practical one, and I'm the hot-tempered one," Han said. "Have you ever heard such character assassination?"

"Don't worry, dear," Leia said, patting his hand. "I won't let him change how I feel about you."

The Wookiee's first grunt was a retort, the second a question.

"Of course—go ahead," said Leia.

Rolling his head from side to side on his neck, Chewbacca loosed a long, well-modulated growl. Before it was over, Han sat up with a start, staring at Chewbacca.

"Go home?" he demanded. "Go home?"

"Of course," Leia said to Chewbacca. "You have a family of your own, a mate and a child. Your responsibility to them is every bit as important as the obligations you feel toward us. Tell him, Han."

"Huh? Look, who's going to help me put the *Falcon* out of order again?"

Leia poked him in the ribs.

"Ow!"

"Try again," she said.

"I guess it's been a long time, pal," Han said,

wearing a rueful expression. "Family won't recognize you if you don't get back there soon and spend more time hanging around the home tree."

Chewbacca shook his head up and down as he answered.

"Of course we understand," Leia said. "You've been here taking care of our kids instead of on Kashyyyk with your own. You really should be there for Lumpawaroo's coming-of-age. We *insist* you go. I feel bad that we've been so selfish."

The Wookiee answered with an uncharacteristically tentative growl.

"No, we'll manage just fine," Leia said. "The kids are safe here, and we're not going to be running all over the galaxy. And Luke is on Coruscant—"

"Leia—"

"—and he'll be helping us with the children. No, don't give it a second thought. You should leave as soon as you can pack. Tell him, Han."

Han nodded. "Leia's right, old buddy. It's a good time. Things are quiet. We'll miss ya, but you've been standing watch on our bridge long enough."

Subtle movements of muscles under fur marked Chewbacca's relief and gratitude. "*Rrargrarg?*" he asked, cocking his head.

"Shoot, pal," said Han, showing an easy grin. But his face paled and his eyes widened as Chewbacca asked his second favor. "Oh, no—oh, no. You can't ask me that. I just got her back after a hundred and sixty-seven days on the hook."

Chewbacca's grunt was terse and snide.

"I don't *care* if I said I hated new boots," Han said. "I hate having someone else's feet in my boots even more. Friendship only goes so far."

"What are you talking about?" Leia demanded.

"Aw, he's just trying to hold me to my own words. I don't have to be consistent if I don't want to."

With a peevish growl, Chewbacca stood and started to turn away.

"Don't you move, Chewie," Leia said sharply. "Han, come on—you should lend him the *Falcon.*"

"Well, I don't want to," Han said, getting to his feet and pacing nervously. "I don't want her bouncing around hyperspace without me. I want her where I know the worst thing that can happen is that some overeager mechanic with a torque wrench will come along and tighten all the connectors to spec. And you know how Wookiees fly—he'll redline it the whole way there and back."

Leia shook her head. "And you wonder why Jacen gives us a hard time."

"*Arrarrarooerrr,*" Chewbacca said plaintively to Leia.

"You hear that?" Leia said. "Han, dear—how many years of Chewie's life have you taken so far? How long have you kept him away from Kashyyyk?"

"Me? I didn't do it. It's that crazy Wookiee life debt stuff. I'd be glad to let him off the hook."

"The least you could do is let him go back a hero, in the ship both of you made famous. Think what that could mean to Chewie's son, to his mate. It might go a long way toward making up for Chewie's absence to know that he was doing something that mattered, to see him honored."

"I suppose," Han said dubiously.

"And he's your friend. You wouldn't want him to think you were willing to lend the *Millennium Falcon* to Lando—"

Han shook a finger warningly. "That's different. That was war. And I still didn't like it."

"—but not to him. You wouldn't want him to think you were willing to *lose* the *Falcon* to Lando in a sabacc game, but you won't lend it—"

"Her. *Her,* not it."

"—to Chewbacca for his homecoming. You wouldn't want to hurt his feelings like that, would you?"

Holding his head in his hands as though trying to massage away a headache, Han looked from Leia to

Chewbacca and back to Leia again. He squinted, frowned, chewed his lower lip, shook his head. His mouth worked, and he made a noise that sounded something like "Not fair."

"What?" said Leia. "What did you say?"

Han cleared his throat and looked straight at Chewbacca. "I said I guess if we need a lift somewhere while you're gone, either the president or the princess can probably arrange something."

Chewbacca crowed his delight and rushed forward to hug Han. "But you'd better take care of her!" Han added quickly, squirming uncomfortably in the Wookiee's crushing embrace. "I want her back without a scratch, d'you hear me? Not a scratch. And fill the tanks before you leave Kashyyyk. I'm not paying for your conjugal visits."

The only response Chewbacca made was to ruffle Han's hair while he showed a toothy openmouthed grin.

When Chewbacca was gone, Leia drew Han into a gentler and more agreeable embrace. "I'm proud of you," she said. "He'd never say anything to either of us, but he still hasn't stopped feeling awful inside about the kidnapping of the kids."

Han did not have to ask Leia how she knew about Chewbacca's private pain. "It wasn't his fault."

"You'll never convince him of that. He feels guilty for failing us. And he feels guilty for neglecting his own. He really needs to go home and get his confidence back." She drew back and smiled up at her husband. "And from what I hear, looking after Wookiee children is good practice for looking after Jedi children."

"Maybe I should go with him."

"You don't need to," she said, and kissed him.

"Yeah, well, fine," Han said. "I'll tell you this much, though—Luke'd better come teach the kids how to flap their arms and fly. Because I'm *never* giving Jacen the codes to the *Falcon*. Not in *my* lifetime, anyway."

"Why? Didn't you start piloting everything in sight as soon as you could?"

"Of course I did," Han said indignantly. "Why do you think I'm worried?"

The unmarked office of Admiral Drayson lay buried inside five security perimeters and hidden behind a curtain of misinformation and plausible deniability.

The section he commanded had no publicly known name. The private name—Alpha Blue—was known only to the dozen officials with the very highest clearances, and appeared nowhere in either the government's or the military command's data records. Those whom Drayson commanded carried no Alpha Blue identification cards and passed under no Alpha Blue insignia on the way to their jobs. They wore the insignia of a variety of unremarkable units, or—like Drayson himself—no insignia at all, and took their pay as quartermasters' mates and second gunners, ion mechanics and civilian clerks.

Given that context, Drayson was just a little surprised the morning he entered his office and found someone already there, uninvited and unannounced— someone who did not work for him and yet was bold enough to sit in Drayson's chair, with his feet up on the corner of Drayson's desk.

"Well," Drayson said. "Lando Calrissian. You're lucky I didn't shoot you."

Lando grinned. "I was counting on your being too curious how I got in to shoot me right away."

"I said shoot you, not kill you. Blowing apart your knee would have been sufficient," Drayson said. "Now, please get out of my chair."

"Oh, if you insist," Lando said, vacating the chair with a flourish that left it slowly spinning. "I was just following my dear mother's advice."

"On breaking and entering?"

"On avoiding stress. 'Never stand when you can sit down, and never sit when you can lie down.' "

"I see," Drayson said, stopping the rotation of his

chair with a hand and dropping into it. "I haven't heard anything of you in some time—"

"I doubt that."

"—Not since Mara Jade showed such surprising resistance to your charms."

"How kind of you to remember."

Drayson steepled his fingers. "My own theory is that you've been consoling yourself by spending the reward from Duchess Mistal in sabacc halls and on pleasure couches. Anything left of it?"

Lando smiled and sat on the edge of the desk. "I'm sure you could tell me to the half-credit. You never have forgiven me for the fact that because you and your Chandrila goons could never catch me and the *Falcon,* have you? Or for the fact that you caught so many of the dumb and clumsy smugglers, I made a *fortune* on my Chandrila runs. I really should have given you a share."

"You never have gotten over this notion that smuggling is an honorable line of work, have you?" Drayson asked, tipping back in his chair. "What makes you think I would have taken your dirty money?"

"Because I knew what kind of chit the Admiral of Chandrila Defense Fleet was drawing," Lando said. "Every good smuggler knows that bribes will get him places bravado won't."

For the first time, Drayson smiled. "You know, Baron, I really hate the fact that I can't help but like you."

"I know," Lando said. "I have the same problem. I never thought I could be friends with someone who was so fond of *rules.*"

"Well—life is full of surprises. Not that seeing you is one. To tell the truth—"

"Oh, why start now?"

"—I've been half expecting to see you since I heard that *Lady Luck* had docked upstairs. Though I didn't think it'd be with your feet up on my desk like you were taking over." Drayson folded his arms over his chest. "So—what can I do for you?"

"Wrong question, Admiral," Lando said. "What can *I* do for *you*?"

"Pardon?"

"I'm bored," Lando explained simply. "I go in business, I make a little money, I lose a little money—the game isn't interesting anymore. Someone throws a title at me, and I pick up the pieces someone else dropped—until one day I realize I'm sitting behind a desk, turning into you. There's no challenge in smuggling, unless you want to go to the Core—and I'm too smart to be that dumb. And there's hardly a scrap anywhere in twenty parsecs worth getting dirty for. That's why I'm here."

"You're bored," Drayson repeated.

"Exactly. Find something interesting for me to do and I'll tell you how I got past your perimeters." His expression was suddenly touched with regret. "I'm afraid there are a couple of security types you're going to have to let go, though."

"I see," said Drayson. "Any particular reason you happened to find yourself afflicted by boredom at this moment in time?"

"Why do you ask?"

Drayson pursed his lips. "I can't say anything more unless you come back in."

"Will I be sorry if I do?"

"Aren't you always?"

General Lando Calrissian and Admiral Drayson, chief of Alpha Blue, stood before a large briefing screen studying a holo image of a strange space vessel. The vessel's five cylindrical hulls, lying parallel to each other like a bundle of logs, were so dark in color that it was hard to see much detail. But the sensor's scale markings along the edge of the frame betrayed its size.

"I give up," Lando said finally. "I almost want to say it's Mon Calamari construction, but I don't think they ever built anything that *big*. What is it?"

"The Teljkon vagabond." When Lando's face

showed no signs of recognition, Drayson asked, "Are you familiar with the legend of the *Another Chance*?"

Lando cocked an eyebrow questioningly. "The Alderaan armory ship? Of course. Every smuggler in that sector has a story about seeing it. Which means that every smuggler in that sector is a bald-faced liar."

"You don't believe the legend, then?"

"Revisionist history," Lando said, shaking his head.

"Explain."

"I just can't believe that when the pacifists took over Alderaan's Council of Elders, they were cynical enough to pack all the weapons into a ship and send it hopping through hyperspace. They just had reason to wish they had done it, when the Empire came knocking a few years later." Lando sighed deeply. "Believe me, I wish the legend *was* true. I wish they'd recalled *Another Chance* before the Death Star reached Alderaan. But it's just another shaggy-ghost-ship story."

"I agree," Drayson said, reaching out and tapping the surface of the screen. "But this is a real ghost ship—probably the one that's kept the legend of *Another Chance* alive. This holo was taken by the New Republic frigate *Boldheart*, five years ago, right in the middle of that business with Admiral Daala."

Lando smiled wryly, remembering just how close "that business" had come to being the end of the New Republic.

"Just after this image was taken, *Boldheart* fired across the vagabond's bow," Drayson continued. "The vagabond fired back with some weapons we still don't understand, disabling *Boldheart*'s engines with one shot. Then it jumped into hyperspace. It wasn't seen again for almost two years. Bored yet?"

"No, go on."

Admiral Drayson turned away from the briefing display and walked back to a seat at the conference bar. "That was actually the second documented sighting. The first to spot it was a Hrasskis monitor ship working the Teljkon system."

"Thus the name."

"Right. The Hrasskis took it for a derelict and tried to intercept it. Now, mind you, they'd been hailing it for hours, and not a peep in reply. Then the vagabond broadcast a five-second wide-spectrum modulation that nearly burned out every comm circuit on the Hrasskis ship. There's a recording, but it's so distorted it's almost useless. Anyway, thirty seconds after it sent the signal—"

"Let me guess. Skipped into hyperspace."

"On the numbers."

"What about the third sighting?"

"That was ours. We thought we were going to be smart. An Intelligence Service ferret tried to attach a locator limpet to the vagabond's hull. Never even got close."

"And the fourth?"

Drayson leaned back in his chair and drummed his fingertips on the armrest. "It's in deep space near Gmar Askilon right now. We're trailing it with another ferret—"

"Keeping a safe distance, I hope."

"Very safe. But we're going after it," Drayson said. "Intelligence is putting together a small task force this very minute. They mean to catch the vagabond, board it, and unravel the riddles. Colonel Pakkpekatt of the Intelligence Service is in charge. If you'd come to me even a week from now, it would have been too late—they'd already have sailed."

"Is that so," Lando said, his face as unreadable as if he were at a sabacc table. "What fortuitous timing."

"Indeed. So—is that interesting enough?"

"It's an interesting *story*," Lando said pointedly. "I don't see anything interesting to *do* yet, though."

Drayson's expression turned gravely serious. "I'd like to put you on Pakkpekatt's ship—nominally as Fleet liaison. *Boldheart* was regular navy, after all. Intelligence can't deny that they have an interest."

"But I'd really be there for you?"

"No," said Drayson. "I could have put any

number of Alpha Blue agents in the task force. In fact, you don't know that I haven't. No, I don't want you to report to me."

"Then why do you want me on the mission?"

"Because you think like a smuggler, and Pakkpe-katt thinks like a colonel. Because you have a way of getting yourself where people don't want you, past traps that others don't see until it's too late. Because I think the mission has a better chance of succeeding if you're there than if you aren't."

"That's all?"

"That's all. That's my job," Drayson said. "To make sure that some things happen, and make sure others don't. So, make up your mind. Are you interested? Want to go chase the Teljkon vagabond?"

Lando just grinned.

Chapter 4

◆

In the first quiet moment of the day, Han's comlink unit chirped at him.

"Han, this is Luke," a familiar voice said. "Will you come see me?"

"What? Luke? Hey, kid, your sister's been looking everywhere for you—"

"I know," Luke said. "Will you come see me, alone?"

"Uh—all right. Where are you? Are you really on Coruscant, like Leia says?"

Luke did not answer directly. "Take your speeder due west from Imperial City. When you reach the coast, turn off your nav system and release the controls. I'll bring you here."

"Well—okay. That's easy enough. But it'll have to be later," Han said apologetically. "Tonight. Somebody's got to watch the kids."

"Of course, I'll see you tonight."

"Wait," Han said quickly, before Luke could break the link. "Is this supposed to be a secret? Can I tell Leia where I'm going?"

"If you need to. I don't want you to lie to her."

"You sure you don't want to just call her yourself, talk to her?"

"I'm sure," Luke said. "Tell her what you need to. But please come alone."

The shore of the western sea had been a glittering playground, a gay and glorious world that never slept, before the clone Emperor's Force storm had ravaged Coruscant. It had yet to fully recover. Only the lights of a few scattered resorts marked the broken lines of the coast as Han's speeder flashed overhead and bored into the dark sky over the western sea.

Han waited several long seconds, until he realized he couldn't say what exactly he was waiting for. "Okay, Luke. Hope you're listening, wherever you are. I really don't want to go swimming tonight."

Leaning forward, Han reached out and switched off the nav system, a process that took three confirmations and two overrides. A third of the speeder's cockpit controls went dark, while a bright orange legend across the bottom of the viewshield warned MANUAL FLIGHT MODE.

"Here goes nothing," Han said with a sigh, sitting back and crossing his arms over his chest.

Almost immediately the speeder veered sharply right and dived toward the water. It was all Han could do to stop himself from grabbing the controls again.

But the speeder soon leveled off, though at an alarmingly low altitude. The moon was still well below the horizon, but Han could see the undulating surface of the sea by the pale phosphorescent light of millions of tiny creatures riding the swells and currents. The sight was eerie and marvelous, but it was also barely an arm's length below the flat underside of the speeder, and racing by at a dizzying clip.

"Hey, Luke—you out there?" Han said, slouching as much as the speeder's seat and his long legs would allow. "Is this gonna be a long flight? Do I have time for a nap? Hey, pal, you can start food service anytime."

There was no response.

"Lousy spacelines," Han muttered, closing his

eyes. "They're all smiles till they have your money and herd you on board. *Then* see if you can get a glass of water—"

A long-winged sea shrike rose from the rocks to fly in formation with Han's speeder as, slowing, it arrowed toward the beach. Wakened by the change in the pitch of the speeder's thrusters, Han strained to make out where it might be headed.

Then a hole opened in the sky ahead, a brightly lit oval that hung above the beach like a doorway to morning. The sea shrike veered off, and the speeder coasted through the oval of light and settled on the floor of an otherwise empty high-ceilinged chamber. Han twisted sideways in his seat to see where he had come from, just in time to watch the opening seal itself behind him.

Hello, Han, a voice said in his mind. *Come up.*

"Come up?" Han said, scrambling out of the speeder. "There's no—"

As he began his protest, the nearest wall deformed into a ladder, and an opening appeared in the ceiling above it. "Sure," Han said. "As if it would have been any more trouble to make *stairs*."

But he reached out and clambered up the rungs all the same, taking them two at a time as a point of pride. He wasn't happy, though, to hear his own grunts at the bottom or feel his heart racing at the top.

Han found himself standing at the bottom of a large spherical room containing no furniture or technology—at least, none that he could spot. "Now what?"

Keep coming, said the voice in his head. *Walk up the wall.*

"Easy for you to say," Han said, starting to feel annoyed.

But the opening he had climbed through had already vanished, leaving him with little choice. He started up the curving wall, and found to his surprise that wherever he stood seemed to be the bottom of the sphere.

There was no telling whether it was a trick with grav fields, some sort of Jedi legerdemain, or the room itself was turning under him. Han tried not to think about it, though his steps became cautious as he went past the halfway point up the wall—or, at least, what should have seemed like halfway up the wall.

After he had gone a dozen more tentative steps, a section of the floor—wall? ceiling?—ahead of him dropped away to form a ramp leading out of the sphere. It seemed to Han as though he must be upside down in relation to the rest of the structure, but he found himself, apparently right side up, entering a large pyramidal room from one of its three sloping sides. It was as lacking in amenities as any space he had seen so far, and lit by the same curious uniform glow that seemed to come from behind the walls without making them bright to the eyes. The light was as cold as the air.

"Nice little tree house," Han said, moving slowly toward the center of the room, looking up at the apex of the chamber. "And you've done a wonderful job of cutting down on clutter. I think you've taken the idea of concealed storage to a new level. You'll have to give Leia the name of your decorator."

"Thank you for coming, Han," a voice said behind him. "It's good to see you."

Han spun around and found Luke standing one long stride away, almost as if he had been following Han. Han's face broke into a boyish lopsided grin. "Well, hey, I wanted to get out of the house, and since I was in the neighborhood— You know, you could've come to see us, too."

"No, I couldn't," Luke said. He wore an ankle-length patchwork robe that seemed to be made from bits of several other garments, including a pilot's uniform and a Tatooine sand cape. His demeanor was relaxed but remote, quelling Han's impulse to grab him in a bear hug and clap him on the back. "I hope by the time you leave, you'll understand why."

"Well—you'll have to start at the beginning, because I don't understand a thing about what's going on," Han said. "What is this place? Why are you here? Why are you hiding? Why am *I* here? Why didn't you want Leia to come?"

"Leia wants something from me," Luke said. "You don't. Your other questions will take longer to answer."

Han looked around with a frown. "If this is gonna be a long conversation—I don't suppose you have anything like a chair anywhere?"

"Sorry," Luke said, dropping gracefully into a cross-legged meditation posture. "Sit where you like, and I'll put an air cushion under you." He waited until Han was comfortably settled, then went on. "As you see, I can hide well enough, even from Leia. But I'd rather be left alone. I hope that you'll go back and ask her to accept that. If she doesn't—well, she's not going to get what she wants. She's only going to drive me away from Coruscant."

"I don't get it," Han said. "Why? You two have always been close. What happened?"

"Nothing," Luke said. "I just can't be close with anyone right now."

"Go on. I'm listenin'."

Luke nodded, but looked down into his lap before continuing. "I don't know if you can understand or not. When I first met Obi-Wan, he'd been a hermit on Tatooine for ten years or more. When I first met Yoda, he had been a hermit on Dagobah for a *hundred* years or more. I never thought to ask either of them why."

"A little late for that now," Han said with a wry smile.

"At the time, I assumed they were both in hiding. Hiding from the Emperor, from my father. But that makes no sense."

"No? Nothing personal, but hiding from that pair

makes great sense to me. I can think of a couple of times I'd have been glad to do it if I could have."

"But why in the middle of a desert, or a jungle?"

"Eh—isn't that obvious?"

"No," Luke said, shaking his head. "It's much easier for Han Solo to hide—even with a price on his head—than for a powerful Jedi, whether Knight or Dark Lord. A Jedi's physical presence is only a small portion of his connection to the universe. Change his face, hide him from sight, and I'll still feel his presence when he draws on the Force. It doesn't matter if he's in the next room or across the system. Remember when we were taking the stolen shuttle to Endor, to destroy the second Death Star's shield?"

"Yeah," Han said. "You were pretty jumpy. You said Vader could sense you."

"He did sense me," Luke said. "I didn't have the skill yet to make the waters still. But Obi-Wan and Yoda were Masters. If they could hide from the Emperor—and I believe they could—why, they could as easily hide in Imperial City, or on Vader's own Star Destroyer, as anywhere. And if their skills weren't equal to Palpatine's, neither distance nor isolation could save them from being discovered."

"Maybe they hid out in the sticks so no one else would get hurt if Vader showed up," Han suggested. "You've gotta admit, when you guys fight, it has a way of getting messy. We've got a few monuments to that fact downtown in Imperial City."

Luke shook his head. "No. I discovered the real reason while I was on Yavin—the dilemma that every Jedi eventually faces. I discovered a very important and difficult truth, Han—a *frustrating* truth. The stronger you become in the Force, the more that you *can* do, the more that's expected of you, and the less your life belongs to you."

"Is this the answer, then?" Han said, gesturing at the room with one hand. "Running away?"

"Call it that if you must. It's one answer. There's another, even less appealing," Luke said. "Han, I'm convinced that for each Jedi, there comes a point at which he or she must choose. When the world presses in on you, threatens to drive you mad, there're only two ways you can find peace. One is to impose your will on everyone and everything around you. The other is to surrender your will, your ego, and withdraw from those who are always wanting you to 'fix' their lives."

"I don't see it," Han said stubbornly.

Luke smiled. "Try to imagine that you're at home. One of the children is screaming, and the other two are tugging at your elbows, each demanding that you punish the other for some slight—"

"Routine," Han said.

"Chewbacca is playing tree-drum music at ear-splitting levels. See-Threepio is nattering on about nothing. Artoo-Detoo is behind your chair, arguing with the household droids in Basic. The hypercomm is blaring two channels at once, both too loudly. Your comlink is chirping in your pocket. You have three messages from people who want you to come do them a favor, and Leia's insisting on your attention. Lando has a raucous sabacc game going in the next room, there's someone at the front door, and a flight of airspeeders keeps buzzing right over your head."

"Okay, that'd be a little worse than routine," Han conceded. "A little."

"Now imagine it goes on around the clock for a day, ten days, a month, half a year, a year—not only without a break, but getting worse all the time. Until you reach your limit, whatever your limit might be. What are your choices? Control your environment, or leave it."

"Or go mad and destroy it," Han said. "Which hardly counts as a choice. Yeah, I think I get the picture now."

"Do you see what a thin line separates Palpatine and Yoda?" Luke said earnestly. "Palpatine sought power over others. Yoda sought power from within. Palpatine wanted control of everything, in the hopes of building what he thought would be a perfect universe.

Yoda gave up the idea of controlling or perfecting the universe, in the hopes of understanding it."

"You know," Han said slowly, "I always kind of wondered why you drew the short straw, why Yoda and Obi-Wan didn't team up and take on the Emperor themselves—"

"Yes!" Luke said, his face more animated than Han had seen it since arriving. "I think that's why it fell to me, Han. That's why I had to be the one to face Vader. I still had the passion to reshape things, a passion Obi-Wan and Yoda had moved beyond. Surrender disarms you."

Han's expression showed his disgust. "It's pretty useless, then, isn't it? Jedi Knights who won't fight?"

"Han, try to understand. The essence of the dark side is using the Force to control others. I know that temptation firsthand. If you champion that idea, you're thinking just as Palpatine and my father did—'I have the power, and it's mine to use as I wish.' Do you want that to be the code we live by? Should the Jedi rule the galaxy, simply because we can?"

"Well—now that you put it that way—"

"Good," Luke said. "But then understand that there's a price. When a Jedi renounces that path, it becomes very hard to be a warrior, to lead a crusade. Obi-Wan and Yoda weren't afraid to fight, or to die. They felt the suffering the Empire was causing just as acutely as any of us did—probably more so. I wasn't stronger than them, or wiser. I was raw, headstrong, reckless. But I had to be the one to challenge the Emperor—*because I still could.*"

Han frowned and cocked his head. "What about now?"

"Now? I don't know," Luke said, shaking his head. "I don't know if I could do it now. I don't know if I could summon the outrage. I feel myself standing on a dividing line, at a cusp. I don't know what I should be doing with these gifts—these burdens. It's the question I've come here to explore."

"And you want to be left alone to do it."

"I need to be, Han. Will you help Leia understand?"

"I can try," Han said dubiously.

"I can't ask more than that."

"Um—look, with everything you've said, I already know the answer. But I gotta ask, so I can tell her I did. Leia wants your help with something."

"I know."

"She wants you to come live with us for a while. She needs help with the kids."

"She thinks she does," Luke said. "I'm sorry. I have to say no."

"Okay," Han said with a shrug. "I had to ask. I guess she thought, you know, family and all, maybe you could become a hermit next month instead of this month—"

Luke stood. "She's important to me, as are the children, as are you. You know that."

"Sure—"

"That's why my answer is no. It has nothing to do with this other matter."

"It doesn't?" Han asked, struggling to his feet.

"My sister Leia has all the talent and wisdom she needs to be not only the mother, but the model, your children need," Luke said. "She has only to believe in herself, and she'll find that nothing is beyond her. Which is why the worst thing I could do for your family right now is come to her rescue, to encourage her to look to me to solve her problems. She'll only undercut her own authority with the children, and yours with it. They must learn their first and most important lessons from you. In that, they're no different from any other children."

Han pursed his lips as he considered Luke's answer. "All right," he said, offering his hand. "Good luck, Luke. I hope this won't be the last time I see you. But you call us—we won't call you. Okay, buddy?"

Taking the offered hand, Luke looked intently into his visitor's eyes. "Thank you," he said, with a small but affectionate smile. "I couldn't ask for a better friend than you, Han."

As always, the open emotion made Han uncomfortable. "You could ask, but you don't deserve one," he wisecracked, patting Luke on the arm and then pulling away. He circled around Luke toward where the chamber's entrance used to be. "You get right to work moving that mental furniture around, or whatever it is you hermits do. I'll just go home and tell Leia you've cracked up—it'll be a lot simpler. No, don't bother, I can find my way out. I never have seen a maze that couldn't be greatly simplified with a good blaster—"

The golden sheen of the droid's metal skin made a brilliant contrast to the tangle of broad green leaves and dangling vines through which he was noisily making his way.

"Impossible! Such arrogance!" the droid said aloud as he struggled with the thick growth, though he did not yet know there was an audience for his thoughts. "For all he listens to me, you would think that he is the protocol droid and I the astromech."

Flailing his arms at a snarl of branches blocking his way, the golden droid stopped and looked back the way he had come. "I hope the stonebats rip out your circuits and nest in your equipment bays," he called into the jungle. "I hope a kitehawk drags you off to the temples and feeds you to her kits. It would just serve you right."

But when he turned back to consider his own plight, the droid found his way blocked not only by the flora of Yavin 4, but by a tall, broad-shouldered man in a military flight suit.

"Oh!" See-Threepio exclaimed, and fell back a step. "General Calrissian! You startled me, sir. Where did you come from?"

Lando grinned. "With all the noise you were making, a platoon of stormtroopers could have snuck up and startled you. Don't tell me you're still fighting with

Artoo after all this time. You two are worse than brothers."

"That stubborn, contrary pile of tin is no brother to me," Threepio said with stiff pride. "If I had been as carelessly constructed as he was, I would return myself to my maker to be scrapped. In all my years, I have never met another R unit as erratic and egotistical as Artoo-Detoo. A simple rebuild of the secondary power grid, and Artoo turns it into a major project. I could give you a list of his operational anomalies as long as—"

"That will have to wait," said Lando. "Right now you need to pack your polish and power couplings. You're coming with me on a little trip."

"Sir, I would be most delighted to accompany you. For all *I* care, Artoo can fall in a mud bog and rust away," Threepio said, extracting himself from the snarl of vines and circling a tree to join Lando. "But Master Luke brought me here to manage the administrative needs of the Academy, and he did not change those instructions before he left."

"What *did* he say when he left?"

"Not a word to either of us, General Calrissian. He simply vanished in the night. I have not heard from him or of him in nineteen local days. Do you have news of Master Luke, sir? Is he well? Do you bring new instructions from him?"

Lando pursed his lips and considered. "Yes, I do, Threepio, new instructions for the both of you. Luke's fine, but he's gone off on some sort of retreat, and he's assigned you to the Fleet Office until he returns. And the Fleet Office has assigned you to me."

If I could have found Luke to ask him, I'm sure the end result would have been the same, Lando told himself.

"I am glad to hear that Master Luke is well, General Calrissian. No one has been able to tell me anything. And I will not miss Yavin Four. It is so humid here that my circuits are always corroding. Look at me—I can't go into the jungle without getting filthy. But must we take Artoo with us?"

"I'm afraid so, old man," Lando said, patting the droid's metallic shoulder. "But look at it this way—*you* only have to deal with Artoo. I have to deal with the both of you. If I can cope, so can you."

Threepio tipped his head back, and his eyes flashed. "Sir, I don't understand—"

"I'll explain later," Lando said, glancing at his chrono. "Call Artoo in. We've got a deadline to beat, and this isn't our last stop."

"I will have to inform Master Streen of our departure."

"Already taken care of," Lando said, thinking of a different set of lies he had just told to Streen. *Still can't get used to being trusted—it's better camouflage than I thought.* "Come on, tin man, *Lady Luck*'s waiting for us."

Coppery clouds rich in oxides of Tibanna gas churned outside the viewpanes of what had once been Lando Calrissian's office in Bespin's Cloud City. Inside as outside, nothing had changed since the last time he had seen it. The walls and shelves were heavily laden with the eclectic collection of objects that only a rich man or a well-traveled smuggler could amass.

"I like what you've done to the place," Lando said to the cyborg that sat behind what had once been Lando's desk. "I guess I never did get around to sending for my things, eh?"

"I don't mind," said Lobot. The activity lights on the interface band he wore from ear to ear were flickering busily. "You have better judgment in subjective matters than I do. The calculus of room decoration still eludes me."

"Well—at least you have the good taste to recognize my good taste," Lando said with a grin. "Still, a man can get tired of the same surroundings day after day, no matter how splendid they are. When's the last time you got yourself out of here for a while?"

"I go out on inspection walks twice a day," Lobot said. "It takes ninety-seven days to complete an inspection schedule."

"Let me put it another way. How long has it been since you broke your connection to Cloud City?"

A puzzled expression flashed briefly across the cyborg's face. "I have never broken my connection to the administrative interface."

"Just as I suspected," Lando said. "And exactly why I'm here. Lobot, you work too hard. You're long overdue for a change of scenery—a vacation."

"How can I leave Cloud City without an administrator?"

"Lobot, I have a secret to tell you—the people who work for you will enjoy the novelty."

Lobot frowned. "But systems will randomize without monitoring and supervision."

"Then think about how much fun you'll have putting them right when you get back," Lando said. "And the trip will do you good, too. Frankly, you could use a little practice in conversation. Am I still the only one around here who knows you can talk?"

"Direct input is more efficient."

"Efficiency is overrated, my friend," Lando said, sitting back in his chair and crossing his legs, ankle over knee. "Come on, what do you say? Knowing how much you *like* to work, I cooked up a vacation where there'll be plenty of work for you to do."

"What sort of work?"

"I can't tell you unless you say yes," Lando said, tapping the insignia on his uniform. "I've got a temporary commission in my pocket, and the security clearance to go with it. All I can promise you is problems a lot more interesting than the ones you're working on now. And I really could use your help. It'll be like old times."

Lobot stood, looking slowly about the room. "I'll trade you my help for your 'things,' " he said finally. "I want them to stay, for old times."

"Why, you old horse trader, you. Who's been teaching you the art of the finagle?"

"You did," Lobot said. He closed his eyes and lowered his chin to his chest. The lights on his interface bar all flashed green, then all flashed red, then went dark. Raising his head, he opened his eyes and looked at Lando. "It's too quiet."

"Go ahead and leave a few channels open, then," Lando said, standing. "Bring with you whatever you need to be comfortable."

A few scattered lights on Lobot's interface sprang back into activity. "Better," he said. "Let's go. What is my rank? What problems need solutions?"

"I'll tell you all about it on the way."

The Teljkon task force, seven vessels in all, had gathered in orbit around the sixth planet of the Coruscant system, where it would not so readily attract attention. *Lady Luck* was the last to join them and the smallest ship among them, save for a pilotless Intelligence ferret. Lando's yacht was dwarfed by Pakkpekatt's command ship, the cruiser *Glorious*.

"I don't like the looks of that heavy artillery," Lando said, sizing up the situation from *Lady Luck*'s cockpit. "I thought we were being sent to outsmart our quarry, not outgun it."

"The fact that the vagabond disabled a frigate with apparent ease may have dictated the choice of a cruiser," Lobot said.

"I'm sure it did," Lando agreed. "I just don't like the way things are shaping up." He reached for the comm unit. "This is General Lando Calrissian aboard the *Lady Luck*, hailing the *Glorious*. Request permission to come aboard."

"General Calrissian, sir," said a young-sounding voice. "This is Lieutenant Harona, officer of the day. We've been expecting you, sir. Would you like us to send out the captain's boat?"

"I'm afraid there's been some misunderstanding,

Lieutenant. I'm not looking for a ride in. I'm looking for parking space on your flight deck."

There was a static-filled pause, which ended when Harona cleared his throat. "General Calrissian, I'm afraid you're right, there *has* been some confusion. Our flight decks are filled with mission gear and our own baby birds. There's no room for *Lady Luck* inboard."

"Then make room, Lieutenant. Unless you were planning for our best speed to be your convoy speed." Lando thumbed the mute switch and added to Lobot, "Now we'll find out if they know how fast my little ship really is."

The second pause was longer. "Sir, Colonel Pakkpekatt suggests that you come aboard *Glorious* and let a relief crew ferry your yacht back to Coruscant."

"Aha," said Lando. "That tells me that they've got it in their minds that I'm an observer." He released the mute switch. "Lieutenant Harona, we have our own mission gear aboard. Do I understand you to say Colonel Pakkpekatt is willing to hold here for another day or two while you set up secure holdings for file and equipment transfer? If so, put your quartermaster on, and we'll start telling him what we'll need—"

"Uh, no, sir, that would not be the colonel's first choice."

Lando winked at Lobot. *Now I've got 'em,* he thought. "Lieutenant, maybe I should just talk to Colonel Pakkpekatt directly."

They could almost hear the OD squirming. "Sir, the colonel is very busy at the moment with predeparture matters—"

"I'm sure he is. Tell you what, Lieutenant. I can solve your little problem for you without disturbing the colonel. I see that your Number Five external dock is open. You pull that cap and we'll hook on there."

"General Calrissian, I'm *very* sorry, but I can't authorize that—"

"Then why are you wasting my time, Lieutenant?" Lando said sharply. "Go get your senior officer and put him on the line. I want to talk to someone who can make a decision. And when we're finished with our business—which should take about two minutes—I'm going to ask him to conduct a review of his bridge procedures and staff. I want him to find out why a flag officer and the Fleet Operations delegation to this mission were kept waiting while the officer of the day thumbed through the manual for a regulation to follow."

The subsequent silence was the longest yet. "*Lady Luck*, Number Five External Hard Dock will be ready momentarily. Prepare for autodocking."

"*Thank* you, Lieutenant," said Lando. "*Lady Luck* out."

"Well done, sir," Threepio gushed. "That seems like an excellent compromise."

"Compromise, nothing. I got what I really wanted," Lando said, starting the autodocking sequence and climbing out of the pilot's seat. "I wasn't about to give up my ship, and I didn't want it locked up inside where I'd need their permission to use it."

"Then you achieved all your objectives," Lobot said.

"Oh, no. We're just beginning. Now we have to reeducate them about our role on this mission," Lando said. "Get ready to disembark. I'm going to need all of you on this."

"Colonel Pakkpekatt, sir, General Calrissian to see you." The ensign's voice was a bit shrill with nervousness. Lando guessed that he had never been on the combat bridge before, or had reason to speak to the mission commander—if he had seen him at all.

The ensign had been the first member of the crew Lando saw after ducking through the inner airlock of Number 5 Dock, and he had commandeered the young technician to escort them to Colonel Pakkpekatt. Lando was familiar with the layout of the *Belarus*-class star cruiser, and could have hazarded a guess as to where Pakkpekatt could be found. But being escorted, with his entourage following at his heels, allowed him to make an entrance.

Several heads swiveled at the ensign's announcement, but most turned immediately back to their duties after taking in the new arrivals with a glance.

The exception was a two-meter-tall Hortek, whose bony armor plates were a ruddy brown in the bridge's combat lighting. His long neck twisted toward the group standing by the bridge's aft blast door, and the intense gaze from his unblinking eyes was nearly hypnotizing.

Curse you, Drayson—you could have told me he was a Hortek, Lando thought reflexively. But after that he guarded his thoughts as best he could. Besides being one of the few predator species in the New Republic, the Hortek had the reputation of being telepathic not only with their own kind, but, to an unknown degree, with a number of other species as well. It was an intimidating combination.

"General," Pakkpekatt said, curtly acknowledging Lando. His gaze flicked to Lobot and the droids. "Who are these—people?"

C-3PO stepped forward smartly. "Sir, I am See-Threepio, human-cyborg relations. I am fluent in over six million—"

"Shut up," Pakkpekatt said sharply.

"Yes, sir," Threepio said, retreating behind Lobot.

Lando stepped forward. "Colonel Pakkpekatt, this is my staff. I'd be happy to make introductions, but I have some late updates for you which perhaps ought to have our attention first. Is your ready room available?"

Pakkpekatt held his head high, studying Lando.

Reaching into my mind? You and I need to talk, and no one else here needs to hear what we say.

Pakkpekatt lifted a hand in the direction of the ready room door. "Captain, continue with preparations for departure," he said.

The moment the door wrapped privacy around them, Pakkpekatt drew threateningly close to Lando.

"So," he said, "you're the man who browbeat my officer of the day. Don't expect to do the same to me."

Lando smiled and opened up the distance between them again by slipping into a chair. "I wouldn't even try, Colonel," he said, adopting a relaxed posture. "Nor would I expect to need to. We're here with the same goal, working for the same people—Princess Leia, the Senate, the Republic."

Pakkpekatt made a sharp barking sound, the Hortek equivalent of a grunt. "I was told to wait for an observer from Fleet Command. Nothing was said about staff."

"Why should anything need to be said? Do you go anywhere without your aides?" asked Lando, gesturing with both hands. "My staff has technical expertise which very well may be the difference between success and failure for this mission."

"We have five protocol droids on board, all E series or newer," Pakkpekatt said. "Yours are superfluous."

"On the contrary, I consider my staff indispensable," Lando said. "And I expect them to be extended every consideration due me as the Fleet Office's field operative for this mission."

Pakkpekatt moved closer, looming over Lando. "*Operative*—now, that's a curious word, General. Were you led to believe that you'd have an active part in the conduct of the mission?"

"Were you led to believe otherwise?"

"I have been assigned to recover the Teljkon vagabond," Pakkpekatt said. "I have no instructions about sharing my command or that responsibility with you."

"I don't want to share your command, Colonel. All I want is mutual cooperation. After all, the Fleet Office's interests in this matter are at least equal to the Intelligence Service's interests," Lando said. "We were the ones who nearly lost a frigate to the vagabond."

"Then you should understand that this is an extremely sensitive matter. We have no idea what we may find out there."

"Colonel, if we find anything of value out there, it's not going to belong to either one of us," Lando said, flashing his best conciliatory smile. "Unless you simply don't trust the Fleet Office, there's no reason we can't work together toward a common goal."

Pakkpekatt loosed an eerie chittering sound, which caused a chill to run down Lando's back. "What are you asking?"

"No more than you would. Run of the ship. Full and timely access to tactical data. Consultation on strategy. And if and when we board her, include us in."

"Only that?"

"That's it. All other command prerogatives remain yours."

"I see," Pakkpekatt said. "All we need do to keep you happy is take you along on the most sensitive part of the mission, and one for which you're completely unprepared."

"Now, Colonel—"

"Do you take me for wounded prey?" the Hortek demanded, showing his teeth. "We are prepared to assemble an assault team tailored to whatever challenges the vagabond presents. I am *not* prepared to assemble one based on who thinks it would be fun to go along."

"Do you have a lockpick?"

"What?"

"You said you're ready for anything," Lando said. "But it's been my experience that when someone in uniform says that, he really means 'We have little guns, we have big guns, we have bombs of all sizes.' There are other ways to get past a locked door. Are you as ready to pick a lock as you are to blow one up? As ready to wheedle as you are to demand? As ready to coax as to capture? If not, you'd better think again about how ready you really are."

"My tactical team has over fifty years' intelligence experience—"

"Listen, Colonel," Lando said, coming to his feet

and thrusting his face close to the Hortek. "I'm sure you have good, solid veteran players on your team. But I've got some ringers on mine. I've got a human with a machine interface, a droid with a universal linguistic interface, and a droid with a universal machine interface—"

"There is nothing special about your staff's abilities."

"Maybe not in the specs," said Lando. "But they know how to play together, and they know how to win. We beat Darth Vader, and we beat the Emperor, on their turf and on their terms—"

"Ancient history. And you were lucky."

Lando smiled. "Any gambler knows you don't bet against a lucky man. If you keep my players out of the game, and you lose, you're going to have a hard time explaining that to the people who sent us out here."

"A commander's burden."

"I wouldn't want yours right now," Lando said. "Look, Colonel—no matter who or what's inside the vagabond, we have to be able to outthink them. Because if we don't, we lose both ways—if we have to destroy that ship, or it has to destroy us."

"I am very aware of that."

Lando pointed toward the door. "Well, that's R2-D2 and C-3PO out there, *Luke Skywalker*'s personal droids. And Lobot and I made a living making fools of Security and Intelligence in one system after another. We've beaten tricks your people haven't even thought of yet. How sure are you that you don't want us on your team?"

Pakkpekatt's nostrils flared. Then he bowed his neck, the Hortek counterpart to a nod of agreement. "Very well. We will work together."

"Good. That's all I want," Lando said.

"I do not believe that. I know who you are," Pakkpekatt said with a menacing stiffness. "Do not think I do not. I will be watching you."

Lando kept his mind clear. "We're going to get along just fine, Colonel. You'll see."

Chapter 5

◆

On the morning of her first meeting with Nil Spaar, Leia climbed out of bed with an aching shoulder, tired eyes, and a blanket of fatigue in her limbs that made her feel as though she was on the verge of being ill.

Anakin had awakened from a terrifying nightmare in the small hours, and Leia had allowed him to climb into bed between her and Han in the hope that it would help him sleep. But the unfamiliar presence of a third little body had forced her into unnatural sleeping postures. Worse, Anakin had become a restive sleeper, and she had found herself aware of his every move, coming fully awake time and again as he turned and squirmed beside her.

Han, Leia had been annoyed to discover, slept through it all, including his own snoring.

Her grogginess persisted through breakfast. As she dressed for her meeting with the viceroy of the Duskhan League, she thought only about falling back into the now empty bed for a nap. It was the kind of morning that sorely tempted her to break her own rule about stimulants and take a cup of naris-bud tea or chew a stick of brightgum.

The temptation got stronger once she reached the final briefing. The conference room seemed to be full of bodies, and everyone seemed to be talking to her at once.

"Try to get emergency transit and landing rights on a provisional basis, as a stepping-stone to full navigation rights. We've got members in Joruna and Widek, and it's a long way around for the freighters."

"Almost everything we know about the Koornacht Cluster is thirty years old. It was in Imperial hands from the time of the Clone Wars until shortly after the Battle of Endor. The Empire didn't allow anyone in, and—until now—the Yevetha haven't seemed interested in coming out."

"As near as we can tell, the Duskhan League only includes the eleven worlds populated by the Yevetha. We believe that there are as many as seventeen worlds in the Koornacht Cluster which are populated by other species, and not part of the Duskhan League. But it hasn't been possible to survey or contact them."

"Intelligence hasn't been able to find a single civilian pilot who'll admit having gone into the Koornacht Cluster. We've gotten a deposition from one of our Imperial prisoners, a former bridge officer on a Star Destroyer which he says visited there on patrol. It's pretty wild stuff, though, and nothing he says can be confirmed."

"Mineral resources available for trade? Isn't that information in the Duskhan application file? It's supposed to be."

"There isn't any application. They're not applying for membership. It's more like an audition—for us. Nil Spaar seems to think this is some sort of summit meeting. He doesn't want to be called 'Ambassador,' either."

"Why doesn't Intelligence have better information for us? Where does a viceroy stand in the Duskhan power structure?"

"I don't think there's any question but that Nil Spaar represents more worlds, a larger population, greater material riches, and a more advanced industrial-technological base than anyone who's come to Imperial City in the last twelve years. And he probably knows it, too."

"Leia, from a strategic standpoint, it sure would be nice to have a friend that big sitting between us and wherever Daala's gotten herself to, in the Core. Right now Koornacht is one of the soft spots along the Inner Line."

"Does anyone have any solid information on what *he* wants?"

"A link to the New Republic hypernet and the Coruscant information went in the second day. His staff did all the inside work, though. At least we know they couldn't just eavesdrop on the net."

"Where's the technical analysis of the Duskhan embassy ship?"

"Does anyone else think that the Yevetha might be related to the Twi'lek?"

"Have you had a chance to review the results of the Obra-skai library search?"

"Leia, are you all right?"

"Princess Leia?"

Shaking her head, Leia pushed herself away from the table and started toward the door. Lightheadedness halted her steps halfway across the room. As she swayed unsteadily, Admiral Ackbar hastened to her side and took her arm.

"Help me to my office," she whispered.

In the privacy of the president's suite, one floor up from the conference room, Ackbar helped Leia settle on a thickly padded couch.

"What is happening to you?" Ackbar asked. "Should I signal the medical droid?" An MD-7, a mobile droid specialized for emergency medicine, was permanently assigned to the executive section.

"No. I'll be all right. I just want to lie down for a few moments. There was no air in that conference room."

"You don't look well. Do you want to postpone?"

She shook her head almost imperceptibly. "No—no, it would just complicate things. There've been too many delays already. I got up too quickly, that's all."

"Perhaps someone else should take over today's session—"

"No one else can," Leia said sharply.

"Then someone should be in there with you."

"Nil Spaar expects to meet in private with the Chief of State of the New Republic. That's what he insisted on. That's what we agreed to. We can't make any changes an hour before the session—not without giving offense," Leia said, and closed her eyes. "Just go away and let me have a few minutes of quiet. I'll be ready when the time comes. This isn't a crisis. Everything will be fine."

In a subtle bit of choreography arranged by the protocol attachés for both sides, Princess Leia Organa Solo, president of the New Republic, and Nil Spaar, viceroy of the Duskhan League, entered the Grand Hall from opposite sides at exactly the same moment.

Leia's strides were measured and steady. She had spent the time alone in meditation, opening her connection to the Force and drawing on its deep, powerful currents, allowing the flow to cleanse and refresh her body and mind. Doing so meant surrendering a bit of her pride, just as drinking naris-bud tea would have—an admission that she needed a crutch. But it left her more ready to face the responsibility in front of her.

Nil Spaar matched her pace, stride for stride. He was not an imposing figure, no taller than Leia, perhaps even a touch shorter without his thick-soled, block-heeled boots. His eyes were strikingly human, distracting Leia at first from the high ruff of bony armor at the back of his neck and the bold streaks of facial color that disappeared under the soft swirl of fabric he wore on his head. Nil Spaar's gaze was open and friendly, his smile disarming.

The Yevethan was dressed as he had been on the streets in all the surveillance recordings Leia had seen: in a close-fitting, long-sleeved tunic with tan shoulders and a brown body, darker narrow-legged pants that tucked into his boots, and beige gloves that disappeared up the sleeves of his tunic. There was no sign of jewelry or insignia save for the pin that held his head wrap in place. There were no signifiers of rank or station, as she might expect on a uniform or ceremonial garment.

By unspoken agreement, each of them stopped when the other was a long stride out of arm's reach. "Viceroy," Leia said, and bowed.

"Princess Leia," Nil Spaar said, bowing in turn. "I am so pleased to be here with you. This is how it should be. You, the head of a confederacy of worlds, strong, proud, prosperous—me, the head of a confederacy of worlds, strong, proud, prosperous. You have welcomed me as an equal, and I welcome you in the same fashion."

"Thank you, Viceroy. Would you like to sit?" Leia said, gesturing toward the two chairs, each with a small side table, that rested in the middle of the room facing each other.

"By all means," Nil Spaar said. His chair, provided and set up by his majordomo, was an S of open wire mesh. On the table beside it were two black cylinders with feeding tubes. "We should be able to sit down with each other and talk honestly, as statesmen and patriots. You yourself fought in the great rebellion against that black beast, Palpatine, did you not?"

"I got my knees and elbows dirty a few times," Leia said. "But many others did far more than I."

"Such practiced modesty! But, here again, we can hardly help but understand each other," said Nil Spaar. "I had my own small part to play in reclaiming Koornacht from the pestilent minions of the Emperor. So we both know what it means to take up arms in a cause to which we pledge our lives and honor. Indeed, as we sit here this moment, I warrant we are both still answering the call to duty which honor imposes on us—is that not so?"

Leia did not want to be led onto such personal ground. "Life is what happens to you while you're busy making sensible plans—or so I've heard," she said with a smile. "I do what I can to preserve that which I love. I don't know that that makes me any different from most of the people I meet."

"Ah, you are wiser than your years," said Nil Spaar. "But of course you know that it is what you love which makes you stand apart. Yourself, of course, and your children, and your mates—but beyond that, a circle of friends, a community of kin, and a collection of ideals. And so it is with me. How pleased I would be, if, here, away from interference and distraction, we should be able to forge an alliance which will benefit those we love."

"That's the entire purpose of the New Republic," Leia said, sidestepping the word *alliance* as if it were quicksand. "I think that if you'll speak to the leaders of some of the hundred worlds which have become members in the last twenty-eight days, you'll hear that the benefits are substantial and immediate."

"I do not doubt it," said Nil Spaar. "One need only look at the miracle of Coruscant. Was it not but half a dozen years ago that this world was ravaged by the clone Emperor himself?"

"Yes—"

"And now I find it rebuilt from its own ashes to a new glory that rivals the stories of old," Nil Spaar said, his tone admiring. "I have walked your city for hours on end, marveling at the industry of your people, the cleverness of your inventions, the grandness of your visions. Such proud edifices you erect out of hope and clay. Such bold dreams you build on the ruins of past failure."

"We do what we can—what we must," Leia said. "I like to think of Coruscant as a symbol of what's possible, a mirror in which we can see our best face.

The vitality you've seen is a reflection of the vitality of the entire Republic. I want Coruscant to stand for the idea that there's an alternative to war and tyranny. Co-operation and tolerance—the best of all of us, available to all of us."

"And there are so many of you! I am certain I saw more different species in my first hour here than I did in my entire previous life. Dozens, if not a hundred," Nil Spaar said. "How does it all work? Is membership political or genetic?"

"The New Republic is a mutual self-protection pact among over four hundred sentient species, and an economic partnership between eleven thousand inhabited worlds," said Leia. "But you'll find that the autonomy of member worlds is hardly compromised at all—"

"So long as they are willing to be cooperative and tolerant," Nil Spaar said.

"That goes without saying."

"Perhaps it ought not," said Nil Spaar. "It might lead to misunderstandings, and mistaken assumptions."

Puzzled, Leia felt as though the ground had suddenly shifted under her. "I don't think a legation has ever come to Coruscant expecting anything else."

"You would know better than I. But you might find some came here more committed to getting Coruscant to fight their fights than to Leia Organa's ideals. The weak are always looking for champions. Are you certain there are none such hiding in your skirts?"

"If the weak can't count on Coruscant's protection, then there is no New Republic—only anarchy. And anarchy can only lead to more tyranny."

"Well answered."

"Thank you," said Leia. "But since you raised the issue, would you mind telling me why you and *your* legation are here?"

"Not at all. I think it important that there be no misunderstandings," Nil Spaar said. "As impressed as I am with your ideas, your capital city, and your confederation, the Duskhan League is not interested in membership in the New Republic. Not collectively, and not as individual worlds. Despite the fact that we submitted no application, you seem unclear on that fact."

"I think the Duskhan League would be a valuable member of the New Republic," Leia said. "I wasn't willing to dismiss the possibility without talking to you."

Nil Spaar smiled tolerantly. "You may dismiss it now—please."

"Then what are you seeking here?"

"As I've already said, an alliance. An agreement between equals, to the benefit of both."

Frowning, Leia asked, "Viceroy, are you concerned that what you call the 'weak' members would be too much of a burden on you?"

"No. That is not an issue."

"Very well," Leia said. "But I think you should know right now that it'll be very hard for us to come to an 'agreement between equals' that'll allow us to respond militarily if you're threatened. The charter under which we operate allows for mutual defense and enforcement of the articles of membership—and that's all."

"Truly, you do not yet understand. We do not want or need your protection," Nil Spaar said. "We enjoyed the 'protection' of the Empire for half my lifetime, and we are determined to avoid such blessings in the future. What we want more than anything is to be left alone. Bear that in mind, and we may begin to speak the same language."

At Leia's prodding, Nil Spaar shared with her some of the Yevetha's experiences at the hands of Emperor Palpatine's generals and stormtroopers. The stories were familiar enough in flavor, if not in detail.

The Imperial governor of Koornacht had been given a free hand in subduing the Yevetha. In his turn, he had Yevetha women taken as pleasure slaves for his staff, and Yevetha men taken as live targets for his troopers. The brutalized bodies were displayed in schools, at sacred sites, and on the public information channels everyone was required to watch twice a day.

When that did not produce the desired degree of cooperation, the Imperial governor had children taken instead. Dissent crumbled, but the terror of random seizures continued. When the Imperial occupation army was finally driven from Koornacht, seven thousand Yevetha hostages were found in the governor's garrison—and the bones of more than fifteen thousand dead.

"Enough," Leia said. "Please. I'm afraid we've already reawakened enough nightmares."

"I wanted you to understand the depth of our feelings in this."

"I do," said Leia. *I may understand one of our own better now, too.*

"Then let us turn our attention to the future," Nil Spaar said.

For the next hour, they worked at teasing out what the language of alliance might sound like. Despite apparent good faith, they constantly stumbled over conflicting assumptions, and their progress was hard to measure. But at midday, when the viceroy gathered himself and stood, he pronounced, "This has been valuable and enjoyable. Shall we resume in one hour?"

"I'd be happy to continue through lunch," Leia offered. "We could have food brought to us."

Nil Spaar looked momentarily shocked. "With all apologies, that is not possible," he said. "My people hold it a great affront to propriety to take food in mixed company. And I personally believe it foolish to dilute a worship meal with distracting conversation."

"My apologies," Leia said, standing. "In an hour, then."

"I look forward to it."

The debriefing session included Leia, Admiral Ackbar for the Fleet Office, Admiral Drayson standing in for Intelligence director General Rieekan, Behn-kihl-

nahm for the Senate, First Administrator Engh, two recorder droids, and half a dozen senior aides.

Everyone listened without interruption as Leia
quickly recounted as much of her conversation with
Nil Spaar as her memory would allow. Then all had a
chance to question Leia or offer their comments.

The comments were largely predictable. Ackbar,
always thinking about strategic issues, was concerned
that navigation rights hadn't come up yet, and wanted
that issue given priority in the afternoon session.
Drayson, always looking to open intelligence channels,
wondered how the viceroy would react to a proposal
to revive the Intersystem Library Exchange, in which
some of the Yevetha worlds had once participated.

Behn-kihl-nahm, always cognizant of the ebb and
flow of power, questioned whether Leia had the authority to negotiate at all without a pending application. And Engh, always aware of the power of money
to cement political bonds, urged Leia to dangle the entire catalog of trade goods before Nil Spaar as an in-
ducement to reconsider membership.

"After hearing your report, I expect them to insist
that all trade into and out of Koornacht be on Yevetha
ships," Engh said. "Fine for their traders, but not what
ours are accustomed to."

"I'm not sure the Yevetha are terribly interested in
trade," said Leia.

"Interesting," said Drayson. "If they don't want
membership and they're not interested in trade, why
are they here?"

"I think they're here because the New Republic
has grown large enough and strong enough to begin to
worry them," Leia said. "They don't want to join us,
but they don't want to be overrun by us, either."

"How strong are they militarily?" Behn-kihl-nahm
asked.

"I don't think we know," said Drayson.

"Before the Imperial occupation, there were three
systems in the Koornacht Cluster with a Class Two
military rating," said Ackbar. "But that was before.

The Empire may have seized or destroyed most of those vessels."

"According to the viceroy, it's been nine years since the occupation ended," said Drayson. "At this point, I don't think we can guess how extensively they may have rearmed. That ship sitting over at Eastport certainly testifies to their engineering abilities."

"I don't think it matters," Leia said. "There's no question in my mind that they feel threatened by us. I think it's critical that we give them reason not to be."

"If they do feel threatened, that should provide you with useful leverage," said Behn-kihl-nahm.

"I'm not looking for leverage," Leia said. "That's the wrong tone for these talks. The Yevetha have good reason to be wary of us—reasons that everyone here ought to be able to identify with. I don't want to twist their arm. I want to win their trust. It's not going to be quick or easy. But I think Nil Spaar and I have a chance to develop the kind of personal rapport that will carry us through the hard parts. I don't know if we're going to end up with an alliance or an application for membership. But I'm not going to worry about that now."

"Five minutes," an aide called.

"Thank you, Alole."

"Please—be very careful with your promises, Leia," said Behn-kihl-nahm as they all rose. "The idea that we are all equals in the eyes of Coruscant is very important to the strength of the New Republic."

"I realize that, Chairman."

"Then you must realize that if the Yevetha win the benefits of membership without the obligations, there'll be an uproar in the Senate, and in thousands of capitals. And if the Yevetha are granted privileges not available to our members, you can expect hundreds of member worlds to resign."

"That won't happen," Leia said. "I expect that any treaty with the Yevetha will provide them with only a subset of the rights contained in the articles of confederation—no open markets, no monetary controls, no dispute resolution, no voice in the Senate, no military umbrella—"

"The presence of a shepherd is frequently undervalued in the absence of a wolf," said Behn-kihl-nahm.

"Maybe so," Leia said. "But there's a lot to be gained by forging a link—any link, to start—with the Yevetha. The Senate will understand that."

"Many a foolish notion has won support in that body," Behn-kihl-nahm said, "and many a falsehood has enjoyed currency in that room. Princess, no matter how much we want that ally on the Inner Line, or access to Koornacht's metals and the Yevetha's technology, we must always be aware of the price. We are not the suitors—they are."

"Thank you for your counsel, Chairman."

"Remember that Cortina and Jandur also came here full of prideful bluster, and both eventually signed the standard articles of confederation. And that was long ago, when membership meant less than it does today."

"Time!" called the aide.

Leia emptied her glass quickly. "If you'll excuse me, Chairman—"

Behn-kihl-nahm nodded and backed away, leaving her alone with Admiral Drayson and a recording droid.

"End recording," said Drayson. A black droid controller was all but concealed in his hand. "Princess, may I have a moment?"

"A moment, but not much more."

"I'm concerned about the process, about the fact that all your advisers must rely on secondhand reports. It makes it difficult for them to provide you with the independent counsel you expect from them."

"What are you suggesting?"

"That I arrange for more eyes and ears in the room with you. I could provide you with a burst-transmission comlink small enough that even General Solo would be hard pressed to find it."

"I don't expect to be frisked by the viceroy," Leia said curtly. "And you can't promise me the comlink would be undetectable by the Yevetha—can you? If we can listen in, in theory so can they."

"Quite true," said Drayson. "Technical assets are always subject to discovery. Of course, if they were covertly monitoring the sessions themselves, they wouldn't be likely to—"

"Do you have evidence that they are?"

"No. But sometimes I find it more prudent to assume what's not in evidence than believe that what I can't see isn't there."

"Admiral Drayson, I'm afraid I don't understand that thinking. Especially in this instance."

"Time, Princess Leia," called Alole, peering back into the room from the corridor.

"Coming," Leia called. "No 'technical assets' in the Grand Hall, General. We'll have to make do with my eyes and ears. I won't take the chance of confirming their worst fears by being caught spying. Understood?"

"Of course, Princess."

The Yevethan ground skimmer that picked up Nil Spaar in the bowels of the Imperial City administrative complex discharged him a few minutes later in the bowels of the embassy ship *Aramadia*.

There was no one there to greet him, but that was no surprise. Nor was the fact that the driver waited inside the skimmer for Nil Spaar to climb out on his own and walk the few steps to the airtight exit hatch on the front wall. As soon as the hatch closed behind him, a thick yellow gas began to fill the chamber where the skimmer hovered. Shortly afterward a scalding spray poured down on the skimmer from thousands of tiny jets, chasing the yellow mist down vents and drains.

Behind the hatch, Nil Spaar found himself in a sanitary entry station. The drill had already become familiar to him, but that day there was more urgency to his motions. Quickly removing his clothing, he dropped it into a sterile incinerator. There was a reas-

suring pop and hiss when he sealed the loading chute.
The face of the incinerator grew warm to the touch.

Then Nil Spaar stepped into the scrub chamber.
With eyes closed, he invoked the needle-spray showers—
first the gentle rain of the fumigant, then the agonizing
bite of the scrub jets. As the water pelted his body, his
expression softened to one approaching bliss. He lingered
in the scrub chamber, willingly enduring a second cycle
of cleansing. Then he passed through the inner door,
where waiting hands draped his body in a fire-blue
gown.

"Viceroy," the attaché said, bowing.

"Thank you, Eri," he said, accepting the heavy silver viceroy's neckguard and fastening it in place. "I
must resign myself to it—their stink never leaves my
nostrils, no matter how long I stay in the scrub chamber."

"You carry no taint to my senses," Eri said.

"I will trust that is more than politeness," said Nil
Spaar. "Is Vor Duull expecting me?"

"Yes, Viceroy."

"Good. See that abstracts of today's reports and
examinations are waiting for me in my quarters. I'll be
there shortly."

An aircart whisked him up eleven levels to the domain of Vor Duull, proctor of information science for
the *Aramadia*. Nil Spaar was greeted with a quick
bow. "Welcome back, Viceroy."

"More welcome for me than for any of you," he
said. "Were you able to receive a signal?"

"Without interruption," Vor Duull said. "A recording was made per your instructions and placed in
your library."

"Did you watch?"

"Only enough to make certain that the decoders
and stabilizers were functioning."

Nil Spaar nodded. "What do you think of them?"
When Vor Duull hesitated, the viceroy prodded, "Go
on, I excuse you."

"They seem to me weak, gullible—eager to please. She is no match for you."

"We shall see," Nil Spaar said. "Thank you, Proctor. Continue your fine work."

The aircart carried him swiftly up the central spiral of the ship to the third level, above which only command personnel could go. He accepted the salutes of the honor guard and a kiss from his *darna*, then disappeared behind locked doors.

In the privacy of his quarters, Nil Spaar sat in front of a cryptocomm. His brief message was beamed to N'zoth, capital of the Duskhan League, as a scrambled string of bits mixed into the stream of ordinary open dispatches.

"I have had my first meeting with the vermin," Nil Spaar said. "All is going well."

The datacard Admiral Hiram Drayson dropped into the datapad on his desk looked for all the world like a standard Universal Data Exchange card.

But the cards used by Alpha Blue for sensitive data used a nonstandard encoding, which made the card appear blank when placed in a standard datapad. The little plastic rectangle could even be erased and reformatted without destroying the information it bore—in this case, excerpts from a recording made earlier that day by a tiny audio telescope concealed in the ornate scrollwork on the ceiling of the Grand Hall. The excerpts had been selected for Drayson by an Alpha Blue analysis droid, using sophisticated context-processing protocols.

Tipping back in his chair and folding his hands over his abdomen, Drayson listened to the recording that no other sentient had heard—or would hear, unless he chose to share it with them.

He listened as Princess Leia said, "I want Coruscant to stand for the idea that there's an alternative to war and tyranny. Cooperation and tolerance—the best of all of us, available to all of us."

He listened as Viceroy Nil Spaar said, "We do not

want or need your protection. We enjoyed the 'protection' of the Empire for half my lifetime, and we are determined to avoid such blessings in the future."

And he thought as he listened, *I wish that you'd chosen to let us into that room with you, Princess. But I'll do all I can to make certain you don't look back on that choice with regret.*

Chapter 6

◆

Inside the protective cocoon of Luke Skywalker's secret hermitage, time had no meaning.

To be sure, the elemental cycle of day and night was echoed in the ebb and flow of the Force, as the living web of Coruscant stirred and slept, fought and foraged. The turning of the seasons was a longer, slower rhythm, an almost imperceptible crescendo and decrescendo of vitality and dormancy, fecundity and death.

Beyond that, a mere whisper, lay the almost unimaginably deep, subtle echo that was the birth of stars, the creation and extinction of life, the blossoming of consciousness. Deep in meditation, profoundly connected to the mysteries of the Force, Luke could see that through the manifestations of life, the universe knew itself, and beheld its own wonders.

But to extend himself that far, and reach that degree of oneness, Luke found it necessary to let go of his everyday senses to a degree he once would have thought impossible.

Sealed behind opaque walls, he lived in darkness for days at a time, barely conscious of hunger, thirst, or other bodily demands. He wore clothing only out of habit, but the habit weakened. The winds howled outside the hermitage, but Luke was oblivious to them.

He took no notice of the sun or moons in their courses, the rise and fall of the tide, the ever-changing sky painted in light and cloud.

The sea began to freeze, as the northern hemisphere slid deeper into Coruscant's short winter. Over a period of many days, the rocks and beach were draped with a heavy crust of sculpted ice. But the sight would have surprised Luke, had it mattered enough to him to seek it out.

Even Leia had stopped reaching out for him, though more in anger than in understanding. The result mattered more to him than the reason. His solitude was complete, timeless and undisturbed.

Then a visitor came, and everything changed.

It was his ordinary senses, reawakened, which informed Luke of the visitor's presence. First, a sound, which he later realized was his own name.

At that point, it had been many days since he had spoken, or even thought in words.

He concentrated. "Lights, medium."

The meditation chamber reappeared around him. Sight told him that a woman stood in the chamber with him, half a dozen steps away. Her shoulders were bare, her throat covered by a long scarf that vanished down her back. Her hair was long and braided, her clothing soft and flattering. Her eyes were dark, intent, and knowing.

He took her at first for a projection, because it was unthinkable that anyone could have passed through the walls, his screens, without alerting him. But then he touched her bare arm, and touch told him her skin was real, and warm. He circled her, and scent told him of salt air, dead quarrelgrass crushed underfoot, a body bathed in flowers, a hint of the taint of the old oils and clinging vapors that hung on one's person after a long flight.

"Explain yourself," he said when he had circled around to face her again.

"You *are* him. You are Luke, son to Anakin." She smiled with bright delight. "Forgive me. I thought I would never find you. It must have been the working when you built this place that I felt. That was what led me here."

"You *felt* what I did? From where?"

"From Carratos," she said, naming a planet in a system forty parsecs from Coruscant.

As rudely as his visitor had invaded his hermitage, Luke suddenly invaded her mind, probing the secret place where sensitivity to the Force resided. If she possessed the sort of talent her words claimed for her, he should be thrown halfway across the room when the ancient reflex repelled his mental touch. It was so with every Jedi he had probed, every candidate he had brought to Yavin for training.

Luke's probing met no resistance. He felt no shields blunting or deflecting his examination. Her mind was open—and yet there was no reflexive response. So sure was he of that test that he wouldn't have considered her for a moment as a candidate for the academy.

But, still, she *had* found him. She *had*, somehow, entered a space she should not have been able to enter unless her gifts in the Force were the equal of his.

"Who *are* you?" he asked wonderingly.

She laughed. "Forgive me. I am Akanah, of the Fallanassi, an adept of the White Current."

"I'm afraid I don't know your people, or that path," he said.

"I know," she said. "You won't find us in your census, or the Emperor's, or the Old Republic's. It's not our way to claim lands and raise flags, or stand queue to be counted. But you *should* know us. That's part of why I've come."

His brows showed puzzlement. "If your people are such ciphers, why should I know you?"

"Because your mother is one of us, Luke Skywalker. Because you are bound to us through her."

Luke stared. "My mother? How can—do you—what do you mean, 'is' one of us? Leia told me my mother is dead."

"Yes—I know. As Obi-Wan told you that your father was dead."

"Are you saying my mother might be alive?"

"I don't know," said Akanah, suddenly sad-eyed. "Who saw her fall? Where is her grave? I wish I could answer your question. But I don't even know my own mother's fate. I've been separated from the body of my people for too many years."

"Separated? Why?"

"I was away when the Empire came to the world we called home then. The Fallanassi had to take flight, because they would not let themselves and their gifts be used for violence and evil. I don't blame them. I know they must have waited for me as long as they could. That was nineteen years ago. I was twelve—not much more than a child."

"And you never found them again?" There was a touch of suspicion in Luke's voice. "You found me."

She smiled tolerantly. "The Fallanassi are more practiced at hiding than you are, Luke Skywalker. And there isn't much an abandoned child can do in the middle of a war to search for a family that doesn't want to be found."

"I suppose not," he said slowly.

"It wasn't until the Emperor was overthrown that I could even think of looking—I was too afraid I would betray them. And even then, it's hard for a young woman on Carratos to become wealthy enough to leave it. Especially to leave in her own ship, owing and answering to no one."

"So you're looking for them now. And you say my mother could be with them." He shook his head. "My mother—she's been such a mystery to me my whole life that I can't let myself believe you know anything of her. I don't even know her name."

"She may have had other names," Akanah said. "Many of us do. But among the body, she is known as Nashira. It is a star-name, and thought a high honor."

"Nashira," Luke echoed in a whisper.

"Yes," she said. "Luke, I know that there's an emptiness inside you where memories of your mother should be, a weakness where what she would have taught you would have strengthened you."

"Yes—"

"There's an emptiness in my life, too, and for the same lack. I've come here to ask you to go away with me, and help me find our people, so you and I can both be whole again."

"I don't think I've ever been whole," said Luke, turning his face from her. "The pieces of my life were scattered by a storm before I ever had a chance to tackle the puzzle. And every missing piece that turns up completely changes the picture. I was alone, and then there was Leia—my sister. I was an orphan, and then there was Anakin—Vader—my father."

He laughed to himself. "I wanted to go to school just to get off the farm, and then my father's mentor came to me, and taught me the secrets of a power I didn't know I had. I was the adopted son of a moisture farmer living next door to nowhere, and then there was a lightsaber, and enemies—the most powerful men in the galaxy—who wanted me dead."

Luke turned and looked back at Akanah. "I don't know if I'm ready to redraw the picture again. Maybe that's what keeps me from believing you. I want to know my mother. You're right about that. But maybe I'm just a little bit afraid to. And that's a feeling that I haven't felt in a long time."

"I knew when I came here that this would be a great shock," she said. "But you must reclaim this piece of what you are."

"I don't know who you are," Luke said stubbornly. "I don't know that anything you've said is true."

"Then I will tell you some things that you know are true," said Akanah. "Your father was lost to the dark side, and you were forced to try to kill him. You were nearly lost to the darkness yourself. That must weigh heavily on you—wondering if you carry his weakness."

"I've faced that test," Luke said defensively.

"And would you have survived it without Leia?"

Luke Skywalker had no answer for that question.

"Perhaps that is why you cannot let yourself love without fear," Akanah said softly. "Perhaps that is why you have no children of your own. You must fear that you will repeat your family's tragedy in another generation. You must fear that someday you will find yourself ready to kill your own son, and him ready to kill you."

"No—"

"You must fear yourself. How could you not? How could anyone, if he had walked your path? The bond that links you to all the horrors of Darth Vader's reign is a terrible burden. Is that not why you're here?" she asked pointedly. "Isn't that the meaning of this structure? You may have forgiven Anakin Skywalker— but you know the Republic can never forgive Vader for his crimes in the service of Palpatine."

Luke was beyond denial. "How do you know all this?" he asked hoarsely.

"I've studied you—before I came here, and since. Hero of the Rebellion, Jedi Master, defender of the Republic," she said. "Even on Carratos, we hear all the stories. And I saw in them all the things I've said to you."

Turning half away from her, Luke shook his head. "No. That can't be. I've voiced those fears to no one. No one."

Akanah glided closer. "They're written in your eyes, and lie heavy on your spirit. You'd see them yourself, but for the blindness we all have when we look in a mirror," she said. "But remember this, Luke—your strength in the Force did not come only from your father. The gift of the Light came from your mother— and your mother was of my people. *That* is why your heart is telling you you must come with me."

Their eyes met. Luke felt her gaze like a light cast into the dark corners of his psyche. Her voice disarmed him. Her words unveiled him. She had taken down all his shields, and he was defenseless against her, his mind wholly open to her. But it was a strangely safe feeling. She already knew his most unthinkable thoughts, and still she held her hand out to him.

"Test me, if you must," Akanah said.

"No," he said. "It's not necessary."

"I will wait here, if you want to return to Yavin for your testing equipment," she offered. "But I can tell you what you would see—nothing. The White Current is not the Force you know, only with a different name. But it is a manifestation of the All. I will teach you what I can."

"You assume a great deal."

"I speak from hope only. Will you come with me, Luke Skywalker?"

"I don't know," he said. "There's something I must do first—someone I need to tell."

"Leia."

"Yes. Is there any reason I shouldn't?"

"No reason," she said, and smiled. "You said it was not necessary to test me. But that question—"

"You're right," Luke agreed. "If you'd said, 'No, this has to be our secret,' I would've doubted you. But there's another reason I have to do this. I have no memories of my mother. Leia has but a few, no more than glimpses touched by emotion."

"There are more memories there. Nashira was protected, just as you were."

"I can believe that. But what you've already told me may be enough to unlock any hidden doors, allow me to probe her mind with more success than I've had in the past. And to find another few glimpses of her here"—he touched his temple with his fingertips—"would mean a great deal. If you could tell me even more—"

"I'm sorry." Akanah's sudden smile was touched by humor. "Fifteen years ago, you weren't important—just Fallanassi gossip. If I had known what was to come, I would have paid more attention."

He laughed. "Will you wait here while I go see Leia?"

"Of course," she said. "I've waited long enough for this night. I can wait a little longer for our journey to begin."

Luke's flight suit felt strange on his body, both too loose and too confining. The E-wing looked like an inert sculpture in its hangar, covered by a fine, pale coating of dust that had fallen out of the still air.

"Artee," Luke said. "Exit standby mode."

Almost instantly several lights of different colors glowed on the dome and faceplates of the astromech droid. A moment later it gave an answering chirrup.

"Preflight the ship," Luke said, starting his own quick but thorough inspection.

The droid whistled, and Luke glanced down at the display bar on his flight suit.

"Yes, you can stop monitoring the house systems," Luke said.

R7-T1's response had the stridency of an alarm.

"Yes, I know there's someone in the house," Luke said, ducking under the left wing. "Just leave some lights on and the upper passways open. She'll be fine."

The E-wing passed both Artee's and Luke's checks with flying colors. Both the design and the example before Luke were relatively new, far more able and robust than the T-65 X-wing he had flown against the first Death Star at Yavin. And the E-wing he was about to climb into had been overhauled to factory-new condition after its last taste of combat.

Still, he hesitated.

Technically, the E-wing was on loan to the Jedi academy for training purposes, but only because there was no provision in the quartermaster's regulations for loaning a front-line starfighter to a civilian. Ackbar had persuaded him that, given the unpredictability of life, it was far more sensible for him to have a fully armed E-wing at his disposal than an unarmed sprint, ketch, or runabout.

"Think of yourself as a member of the Republic's militia. And a militiaman should have his weapon at home with him, in the event he is called on again," Ackbar had said.

Luke had accepted that argument reluctantly. But in the months before he returned to Coruscant, he had become more and more uncomfortable in the E-wing's cockpit. It was a heavily armed killer, an intimidator, an unspoken threat wherever it appeared. As such, it represented a part of his life that he was trying to leave behind.

His X-wing had fit him like a second skin, like an extension of himself. He had taken joy in flying it, even in battle. But that had been another, younger Luke. The E-wing was different. It was an embarrassment, an ugly set of clothes he was forced to wear when he went out in public. And he missed the familiar presence of Artoo, who simply did not fit—physically or electronically—in the E-wing's R7 astromech interface.

One last time, he thought. *Then maybe they'll let me give it back.*

"Open the canopy, Artee," he said, and directed his concentration at the hangar's front wall. Seams appeared in the unbroken expanse of silicon and quartz crystal, and the wall opened on hinges that had not existed just moments before. Bitter air filled the hangar as the wind screamed past the opening.

In the absence of a boarding ladder, Luke leaped lightly to the edge of the open cockpit and clambered in. As the canopy closed over him, he pictured in his mind the E-wing hovering a few hands above the hangar door and gliding silently out into the night. As he pictured it, it happened—except that the silence was broken by Artee's insistent squawking. There was no explaining to the rigid-minded astromech that hovering with no engines did not necessarily represent an emergency.

"Power up engines," Luke said.

Artee cooed in relief and complied.

Luke climbed out from the hermitage in a widening spiral, scanning the ground for further clues about his visitor. As he passed over the cliff for the second time, he spotted her ship—an elderly Verpine Adventurer—resting a hundred meters back from the precipice.

I can't believe I didn't hear that clunker coming, he thought. *Pre-Empire, lifting body design, hoverjets for atmospheric mode*—

Memories stirred, crossed, linked. He heard Leia's impudent voice saying, "You came here in that thing? You're braver than I thought." That had been aboard the Death Star, the first time they'd met—when he'd seen himself rescuing a princess, not a long-lost sister. A long time ago.

Luke pulled the stick hard over, and the E-wing wheeled nimbly toward Imperial City. With a thought directed ahead of him, he let Leia know he was coming. For now, he kept the reason to himself.

He did not see Akanah watching from the tower, her hopeful gaze following the track of the engine exhausts as the E-wing disappeared into the night.

Without warning Leia sat bolt upright in her bed, breaking Han's embrace.

"What is it *now*?" he asked plaintively.

"He's coming here tonight."

"*Who* is?"

"Luke." She threw back the soft coppery sheet and climbed out of bed. "He's coming to see us."

"How do you know?"

"I heard his voice. You know, what you fondly refer to as that semimystical twin thing?"

"Well—he's not ringing the doorbell yet," Han said hopefully. "It'll take him a while to get here."

Leia seemed not to hear him. "It's about time. All I have to do is tell him about the way the kids were today—that'll give him the whole catalog of problems."

"Are you sure that's why he's coming?"

"He said he needed to talk to me about family matters."

Han received that news with a dubious expression. "I dunno, Leia—the kids aren't the only family you two have," he said, trying to dislodge her from her certainty without revealing where Luke was living. "Isn't it more likely to be something about your father?"

"Why do you say that?"

"I kind of got the impression he's still having trouble with some of that."

"What? No, that's silly," Leia said dismissively. "Why should he feel guilty about what Father did under the control of the Emperor and the dark side? Luke forgave Father at Endor. You were there—you saw."

Han frowned. "Well—maybe it didn't turn out to be that simple for Luke. After all, a few billion people around the galaxy are still pretty unhappy with dear old Dad."

"You don't have to remind me about that," said Leia, shrugging into a white robe and tying the sash in a bow. "But I'm the one who has to deal with it, not Luke. I'm the one who gets accused and screamed at and threatened, not Luke. And I'm handling it."

As she was speaking, she moved toward the bedroom door. When she reached it, she stopped and turned back toward Han, still sitting bare-chested on the bed in a jumble of sheets. "No, I'm sure you're wrong. That's not why Luke's coming here. He seemed—excited. Almost happy."

Han surrendered. "All right. Whatever you say. Where are you going?"

"I've been keeping notes on the children. I want to bring them up to date before Luke arrives." She threw him a quick smile and disappeared through the doorway.

"I guess we're done here, then," he said to himself. Sighing, he climbed out of bed. "I've got a bad feeling about this. Oh, yes, I do."

Even in the middle of the night, it wasn't possible for Luke Skywalker to make a quiet visit to the Chief of State of the New Republic. The entire area surrounding the president's residence was secured airspace and protected by its own local shield generator. That ruled out a convenient landing right on the grounds, or even close by.

Instead, Luke was directed to land his E-wing on a military pad at Eastport. Even before he could climb out of the cockpit, a sizable crowd of ground crew and other port workers gathered at the pad. But it was different from the kind of crowds Han still drew. Everyone hung back, even after Luke jumped down from the cockpit to the tarmac.

It was as though they couldn't pass up a chance to see Luke Skywalker but were too intimidated by his status to risk trying to shake his hand, clap him on the back, or even speak to him. He felt less a celebrity than a curiosity, more a dead legend than a living hero.

Luke wished they would all just go away. He had no interest in being celebrity *or* curiosity, legend or hero.

"Security Protocol One, Artee," he said. As the E-wing's canopy and engine intake covers closed, Luke strode toward the airspeeder waiting for him just outside the landing circle. The crowd parted for him in silence. But their excitement buffeted him, and their ambivalence tore at him. He heard them whispering to each other, read their faces, and he filled in the rest.

Children—you'll never guess who I saw at the port tonight—

He's here? What did he say? How did he seem? Where did he go? I wonder what it means.

The airspeeder was a standard government model, with a speed governor, an altitude limiter, and a pilot droid at the controls. To Luke, it was as welcome a sight as an escape pod on a doomed ship.

"President's residence, north entrance," Luke said.

He seemed so serious—

So mysterious—

He floated to the ground like a leaf—

He was as close to me as I am to you—

He smiled at me—

I never thought I'd have a chance to meet him—
You can tell just looking at him that he's a Jedi—
You can tell just looking at him what he's been
through—

Luke closed his eyes in relief as the airspeeder took flight.

While they were waiting for Luke, Han had lingered in the front rooms, thinking that he might be able to get to his friend first and warn him what his sister was expecting. But when the signal from the north gatehouse finally came, Leia was past Han and out the door before he knew it.

"Let him in," Han told the gate guard resignedly, and hurried after his wife.

He caught up just as Leia and Luke met on the north garden trail.

"Leia," Luke said with a warm smile, and they embraced.

"I knew you'd come," Leia said, kissing him on the cheek and taking his arm. "I knew you'd change your mind. I can't tell you how glad I am to see you. How long can you stay?"

"We have some work to do together," Luke said. "I don't know how long it will take. And then I have some things to tell you. Hello, Han." Luke clapped the taller man on the back with his free hand. "It's good to see you again."

"You don't know the half of it, kid," Han said wryly.

"Come on—let's go inside," Leia said. "Did they make you leave your bag at the gatehouse? That's so foolish of them—"

"I didn't bring a bag," Luke said. "I didn't plan on staying. But if it's too late for you, I can pass the night out here, and we can work in the morning. I've always liked these gardens."

Leia stopped, turning toward Luke and frowning. "I think I've missed something here," she said. "The children are sleeping—at last—so we couldn't start work until morning anyway. But I'm sure it's going to take days, more likely weeks, to make any progress."

"Leia. I haven't come to train the children. Didn't Han tell you my feelings on that?"

"I told her," Han said.

"Han told me you said it was my problem," Leia said. "And that was so unlike you that I was sure he'd gotten it wrong."

Luke shook his head. "It suffers a bit for being condensed, but I suppose the kernel is still there," he said. "Leia, there's nothing I can do right now that won't make your lives and theirs harder in the long run. I've meditated on this for a long time. I'm sure this is the right decision."

"Then—you came here because *you* want something? Not because we need help?"

"I'm here because I may have some new information about our mother."

Han was startled by Luke's words, but, so far as he could see, Leia's expression didn't waver or soften in the slightest. "What new information?" she asked. "Where does it come from?"

"I don't want to tell you yet," Luke said. "I'm hoping that you'll let me probe your mind again first. I have an idea what to look for now."

Her body language foretold her answer. She held herself back from him, arms wrapped around herself, her mouth hard, her eyes darting, angry. "No," she said. "Go back to wherever you came from." She turned abruptly and started back toward the residence.

"Leia—" Han said, reaching for her as she neared where he stood.

She eluded his touch with a twist and a sidestep. "And you, if you take his side, you can go with him."

"Leia—" Han's tone was plaintive now, and it had no effect. In moments, the two men were alone on the path.

"I thought I was just out of practice flying," Luke said with a sigh.

"For what it's worth, kid, she had kind of a hard

day," Han said. "Leia's been negotiating with the same guy for a month now, and it's starting to drive her nuts. And I don't know how they do it, but the twins seem to know when she's not up to dealing with them, and really push the limits."

"If she'd just draw on the Force," Luke said, shaking his head. "It's inexhaustible."

"Well—she's not. For whatever reason. I guess you'd better come back."

"No," Luke said. "I'm going to talk to her. She has to realize how important this is to both of us."

"Kid, I can't recommend it—"

"It'll be all right," Luke said, and started up the path.

The valet droid helpfully told Luke that Leia was in the private kitchen. He found her sitting on a stool at the meal bar, cupping a tall glass in both hands and staring out the window with faraway eyes.

"That's perfect," she said as he entered. "I was just trying to remember if you'd ever done anything I asked you to."

"Once or twice, by accident," he said lightly, hoping to draw a smile from her. "But we made it through anyway."

Leia said nothing, choosing instead to sip from her glass.

"This is important for both of us, Leia. For your children, too," Luke said. His glance acknowledged Han, who had followed as far as the doorway and taken up a position leaning, arms crossed, against the frame. "I think there really might be a chance to break through and discover our mother as a real person."

"Why?" She turned her face toward him for the first time, and he saw the weariness in her eyes. "You've probed me more times than I can remember. You had Artoo and Threepio on Obra-skai for months, searching the libraries for any clue." She emptied her glass and set it down on the bar. "You and I sat in a Jedi meditation circle for hours on end, night after night, calling on Obi-Wan and Anakin and Yoda, Owen and Beru, my foster parents, anyone we knew of who might have known her. Calling her, too—remember?"

"I remember."

"And when we were done, we knew exactly as much as we had before. A conspiracy of silence, you called it."

"It seemed that way," Luke said. "But I think the silence has just been broken. I think I know why we never found any trace of her."

"You're obsessed with the past," she said, her tone sharp. "I just can't let myself keep caring that much. Father and Mother are dead, and nothing you do can change that. My children are the future."

"How do we know that Mother's dead?" Luke asked, easing onto a stool on the opposite side of the meal bar. "Where's her grave? Who saw her die? Did you?"

"No—"

"How do we know she didn't leave Alderaan, leave *you* on Alderaan, to hide from Father? How do we know she didn't succeed?"

"There's a simple answer to that," Leia said, raising her head. "She's dead, Luke. If she were still alive, there'd be nothing to stop her from coming here for a reunion."

"She might be as young as fifty," Luke said. "It could still happen."

"It's been *twelve years,* Luke," she said. "And we're not hard to find—at least, I'm not."

"What does that mean?" asked Luke.

"I'm going to tell you something I've kept from you, just because of the way you are about this thing," Leia said slowly. "Since the end of the war—since I made Coruscant my home, and the work of the New Republic my life—there's been a steady stream of women coming here and claiming that they're our long-lost mother." She looked to Han. "How many have there been now, honey?"

"More than two hundred," Han said, nodding. "More of them lately, for some reason—almost one a week so far this year."

"The security staff calls them 'mad grannies,' " Leia said. "Some of them aren't old enough by half—some aren't even human. But they're all firmly in love with the idea that they married the monster and gave birth to the heroes of the Rebellion." She shook her head sadly.

"But there might be reasons we don't know of for her not to come," Luke said earnestly. "She may need to protect those who protected her. She might not want to face our questions. For all she knows, we curse her memory. That's why we may have to find her. Please, Leia—let me look into your mind one more time. I have a signpost this time—a name."

"And what if you find what you're looking for?"

"Then I'm going away with the woman who brought me the name, to find the rest."

Leia raised her hands in exasperation. "You see? You see? There'll never be an end to it—you'll never be able to let it go."

"I just have to know the truth," Luke said. "I don't understand why you don't feel the same way—"

"Listen to me—we're never going to have a tidy family tree," Leia snapped. "Why can't you realize? We're never going to know our parents better than we do right now. We're never going to have fond stories of our grandparents to tell our children. We're better off telling them about Owen and Beru, about Bail—the real people who cared for us, protected us, loved us like we were their own. You make too much of blood."

"It's more than blood—" Luke began.

"I don't care," Leia said, slapping the top of the bar with the flat of her right hand. The noise was so sudden and loud that it made Han jump. "You can't invent a normal childhood for us, no matter how much you turn up about Mother and Father. And if you do find the truth, as you call it, you just might find you don't like it very much. You might end up wishing you'd let them stay dead."

"Could anything be worse than what we already know?"

"I'd rather not know the answer to that question," Leia said curtly, pushing herself back from the bar so violently that her stool toppled to the floor as she slipped off it. "You and I are foundlings, Luke. That's how it is, like it or not. Our family tree starts here—with this family, and these children. And *they're* going to know their parents, and their uncle, and all our wonderful friends."

Leia's face and voice filled with a rising fury as she spoke, fury at the world, the past, at Luke, at all who stood as obstacles to her vision of what should be. "My children are going to have normal family stories to tell *their* children, little funny stories about everyday nothings, stories where no one dies too young or has to carry a burden of shame. I'm going to see to that, with your help or without it—"

Han approached from the doorway. "Leia—"

"Nothing matters more to me, do you understand?" she demanded, jabbing a finger in Luke's face. "Nothing. So you do what you think you have to, brother—go wherever you have to with whoever you want to, chasing whatever shadow of a hint of a promise of a clue you like. I don't care about any of it. Don't ask for my help again. And don't bring the past into this house. It's all just pain and death. You wallow in it if you want to. I've had enough of it for ten lifetimes."

Stunned by the vehemence of her outburst, both men stood mute as Leia stalked out of the kitchen. "I'm sorry," Luke said at last. "You were right. I let myself think I know her better than you do."

"I don't know who's right and who's wrong, kid. I just know you're both stubborn as tauntauns," Han said. "And that this would probably be a good time to be leaving."

Luke did not argue.

* * *

Like most small sport spacecraft with bold names, Akanah's Verpine Adventurer offered few amenities, technical or personal.

It had no weapons, combat shields, or astromech droid, and its sublight speed rating was a meager 2.5. The navigational deflector array had been upgraded to the Block 3 standard somewhere during its history, but its hyperdrive motivator was still Block 1. There was only a single pressurized compartment, which the flight stations shared with a single-width sleeper and tiny curtained refresher unit. The meal-service console was limited to three drink selections, Akanah explained apologetically, since she hadn't been able to afford repairs to the food dispensers.

But the pilot's station was roomy enough for Luke to forgo his service flight suit in favor of looser, more casual clothing, and the small cargo hold had more than room enough for Luke's one modest bag beside Akanah's luggage and supplies.

"Is that all?" Akanah shouted over the wind.

"That's all," Luke said, retrieving a comlink from a concealed pocket. "Go on, get inside—you're shivering. Artee, can you hear me?"

The comlink chirped brightly.

Luke helped Akanah climb through the narrow access chute, then moved away from the Adventurer. "Artee, I'm going away for a while," he said, cupping the comlink in one bare hand. "Maintain Security Protocol Five. If anyone breaches the perimeter, send Code Alpha-five-zed-alpha on Control Channel One. Acknowledge."

R7-T1 acknowledged the instructions obediently. It was innocent of the fact that the code it had been given would topple the hermitage into the sea, shattering it on the rock spires and plunging the E-wing below the waves.

"End link," Luke said, and switched the comlink off. Turning away, he returned to the Adventurer and climbed the access ladder two rungs at a time.

"Is everything all right?" Akanah asked as he joined her.

"Everything's fine," he said, pushing the lever that folded the ladder and sealed the hatch behind him. "Do you want the controls?"

"That's not necessary," she said, slipping in the second seat.

"If you don't mind, I'll help," Luke said as he buckled himself in. "But first you have to tell me which way to point the little end of the ship."

"Our destination is Lucazec," she said. "That was our last home. We'll start our search there."

Chapter 7

◆

In deep space far from any star, the Teljkon vagabond drifted in the darkness, silent and inert. Gmar Askilon, the nearest of the cold lights woven into the eternal curtain of night, was too far away to raise more than the faintest gleam on the vagabond's gray metal skin.

Trailing well behind was the much smaller black-hulled Intelligence ferret *IX-44F*—one ghost shadowing another. The ferret was nearly as inert as its quarry. It announced itself only with periodic position updates broadcast to Coruscant by hypercomm, and by an optical-laser pulse aimed directly aft.

The laser pulse was the rendezvous target for Pakkpekatt's approaching armada, which had come out of hyperspace on tiptoe, one ship at a time, hundreds of thousands of klicks behind the vagabond. Following the ferret's beacon, the armada had taken days to close the gap, its slow, silent approach that of an infinitely patient predator.

For most of that approach, the armada was arrayed single file on a heading that allowed the hull of the tiny ferret itself to hide the approaching ships from the vagabond. Only two days ago had the armada broken file and, using thrusters only, begun to spread itself out into the intercept formation.

The three pickets that made up the interdiction screen moved the farthest out and forward. Their orders called for them to flank the vagabond on three sides, and move ahead of it. By the time the rest of the armada caught up to the ferret, the interdiction pickets were to be in position to cut off a hyperspace escape.

Spreading out almost as widely were the three spotter ships—two escorts and the *Lightning,* a converted Prinawe racer—assigned to make complete visual and full-spectrum recordings of the intercept attempt. If the vagabond tried to run in real space, it was *Lightning*'s job to run with it.

Glorious, the gunship *Marauder,* and the pilotless ferret *D-89* remained on the initial intercept heading, closing with the shadowing ferret so slowly that at times an impatient Lando thought they would never reach it.

"This Pakkpekatt is so cautious, he makes you look impetuous, Threepio," Lando complained in the privacy of *Lady Luck*'s main cabin.

"I agree with his tactics," said Lobot.

"You would," Lando said wryly.

"Is it not prudent to take all pains to avoid alarming one's prey?"

"We've gone far beyond prudent," Lando grumbled. "I'm beginning to suspect the Hortek hunt by boring their prey to death."

But finally the hour came when all ten ships were in position, and *IX-44F* and its three-man crew were relieved from their seventy-nine-day deployment.

"Captain, you are free to return to base, with our thanks," Pakkpekatt signaled the ferret. "I'm afraid you will have to make a stealth withdrawal from the target zone, however."

"Thank you, Colonel," came the response. "A couple of days more or less in this closet don't mean much to us at this point. Good luck and good hunting."

As *IX-44F* veered slowly off the intercept heading

and fell behind, the cruiser *Glorious* took up its position.

"What do you think is inside, General Calrissian?" asked Pakkpekatt as they stood together at the main bridge viewport. "Why is it here? Where is it going? Tell me what you're thinking."

"Wherever it's going, Colonel, it's not in a hurry," Lando said easily. "Just like us, eh? Have you made a final decision on when to send in your ferret?"

"I intend to establish an observation baseline before making any approach," Pakkpekatt said. "Have you and your staff made any progress on the signal fragment from the Hrasskis contact?"

"Colonel, you know our hands have been tied by your blackout orders. We've had hardly any bandwidth available to us on the HoloNet. *Lady Luck* doesn't have the kind of data capacity you have here on *Glorious*. We depend more heavily than you do on access to records located elsewhere."

"I will take that as a report of 'No progress,'" Pakkpekatt said. With a light touch on the main viewport's controls, he increased the gain on the photoamplifiers until the outline of the vagabond sharpened and the body of the vessel brightened enough to show the gross detail.

"Look at it, General," he went on. "For all we know, it may be five hundred years old, or fifty thousand. It may have been roaming space since both our species were too young to raise our eyes to the stars. Perhaps the only reason we can get this close is that the work of some ancient engineer has at long last begun to decay and fail."

"The odds favor a shorter history," Lando said, surprised at the Hortek's sentimentality. "There are many dangers in space."

"Yes," said Pakkpekatt, "and to the vagabond, we are one of them. Do you know, General, that no ship like this, no plan or design, appears in any registry of any New Republic world? No shipwright we've found will claim it as his handiwork, though all seem to admire the craft evident in it. If the vagabond was built by any species we know, no other like it was ever made."

"Our catalog of everything that ever was is a long way from being complete," said Lando. "The odds favor a less exotic history."

"How can a gambler post the odds without knowing the game?" scoffed Pakkpekatt. "Perhaps this ship before us is home to a species which has no other home. Perhaps it's a new and curious visitor to this part of the universe, from places for which we have no names. Or perhaps it comes here from deep in the Core, where we have vanishingly few friends. All are possible—as are a universe of possibilities beyond our present imagining."

"Yes, possible," Lando admitted. "Not likely."

"But reason enough to be cautious, wouldn't you agree?" Pakkpekatt said pointedly. "Reason enough for patience, even to the point of pain. Even to the point of boredom. We will watch them for a while, General. We'll let them watch us for a while as well. And I'll tell you when we're ready to do more. Can you live with that, General?"

Lando's skin prickled to hear echoes of his private conversations in Pakkpekatt's words. It seemed more than a coincidence, and yet he had, on many occasions, seen charlatans perform even more convincing feats of mind reading through trickery.

"For now, Colonel," Lando said. "I just hope whoever or whatever's inside that thing isn't busy making plans to destroy it to keep it out of our hands. That's part of your universe of possibilities, too. I hope you won't forget it."

Pakkpekatt's expression was unreadable. "I will ask the communications officer to allot what slack time there may be in our HoloNet queue to your staff. Perhaps that will allow you to make faster progress."

"Thank you, Colonel," Lando said with courtly politeness. "That'd be a step in the right direction."

*   *   *

"What a mess," Lieutenant Norda Proi said, studying the high-resolution scan of space directly ahead of the *Steadfast*. The three-D display showed more than twelve thousand objects, from hundreds no larger than a stormtrooper's combat boot to one that promised to be the aft third of an Imperial Star Destroyer. "Must have been one wild party."

Captain Oolas nodded. "We'll be here a month, at least. Where would you like to start, Lieutenant?"

"The big piece of cake, of course," Proi said, pointing. "But we can launch droids on the way in, and let them start picking up the crumbs."

For nearly a year the fleet hauler *Steadfast* had traced a solitary course through some of the most famous regions of what had once been Imperial space. Known in Fleet Office slang as a junker, *Steadfast* had served in the Battle of Endor, in the defense of Coruscant against Admiral Thrawn, and in the pursuit of the *Knight Hammer*.

But with the cessation of hostilities, the four oldest fleet haulers had been recalled—at the request of the Intelligence Section—from the combat groups they usually served. Equipped with dozens of specialized droids and with Intelligence officers supplementing the usual crew, the junkers were reborn as scavengers. Their mission orders took them to the coordinates of major battles between the Empire and its enemies, where they searched through the wreckage for objects or information of potential value.

"Do you think we're the first ones here this time?" asked Captain Oolas.

Norda Proi studied the spectroscopic analysis of the objects being tracked. "Just possibly so, Captain. I don't want to get my hopes up, though. We'll know pretty quickly when we board the wreck if the mice have been here before us."

Operation Flotsam had been launched when military artifacts, Rebel and Imperial, began showing up on the private collectors' market. When further investi-

gation showed that the artifacts had not been stolen
but had been salvaged from battle zones by smugglers
and other entrepreneurs, the Senate acted with unusual
speed and unanimity.

The Historic Battle Site Protection Act established
more than two dozen restricted areas and claimed
ownership of all combat debris everywhere in the name
of the Alliance War Museum. But security, not history,
was the prime concern. Many observers credited the
explosion of a thermal detonator in a wealthy residen-
tial zone on Givin and a Rudrig crime ring's use of an
Imperial interrogator droid on a kidnap victim with
putting the fear into the Senate.

But a declaration of ownership by Coruscant only
made the traffic in artifacts illegal—it didn't end it.
That took gunship patrols through the restricted areas,
the arrest of the notorious Huttese smuggler Uta, and
the seizure of weapons and other exotic collectibles
from the upper-class customers of a well-known Imperial City art dealer. Even at that, the arrival of *Steadfast* had twice sent would-be poachers running, and the
debris fields it had surveyed so far had all seemed
picked over.

"I have a positive identification on the wreck,
Lieutenant," a junior Intelligence officer called out.
"It's the I-class Star Destroyer *Gnisnal,* our registry
number SD-489. Reported destroyed by internal explo-
sions during the Imperial evacuation of Narth and
Ihopek. The report is from Alliance sources."

"All right," said Norda Proi, nodding. "Let's
move in."

First aboard the wreck were half a dozen scanning
and monitoring droids, which jetted across to it on
their own power while the *Steadfast* held station a safe
distance away.

Working in pairs, so that anything that happened
would be documented by the other, the droids
according to a search plan tailored to that
The priorities were live weapons,

known booby traps, and other possible hazards to the living, breathing search teams that were ready to follow.

The threats were not merely theoretical. The junker *Selonia* had been badly damaged when a poacher's bomb disguised as a datapad went off in its hold. A year earlier, the ironically named surveyor *Foresight* had been destroyed by autofiring laser cannon when search teams tripped an alarm inside an abandoned Imperial cruiser.

But one rule of thumb had never failed the scavengers—if the droids found bodies aboard, there would be no bombs. Imperial guile did not extend to using the bodies of their own as bait for their enemies, and poachers—out of superstition or respect—always cleared the corridors and compartments of corpses.

Still, Norda Proi found that it made him uncomfortable to be gladdened by the sight of bodies aboard the *Gnisnal*.

"Did you hear about the fellow Republic Security arrested on Derra Four last month?" Proi asked, studying the images being relayed to *Steadfast* by SM-6. "He had eleven Imperial corpses in cryotanks in a hangar, all of them in full armor or deck uniform. Crazy."

"I heard," said Captain Oolas. "Crazy and sad. Apparently he was keeping them until his son was old enough to be told what happened to his mother during the occupation. Seems he planned to hand his son whatever weapon he wanted and let him take his revenge."

"I'm glad I had a normal father," Proi said, switching the display to the signal from SM-1.

Captain Oolas sat back and folded his hands on his lap. "I'm glad my homeworld was never occupied by the Empire."

At that moment, SM-1 bumped against a floating body, sending it slowly cartwheeling away. But for just a moment, the face of a dead Imperial petty officer— burned by fire or explosion and blistered by decompression—seemed to hover in front of the droid's optical scanner.

"You know, Lieutenant," said Oolas, "even a just war doesn't look quite so gloriously heroic to those of us who have to pick up afterward."

"I won't disagree," said Proi. "I'm glad it's over."

The droid team of SM-3 and SM-4 found what was left of the power and propulsion decks of the *Gnisnal:* a jungle of scorched and twisted durasteel yawning open to space.

"The explosion was internal, all right," Norda Proi said after studying the side-by-side images sent back by the droids. "Looks like a failure of the primary transfer coupling for the solar ionization reactor. Which is about as foolproof a piece of equipment as there is aboard a Star Destroyer."

"Sabotage?"

"Or plain bad luck," said Proi. "Whatever happened, it dropped the hyperspace motivator right down the pipe into the reactor core. The secondary explosion broke her back and carried away just about everything below the twenty-sixth deck. Poor sods wouldn't have had any warning at all. Concussion alone probably killed most everyone on the upper decks."

Proi switched to the signal from SM-5 and SM-6, which were slowly making their way to the bridge.

"Ensign, what would the normal ship's complement be for the intact portion of the *Gnisnal?*"

"One moment, sir," said the rating, leaning over his console. "At battle stations, approximately twelve thousand. At normal watch stations, approximately seven thousand, four hundred."

"Too many to take home," said Oolas.

Norda Proi shook his head. "Chances are half the crew or more was comprised of conscripts, most of them from what are now New Republic worlds," he said. "I'll put in a request to have a fleet transport diverted here to take the overflow."

*   *   *

The primary operator for SM-1 sat beside data analysis droid DA-1 at a console in *Steadfast*'s forward hold. Together they monitored in real time the steady stream of images and sensor data from inside *Gnisnal*. A few steps away sat the operator for SM-2 and his analysis droid, performing the same tasks in parallel.

The primary task for the droids and their operators was to inventory the ship's hangars, which had been located forward of the reactor, and its gun batteries, which ordinarily bristled from every face of the wedge-shaped main hull. But enough of the ship was missing that that task was well ahead of schedule. Both droids were already well aft, in the sections below the Star Destroyer's superstructure.

Gnisnal's hull was intact there, and the droids moved through the outer corridors on the port side without difficulty or obstruction. But when they turned down an inner corridor leading to the aft emplacements, alarms began sounding at both consoles.

"Ambient light detected," DA-1 announced. But it was obvious to both operators without interpretation—the corridor ahead was brightly lit by its own overhead lights.

Immediately, the operator paged the *Steadfast*'s bridge. "Lieutenant Proi, this is Makki on Number One. Sir, the lights are on in Corridor R, Level Ninety. There's still power aboard." The operator's voice was shadowed by concern.

"Interesting," said Oolas, glancing at the range marker on the navigation display.

"Redundant systems," Proi said, frowning, calling a three-view plan of the ship to his display. "That section is served by the Number Four power cell, backed up by the Number Eight. I guess one of them's still working. Give the Imps credit, they built those babies to last."

"Should I have the helmsman put a little more distance between us and the wreck?" Oolas's upper tentacles wrapped themselves protectively around his thin neck as he spoke, showing his nervousness.

"No," Proi said. He frowned, seemingly lost in thought. "That's combat lighting, not emergency lighting. You know—as quickly as this ship went bad, there's a chance they didn't have time to initiate a purge— Makki, you there?"

"Yes, sir."

"Any signs of movement? Any vibration or hot spots in the bulkheads?"

"No, sir."

"Then I want you to check something for me," he said. "Send the droid up to Level Ninety-six, Corridor Q."

"What's there?" asked Oolas.

Norda Proi shook his head. "Wait. I'm superstitious about wishing out loud."

With its twin following, SM-1 entered a turbolift shaft and began rising toward Level Ninety-six. Oolas watched anxiously, while Proi watched with silent anticipation. When the first droid had cleared the shaft, they saw an abandoned guardpost by a set of open blast doors. Thousands of jagged, glittery fragments drifted in the air like snow.

"The viewports on this level must have imploded after the explosion," said Oolas.

"No—too thin. Those are fragments from display screens," Proi said. "Which tells me we're in the right place. Makki, turn to starboard. Forward, now. Through the blast doors. Look for an access corridor on the right, about twenty meters ahead."

The droid's maneuvering jets stirred the cloud of fragments into frantic motion as it made its way along, finding and turning down the access corridor. Before long, the corridor opened into a large, high-ceilinged room.

More than forty workstations, their displays all shattered, were arrayed in two half-circles. All faced the two-meter-tall metallic cylinder that stood like an unfinished sculpture on a platform against the far wall. Hanging on the wall to either side of the cylinder were digital display panels as wide as blast doors. An ever-changing array of multicolored messages in Basic and binary filled most of the face of the left panel.

"By my mother's jewels—" Proi said in awe.

"What is it?"

"Our express ticket back to Coruscant," said Lieutenant Norda Proi. "An intact Imperial memory core."

The Number 4 memory core from the Star Destroyer *Gnisnal* stood in a Technical Section laboratory coupled to three heavy-duty power droids in a cascade chain. One droid was sufficient to keep the core's tiers and channels from collapsing; the others were insurance. The contents of the memory core were too valuable to risk.

Accessing the contents, though, required knowing which of more than a hundred Imperial data sequencing algorithms had been used to write information to the core. And that knowledge was not stored anywhere in the core itself, but in the dual system controllers—which had not survived the destruction of the ship.

Only fourteen of those algorithms were known in detail to the experts of the Technical Section. In the first day the *Gnisnal* core was in the laboratory, all fourteen were tried on it, without success. The contents of the core poured out as seemingly impenetrable gibberish.

Five different teams made up of crack information-science specialists aided by speedy analysis droids immediately set out to find the patterns in the gibberish. Using files captured from other Imperial vessels as a guide, they searched through the digital jigsaw puzzle for pieces that went together. Even a few short strings could be enough to allow the droids to re-create the unknown algorithm, and unlock whatever secrets the memory core held.

Jarse Motempe's Team 3 assembled the first fragmentary string, made up of the names and ranks of two of *Gnisnal*'s command officers. Within a day Team 5 had found an even longer string containing a standard Imperial hypercomm message header.

The final breakthrough belonged to Motempe again—the complete fifteen-point standing maintenance order for a TIE bomber. Its more than fourteen hundred sequential data bits seemed to map every detail of the new algorithm. Confirmation came quickly: The first file reconstructed was the ship's duty roster. The second was its daily communications log for the day it was destroyed.

After that, things moved very quickly. An interface droid was programmed with the new algorithm and linked to the *Gnisnal* core, and this time tens of thousand of object and data files poured forth instead of gibberish. Each file was copied, tagged, classified, and forwarded to the Analysis Section for distribution.

One of them, given the ID number AK031995 and a priority code of Most Urgent, ended up in the hands of Ayddar Nylykerka.

Officially, Ayddar Nylykerka was a cataloger, and his assignment was Asset Tracking. Practically, that meant he made lists, requested lists, collected lists, collated lists, cross-indexed lists. All of the lists concerned the same subject—Imperial warships.

The Asset Tracking office had been set up in the wake of an intelligence failure that had nearly led to disaster. Grand Admiral Thrawn had been the first to rediscover the more than a hundred hidden Old Republic Dreadnaughts known as the Katana fleet, and had managed to seize the great majority of them before the New Republic caught up. Thrawn's vastly strengthened fleet then attacked more than twenty New Republic systems. By the time he was defeated, a great price had been paid in lives and material.

Asset Tracking existed to make sure that there were no more such painful surprises.

But the office had undergone many changes since it had been established. At first it enjoyed a staff of fifteen—eight researchers, three catalogers, two analysts, and two clerical droids. The size of the staff reflected the importance given the task, and the chief analyst was invariably well connected in the Fleet Office. Reports from the Asset Tracking office regularly received high-level attention.

Over time, however, the office's star faded. The easy work was done early, and each report contained less new and useful information. The passage of time raised doubts about the usefulness of Asset Tracking assessments, since it gave potential enemies the chance to build and launch new vessels. Little by little, staff was reassigned to higher-priority tasks, and the positions that remained came to be viewed as career dead ends. Those who could get out, did—except for Ayddar Nylykerka.

At the time the *Gnisnal* intelligence reached him, Ayddar Nylykerka *was* the Asset Tracking office. Starting out as a researcher, he had moved up to cataloger when no one else had seemed to want the job, and had added the analyst's hat when the office's last licensed analyst had been reassigned. For more than seven years he had carried the burden alone. He had the smallest cubicle in the Threat Assessment section, no more than a box with a door. To go with the absence of creature comforts, he also had no staff, no status or perks, and no contacts to tell him where file AK031995 had come from.

Ayddar Nylykerka did not know about the evacuation of Narth and Ipotek, the destruction of the *Gnisnal,* or the discoveries of the *Steadfast.* He had never heard of Captain Oolas, Norda Proi, Jarse Motempe, or any of the others whose work had brought the file to him. He was not aware that outside his cubicle walls he was considered laughably humorless and harmlessly obsessive.

But he knew his job, which had not changed since the office had been established: to inventory and determine the status of every warship known to the New Republic and not under the control of the New Republic.

And he knew that in the entire history of the Asset Tracking office, it had never before had available to it what he now had before him: a complete Imperial order of battle.

It was all there: Every warship, by name, class, callsign, and commander, assigned to every fleet and combat command. Every fighter, interceptor, bomber, and assault squadron posted to every SD, SSD, carrier, and Dreadnaught, with squadron strengths detailed. Every stormtrooper company and infantry battalion assigned to every transport, occupation force, outpost, and fort. Every cripple in a drydock and every keel in a shipyard, with projected repair and completion dates. Even the second-tier vessels allocated to training commands were included.

The datestamp on the file was more than ten years old, but it was still a treasure beyond price. The order of battle encompassed information far beyond that which ordinary ship captains and task force commanders would have at their disposal, information that only a ranking sector commander or the Emperor's own military aides would possess.

And that made Ayddar Nylykerka suspicious—suspicious enough to spend the next several hours trying to show that the file was a fraud, a late-discovered Imperial disinformation trick.

When he could not do so, he called his wives and told them not to expect him that night.

Then he threw himself into the real task before him: finding something in AK031995 to justify the last seven years of his professional life, something to remind everyone in the Fleet Command that the Asset Tracking office existed for a reason. Having authenticated the order of battle with his highest-confidence intelligence, he put his faith behind it, certain that he would never have such an opportunity again.

As he studied the data, the unofficial motto of the Intelligence Section lingered in his mind: *As dangerous as what we don't know are the things we "know" that aren't so.*

Ayddar Nylykerka did not leave his desk for three days. When at last he did, it was not to go home. With his datapad tucked tightly under his arm, he ordered an airspeeder from the pool and headed for Victory Lake.

The Coruscant home of Admiral Ackbar was made up of two squat off-white cylinders. One cylinder, windowless, rose from the grassy shore of Victory Lake. The other, half transparisteel, rose from the tranquil blue water. They were linked by a third cylinder, a long, slender shape that enclosed a second-story skywalk. A graceful single-seat Calamari water skimmer was moored to a pylon in the lake.

Ayddar's Fleet ID was enough to get him past the guardpost at the security perimeter, though he was obliged to surrender his datapad for screening, then park the airspeeder and walk up to the house. There he presented himself at the entrance to the lakeshore cylinder.

"Ayddar Nylykerka, chief analyst of the Asset Tracking office, Intelligence Section, Fleet Command, to see Admiral Ackbar."

A few seconds later the curved door flashed open with a hiss to reveal a Fleet valet droid. Folding its arms across its chest, it seemed to take up the whole doorway. "Analyst, Admiral Ackbar doesn't see anyone below the rank of commodore when he's home," the droid said. "He spends enough time out of water as it is. Call his office in the morning and ask for an appointment."

Ayddar stared disbelievingly. "You don't understand. This is *important*."

"Then it's important enough to disturb your immediate superior first," the droid said. "Run it up through channels. The admiral will consider it if and when it reaches his desk."

"No," Ayddar said stubbornly. He tried to look beyond the droid into the house, but all he saw was the inner door of the security lock. "Not acceptable. I have to see him personally. I can't take the chance that this information won't be brought to his attention."

"Mr. Nylykerka, Admiral Ackbar is resting. He is not available to see you," the droid said implacably. "Now, will you leave, or do I need to signal the guard?"

Hugging the datapad to his chest, Ayddar squinted angrily at the droid. "Very well," he said finally. "I'll go."

"Thank you, Mr. Nylykerka," said the droid. It waited until Ayddar had turned and taken his first steps down the path before closing the door.

The moment the door closed, however, Ayddar wheeled around on the path and ran past the entrance toward the shore. Gritting his teeth and cringing, he waded clumsily out into the water, splashing wildly. Alarms began to sound, and a brilliant bank of lights on the underside of the skywalk suddenly cut short the twilight. With an animal cry, Ayddar flung himself headlong into the waist-deep water and began to thrash his way toward the lake cylinder in a wretched imitation of swimming.

His simple and single-minded impulse had been to pound on the lake-level viewpanes to get Ackbar's attention. But as he got closer, he saw that the cylinder was an aquahab, filled with water nearly to the level of the skywalk.

A security airspeeder swooped low overhead, and an amplified voice bellowed orders at him. "Attention, intruder—this is your only warning. You are trespassing on government property. Antipersonnel blasters are aimed at you. Stop where you are, and you will not be fired on. If you do not surrender, you will be shot."

Panicked, Ayddar raised his arms. When he did, his fragile grasp of swimming abruptly ended, and he slid below the surface. Before he realized what was happening, he found himself mired hand and foot in a layer of muck on the bottom, unable to push off and free himself to return to the surface.

A ring of lamps around the base of the aquahab flooded the dark waters with light. For the first time Ayddar could see that there was an underwater entrance to the cylinder. He fought his way along the bottom to it, reached up with his free hand, and squeezed the Open lever.

Nothing happened.

In final desperation, with the sound of a jetboat's engines surrounding him and quickly growing louder, Ayddar reached up and swung the datapad against the hatch. It seemed to move in slow motion and to make hardly any sound when it struck.

But to Ayddar's surprise, the hatch slid open. A blur in the water grasped him firmly by the front of his shirt and dragged him inside with an ease that spoke of impressive strength. Moments later Ayddar found himself breaking the surface at the top of the aquahab. Gasping noisily, he grabbed wildly for the edge. Only when his fingertips had found precarious purchase there did Ayddar realize that he no longer had the datapad.

He looked around wildly and found Admiral Ackbar watching him. The Calamari glided easily through the water on the far side of the pool, making barely a ripple.

"You are Tammarian, are you not?" Ackbar said.

Ayddar was shaking uncontrollably as he clung to the edge of the walkway surrounding the water. "Yes, Ad-Admiral."

"I have heard that Tammar has an unusually thin atmosphere for an inhabited world," said Ackbar casually.

"That is t-true, Admiral."

"I have heard," the admiral went on, "that as a consequence your people evolved a sort of chemical pouch where you store oxygen while at rest."

"Yes," Ayddar said through chattering lips. "The *chaghizs torm*. It al-allows us to expend en-en-energy faster, for—for a short time, than res-respiration alone would al-allow."

"I am told," said Ackbar, "that this is why your people can free-live in vacuum for short periods of time."

Feeling nauseous, Ayddar closed his eyes and rested his head on his arms. "Yes," he said, his voice small and muffled.

"I have also heard," said the Calamari, gliding nearby, "that your planet is wholly without surface water, and that your people's most powerful fears have come to involve being immersed in standing water."

Ayddar nodded weakly.

"I confess that such fears are completely alien to me," said Ackbar. "Yet you willingly entered the lake in an effort to see me."

"Y-Yes, Admiral. I thought it was my d-duty."

Effortlessly, the big Calamari eased himself out of the water and onto the ledge. Ayddar saw that he held the datapad securely in one big hand.

"Well," Ackbar said, extending his empty hand to Ayddar, "I find I am not resting any longer. So perhaps you will come to my study with me and tell me what news has inspired such reckless devotion to duty."

The track outside the officers' gymnasium at Fleet Headquarters wound its way for a kilometer over hilly, wooded ground. Secured, shielded, and privacy-screened, it had been used many times for discreet, deniable meetings—not least by the man for whom Admiral Ackbar waited in the cool morning air.

Ackbar stood at the edge of the line of trees, a few strides from the cinder track, and looked back toward the rising sun as a solitary runner crested a small rise. As the runner drew near, Ackbar stepped out from the trees. "I see you are a still a creature of habit, Hiram," he said with cheerful gruffness.

Admiral Hiram Drayson slowed from his brisk jog to a walk. "I see you're still as slothful as ever. It's been a long time since you've been in the gym."

"I do not much enjoy coming here, but sometimes I have no choice," Ackbar said, falling in beside

Drayson. "Will you take pity and walk with me a while?"

"I think I can accommodate myself to your pace," said Drayson. "What's new?"

"I had a visit last night from the senior analyst of Asset Tracking," said Ackbar.

"Indeed."

"So—you have already heard."

"I heard there was a disturbance at your residence—nothing more."

"I will choose to believe that," Ackbar said. "Ayddar has uncovered something which concerns me, and about which I would like your counsel. But I did not want to be seen coming to your office, or allow this to be placed on the Fleet net."

"Go on."

Even at their modest pace, Ackbar was beginning to pant. "Ayddar has been studying the Imperial order of battle taken from the *Gnisnal* a month ago. He has found a discrepancy."

"Another Katana?"

"Nothing so large or clear-cut," Ackbar said. "What the young man has discovered is this: There are an unusual number of vessels assigned to the Empire's Black Sword Command which we cannot account for."

"Black Sword Command defended the center of the Empire's Rim territories," Drayson noted. "Praxlis, Corridan, the entire Kokash and Farlax sectors."

"Yes," Ackbar said, nearly gasping for breath. He placed a hand on Drayson's shoulder and turned him. "Please—may we stop?"

"Of course."

"Thank you," said Ackbar, his neck and upper chest heaving. "I apologize. The older I get, the harder it is for me to keep my lungs wet in air."

"Apology not necessary. You were saying—"

"Yes, of course." Ackbar glanced up and down the track, then dropped his voice. "According to Ayddar, the order of battle for Black Sword includes forty-four capital ships which we have not seen nor heard of since the fall of the Emperor. None smaller than a *Victory*-class Star Destroyer. Three are *Super*-class vessels."

Drayson whistled. "What do you think of his analysis?"

"I find it indisputable."

"You know that that's more than enough fire-power to overwhelm any planetary system in the New Republic," said Drayson. "Coruscant included."

"Yes," said Ackbar. "If those ships still exist, they would represent a serious threat."

"If?"

"If," Ackbar repeated. "You see, there are many wrinkles to this matter. All but five of the forty-four were either newly laid keels or in a yard somewhere for refit or major repairs."

"Which yards?"

"Ayddar cannot say. The names given are either not known to us, or are unknown code names for places we do know."

"Or they may not exist at all—the yards or the ships," said Drayson. "Don't rule out the possibility that the order of battle is padded with paper assets. If neither Daala nor Thrawn could lay hands on these ships to throw at us—"

"That is a consideration."

Drayson frowned. "What are the chances that some or all of them were simply renamed, and we *have* seen them since? We've certainly known Imperial Command to play that game."

"Ayddar tells me that, at most, that could account for five of the missing vessels."

"Which would still leave a substantial force unac-counted for," mused Drayson. "How long after the destruction of the *Gnisnal* did the Black Sword Com-mand withdraw from the Rim?"

"Less than a year."

"Long enough for at least some of those vessels to have been completed or repaired," said Drayson.

"More than half, if the projected commissioning dates in the order of battle were met."

"So the Empire may have taken upwards of twenty more ships than we knew back with them to the Deep Core."

"Yes. But there's another possibility, which concerns me rather more," said Ackbar. "The Empire preferred to establish military shipyards in every sector they controlled, so that no one facility was critical to the war effort, and damaged ships did not need to travel far for repairs—"

"Which would suggest that those unidentified yards were likely located somewhere in Black Sword Command's patrol area."

"Which would mean that as many as twenty Star Destroyers could be very much closer to us than the Core."

Drayson squinted at Ackbar. "Ordinarily, I'd expect the Empire to destroy any assets they couldn't take with them."

"I would be happy to know that they had done so," said Ackbar. "But we haven't found any ruined shipyards in that area. Though that is not conclusive— there are large areas of Kokash and Farlax which have never been properly surveyed. Including the Morath Nebula and the Koornacht Cluster."

"Ah," said Drayson. "I see where this is leading."

"Hiram, I don't want to know how you might know the answers. But I know you have resources not available outside your office. I am concerned by this business with Nil Spaar. Negotiations have been at a standstill for weeks, and yet Leia still urges patience. And I wonder to myself, could the Yevetha be hiding these ships for Daala? Is it possible the Duskhan League is still allied with the Core?"

After a moment's measured consideration, Drayson said, "I have no information to support such a thesis. Or to rule it out."

"Then I am at a loss as to how to proceed," Ackbar said. "The negotiations in progress make this a delicate matter. I cannot make accusations without evidence. Nor can I ignore a potential threat of this magnitude."

"What would you do if the decision were yours?"

"I would begin a search for this Black Fleet, and not stop until we have found it, or its wreckage, and made certain it is not sitting on our doorstep. We must know the fate of these ships."

Drayson nodded thoughtfully. "Then I think you should take Ayddar's information to Princess Leia, and make that recommendation. Perhaps she'll allow you to persuade her."

"I fear otherwise," said Ackbar. "Still, I can but try."

"I wish you success. In the meantime—can you see your way to—"

Ackbar pressed a datacard into Drayson's hand. "The list of the missing ships, and the mystery shipyards."

Two other runners were in sight now and drawing nearer. With a perfectly practiced casualness, Drayson made the datacard disappear into a pocket. "I'll do what I can," he said, and flashed a stage smile. "Nice seeing you again, Admiral."

At the pace at which Drayson then struck out down the track, Ackbar doubted that any other runner would head him.

Chapter 8

◆

"Let me make sure I understand," said Princess Leia, turning away from the broad windows of the executive conference room to face Admiral Ackbar and General A'baht. "No one has seen any of these vessels for ten years—and that's why you're worried about them?"

Ackbar and A'baht exchanged looks, negotiating who would answer.

"Essentially, that is correct—" said Ackbar, who lost.

"Why doesn't it sound as silly to you as it does to me? I believe you're worried about literally nothing."

Ackbar cleared his throat. "Princess, you know the price of being wrong. It can be a fatal error to underestimate an enemy's strength, or the seriousness of a threat. Our own success against the Empire owed much to the Emperor's making exactly that error."

"Better to take precautions that aren't needed than to fail to take them when they are," A'baht said, almost to himself.

"No one is going to attack the New Republic," Leia said flatly.

Both Ackbar and A'baht were taken aback by her pronouncement. "If you're so sure of that, then let's mothball the Fleet and muster out the troops," A'baht said scornfully. "I'm sure we all have better things we could be doing."

"General, it's *because* of the Fleet that no one's going to attack us," said Leia. "Ackbar tells me we can now call on more ships than fought on *both* sides in the largest battle of the Rebellion. Do I have that right, Admiral?"

Ackbar nodded silently.

"That's more than enough to bloody the nose of anyone who makes the mistake of taking a swing at us. And everyone out there knows it," she said. "They have more to gain by joining us than they do by opposing us. Look at the Duskhan League—they clearly represent a first-order civilization, economically and technologically. What are they doing? They're here negotiating with us."

The general remained undeterred. "To take your metaphor, Princess, one swing can both start and end a fight if it comes without warning."

"Are we suddenly more vulnerable to surprise attack than we were a week ago?"

"No, Princess—"

"Then are you telling me that we've always been vulnerable to a surprise attack?"

"I'm telling you that there's more to being ready to defend yourself than posting sentries at the border," said A'baht, a touch of impatience in his tone. "You must plan, and you must train, for the battle you don't want to fight, against the enemy you don't want to face, on the ground you don't want to defend. Then, and only then, do you have a credible deterrent."

She turned quickly to face Ackbar. "And haven't you done that, Admiral? Haven't you seen to it that our forces are thoroughly trained and thoughtfully deployed? If not, I'm afraid I may have to fire you."

"Yes, we have done those things, Princess—"

"Then will you explain to General A'baht—"

"—but there is more to consider," Ackbar said forcefully. "If this Black Fleet exists, and if it is operational, it represents a secret weapon. And it is the nature of secret weapons to upset all the careful planning of one's adversaries. Indeed, Princess, that is their purpose."

Leia looked down and studied the list displayed on her datapad, then shook her head. "Do these ships really represent a threat on that scale?"

"Yes," A'baht said firmly. "The Empire's standard Sector Group strength was only twenty-four Star Destroyers. They were able to exercise control over an entire system with a single *Imperial*-class ship. They were able to overwhelm anything up to a Class Four planetary defense with one-third of a Sector Group."

Closing her datapad, Leia studied A'baht next. "But those were the Empire's best, and fully equipped with the Empire's best. When a capital warship is in the yards, does the crew ordinarily stay aboard?"

"No, of course not."

"What about the troops, the fighters? Are they kept aboard?"

"I suspect the Princess knows better," said A'baht. "When a ship is laid up for any significant time, its complement would normally be reassigned."

"So—let's say that all of these ships fell into other hands when the Empire withdrew. They'd be empty shells. They won't have six TIE squadrons aboard. They won't have a division of stormtroopers. They won't have assault gunboats. They won't have an army of AT-ATs."

A'baht was unmoved. "The Princess is grasping at straws," he said. "The greatest threat in this situation is that those ships never left Imperial hands, or that region of space."

"They couldn't have been on continuous deployment for ten years," Leia protested.

"No," said Ackbar. "But there are more than two hundred inhabited worlds in Hatawa and Farlax, many of which we still know little about. Some may still be friends with our enemies. And there is still the matter of the five unknown shipyards used by the Black Sword Command. No matter who owns them, I would like to know what has come off the ways in those ten years."

Pressed from both sides, by one she knew and trusted and by another she did not know but respected, Leia relented. "I really don't need this right now," she said, sighing. "What exactly are you recommending?"

"Princess, the Fifth Fleet is about to sail on its show-the-flag excursion," said A'baht. "I would suggest to you that searching for the Black Fleet would be a better use of those ships."

"You want to take the entire Fifth into Hatawa and Farlax?"

"I would not want to *find* the Black Fleet with anything less at my command, Princess."

"You realize, of course, that the Koornacht Cluster is in Farlax."

Ackbar nodded. "Yes—of course."

"Then you realize that you'll have to exempt Koornacht from any search. Nil Spaar has been adamant about territorial integrity," she said. "Their claim extends to the entire cluster. He hasn't even agreed to grant emergency landing or pass-through rights yet. Any intrusion by Republic warships, no matter what the mission, is completely unacceptable—to him and to me."

Once again Ackbar and A'baht exchanged glances. This time A'baht lost. "Princess, perhaps you can explain to me the logic in starting a search and announcing a safe hiding place at the same time."

"Ackbar said there're over two hundred inhabited worlds in that region," Leia said. "That should give you enough to keep you busy until I've reached an agreement with the Yevetha."

"Koornacht is centrally located, and the Yevetha are technologically adept," said A'baht. "It's a likely location for at least one of the shipyards."

"The Yevetha hate the Empire as much as anyone," said Leia. "They ran them out of Koornacht at the first opportunity. You can be sure there are no secret weapons hidden *there*."

"Perhaps. And perhaps Nil Spaar will view the missing vessels with more alarm than you have," said A'baht. "Why not ask him for permission for my ships to search the Cluster for the Black Fleet? Make him say no for himself."

"You obviously don't understand the situation with the Yevetha, or you would never make such a request," Leia said sharply. "Admiral Ackbar, I know *you* understand."

"I understand your reluctance, and I understand General A'baht's concern," said Ackbar. "Given that, as you say, the Yevetha are no friends of the Empire, I would like to see the question put before the viceroy. He could surprise you."

"No," said Leia with a shake of her head. "The question alone is a threat. The presence of warships would be an open provocation. He could never agree to such a thing."

A'baht pressed her again. "Let him say so. Put the question before him, as the admiral suggests."

"No," Leia said firmly. "Don't ask me again. General, you may take the Fifth into Hatawa and Farlax to search for Nylykerka's phantoms. You will respect the boundaries asserted by the Duskhan League, and not enter the Koornacht Cluster without explicit permission from me. Is that understood?"

A'baht rose from his seat and made himself tall. "I understand," he said. "Please excuse me, Princess. I have a great deal to see to."

"Good day, General."

He saluted smartly and was gone.

"I want your word, too, Admiral," Leia said, turning to Ackbar. "I won't have all my efforts with Nil Spaar compromised. I've worked very hard to earn his trust. I don't intend to lose it because some junior intelligence analyst couldn't get his lists to agree."

"You are Chief of State, and my superior," said Ackbar, standing. "You do not need my word, but I give it to you—your orders will be obeyed. But I cannot give you my approval. I believe you've wrongly placed a lesser matter above a greater one."

"Curious—that's exactly how I felt listening to you and General A'baht," Leia said. "I considered it quite a concession on my part to agree to send the Fifth into those sectors at all. You might try to appreciate that a little more, and lecture me a little less."

"Han, darling?"

Han's face was buried in a pillow, and his answer was muffled. "Um—what?"

"I'm thinking something I don't like thinking."

Rolling over, Han made as polite a show of interest as he could manage half asleep. "What's that?"

"These aren't negotiations anymore. With Nil Spaar. All they are is conversations."

"What do you mean?"

Leia sat up in bed. "In the beginning, I thought what I had to do was learn enough about them to find something they wanted—wanted enough to make them reconsider their position."

"You can't bargain with a man who doesn't want to buy," Han said.

"No," said Leia. "You're right about that. The viceroy was sent here to preserve the status quo. No trade, no cultural exchange, no technical or scientific information access, mutual agreement on borders and territories, strict border controls. To the Yevetha, only the status quo is acceptable—and the status quo is isolationism."

"Well—that's their choice, isn't it?"

"But I want to bring N'zoth and Coruscant closer together. This could be the most important alliance of the last ten years—or the next fifty."

"There's always someone who doesn't want to join the club," said Han. "Sometimes to be contrary. Sometimes because they like not having to answer to anyone, follow anyone else's rules. Independence is worth something, Leia. I knew a man on the Praff

runs, name of—oh, blast, what was his name?—
Hatirma Havighasu. He always worked alone. Said cooperation was for cowards."

"How did that work for him?"

"Well—he couldn't take the big jobs, of course.
Or the ones where you've *got* to have someone to
watch your back. But he was still alive when I moved
on. I imagine he probably still is, tough as he was."

Leia sighed. "Maybe that's it," she said. "Maybe
the way the Yevetha see themselves, they have to be
standing alone, owing no one anything. The viceroy
hasn't given me a single concrete reason to hope for an
agreement on any terms but his—except for the fact
that he comes back day after day."

"Then why continue?" Han said, propping himself up on his elbows so he could see her better in the
dimly lit room. "It's been eating up your time and
stealing your energy for two months now."

"Because Nil Spaar's not like that," said Leia.
"He's reasonable, even though the League isn't ready
to be. He's even friendly at times, even though the
League doesn't want to be. Right now, the only thread
that connects the League and the Republic is our personal relationship."

"Pretty thin thread, isn't it?"

"I don't think so. The viceroy is more open-
minded than whoever wrote his orders. I have a very
clear sense that he wants me to succeed—he's trying to
give me time. He hopes I'll find a way to bring us together."

"Are you sure you're not just trying one more
time to win your argument with Luke?"

"What do you mean?"

"If the Yevetha want to hide away out there like
so many hermits, I'm not sure why they should care
how we feel about it," Han said, shrugging. "Unless
you're thinking about twisting arms. Which you probably could, this time."

"I'm not thinking about any such thing," Leia said
tersely. "Haven't you been listening?"

"I'm just trying to figure out why it matters so much to you to make something happen when this business with the viceroy is obviously going nowhere," Han said defensively.

"Maybe that's why," Leia said, looking down at her hands. "Maybe because I'm the only one in that room with him. No one else can do this but me." She hesitated. "Maybe some little part of me is still trying to prove that I belong here."

"No one questions that."

"That's kind, Han, but it's not true. It'd be no trouble at all to make you a list of a hundred senators who'd be delighted to see me go."

"Well—you can't please everyone. If everybody likes you, you're probably not doing your job."

"It's not about being liked," Leia said, then hesitated. "I guess *I* question whether I belong here."

Han rolled toward her. "Now that's just crazy."

"No, it isn't. I never realized how much Mon Mothma did, or how hard it was. This job is so overwhelming. Everyone always wants a piece of you. It takes someone special to deal with it all."

"You *are* someone special, boss lady."

"Some days I just don't feel up to it," she said, shaking her head. "Behn-kihl-nahm, now, he'd be a terrific president. He's got the experience, the insight, the patience—he's been here more than thirty years, Han. Half the time I feel like an accident of history. What happens if you and Luke don't get it into your heads to rescue me? *Poof.* No Princess Leia."

"I seem to remember a certain feisty young princess taking charge of her own rescue," Han said dryly. "I don't know if any of us would have gotten out of there without all of us."

"The point is, I could easily have died on the Death Star," Leia said. "I don't doubt that my father was capable of killing me to get what Grand Moff Tarkin wanted."

"You never have talked about that."

"I don't like even *thinking* about it," she said.

"He didn't know you were his daughter."

She smiled sadly. "That says something, doesn't it? Oh, listen to me—I'm sounding more and more like Luke all the time. This is why I hate looking back. Nothing good comes from looking back."

"So why are you doing it?"

"Because you asked me why these negotiations matter to me," she said. Then she quickly amended her answer, saying, "No—that's not fair to you. It's not your doing. I've been lying here for an hour afraid to go to sleep, and I can't think of anything else but."

"Oh," said Han. "Did you dream about Alderaan again?"

"Twice in the last week," said Leia. "And that's another reason to question myself."

"Because you have bad dreams? Anyone who was there would."

"Tarkin said I had dictated the choice of targets for the Death Star's demonstration," Leia said softly. "I haven't been able to make myself stop hearing that. I still see the explosion." She looked away. "And sometimes I can't help feeling as though they died because of me. That I survived because I betrayed them. And what kind of qualification is *that*?"

"Nonsense. They died because of Tarkin," Han said. "He only said that to manipulate you. I hate to see that it's still working."

"Memories have a long reach," she said, settling back against her pillows. "I just realized something else, Han. About why this matters. And it's a better answer to your question than my doubts about belonging where I am." She shook her head slowly and closed her eyes. "My father did so much to divide the galaxy. I feel as though I *have* to do what I can to unite it."

"You can't take all that on—"

"I can't *not* take it on. I have my demons, too—Luke's not the only one. That's why you can never ask me to walk away," Leia said. "I don't know if I belong in this job, and it makes me bone-tired and half crazy sometimes, but I want to be here. Here, maybe I can make a difference." She turned to her husband in the darkness. "That's all I'm trying to do in that room with Nil Spaar, Han—make a difference. Is that wrong?"

Han reached for her hand and squeezed it affectionately, forgivingly. "No. There's nothing wrong with that. But you might think about throwing in a vacation here and there, when you start to feel the walls closing in. Let someone else mind the store for a while."

"There isn't anyone else," she said, with a hint of sadness. "They come here to see the president. So that's who I have to be."

"Viceroy, before we recess for the day—I wonder if I could ask a favor of you."

"What is that?"

"I wonder if you might be able to satisfy my curiosity on a historical matter."

Nil Spaar bowed his head. "If I can, Princess. I am not a historian."

"This is recent history," Leia said, "well within your own lifetime."

"That is no guarantee that I am acquainted with the answer," the viceroy said with a smile. "But ask, and I shall see what I can tell you."

"When the Empire occupied the League worlds, did they establish any shipyards there?"

"Oh, yes," Nil Spaar said. "Several of them. This history I am well acquainted with. We Yevetha are skilled in matters of making. It is a gift of our very being. These hands"—he waggled six long, glove-covered fingers before his face—"are sure. These minds"—he tapped his thorax, just below his neck—"learn quickly. But the Empire made our gifts our curse. Thousands of my people were made to work as slaves to repair the very machines that were used to oppress us, and to wage war on your Rebellion."

"When the Empire left Koornacht—"

"They took all that they could with them, and destroyed what they could not. The shipyards, the spaceports, the power stations that fed them, even our own few vessels—killing more than six thousand Yevetha in the process. It was one final act of savagery to end a reign of cruelty," said Nil Spaar. "But, tell me, Princess—how is it that you ask this question? I know your face, and this is not idle curiosity."

"No," Leia admitted. "My defense advisers have become concerned about the possibility of old Imperial capital ships in the patrol area of the Black Sword Command—Farlax and Hatawa. It's more a matter of bookkeeping than anything else, but I've had to give my permission for some further investigation."

"Your advisers are only prudent to insist on it," said Nil Spaar. "They serve you well to worry over such things. Tell me, how many ships are they seeking?"

"Forty-four. Viceroy, I can't offer you anything but my goodwill. But you could be of great help to me in what should be a small matter," she said. "If you could ask your historians to look at the list of missing ships, and relay what you can about the fate of any that may have been in Koornacht—"

"You ask us to revisit old unpleasantries," said Nil Spaar.

"I'm sorry. I was only hoping to keep the search vessels as far from Koornacht as possible—perhaps even make the search unnecessary."

"I did not say you should not have asked. I would, in your position."

"Thank you for understanding."

"Nor did I say we would not help," Nil Spaar went on. "My mission is to protect my people. If I can help put the fears of your advisers to rest, then I am serving that duty. Give me the list. I will transmit it to the proctor of records and antiquities, and we shall see what can be learned."

"I want you to know, Admiral, that I do not plan to make a habit of idle exercise," said Ackbar, wheezing as he walked along the cinder track beside Drayson.

"I thought you should know that Leia gave him the list."

"What?"

"At the third session, this evening."

"She should not have done that," Ackbar said darkly. "What could she be thinking?"

"She asked the viceroy for a report on what the Yevetha know about the missing ships," said Drayson, his voice calm. "In effect, she asked him to search his own pockets, so the Fifth doesn't have to frisk him."

"How foolish of her."

"But logical, from a certain point of view. She trusts him."

"Do you?"

"I'm not paid to be trusting," said Drayson.

"And if the Yevetha are holding those ships?"

"Then these conversations with Nil Spaar are every bit as important as the princess believes them to be."

"I do not like the way he has separated her from her staff. She should have talked to us before doing this," Ackbar said, shaking his head slowly.

"But she didn't," said Drayson. "There's one bright spot to consider, though. When he transmits that list home, we should finally be able to break their encryption key. The list is more than long enough, with highly distinctive sequences."

Ackbar did not seem to take much comfort from Grayson's words. "In the meantime, we may have tipped our hand—and the Fifth Fleet sails in two days. What am I to tell General A'baht?"

"Nothing," Drayson said firmly. "There's nothing we *can* tell him yet. Let's see how the viceroy responds to Leia's request. That may tell us something useful."

The list Leia had given Nil Spaar was now yellowed by disinfectant and sealed behind a heavy layer of transparent isophane. It was the first Republic artifact the viceroy had allowed into his quarters on the *Aramadia*—and that only because he needed to think at length about what it meant.

For more than an hour he carefully reviewed the plan he had been following, considering whether the list before him altered any of its assumptions. In the end he concluded that it did not. All would continue as before. Only the timetable might change.

"They know," he signaled his lieutenant on N'zoth. "Make ready. It will not be long."

Then he walked to the bulkhead and opened the night-womb where his nesting awaited him hopefully. He sank back into its comforting softness and soothing scent, letting it enfold him in darkness, enclose him in shelter, embrace him in fond, tender concern. Bliss came on him, and he surrendered to the joy of reunion.

"I have good news for you, Princess," said Nil Spaar as they met the next morning in the center of the Grand Hall. As he spoke he handed a copy of Leia's list back to her, and she scanned it quickly. The majority of the forty-four names had been marked, in one of two colors.

"I have consulted with those most knowledgeable in this matter," he went on, "and they can account for all of the vessels I have indicated. The greater number were destroyed in the shipyards at N'zoth, Zhina, and Wakiza. The others are known to have taken part in the destruction and retreat."

"Viceroy, I'm overwhelmed. This is most welcome news—more than I'd hoped for. And to have an answer so quickly makes me all the more grateful."

Nil Spaar nodded. "No great difficulty was involved, Princess. It was simply a matter where we had knowledge that you did not. Shall we sit?"

"Of course," she said, and they settled in their familiar places. "Viceroy, I wish that I could repay this favor in kind. Is there no question that we could answer for you? A matter of science, of history—perhaps even your own history? The Republic has full access to the galactic libraries of Obra-skai."

"No," said Nil Spaar. "I'm sure your offer is well meant. But I do not think your libraries give importance to that which the Yevetha value. I feel I must tell you that those who gave me the information you asked for urged me to also bring you the names of the six thousand, four hundred and five Yevetha who died that day. I was told I should correct you, as parent corrects child, telling you that your interest in the fate of machines over the fate of living beings is unseemly."

"But, Viceroy—"

"Now, I know you as they do not, and I know that your heart is not cold to our loss. But, you see, here is another way we are different, your people and mine. And when the differences run so deep, it is easy to give offense. Perhaps inevitable. It is one of the dangers of closer contact."

"I am so sorry, Viceroy," Leia said. "I meant no insult to those who died. You know I only want to try to see that no one else need die. Please—will you accept my apology?"

"Your apology is unnecessary," said Nil Spaar. "I do not judge you as I would judge Yevetha. It is enough. Let us speak of something else."

"Good morning, Admiral," the voice on the comlink said. "Are you alone?"

Ackbar was momentarily taken aback. "I— Yes, go ahead."

"There's something you should know before you talk to the commander," Drayson said. "Nil Spaar gave her his answer a little while ago, and it was what she wanted to hear—that most of them are gone. But he never transmitted the list home."

"Are you sure?"

"Yes. I don't know what he did send, but it was far too short to have been the list. And there's been no reply."

"Does this mean that he is lying—or that he already knew where they are?"

"It may only mean he had all the records he needed already at hand. It's impossible to say."

"You should be telling Leia this, not me."

"You know that's not possible. She's set on playing by the rules."

"So what do I tell the general?" Ackbar said, his voice rising in exasperation. "The Fifth sails in less than forty hours."

"You'll have a fight on your hands before that happens," said Drayson. "But tell him to be very, very careful."

"—So you see, we can go back to the original plans for the Fifth Fleet," Leia said. "This needlessly provocative mission to Hatawa and Farlax isn't necessary. There's no Black Fleet hiding there."

Admiral Ackbar scanned the list and handed it on to General A'baht, sitting to his right at the great conference table. "Princess, I do not believe this changes anything," Ackbar said. "It is my intention that General A'baht carry out the search mission as planned."

"I don't understand, Admiral," Leia said, her face showing open surprise. "I went to the viceroy and got you the answers you wanted. Why won't you accept them?"

"This is meaningless," General A'baht said, dropping the list on the table. "There's no documentation, no proof. It's only their word."

"I'm satisfied that the viceroy's word is good," Leia said.

"Why?" challenged A'baht. "Because you like him? Have you led such a sheltered life that you've never been lied to by someone you liked before?"

"I believe him because he wants the same things I do—"

"Or is smart enough to let you believe he does."

"General," Ackbar said reprovingly. "Princess, I must remind you that you are the one who agreed to meet with him alone. We are at a disadvantage in judging his motives. But that is not the issue."

"What is?"

"Whether we are ready to accept that we are now a great power," said Ackbar. "Princess, a third of that region is now aligned with the Republic. Another third or more is unclaimed, uninhabited, or under dispute. Even if you accept the Duskhan hegemony over all of Koornacht, they control barely a tenth of the region. We have every right to be there."

"Because no government there can stop us?" demanded Leia. "Is that the morality you think the New Republic should be following? You sound more like an adviser to the Emperor."

"Leia, we must follow our own principles, or they are meaningless," said Ackbar. "Under Article Eleven of the Charter, we proclaim a principle of free navigation. Both interstellar space and hyperspace are owned by none, and open to all. We recognize no territorial claims beyond the boundaries of a single star system. Do you believe in the principle of free navigation?"

"Of course."

"Then there is no precedent for the Duskhan League's claim to an entire star cluster," said Ackbar. "I am willing to accept that we will *choose* not to enter Koornacht at this time. I am not willing to accept that we have no right to go there."

"It's what the Duskhan League is willing to accept that matters here."

"Not more than our principles," said A'baht. "And not more than our own security. The idea that we should stay away from Farlax because it might upset the Yevetha is absurd. If it comes from them, it's unreasonable paranoia. If it comes from you, it's unreasonable timidity."

Leia's eyes flashed dark anger. "General, you sound like you don't care about the possibility of alienating the Duskhan League."

"If you're afraid to offend someone, they control

you," A'baht said. "And that's no way to govern. Or negotiate. No one respects weakness."

"Is that all friendship is to you—weakness?"

"Treaties aren't built on friendship. They're built on mutual self-interest, or they're no more than polite lies."

"You are quite the cynic, aren't you?"

"I'm afraid the general is right," said Ackbar. "We must honor the same claims we make on our own behalf. But we cannot sacrifice our freedom of action simply to please a would-be ally. We cannot shackle our own hands simply to appease a possible enemy. If we do, we have given away our strength to them. We have raised them up and made them equal to us— when they are not."

"I thought equality was another of our principles."

"Between members of the Republic, yes. But even there, you must admit, some are more equal than others," Ackbar said. "We must look to our own interests first, Princess. And our first and strongest interest here is to learn the fate of the Black Fleet. I would be more than glad if we confirm what the viceroy has told you. But we *must* confirm it."

"The ships about which Nil Spaar could say nothing are enough in themselves for concern," said A'baht.

Leia ignored him, focusing her attention on Ackbar. "You feel that strongly about this?"

"Yes. If you do not agree to let the Fleet's orders stand, you will have to find someone to replace me," said the Calamari. "I will have no choice. I cannot continue without your confidence."

Leia closed her eyes and bowed her head slightly. Searching her heart, she could not find the strength to resist Ackbar's earnest certainty. How could she place her judgment above his? This was his domain. She did not trust herself that much.

"Very well," she said. "The orders stand."

*   *   *

Han Solo knew that something was up when Leia came back to the president's residence in the middle of the afternoon. But he could never have guessed what she was going to ask him when she found him in the garden.

"Han, I need you to go with the Fifth Fleet on this mission."

"What? That's crazy. What do you need me for?"

"It's A'baht," she said. "I don't know if he really accepts my authority and judgment."

"Then ask Admiral Ackbar to relieve him of command. You have a right to senior commanders you have confidence in."

"There isn't anything I can point to to justify it," Leia said. "He hasn't done anything wrong. I'm just not sure what he'll do when he's on his own out there."

"That's reason enough," said Han. "Ackbar will understand."

"No," Leia said. "He won't. Han, I just have a feeling that I need to be there, by proxy, right at General A'baht's side. I can't explain it. The idea of watching the Fleet sail tomorrow without a friend on board makes me very afraid."

"Why me?"

"You're the only person I trust completely," said Leia. "And you have all the necessary clearances in place."

"What about the kids?"

"I've already talked to Winter. She's willing to come back and take over while you're gone."

Han glowered. "That's not the way we decided it was going to be."

"It'll be all right. I'll spend more time here."

"You know A'baht's going to hate this," said Han. "Commanders always hate feeling like they're being watched. And he's gonna take it out on me."

"You'll bear up."

"He's gonna expect me to be in full uniform. I'm gonna have to *shave* every morning—"

"I know I'm asking a lot, Han. The chances are it'll be a long, boring deployment. I *hope* it will be."

"So why am I going?"

"Just in case I don't get my wish."

He combed his fingers through his hair, then scratched the back of his neck vigorously. "Son of a— How you get me to do these things—"

Leia hugged him and rested her head on his shoulder. "Thank you, darling."

"Yeah, that's how." He sighed. "I'm gonna need to catch a shuttle up tonight, aren't I."

"By nine or so. They're holding a Fleet four-place for you at Eastport."

"Then I'd better go in. I need to pack."

Her arms tightened around him. "I already sent the valet to pack for you," she said. "You need to stay here and hold me until the last possible second."

"Right," said Han. "That's what I was about to say."

Chapter 9

◆

For twenty-two days Colonel Pakkpekatt's little armada had flown station with the Teljkon vagabond in deep space near Gmar Askilon. In all that time the mystery ship had done nothing to acknowledge their presence.

The vagabond had not changed course, accelerated, decelerated, emitted any radiation, transmitted any coherent energy, altered its heat signature, or scanned the armada by any means known to the New Republic. It was coasting, seemingly inert, on the same heading it had been on when spotted by ferret *IX-44F* nearly three months before.

The armada had done its part to preserve the silence. No messages had been sent to the vagabond. No active scanners had painted it with energy. No ship had approached closer than fifteen kilometers—respecting the facts that the Hrasskis contact had been at a radius of thirteen klicks and the debacle with the frigate *Boldheart* had been at a distance of ten.

Pakkpekatt's technical experts had captured countless images of the ship, using every band of the spectrum. They had modeled it in three dimensions for structural analysis. They had tried to correlate the visible structure and mechanisms with known technologies.

And for all that, there was still not much basis for choosing among the many possibilities: There were no sentient beings aboard. There were beings aboard once, but they had abandoned it. There were beings aboard once, but they were long dead.

There were beings aboard, but in hibernation. There were beings aboard, but their ship was disabled. There were beings aboard, but they didn't consider the armada worthy of notice. There were beings aboard, waiting for Pakkpekatt to make the first move. There were beings aboard, waiting for Pakkpekatt to make a *wrong* move.

It was nearly impossible to have a conversation of any length without someone asking, "So, what's your guess?" Betting on one outcome or another had become rampant, and it was all Lando could do to make himself stay out of the action.

But when Lobot asked him privately, Lando opted for one of the less popular choices.

"Seems to me that this isn't much of a destination, but it's a pretty good place to hide," Lando said. "Same with the other known sightings—all in deep interstellar space. There's nothing out here to bring in even the low-rent crowd—prospectors, smugglers, short haulers."

"Virtually all interstellar traffic goes by way of hyperspace."

"Which skips right over this neighborhood," Lando said. "Nobody goes to deep interstellar except pirates, and not many of them. This is about the loneliest place I've ever seen. And, something else—this ship doesn't seem to be in a hurry to get anywhere else. I don't think there's anyone on board."

"Then what would be its purpose?"

"To hide something," said Lando. "To keep something safe. Something *incredibly* valuable, considering the effort. I'm thinking what we have here is some sort of treasury ship."

"There are twenty-two thousand, four hundred

eight known cultures which entomb riches with the dead," said Lobot, opening a link.

"That many? See, this could be some planetary potentate's tomb, packed to the scuppers with all his worldly goods. That'd explain a lot about why it's here, doing what it's doing." Lando pursed his lips as he thought. "I like this notion a lot."

"Tomb robbers are reported to be a common problem," said Lobot, still processing the link he had opened. "Tomb design frequently incorporates traps, barriers, dead-end passages, false entrances, and other defenses against intrusion."

"Sounds like fun," said Lando, showing an easy grin. "Maybe you'd better catalog all those defensive tricks, though."

"I am doing so," said Lobot. "Lando, my information suggests that tomb thefts are common immediately after construction is completed, unless the construction workers who have knowledge of the defenses are executed. Perhaps this vessel has already been entered."

"If anyone else'd gotten inside that ship, they'd have taken her home with them," said Lando, shaking his head. "She's still locked up tight and ready to fight. You watch tomorrow, when we violate the perimeter. If she doesn't put up a squawk, I'll walk back to Coruscant."

The pilotless ferret *D-89* had an appointment with an imaginary spot in space, twelve kilometers directly astern of the Teljkon vagabond.

Racing in on a trajectory at right angles to that of the vagabond, it would slice across the imaginary defensive sphere surrounding the vagabond in the maneuver sailors call crossing the T. *D-89*'s mission was to breach the perimeter much as the Hrasskis ship had, but not as aggressively as the *Boldheart* had.

"Minimal provocation, minimal risk to our assets," Pakkpekatt had ordered.

According to the plan, the ferret would be inside

the vagabond's defense perimeter for less than a second. If the alien vessel tried to jump into hyperspace, the interdiction pickets were directly ahead, ready to stop it.

"Like clapping your hands behind a sandfrog to make him jump into your net," said Lando. "I hope the net holds, Colonel."

"Do you have any reason to think it won't?"

Lando shrugged. "We don't know what sort of hyperspace drive that ship has. An interdiction field designed for our engines might not work on it."

"It is not a matter of design, but of principle. No hyperdrive can operate in the shadow of a planetary gravity well. Or so I am assured by my technicians. And I have confidence in their expertise."

"I'll bet the captain of the *Boldheart* had confidence in his shields, too," Lando said. "A pity the Intelligence Service couldn't lay hands on a full-fledged *Interdictor* for this mission—"

"Here it comes," Pakkpekatt said quietly.

"All recorders are on," sang out Lieutenant Harona. "All shields at full strength. All commands report ready. Interdiction field is ready. The captain of the *Lightning* reports he is standing by to pursue if needed."

"Nobody blink," Lando said under his breath.

In preparation for the intercept, Pakkpekatt had ordered that the *Glorious* be moved back from its usual trailing position fifteen klicks aft of the vagabond to the safer distance of twenty-five kilometers. At that distance, the ferret would have been visible as a dot moving in swiftly from the right, the vagabond as an oblong dead ahead—if either ship had been lit by a nearby sun, carrying running lights, or highlighted against the background of a bright nebula. None of those was the case, so there was nothing to see.

"Tracking," said Pakkpekatt.

A red circle appeared around the position of the alien vessel. A moving green circle marked the progress of the ferret.

"Magnify center, right," said the colonel.

The now familiar shadowy view of the tail of the vagabond ship filled the right third of the viewscreen.

"Let's have the feed from *Lightning,* left," Pakkpekatt said. The left section of the forward bridge viewscreen acquired a pale blue border and shimmered into a profile view of the strange vessel.

"I want to see the range," Pakkpekatt said.

Numbers appeared at the top of the forward viewscreen decrementing quickly at first, then ever more slowly. The two circles on the display merged for a moment as the range paused at the number 12.001, then began to increase.

Suddenly the bridge's speakers began blasting out a wildly modulated sound. It could not be called musical, but there was no other ready word to describe the experience of it. Three men with headsets on tore them off and threw them down, only to find the sound still hammering at them, nearly as loudly, from the ship's comm system.

Lando smiled in surprise when he discovered that the sound was both familiar and new to his ear—the same as the Hrasskis recording, but much more distinct. For the first time, he could tell that there were two "melody" lines, something that only signal analyzers had been able to detect before.

There was relief on the bridge when the signal from the vagabond abruptly ceased. Its job done, *D-89* continued out of the intercept area and off the bridge display.

Almost at the instant *D-89*'s tracking circle vanished, a brilliant white flash filled all three sections of the display, so intensely that those looking that way were left momentarily blinded. When the flash faded, the vagabond was gone from the *Lightning* feed and suddenly smaller in the magnified view.

"What was that?" Pakkpekatt demanded.

"Target jumped—but the field held it in realspace," said Harona. "Target has moved ahead about three kilometers. Just sitting there now—no sign of sublight engine activity."

"My heart jumped, too," said Lando. "For a moment there I thought she'd blown up. Or taken a shot at us."

They waited for nearly an hour before deciding that nothing else was going to happen. Then Pakkpekatt ordered the spotter ships to move up, and had *Glorious* brought back to its accustomed position, trailing fifteen klicks behind the vagabond.

"Briefing in my wardroom, thirty minutes," he announced to the bridge. "I want preliminary encounter data from all teams at that time. And I want the commanders of the landing teams present."

"Did you get it?" Lando asked Lobot eagerly.

"We could not help but 'get it,'" said Lobot. "The same pattern was broadcast at multiple frequencies along the energy spectrum, and not only monitored by active receivers, but induced in passive circuits."

"Is it the same as the Hrasskis signal? It sounded like it to me."

Artoo-Detoo chirped a short, emphatic response.

Threepio straightened himself to a formal standing posture before translating. "Artoo reports that if he allows for the missing and distorted sections of the original recording, the probability that the new signal is identical is greater than ninety-nine percent."

"So we've filled in all the blanks? That's something. Do you recognize the language now, Threepio?"

"No, Master Lando," Threepio said with a convincing emulation of regret. "Although I am fluent in more than one thousand languages and codes which employ single-frequency vibrations as meaning units, this does not match the syntax of any of those methods of communication."

"Blast," said Lando. "I think Pakky's about to send in the landing teams, and we still don't know what that ship's been trying to say to us. Keep working on it, everyone. We'll talk more when I get back."

The captain's wardroom aboard the *Glorious* had not been built to accommodate as many bodies as were crowded into it. By the time Lando arrived, there was no room left at the table, and all but one of the auxiliary seats along the walls were occupied.

The vacant chair was directly behind Pakkpekatt, who was seated in the middle along one side of the oblong table. Lando opted to leave the chair vacant, settling instead for standing in front of the panels where the ship's history was recounted.

"We can begin now," Pakkpekatt said, indirectly acknowledging Lando's presence. "I'd like the report from the tracking team first. Keep it succinct."

"Yes, sir," said a slender officer seated to Lando's right. "Close approach was twelve-point-zero-zero-one kilometers. Initial target response occurred point-eight seconds after close approach and lasted six seconds. Secondary target response occurred six seconds later—"

"Not long on patience, are they," Lando said. Two officers laughed, then immediately looked sheepish.

"—and resulted in an aborted jump of two-point-eight kilometers along the flight vector."

"Nor am I, as a rule, General Calrissian. If you could confine your comments to matters germane to this meeting—"

"I think the quick trigger these folks have shown is absolutely one hundred percent germane," Lando said. "Whatever the meaning of that signal we all heard, they don't wait very long for the right response on our part. We'd better be awfully sure of ourselves the next time we cross that line."

"Thank you for your thoughts, General," Pakkpekatt said in a decidedly ungrateful tone. "Was there anything else, Agent Jiod?"

The slender officer shook his head. "Only that by

all appearances, the hyperspace entry and exit of the target were indistinguishable from those of a ship equipped with our standard Class Two fusion engine and motivator."

"Very good," Pakkpekatt said, glancing meaningfully at Lando. "Report of the scanning team, please."

"There were a total of twenty-eight distinct variances and events detected by the combined sensor array during the encounter. The six we've been able to identify . . ."

Leaning his broad back against the plaque, Lando suffered silently through six more reports before Pakkpekatt called for the one which most concerned him.

"Foray commander, your report on team readiness."

The foray commander, Bijo Hammax, was one of the few officers under Pakkpekatt's command for whom Lando still had any respect after a month's exposure. Technically astute and mentally tough, Bijo had been a member of the Narvath underground and fought with the Alliance regulars through the last year of the Rebellion.

"The team is as ready as can be," Bijo said, standing slowly. "We've identified two suspected hatchways and a couple of candidate sites in case we have to cut our way in. Of course, we'll take active soundings right off the hull as soon as we have the cofferdam up, and be ready to adjust accordingly. I've got one man down with a cold and not fit for work in a suit, but that shouldn't affect our ability to do the job."

"Have you isolated this sick man from the rest of your team?"

"He isolated himself, at the first symptoms," said Bijo.

"Can I assume that you'd have no problem being ready for a go order at fifteen hundred hours tomorrow?"

"None at all, Colonel."

"Thank you." As Bijo sat down, Pakkpekatt

turned toward the other end of the room. "General Calrissian, what can you tell us about the vagabond's hailing signal?"

Lando was taken by surprise at being called on. "I can tell you that it's a dual-frequency carrier, modulating up to a thousand times a second. I can tell you that the data capacity is at least fifty thousand units, and could be ten times that. And I can tell you that we still don't know if they're saying 'Halt or I'll shoot' or 'Welcome to the Cold Space Bazaar, transmit credit information immediately.' Have your people had any better luck?"

Pakkpekatt looked down the table for an answer.

"Er, the contact protocol team believes that the signal recorded by the Hrasskis and in today's contact was an automated collision alarm," a young rating said, his voice touched by nervousness. "In our opinion, it has no informational content. It's simply meant to be heard loudly and clearly, no matter what sort of communications receivers an approaching ship might use."

Lando walked forward to the table and leaned down to rest his weight on it. "Are you saying that the vagabond jumped to avoid a collision that was never going to happen?"

"You have another explanation, General?"

"How about that it was trying to get away from us?"

"Do you think the target didn't know we were here until the intercept took place?"

"No, I—"

"Then why would the target wait until now to try to get away?"

"I'll give you three answers for the price of one," Lando said. "Because some animals freeze first when a predator's nearby. Because until now, we hadn't made any aggressive moves. And because we flunked whatever intelligence test it sent us today."

"Mr. Taisdan," said Pakkpekatt, keeping his steady gaze on Lando, "is there as much as a minority opinion on your team that believes we should wait until we have deciphered what General Calrissian has called the 'intelligence test'?"

"No, sir, Colonel."

"General Calrissian, do you have any clear evidence of informational content in the signal recorded during today's intercept?"

"No," Lando admitted reluctantly.

"Thank you," said Pakkpekatt. "Captain Hammax, inform your team that we will begin operations at fifteen hundred hours tomorrow. Foray Team One will make the first attempt, in Assault Barge One. Everyone, make sure your sections are ready. Thank you—that's all."

Lando waited, arms crossed over his chest, as the other officers and staff filed out past him. He was like a rock in the middle of a river.

"Was there something else, General?"

"I'm just trying to find out if you and I are even on the same menu," said Lando. "We waited weeks before taking the first tentative step, and now we're going to rush ahead and try to board her? Shouldn't we allow some time to process what we've learned?"

"I *am* allowing time for that," Pakkpekatt said. "Why do you think we're holding off until fifteen hundred hours tomorrow?"

"That's not very blasted much time," Lando said angrily. "You've bought into this collision-alarm theory because it suits your purposes. If you think you've seen the last of the vagabond's defenses, you should think again. You're treating that ship like a yacht with a burglar alarm, when you should be treating it like— like a warship."

"The assault barges are fully armored and have augmented shields. The agents will be in full armor as well," said Pakkpekatt. "How long would you have me wait for you while your vaunted cyborgs and droids fail to decipher something my experts tell me has no meaning to begin with?"

"Longer than twenty hours."

"No, General," Pakkpekatt said firmly. "Even twenty hours may be too much. I will not relax for a moment until fifteen hundred hours arrives. We took a step forward today. We are no longer just curious companions, traveling in company. Our next step has to follow quickly, before whoever or whatever controls that ship decides to act rather than react. I would rather that the foray team was boarding the shuttle this minute. So use what time I have given you. And surely you can find better uses for it than arguing with me."

Lando frowned, and the frown quickly turned into a sour expression. He started to turn away toward the door, then stopped and turned back, head held high.

"More?" asked Pakkpekatt.

"You promised that we'd be included in the boarding party."

Pakkpekatt showed surprise. "I thought that with your apparent disapproval of my plans, you wouldn't want to risk yourself or your staff. But, very well. There is one space open on Barge One. Choose your representative and notify Captain Hammax within the hour."

"One! That wasn't our agreement—" Lando began, warming up to blister the colonel's leathery hide.

"One or none," Pakkpekatt said firmly. "Your choice. Notify Bijo either way." He swept out of the room, moving swiftly and lightly despite his mass, before Lando could say another word.

"All right," said Lando with a quiet seriousness. "Tomorrow at fifteen hundred hours, Colonel Pakkpekatt's going to send his brush salesmen knocking at the vagabond's door. The colonel's accepted an opinion that the signal is just a warning hail. I think if it were that easy, the vagabond wouldn't be here for us to puzzle over.

"But we're running out of time to offer the colonel any alternatives. We've got one of every kind of brain there is in this room," he said with a grin. "Let's do some serious brainstorming.

"Here's the situation in a nutshell: We've got a good, clean capture of the signal from the vagabond. It looks to be identical to the signal captured by the Hrasskis. A warning hail? Maybe. What *else* could it be? Maybe if we can figure out what it is, we'll be able to crack what it says. I want to hear every idea every one of you has. I don't care if it's been brought up before."

"I am still inclined toward a recognition code," said Lobot. "The telesponders on our ships send out an ID profile when interrogated. This may have been an interrogation of that sort."

"It's thousands of modulations long."

Lobot considered. "Then perhaps our proximity served as the interrogation, and this was the response. We don't know what information they might consider crucial."

"And the way the ship tried to run today, after giving the signal?"

"Failure to respond in kind."

"They said hello, and we didn't say hello back," said See-Threepio. "A clear breach of etiquette."

Lando considered. "A ship closes with the vagabond—the vagabond pipes out its ID code, then listens for the same—when it doesn't come, it treats the approaching ship as a threat, and bolts."

"Call and response," said Lobot.

"Sign and countersign," said Lando. "It wants to hear the password. But why didn't it try again to get away? All it would have had to do is turn to a new heading. The interdiction pickets could never have repositioned themselves in time."

"There is a high probability that this vessel was built before interdiction fields were invented," said Lobot. "If we are dealing with an automated response system, what just happened may have been outside the parameters of the identification and security routines."

"Okay," said Lando. "Maybe their black box doesn't look outside to make sure that the jump actually took place—if the motivator and the drive report normally, it assumes that the ship jumped. And by the time all that was over, *D-89* was long gone—no threat within the threat horizon."

"That seems plausible."

"I'm going to play a hunch here and say it's more than plausible," Lando said. "The ship wants an answer from anyone who comes knocking. No answer, no entry. And it won't wait around for you to keep guessing. It wants the answer right away."

See-Threepio cocked his head. "But Master Lando—what is the question?"

"That's what we have to figure out, Threepio."

Hours of frustrating and fruitless verbal wandering passed before the group finally found a path that seemed as if it might lead somewhere.

"Think, everyone—think. Let's back up and look at this again," Lando said impatiently. "You want to lock up a spaceship you're sending out to the great nowhere. You want to make sure no outsider can get in uninvited, but you and yours always have access—"

"Excuse me," said Lobot. "We don't know that the builders of the vagabond intended to reenter it after it was launched."

"That's true," admitted Lando. "But if they locked the door and threw away the code, we might as well go home before we get somebody killed. We have to assume there's a way in."

"Very well. But I will consider this an axiom rather than a fact."

"Here's a fact: If I'd built it, there'd be at least two ways in—a front door, and a back door for when something goes wrong with the front door," Lando said. "But, I was saying—you don't want to use a physical key, because you don't want to let anyone that close without checking them out. So we're talking about a password, basically. A really long binary password."

"Forgive me, Master Lando, but in my experience

no sentient being could remember a password of this length and complexity," said Threepio.

"The answer might not be as long as the question—" Lando began.

"It could be longer," said Lobot.

"That's not the point. Maybe the question only looks long and complex because we don't understand it. Human beings can remember incredibly long sequences if they have meaning," said Lando. "I knew a smuggler who'd memorized the Hundred Prescriptions of Alsidas when he was a kid taking religious training, and he could still rattle them off thirty years later. My mother knew hundreds of songs and poems by heart. And there are species with much better memories than human beings."

"I don't dispute that. There are many feats of memory recorded in the libraries," said Lobot. "Even so, passwords and access codes, whether mathematical or linguistic, are not error-tolerant. No matter how long the expected response may be, it must contain no errors."

"Well, that's always the problem, isn't it?" said Lando. "How do people remember all the things they have to remember? What do they do when there's something they can't allow themselves to forget? *Some* people have incredible memories, and others have trouble remembering their kids' birthdays, much less their ID numbers and the access codes for digital locks they haven't opened in years. So people cheat."

"Mnemonics."

"Yes, but they cheat in other ways, too," said Lando. "They carry the passcodes with them—"

"But that compromises security. Anything that's carried can be stolen."

"Right. So some try to disguise the passcode as something else—"

"That's little better. Anything that's hidden can be found."

"Right again," said Lando. "A pickpocket on Pyjridj once told me that four of every five belt pouches he saw had passcodes in them, and it rarely took him even a minute to find them. Sometimes the passcode was the only handwritten item in the pouch."

"You could ask a droid to remember the passcode for you," said Threepio. "A droid can be instructed to tell no one but you, does not make mistakes, and will not forget."

"But droids can be stolen, just like pouches," Lobot said. "Droids can have their memories read, or wiped. Droids will dump their memory data under sensor-torture. Droids also know what it is that they know, which can lead to erratic behavior. Droids have revealed criminal acts by their owners, refused orders from their owners, wiped their own memories, destroyed themselves—"

To Threepio's seeming relief, Artoo interrupted the litany of failings with a trill.

"Artoo wishes to remind us that all combat astromechs have protected memory segments which can be used to store sensitive information," said Threepio. "He says that in more than thirty years of operation, no captured R2 unit has ever revealed the contents of a protected memory segment."

"That's fine, Artoo," said Lando. "You can tuck something away in your memory where even you won't know what's in it, so you can't be forced to reveal it. But you can still be blown to bits or snatched away from me—and then what am I supposed to do? A little better shooting by the Empire, and the technical readouts on the Death Star would never have reached General Dodonna at Yavin."

"The key must be replicable," Lobot said.

"Exactly," Lando agreed. "Otherwise the key itself is the weak point. Like having all your riches in a vault, and only one guy who knows where the only key is. Too risky." He stood and started to pace in the confined space of *Lady Luck*'s galley. "Come on, come on—we're getting close to something here, I feel it. What haven't we looked at? Where's the missing piece?"

"What about the fact that there are pairs of tones in the transmission?" asked Lobot.

"Good, good," said Lando, rubbing his hands together. "But are they pairs, or is it two separate channels of information? Do the individual modulations count, or just the pairs? Pairs, long sequences, replicable, securely concealable—what kinds of information fit that description?"

Lobot could no more have explained how he listened to the stream of data that passed through his consciousness in the next few seconds than a blind man could describe fireworks, or a droid could describe giving birth. In the early days of his training, he had imagined himself creating a sieve to place in the torrent, a sieve that would catch only the information he sought.

But that crude metaphor no longer sufficed. Now he immersed himself in the flow and somehow let himself see all of it, not just the pieces of a certain size or shape that fit his preconceptions. Even the flow was under his control—the depth, the speed, the temperature, the colors. But all metaphors ultimately failed. In the end, all he could say was that he sent out his thoughts, and brought back an answer.

"Long, unique nonrandom sequences are found in most genetic codes," said Lobot. "The code for a single distinctive molecule would suffice to meet your conditions."

"A genetic code? But it would only have four different pairs."

"Only if it were human. The number of code pairs varies from one planet's life-forms to another."

"How many pairs are there in the fragment?"

"Eighteen."

"How many species have eighteen different molecular pairs in their genetic code?"

Lobot lowered his eyes for a moment, searching for the answer. "There are six recorded species with eighteen-pair genetic structures. But genetic information is not available for all known species, or for unknown species."

"Do any of the six have a pitch-based language?"

"One," Lobot said. "The Qella. I am passing the genetic sample library marker to Artoo-Detoo for analysis."

Artoo's dome rotated left and right as the droid aligned its processors for the task. Lights flickered on and off across the function panel. After several seconds the droid responded with a single high-pitched beep.

"What?" demanded Lando. "What is it?"

"Master Lando, I believe the closest translation would be 'Bonanza.' "

Lando's face broke into a broad grin. "It matches?" He clapped Lobot on the shoulder enthusiastically. "Son of a— You did it, old buddy!"

Artoo burbled electronically.

"What's he saying?" Lando demanded.

"Artoo says that there is a ninety-nine-point-nine percent certainty that the signal from the ship is a representation of a segment of the genetic code of the Qella," said Lobot. "But the sequence ends in the middle—it's not complete."

"Of course not," said Lando. "That's the answer they're expecting—the rest of the sequence. Is this thing a vocalization, or synthesized? Artoo, can you sing the next fragment?"

Artoo's coo in response sounded almost sorrowful.

"Master Lando, an R2 unit has only a simple vocabulator," said Threepio. "But if I may offer my assistance—"

"Offer away."

"Sir, in order to fulfill my primary function as a protocol droid, I was constructed with the capacity for polyharmony. I believe that *I* can sing the sequence, with Artoo's help."

"Give it a try."

For several seconds Threepio and Artoo huddled together and conversed silently over the droid transmission channel, passing information in binary far faster than Basic or Artoo's own idiosyncratic dialect would allow. Then Threepio straightened up, looked toward Lando, and cocked his head.

Almost at once the room was filled by an eerie echo of the vagabond's hailing signal—distinctively different, but unmistakably the work of the same composer.

"All right," Lando said, punching the air with a fist. "That's the key. We're going in the front door. Threepio, Lobot, tell me all about the Qella. Maybe we can get an edge."

"Master Lando, for some reason I do not understand, I do not have any information on the language and customs of the Qella," said Threepio. "But now that we know the owners of this vessel, we must return it to them. It would be a serious breach of etiquette to enter it without an invitation."

"Are you saying you'd refuse to send the response—"

"One moment, Lando," said Lobot. "I have been accessing all records available to me, and I believe *I* know the reason, Threepio. The best-established fact seems to be that the Qella have been extinct for more than one hundred fifty years."

"Extinct?" Lando said in surprise. "I guess we can't hang that one on the Emperor. What happened to them?"

"According to a report in the Galactic Survey," Lobot said, "their planet appeared to have been struck by several large asteroids, and its ecosystem destroyed."

"That doesn't make any sense," said Lando frowning. "Any world that could build something like the vagabond should have been able to push an off-course asteroid or three out of the way." He shook his head. "One mystery just leads to another."

Nodding, Lando said, "Perhaps the answers to all of them wait for us inside the Qella vessel."

Lando's expression darkened. "Except there isn't going to be any 'us.' The colonel's only giving me one ticket for the boat, and I'm pretty sure it doesn't come with a front-row seat."

"I'm certain that if you tell him what we've discovered, he'll make room for all of us," said Threepio. "It would be the reasonable thing to do."

"Hortek are only reasonable when they don't have the upper hand," said Lando. "And he thinks he does."

He paced. The others waited.

"You know, there's only one way we're going to know if this really is the key," he said finally. "Otherwise, we might just be believing what we want to."

"I agree," said Lobot.

"And Pakkpekatt's going to want evidence. It's clear that, to him, we're just baggage he couldn't manage to dump. I wouldn't exactly say he's been cooperative."

"No," said Lobot.

Lando nodded slowly. "Threepio, Artoo, it's been a long day—or I suppose it's night by now. And tomorrow could be a longer one. I want you both to power down, recharge, and run your system optimizers. Set your reactivation clocks for thirteen hundred hours. That will give us plenty of time."

"Shouldn't we notify Colonel Pakkpekatt first, Master Lando?"

"I'll take care of that," Lando said, with a glance at Lobot's impassive face.

"Very well, sir. Closing down." The droid's eyes dimmed instantly.

A moment later Artoo rolled over to the power port, hooked up to it, and echoed the acknowledgment before its displays also went dark.

Lando slid easily back into a chair at the table and studied Lobot with one eyebrow raised questioningly. "Are you sure about this?"

"It is our theory," said Lobot. "It's right that we should take the risk."

"All right, then," said Lando, leaning back in his chair. "In that case, you and I'd better get some rest, too. Tomorrow's gonna be an *interesting* day."

* * *

A few minutes before 1300 hours, Lando and Lobot slid into the cockpit couches aboard *Lady Luck*.

"I figure we have twelve seconds minimum before they try to get a lock on us," said Lando. "I intend to be inside no-man's-land by then. He's been so scared to even ping the ship that no one on that bridge is going to be in a hurry to point a tractor beam in that direction."

"That will require a very high rate of acceleration."

Lando nodded, his lips pressed tightly together. "Yeah, we just might end up blistering the paint on old *Glorious*. So it goes."

Lady Luck had been flying with her engines cold, a parasite on the side of the cruiser, for more than a month. Respecting that fact, Lando went through an unusually thorough system check in the minutes that remained, bringing the engines to a state of readiness just one step below going hot.

At 1300 hours exactly, Lando thumbed the ship's com unit. "Threepio, are you there?"

"Yes, Master Lando."

"How about Artoo?"

"He reactivated on schedule," said Threepio. "Sir, what did the colonel say when you told him our news?"

"He wasn't exactly ready to hear it," Lando said. "Do you remember the song from last night?"

"Yes, of course, sir."

"Then both of you grab something to hold on to, and, Threepio—you get ready to sing."

The moment *Lady Luck* disengaged from the docking ring, alarms began to sound on the bridge of *Glorious*. In moments the yacht was roaring away from its mooring point and toward the vagabond, its fiery engine exhausts clearly visible from the bridge's forward viewports.

"What in white blazes—" exclaimed Lieutenant Harona. "Sparks, where's the colonel?"

"Down in Hangar Three, with Bijo and the foray team."

"Call him up here," Harona said, and took a deep breath. "*Lady Luck,* this is the *Glorious.* I order you to come about and bring your vessel alongside. If you do not come about immediately, I will order the weapons master to disable your ship."

"You'd better think about that again, Lieutenant," Lando answered breezily. "Blaster fire near the vagabond? Remember the *Boldheart.*"

Harona sighed. "General, what do you think you're doing out there?"

"Research," Lando said. "I'd make sure I was recording this if I were you."

"Turn your ship about, General. This is your last warning."

At that moment the bridge was filled with the sound of the vagabond's keening chorus.

"Tracking! Range!" Harona called out.

"Eleven klicks and closing fast."

"Get a tractor beam on that ship, and I mean now."

"Ready, now, Threepio," said Lando, his face tight with anxiety. "Don't wait for me. Use every band you have. I'll pipe the standard channels out from here."

"Very well, Master Lando. I'm extremely glad the colonel agreed to let us test our own theory."

"He didn't give me a word of argument," Lando said. "Ready—here we go."

There was no more than a heartbeat's hesitation between the end of the vagabond's transmission and Threepio's taking up the song. Throttling the ship back sharply, Lando held his breath and waited, watching the seconds slip by on the bridge chronometer.

"This is exciting," Lobot said. "Thank you for inviting me."

"Dying's exciting, too, I hear," Lando said, shaking his head. "You pick the strangest times—What's the status of the interdiction field?"

"It's up."

Lando peered at his instruments. "Where's that tractor beam? They can't be this slow. What's happening?"

Glancing sideways at a display, Lobot said, "There's a secondary shield up. The tractor beam has been deflected."

"What?" Lando demanded. "The vagabond is protecting us?"

"Yes," said Lobot. "That appears to be the case. We have been recognized. We have left the colonel's armada and joined the Qella."

Chapter 10

◆

In the wee hours of the morning of the Fifth Fleet's departure from Coruscant, a dark-blue bubble-topped Fleet speeder reached the entry gate at Admiral Ackbar's residence on Victory Lake. It slowed only briefly, then was waved through, following the drive up to the house.

There was already a vehicle parked there, a sleek-winged Poranji orbital jumper—the smallest ground-to-orbit spacecraft licensed for use on Coruscant, and a favorite of kids with dreams of the stars. But the adult who emerged from the speeder was not beyond the appeal of such glittery attractions. Despite the hour and the weight on his shoulders, General Etahn A'baht paused to look over the Poranji jumper before turning toward the door.

Light flooded the lawn briefly as Admiral Ackbar admitted the commander of the Fifth Fleet. The light also revealed A'baht's tired eyes and unhappy expression.

"Ah, Etahn, come in," said Ackbar, stepping aside to clear the way. "Thank you for coming. I know you're needed elsewhere, and I will not keep you long."

"I don't know why whatever business we have at this point couldn't have been conducted by holo-comm," A'baht grumbled. "I should have been at Eastport two hours ago as it is."

"I am certain that the Fifth will not sail without you, General," said Ackbar, guiding A'baht through the house. "And I think you will not begrudge the time."

"I wouldn't begrudge it if I had it. I could be on my way to the *Intrepid* right now. I *should* be."

"There is someone I want you to meet before you go," Ackbar said, leading the way into a round-walled inner room.

"It's a curious hour for a *social* call," said A'baht, following.

"It would be," agreed Ackbar as a third man rose from a wide, soft-cushioned chair and approached them. "Etahn, I want you to meet Hiram Drayson."

"Admiral Drayson, of Chandrila?" asked A'baht, caught uncertainly between a salute and taking the hand offered him in greeting.

"Once upon a time," said Drayson, smiling.

"I know of you, sir. I did not know you were still on Coruscant."

"Let us dispense with 'sirs' and saluting," said Ackbar. "This meeting is quite unofficial, so it might as well be informal."

"All right," said A'baht. "What's this about?"

"Etahn, Hiram is the director of Alpha Blue. Have you heard *that* name before?"

"No."

"Good. You should not have, until now," said Ackbar. "Hiram and Alpha Blue work within Fleet Intelligence, and beyond its reach. They have a charter which recognizes the ambiguities of war and politics, and inherit the jobs which require working outside the rules of polite society."

"Diplomatically put," said Drayson, smiling pleasantly.

"Hiram has some information for you," Ackbar continued. "I would listen to him carefully. I myself have found it valuable to do so in the past—and to have his counsel, as well." He nodded at Drayson. "And now I will say good night."

"Wait—where are you going?' asked A'baht.

"This conversation is not meant for my ears," said Ackbar. "I am going to the water column, to sleep. It is quite late, you know."

A'baht watched him leave the room, then turned to Drayson. "I have the curious feeling that being favored with an introduction to you is less an honor than a portent."

Drayson smiled. "It signifies that Ackbar trusts you implicitly, and that's no mean compliment. But I won't deny it—introductions to me seem to have a way of costing folks the blessings of a peaceful sleep."

"Just so. Well—what did you want to talk to me about?"

"Your travel plans," said Drayson. "Come, let's sit."

"I've been trying for months to establish some assets in the Koornacht Cluster," said Drayson. "It hasn't been easy, even for me." He smiled self-deprecatingly. "Traders will go to the fringes of the Cluster, but the deep Cluster worlds belonging to the League are another story. Apparently the Yevetha have a straightforward method of dealing with trespassers—they execute them on sight. And frankly, I find that to be reason for concern in its own right."

"They like their privacy."

"Perhaps a little too much," said Drayson. "Which is consistent with the behavior of the viceroy here. The Yevetha stay in their ship, and the viceroy limits his outside contacts to a few hours every other day with Leia. I don't know if there are ten of them in there, or a thousand—"

"You don't trust them, either."

"No, I don't," said Drayson. "I'm certain that Nil Spaar has been lying to Leia. The viceroy is a player. I haven't quite figured out the game, and I can't tell how far beyond normal diplomatic posturing the lies go.

But one thing I know for certain is that they've been learning about us faster than we've been learning about them. That's another reason for concern."

"You think they've been studying us."

"They'd be fools if they weren't, and I don't think they're fools," said Drayson. "That Yevethan spaceship has had access to the Republic hypernet and the planetary N&I channels since the second day it was here. And the viceroy has had unimpeded access to the Chief of State of the Republic. Meanwhile, I can't even confirm how many League worlds there are, or their names and locations. I've been shut out completely, and I'm not accustomed to that happening."

"Is that why you're having this conversation with me instead of with the princess?"

"That's one reason," said Drayson. "The other is that you're going out there with thirty warships, and she's not."

"Can you tell me *anything* about what I'm likely to find?"

"Some. There are several worlds on the fringe of the Cluster which are inhabited by species other than the Yevetha," said Drayson. "Along the border, there's a sizable colony of Kubaz, two small mining installations owned by the Morath, and a commune of H'kig cultists who apparently left Rishii over a doctrinal conflict. A little farther in, there's a nest of Corasgh established by the Empire and then abandoned, and a droid-run Imperial factory farm, likewise abandoned, which represents a free lunch for any cargomaster willing to risk the trip."

"The droids are still tending and harvesting crops?"

"Yes. Put a ship down at the loading docks, and the droids fill the hold without even being asked," said Drayson. "Now, all of those are new since the last general survey of that sector, and there could be more. Based on that survey, there are also at least five indigenous sentient species in the Cluster, none of which have achieved hyperspace travel. Some haven't even gotten off the ground."

"Not a very likely place for the Empire to put a key forward shipyard."

"Not with the Yevethan worlds nearby."

"Do you think they have the ships?"

"It would have been unusually sloppy of the Empire to allow that to happen," said Drayson. "But I don't rule it out."

"It would be nice to know."

"Wouldn't it? But I don't. Chances are you'll end up finding out and telling me, instead of the other way around." Drayson rubbed his eyes, then finger-combed his short black hair. "But here's something I keep thinking about. The Yevetha had just achieved interplanetary spaceflight at the time of the general survey. Very bright, technically clever, rather proud of themselves, but no threat to anyone."

"Then the Empire shows up."

"And puts the Yevetha to work for a few years in Imperial shipyards, building and repairing vessels which represent a big leap beyond what the Yevetha had been doing on their own. Whether or not the Yevetha acquired any ships or shipyards from the Empire, they almost certainly acquired the knowledge of how to build them."

"They could have created their own Black Fleet."

"Indeed," Drayson said. "How's your memory, General?"

"Why?"

"I'm going to teach you a code," Drayson said. "If you begin a message with it, that message will come to me without ever being seen at Fleet Headquarters. And if I send you a message, that same code will decrypt it."

"I don't like this," said A'baht, frowning deeply. "And I don't believe I like you, Admiral. If Admiral Ackbar hadn't spoken up for you, I would wonder at your loyalty. Now I find myself wondering at his judgment. Is all this necessary? Why would I want to conspire with you to conceal information from the president or from Fleet Command?"

"Let me answer your question with a question—do you trust *Leia's* judgment where the viceroy and the Yevetha are concerned?"

A'baht looked away and remained mute.

"That's why," said Drayson. "The purpose of the code isn't to conceal anything. Just the reverse—it's meant to ensure that you can get the information you need, and that you can provide us with the same in turn. Information that might otherwise be filtered out by the prejudices of those who control the comm channels."

A'baht drew a deep breath and sighed. "This is the real reason for this meeting."

"Only one of several," said Drayson. "I want you to have everything you need to do your job out there, General. I want you and your people maintaining a high level of alertness through the whole deployment. I want you to see the punch coming, if there is one. I want you to come back without ever having had to open your gun ports. But if you do have to open them, I want you to know who you're trying to kill, and why."

"Is that all? I have people waiting for me."

"No," said Drayson. "There's one more thing. I understand you know Kiles L'toth, the associate director of the Astrographic Survey Institute."

"We served together in the Dornean Navy."

"More than that, you were friends. Perhaps he even owes you a favor."

"Now I'm sure I don't like you. You know too much."

"You're not the first to think so, or say so," said Drayson.

"I want a better answer than that, Admiral. What does Kiles have to do with this?"

"Nothing, yet," Drayson said. "I just think it's been much too long since you and Kiles talked. A pity there's so little contact between the Fleet and the civil

service. Sometimes I think they're two completely dis-
connected worlds."

The bark in A'baht's voice betrayed his growing
anger. "Speak plainly! What are you getting at?"

"The Institute is a long way from the Fleet Office,
or the Palace," said Drayson. "About as far away from
the Senate and the president and the inner circle as
could be. It must be nice not to have everyone breathing down your neck. It must be nice to be able to just
do your job, without anyone questioning your every
move. And they've been given everything they need—a
whole fleet of astrographic and survey vessels."

A'baht stared, struck silent.

"Maybe you should call him before you leave,"
Drayson suggested softly.

A frown hardened A'baht's gaze still further as he
weighed the implications. "I don't like you, no, sir," he
growled at last.

"You don't have to."

"No, I suppose I don't," said A'baht, and hesitated. "But I suppose you'd better teach me that
bloody code after all."

"Kiles."

"Etahn? What are you doing calling at this hour?"

"Calling in a debt," A'baht said.

"I'll be glad to have it paid," said Kiles, touching
the stump of his right leg unconsciously. "Long overdue. What do you need?"

"How many of your ships can you put together
quietly, without attracting a lot of attention?"

"How quickly?"

"Very."

"Well—six, maybe. Possibly seven or eight, de-
pending on where you need them."

"Farlax Sector."

"Ah. Not much out there right now. Six is the best
I could do without rolling some people out of bed, and
that can't be done quietly."

"Then six will have to be enough," A'baht said.

"Kiles, I need an updated survey of the Koornacht Cluster and its immediate neighborhood. The old survey just won't do. I can't tell you why—"

"I didn't ask."

"I can't even make this an official request."

"I figured out that this was unofficial on my own," said L'toth. "You know, Etahn, things don't really *change* out there all that fast."

"The things I'm worried about change all too fast," A'baht said.

"It's not navigation that concerns you."

"No. It's all the little flags—the who, the what, and the where."

"Will my people be at risk out there?"

"I don't know, Kiles," A'baht said. "I just know that if it turns out that they are, it'll be the most important work they've ever done."

"All right," Kiles said. "I can live with that."

"I'd take my own people there if I could. You know that."

"I do. I know you that well. You hate to ask for help from anyone. I was starting to think I was going to carry this debt to my death."

"I need your help now, Kiles."

"You'll have it. I'll start diverting the ships right away."

"Thank you, old friend."

"Good luck, Etahn," L'toth said. "Watch your back out there—watch it better than I did."

The Fifth Fleet had marshaled at an orbital parking site called Zone 90 East. It lay just outside Coruscant's planetary shield, but within sight of the vast military space station which served it, and through which the Fleet's crews and supplies flowed.

As the time for departure neared, there was little sign of sentiment or ceremony, either on the station or the ships of the Fleet. All the tearful and earnest goodbyes had been said at the Eastport, Westport, and Newport gates, most of them days ago. Almost everyone on the crew rosters and everything on the manifests were already aboard.

Only the stragglers of the last watch to be recalled from liberty were aboard the tail-sitting shuttles that rose from the surface to the station. Only the most urgent supplies joined the stragglers aboard the tenders and tugs that moved back and forth between the station and the Fleet like scuttling insects.

"You should have just gone on up without me," said Skids, peering worriedly ahead through the viewport for the carrier *Imperious*.

Tuketu's long limbs were sprawled casually across three of the tug's tiny passenger couches. "The heck with that," he said, his tone light. "I never go anywhere without my triggerman."

"We're both going to get black-marked for sure. We'll be lucky if we both don't get taken off the flight roster."

"Well—we've been pretty lucky together, right?"

Skids shook his head, only half listening. "I had it all timed out to the minute—exactly when I had to leave Noria's to get back to Newport. How was I supposed to know that a Duraka gang was going to hit the resort exchange?"

"No way you could, Skids. So stop sweating it."

"The police kept everything bigger than a bird on the ground for almost eleven hours, till they caught them. And then I get pulled down over Surtsey for speeding, trying to make up time—over *Surtsey*, mind you. If they've got enough aircops to patrol *Surtsey*, you think they'd be able to catch a couple of four-foot-tall jewel thieves a little faster—"

"There she is," Tuketu said, pointing toward the upper right corner of the viewport.

"What? Where? Oh—all right. Be there in no time now," Skids said, settling down in an empty seat. "You think they'll move Hodo up to squadron commander? I'd rather it was Hodo than Miranda, myself. I don't know how you feel—"

"Skids—"

"What?"

"You're babbling."

"Am I? Okay. You're right, I am. I'll stop," Skids said, his expression sheepish. "I just feel so bad about all this, is all. I can't believe it happened." He glanced at his watch. "Almost twelves hours late—the captain's going to stuff us in a drone and use us for target practice. Next time, don't wait for me. Just leave me there and go on up by yourself—"

Standing inside the hatch of the four-seat shuttle he had flown up to the *Glorious,* General Han Solo tugged unhappily at the stiff fabric of his uniform, vainly trying to make it more comfortable. He had gained weight on two months of regular family meals, which only made matters worse. He heard Leia's voice telling him, *You look dashingly handsome, dear. It's your head that's uncomfortable in uniform, not your body.* Sighing, he surrendered and pushed the hatch release.

The flight-deck crew already had an egress ladder in place for him, and the deck officer was waiting at the bottom of it.

"Lieutenant," Han said. "Permission to come aboard."

"General Solo, sir! Granted—welcome aboard. I hadn't heard that you were coming to see us off, sir."

"I'm not," said Han, smartly descending the ladder. "I'm coming along for the ride. Have my gear brought off, and then get one of your ferry pilots to take this thing back to the station before you lock down, would you?"

"Yes, sir, right away." The lieutenant's startled look quickly gave way to the slightly worshipful eagerness Han had learned to expect, but never to accept. "I'm just sorry you didn't come up in the *Falcon,* sir. I would have liked to see her."

"I'd kinda like to see her right now myself," said Han. "Where is General A'baht?"

"The general is not aboard, sir. We're expecting

him at any time. Captain Morano is on the bridge. I'd be happy to show you the way."

Looking past the lieutenant, Han scanned the cruiser's bay, making a quick inventory of its contents.

"Looks like a tight pack," he said with a nod.

"Yes, sir. Capacity plus. Took in half a dozen more E-wings this morning. But we can still get things moved around when we need to, so it's not too bad."

"Make sure you can get them launched in a hurry," said Han. "That's what counts most in a scrap."

"Yes, sir. Would you like that escort to the bridge now?"

"If you could just find out where my quarters are, that would do for now," Han said, tugging at the tight collar of his shirt. "Oh, and let me know when General A'baht comes aboard."

Han lay bare-chested on his back in the bunk of what until recently had been the quarters of the ship's surgeon. His shirt hung from a wall clip nearby, and his shoes made a pile at the foot of the bunk.

It had been a long day, and Han's body wanted sleep. But the ship, like the station, was on Standard Time, eight hours out of sync with Imperial City. Han knew from experience that the best way to adjust to it was to extend his day further still, and turn in with the first watch. He had left the overhead lights on as insurance against falling asleep.

But his body welcomed the quietude, and his eyes needed rest from the light, and his mind wanted relief from the thoughts that gnawed at him. Nothing felt right—being away from Leia and the kids, going off alone without Luke or Chewbacca, resenting Leia for asking when she knew he could not refuse her, hating his own inability to say no. Somewhere he had lost the independence he had once cherished as his most precious possession, and the worst part was that he knew he had given it up freely.

No—the worst part was that here he was, on his

own, and he couldn't remember how to enjoy it. It didn't feel right to be alone.

Han flung an arm across his face and tried to make it all vanish. In a little while, it did.

General A'baht climbed out of the Poranji jumper with respectable limberness for someone his age.

"General," the deck officer said, saluting smartly. "Good to see you, sir. Captain Morano's in conference with the task force captains, and the XO is on the bridge."

"Thank you," A'baht said, jumping down and jerking a thumb in the direction of the jumper. "Find someplace to strap this down, will you, Marty? It's borrowed, but I've taken kind of a fancy to it."

"Yes, sir. Will do."

There was something about the deck officer's demeanor—something in his voice, or the way he held his mouth—that wasn't quite right. But it wasn't until A'baht turned to walk forward toward the exit that he got a clue as to what it was. That was when he saw that fully half the bay's crew had stopped work to look his way. Several seemed to be wearing either funereal regret or indignant distress on their faces.

"Marty, what's going on?"

The deck officer swallowed hard. "Sir, General Han Solo showed up a couple of hours ago—"

"Did he," A'baht said thoughtfully.

"Yes, sir. I figured that he was here to see us off, but the captain put him in Dr. Archimar's quarters."

"*Did* he."

"Yes, sir. I— General, there's talk that Solo's here to take over the Fleet."

"If he is," A'baht said evenly, "then Captain Morano gave him the wrong quarters. Where is General Solo now, Marty?"

"I can find out for you. He asked to be notified when you came aboard, sir."

"Find out for me," said A'baht, nodding. "But let me be the one to give him the message."

A smile cracked the deck officer's mask of concern. "Yes. *sir*."

The first that Han knew he had fallen asleep was when he was startled awake by a sharp noise. Sitting bolt upright, wild-eyed, he found a tall Dornean in a Fleet Command uniform looming over him. The age lines on the Dornean's face showed that he was over a hundred years old. The bars on his jacket showed that he was General A'baht.

"General Solo," A'baht said. "There's a rumor all over the ship that I'm out and you're in. Want to tell me what that's about?"

"I don't know what that's about," said Han, swinging his feet over the side of the bunk and grasping for his shirt. Still half addled by his nap, he needed three swipes to grab it away from the clip. "You're the commander of the Fifth Fleet. Nothing's changed."

"You're here," A'baht said, settling back against the vanity. "That's a change."

Han shrugged into his shirt and began struggling with the buttons. "Tell me about it," he said. "Look, General, I know you don't want me here, and the truth is I really don't want to be here. Maybe if we give each other some breathing space on that understanding, this won't be too bad for either of us."

"I see I was prepared to give you too much credit on your reputation," said A'baht.

"What are you talking about?"

"Among the Dornean, a male is expected to know when it is time to put down his babies and take up his weapon. But to be shamed into that duty by his female—"

"Yeah, well, tell it to someone who cares," Han said, annoyed. "I've done my turn, and then some— and if it's not enough to satisfy you, ask me if it's gonna cost me any sleep. You're not exactly diving on the Death Star in a snub fighter yourself, you know."

A'baht laughed. "At least you have enough teeth left to bite back," he said. "Can I see your orders?"

"There wasn't enough time for formalities," Han said, pushing the tail of his shirt down into his waistband. "Look, I'm no diplomat—ask anyone. Let's try talking plainly and see where that gets us. I'm *not* here to replace you. I wouldn't begin to know how to fight this task force, and I wasn't planning on taking a crash course."

"Very well. Why are you here, if not to replace me?"

"Now I'm giving *you* too much credit. I thought you could figure that one out on your own."

"I do not enjoy the princess's full confidence."

"Right. But I do. So if I tell her everything's fine, she'll believe it."

"No, there must be more," said A'baht. "I don't enjoy the princess's full confidence—but she couldn't find a reason to justify replacing me. If you're not here to replace me, are you here to find her that reason?"

"I'm here to help you not do anything stupid," said Han. "If it turns out you don't need any help with that, that's fine with me. I'll sharpen up my *barlaz* game in your rec hall, find where your quartermaster keeps the medicinal dragonjuice, and catch up on my sleep."

"She still fears an incident with the Yevetha."

"You could say that."

"Perhaps she should fear the Yevetha instead," said A'baht. "I'd like to hear your opinions concerning the Black Fleet."

"Outside my jurisdiction," said Han.

"And you said you were no diplomat."

Han grinned crookedly. "I guess Leia's been more of a bad influence on me than I thought."

"Is there enough of the soldier left in you—"

"I was never, ever a soldier, General, even when I was wearing one of these," Han said, tugging at the front of his shirt. "Too independent-minded—taking orders was never my strength. I was a Rebel."

"And now?"

"I'm—a patriot, I guess. If that's what you call

someone who thinks the New Republic has the old Empire beat all hollow."

"Very well," said A'baht. "Then I ask the patriot in Han Solo to let me share with him a soldier's view of why we are taking this ship to Hatawa and Farlax."

"All right," Han said. "If it can wait until all of us are a little more awake."

"It can wait, but not too long," said A'baht. "Have you eaten?"

"Nothing since my feet left the ground."

"Then I suggest you come with me to the captain's mess, and we'll catch a meal while Captain Morano jumps us into the first grid. Unless your stomach takes exception to the combination of food and hyperspace?"

"Not at all," said Han. "That's kind of you. Let me find my shoes."

"Oh—not entirely kind," said A'baht.

"Oh? Is the captain's cook still struggling to master his galley?"

A'baht smiled. "Since you're senior to me—and especially since you're Han Solo—your presence is a problem for me where the crew is concerned," he said. "If you will allow it, I'd like to use your presence to underline the seriousness of this mission, and turn a negative into a positive. And having you seen as my guest aboard will kill the rumors your arrival spawned faster than any announcement I could make."

Han nodded. "Let's do it, then. I'm not here to make your job harder."

At 2440 hours exactly, between the *para* rolls and the Dornean brandy, the Fifth Fleet jumped into Hatawa Sector. The search for Ayddar Nylykerka's Black Fleet had begun.

Chapter 11

◆

By the time Colonel Pakkpekatt reached a comm station, *Lady Luck* had moved within two kilometers of the vagabond and was closing at a leisurely rate that would nonetheless place it alongside in a matter of minutes. The sight of it brought the threat ruffles on Pakkpekatt's back to full flourish, and his throat turned crimson—a display no one in his bridge crew had ever seen before.

"Calrissian, you are a madman," said Pakkpekatt with an icy evenness. "You will lose more than your commission over this, I promise you that."

"Colonel, I'll take that as your promise to do everything you can to help keep me alive long enough to satisfy your fine sense of outrage. I understand the Fleet doesn't allow you to court-martial a corpse."

"There are other uses for corpses," said Pakkpekatt with a cold smile. "While you *are* still alive, perhaps you would like to place your justifications on the record."

"Gladly," said Lando. "Your decision to exclude us from the foray team endangered not only the lives of Bijo and his men, but the whole mission. And your attitude during yesterday's briefing convinced me that you'd never give any real weight to anything we brought to the table—"

"You mean to blame *me* for your recklessness?" Pakkpekatt raged, his frosty reserve vaporizing in an instant. "You brought *nothing* to the table. You obviously came here with secret information about this vessel, which you denied having, and denied to us."

"Secret information? What're you blathering about, Colonel?"

"You as much as admitted it. *You* are the one who knew that the foray team would be in danger. *You* knew that the target was expecting a countersign, which you already possessed."

"Colonel, you don't know what you're talking about. I had a hunch about what the builders of this ship out here were doing, and this was the only way to play my hunch."

"You expect me to believe that you risked your lives and your ship on a 'hunch'?"

Lando chuckled, a low, smooth sound. "You've never played sabacc with me, have you, Colonel? You have to be willing to lose big if you're hoping to win big. No one ever got rich wagering one credit at a time."

"I hope you've enjoyed your little game, General. But I had always understood that hiding cards was considered dishonest."

"Colonel, we didn't have any secret information. We simply happened to look in the right place in the Imperial archives, and just barely in time, too. Now we're in, and we're going to do what we can while we're here. I trust you have the recorders running by now?"

Pakkpekatt muted the link and looked away from the comm unit toward his operations officer. "Do we have the recording of the key signal *Lady Luck* used to enter the restricted zone?"

"Yes, sir."

"Is the tractor beam on *D-89* strong enough to tie up *Lady Luck*?"

"Easily," said the operations officer with contempt. "She's just a civilian pleasure yacht."

"Is the interdiction field up?"

"Yes, sir, the field is operational."

"Then queue up that key, and get ready to send the picket in to yank them out of there." Pakkpekatt turned back to the comm unit and opened the link. "We're doing the best we can," he told Lando. "But some systems were in the middle of a calibration diagnostic, getting ready for our attempt later today, and they're not back up yet. Can you stand off at your present range and give us a little time? A few minutes ought to be enough."

"I guess that's reasonable enough. But I hope you're not thinking about trying to send the foray team in," Lando said warningly. "We've talked about it here, and we have doubts that the key will work a second time."

"No," said Pakkpekatt, "we have no plans to do that. Just stand by." He broke the link. "Ready?"

"Yes, sir."

"Then do it."

Since making its pass at the vagabond the day before, *D-89* had been flying formation with *Glorious*, awaiting its next job as the second spotter platform for the long-range stereo recordings to be made of the foray team's contact. When its realspace engines suddenly roared to life, it had only a few kilometers to cover before reaching the invisible boundary of the vagabond's security sphere.

D-89 was still accelerating when the vagabond hailed it—a signal heard on board *Lady Luck* and *Glorious* as well. Lobot was the first aboard the former to realize the cause. "There's another vessel approaching the vagabond."

Almost at the same time, Threepio said, "Master Lando, that is not the same sequence."

"I know," said Lando grimly. "I can hear it. Ah, I was afraid he was going to try this—"

The signal from the vagabond ended, and the response began, relayed from *Glorious* through *D-89*'s own transmitters. But even before the response was complete, a fierce blue light began dancing over the entire aft third of the vagabond's hull.

"Hold on, everyone!" Lando cried on seeing it. He threw himself across the console, reaching for the control that would boost *Lady Luck*'s combat shields with the full output of her engines.

But his hand had not reached the switch when the cockpit was flooded with light, a light so harsh that even Threepio flinched from it, a light so cold that it made Lando shiver. Half a dozen alarms began to sound at once, as though the yacht itself were crying out in surprise. And piercing the cacophony was the keening wail of a frantic Artoo.

From the vantage of those watching on the bridge of the *Glorious*, it all seemed to take only a moment, a few heartbeats. Those who glanced down at their consoles in that moment missed it. When their heads swiveled and jerked upward at the collective gasp, all that was left to see was the sudden spreading cloud of flotsam in space between the cruiser and the vagabond.

The blue glow had made the vagabond suddenly bright on the cruiser's screens. Then three beams of energy had lanced out from the tail of the ship, knifing across space like searchlights, sweeping toward the same target. The beams intersected, merged, and at that moment, that point, there was a small but spectacularly intense explosion.

At the same time, all the telemetry from D-89 vanished from the bridge consoles of the *Glorious*.

Then the lances disappeared as quickly as they had appeared, and there was silence. The vagabond dropped back into near invisibility as small secondary explosions lit the atomized debris from within, like tiny nova stars inside a hot nebula.

"What about *Lady Luck*?" Pakkpekatt quietly asked a still shaken tracking technician.

"Uh—we can't see through the cloud until it disperses. It's too heavily ionized. But the *Marauder* still has *Lady Luck* on her screens."

"How very interesting," Pakkpekatt said, straightening to his full height.

"Colonel, Captain Hannser of the *Marauder*, asking for your instructions."

"Tell him to wait," said Pakkpekatt, turning toward the bridge windows. "Imaging, replay the attack, half-speed. Everyone, watch your monitors. Let's see what we can learn about the general's friends."

One by one, Lando silenced the alarms—the radiation alarm, the proximity alarm, the contact alarm, the systems alarm, the anomaly alarm. The ship seemed unharmed, even untouched.

"What *was* that?"

"I'm showing an explosion eight kilometers aft of us," said Lobot. "I believe we have now seen a demonstration of the weapons technology of the Qella."

"Holy queen of sailors—tell me it wasn't the foray shuttle, Lobot."

Lobot opened a link to one of *Glorious*'s unsecured processors. "It was the ferret D-89. No one was on board."

"Thank the stars." With a touch on the console before him, Lando signaled the cruiser. "Colonel, one of these days you're going to learn to stop ignoring what I tell you."

"Anytime you care to start telling me the truth, General, I will be happy to listen."

"The truth?"

"Yes, the truth," Pakkpekatt snarled. "You could begin with who you're working for, what's inside the target, and why you chose to become a traitor to the New Republic. The vagabond allowed you to approach, and now it's protecting you."

"General, I warned you that the key might not work a second time. The challenge to the ferret was different than the challenge to us—probably to stop someone from doing exactly what you tried to do, namely snoop and steal the key. If the vagabond's protecting us, it's only because it thinks we belong here."

"Are you still claiming that all this is simply the outcome of a gambler's lucky hunch?"

"Colonel, we're breaking and entering. We're not here to keep an appointment."

"Then why is the vagabond still here?"

Lando looked up and stared out *Lady Luck*'s front port. The weapon that had been used against the ferret would be equally effective against the interdiction pickets. And with even one of them destroyed or disabled, there would be nothing to stop the vagabond's escape.

"I don't know, Colonel," said Lando. "Maybe she's waiting for us. I'm going to start closing with her again and see what happens." With a light touch he edged the thruster control forward. "In the meantime, if you'll stop trying to send in the cavalry long enough to listen, we'll pass along everything we know, or think we do."

Artoo and Threepio had been having their own conversation at the rear of the yacht's flight deck, and now Threepio stepped forward to where Lando and Lobot sat. "Sir—"

"Wait, Threepio."

"Sir, Artoo says that the new sequence sent by the Qella vessel does not appear in the information from the survey archives."

"What?"

"Artoo says he is unable to determine what the correct response might be."

Lando shook his head. "I feel like I'm in a spelling bee and the kid in front of me just went out on a word I don't know either. Colonel, are you getting all this?"

"Getting it, yes. Understanding it, no."

"We matched the original signal from the vagabond to the genetic code of a species called the Qella. The correct response was the next portion of the code," Lando said. "But it interrogated the ferret with a different sequence, and we don't seem to know what comes next. Maybe Lobot has an explanation—he's the one who found the match in the first place."

"An explanation is readily available," Lobot said. "But it will not help us with our problem."

"I'd like to hear it anyway," said Pakkpekatt.

Lando nodded his agreement.

"I have reviewed the history of the records concerning the Qella. They were discovered by the Third General Survey, which was the Republic's first comprehensive examination of habitable worlds in the galactic arms," Lobot said. "But the only report is from the survey vessel. By the time the contact vessel arrived eight years later, all of the Qella were dead, and more than one-third of the planet was covered by ice up to a hundred meters thick."

"*All* dead? What happened?"

"An asteroid impact was postulated," said Lobot. "The contact vessel collected genetic samples and technological artifacts from two sites, but it wasn't equipped for archaeological work, and there were many worlds with live populations waiting for a contact vessel. Qella was marked for a follow-up visit by an archaeological team, and the contact vessel continued on. But there was no follow-up."

"Why not?" Lando demanded.

"The Third General Survey was never completed," said Pakkpekatt. "It was terminated at the outbreak of the Clone Wars."

"The colonel is correct," Lobot said. "All survey and contact vessels were taken over by the Imperial Navy with the Third General Survey only sixty-one percent complete."

"Which means we have all the information we're going to have about the Qella?" Lando asked. "There must be more somewhere. They obviously had interstellar travel. They must have had neighbors, trading partners—"

"Perhaps the colonel's staff can locate such information," said Lobot. "I have been unable to locate any other references to this planet and its inhabitants."

"I have people working on it," Pakkpekatt said curtly. "If I had been given this information when you first developed it, I might have had some results for you by now."

The vagabond now nearly filled *Lady Luck*'s forward viewscreen. "Colonel, you can deal two different players the same hand; one of them will win with it, and the other lose. If we had given you the chance to play our hunch, what would you have done with it? Where would Bijo Hammax be right now?"

After a long pause, the intelligence officer said, "Point taken, General."

"Thank you, Colonel. We're getting pretty close now, as I guess you can tell. The way I see things, I'd better start concentrating on the game going on out here," Lando said. "We'll keep in touch, but that's not going to be my first worry."

"If you would leave an audio channel open—"

"You'll probably want to pick up all our cockpit sensor feeds—Lobot can route 'em to you."

"We will do what we can to assist you," said Pakkpekatt.

Lando knew that those must have been difficult words for the Hortek to say. "You'll hear us yell," he said. "But if you'd really like to help, maybe you want to see what you can do about getting a ship sent to Qella, fast. There may still be answers there that we're gonna need before this is over."

With *Lady Luck* cruising slowly along the hull of the vagabond at a distance of only a hundred meters, Lando felt as though he were seeing the ship clearly for the first time.

At a distance, the hull seemed lumpy and irregular. Up close, it looked like nothing so much as a bundle of massive tree trunks woven round with thick, crisscrossing vines, which had grown into the metallic bark. But the scale was all wrong for that comparison—the "vines" were large enough in cross-section to park the yacht inside one, and the "trunks" would easily have swallowed the bulk of the cruiser.

"Looks a bit like a Foss," said Lando. "What do you think about those extrusions?"

"I can't tell whether the design is symbolic or functional," said Lobot. "There is no repeating pattern that I can perceive."

"Maybe those extrusions are some sort of energy conduit for the weapons," said Lando. "I can't see anything *else* that looks like a weapon."

"It is possible that their weapons use surface-charge capacitance," said Lobot. "SCC is considered unsafe for task force operations, but single vessels can accumulate very large surface charges without affecting internal systems. Deep space is a good insulator."

"So the entire surface might be an accumulator for that weapon we saw?"

"Yes. The extrusions, as you call them, increase the surface area. The actual weapon apertures could be quite small."

"Perhaps we should send a greeting message," said Threepio. "I would be happy to offer my services."

"Not yet, Threepio," said Lando. "Look, there's the primary attach site that Bijo was planning to use—there, swing the spot up and to the right."

"That's not a hatchway," said Lobot after a moment's inspection. "It's a surface marking. There are no seams."

"The secondary attach site is farther forward. We'll go take a look at that."

"General Calrissian," Pakkpekatt said.

"Yes, Colonel."

"I thought you would like to know that *IX-26* has been diverted from its patrol in Nouane to pick up an archaeological team from the Obroan Institute," said Pakkpekatt. "They are on their way to Qella now."

"Thank you, Colonel."

"My chief of data acquisition has asked me to relay a request to you," Pakkpekatt continued. "He would like you to attach a tracking and monitoring limpet to the target at first opportunity. In the foray team's action plan, that was considered a mission failsafe."

"Colonel, I intend to attach this entire yacht to the vagabond, as soon as I can figure out where to do it. We'll do a hand attachment of a TRAML then, if everything's still quiet. I'm not going to fire anything at her if I can avoid it."

"Lando," said Lobot suddenly. "Look."

The surface of the vagabond had suddenly come alive with small, pale patches of light. They appeared and disappeared in orderly patterns along the top of the hull extrusions, forming sequences that drew the eye forward, and then to the edge of the curving hull, where they disappeared.

"Oh, no! Artoo, look out! It's getting ready to attack!" Threepio exclaimed.

"That's not what happened the last time they fired," said Lando.

"The last time they fired, we were two klicks away," Lobot reminded him. "We wouldn't have been able to see this stage from there."

"Some thought here that this is engine activity, and the target is preparing to jump into hyperspace," said Pakkpekatt over the comm. "Suggest you back away and launch that limpet now. You may not get another chance."

"There is another possibility," said Lobot. "This could be the next question for us. If so, it is one we're not prepared to answer."

"General, I strongly suggest you drop the limpet and get your people out of there," Pakkpekatt said forcefully.

"No!" said Lando. "I want to know what's happening on the rest of the hull, the part we can't see. Where do the lights go? Is there a beginning, an end? Lobot, where are those other video feeds?"

"I am monitoring," said Lobot. "The light streams originate at a point aft of our position and diverge into two streams which wind forward along the hull, following the surface contours. Both streams end at separate points on the far side of the ship."

"Threepio, can you make anything out of this? We've got *two* streams again. Is this another duet?"

"I do not recognize this as any form of language known to me, Master Lando. But perhaps it is not linguistic, but symbolic communication."

"What are you talking about?"

"Sir, perhaps they are pointers, not streams."

"Pointers—so which one do we follow?"

"Master Lando, might I suggest that you follow them both, back to the point of divergence?"

"That's backwards!"

"Sir, the conventions of symbolic communication are not universal. You have been conditioned by the customs of your culture to extrapolate in the direction of movement, rather than to look for the source."

"Threepio's right," said Lobot. "You can follow a stream to its origin or its destination. Perhaps we've taken so long since we first signaled them that they've decided we missed the portal, or don't know how to find it."

Lando raised his hands in a gesture of surrender. "Backwards it is," he said, and reached for the thruster controls.

Watching the streaming lights flicker by and disappear in the direction of the bow, Lando could not help feeling they were going the wrong way. But when they reached the spot from which the light seemed to appear, a dark hole irised open there, and the streaming lights vanished.

"They're inviting us inside," said Lobot.

"Well, I'll be the last pup of an ion storm—" Lando breathed in delighted wonder. "So they are, Lobot. So they are. What kind of atmosphere did the survey ship record on Qella?"

"Nitrogen seventy-five percent, carbon dioxide thirteen percent, oxygen nine percent, water vapor one percent, argon one percent, traces helium, neon—"

"That's enough," Lando said, putting *Lady Luck* on automatic station-keeping. "The droids won't mind, but it's a bit thick for my lungs. It's suits for us, pal. Let's go get prepped."

The yacht's outer airlock and the opening in the vagabond's hull were mismatched in both shape and size. The solution was an old invention, elegant in its simplicity, which Lando had made standard equipment on all his vessels—an extensible cofferdam. Flexible yet vapor-tight, the cofferdam could telescope out from the hull of *Lady Luck* and attach itself to the other ship, forming an enclosed tunnel between the airlocks.

Lando locked the helmet of his suit in place with a twist and looked across the compartment at Lobot. "Everything all right?" he called, more loudly than necessary. He'd spent as little time as possible in spacesuits and still had the neophyte's reflex of trying to shout through the faceplate.

"Everything is fine," said Lobot. "I have nominal pressure and temperature, and there is minimal interference."

"All right, then. Extending the cofferdam."

Lando pressed the switch, engaging a specialized autopilot which not only controlled the movement of the tunnel of rings, but took over thruster control for *Lady Luck* as well. The autopilot reported its progress in relentless detail, which Lando ignored until just before contact.

"Beginning cofferdam attach sequence. Attempting magnetic lock," the autopilot announced. "Testing. Magnetic lock failed. Attempting negative pressure lock. Testing. Pressure lock failed. Attempting Chemical Lock One. Testing. Chemical Lock One failed—"

"What's that hull *made* of?" Lando demanded.

"We may have to free-fly over there," said Lobot.

"You sound almost hopeful."

"I've learned that it's something many people try on their vacations."

"—Attempting Chemical Lock Three. Testing. Chemical Lock Three failed. Attempting Mechanical Lock One. Testing. Mechanical Lock One holding."

Mechanical Lock One consisted of thousands of tiny composite barbs attached to monomolecular threads. The barbs were driven into the hull like so many anchors, and then the slack was taken up, pulling the cofferdam's ring seal snug against the surface.

"Any change, Colonel?" asked Lando.

"No change, General."

"She doesn't seem to have felt it," said Lando to his companions. "Pressurizing the cofferdam." They could not hear the hissing, but the transfer pumps made the deck under their feet vibrate. "Looks like a good seal. Pressure is holding."

"Good luck, General," said Pakkpekatt, reduced now to the role of spectator. "I envy you."

Lando drew a deep breath and offered a jaunty grin. "I might trade places with you if I could, Colonel," he said. "Lobot, if you lose contact with me, take the ship out of here. Don't come in after me."

Lobot cocked a questioning eyebrow. "Do you really expect me to follow that order?"

"Well . . . ," Lando said, and the grin returned. "At least wait until I yell *twice*."

"Good luck, Lando," Lobot said, and opened the inner airlock.

"Do be careful, Master Lando," Threepio called after him.

The cofferdam's rigid rings had handholds spaced at intervals, which Lando used to pull himself along through the five-meter-long tunnel between the ships. He paused outside the vagabond's portal to switch on his suit and helmet spots, as the chamber beyond was still lit only by the overspill from the lamps at *Lady Luck*'s airlock.

With his own spotlights on, Lando's shadow no longer led the way for him. But the lights revealed little detail inside the Qella vessel—only an empty space enclosed by blank walls of the same mottled color as the hull itself.

Grasping the upper rim of the opening, Lando raised his feet and floated himself through, twisting to look in all directions. He had half expected lights to come on as he entered, but that did not happen. But the lights he wore were enough to assure him that he was alone.

"All right, I'm in," said Lando. "This chamber is about twice my height in every dimension—plenty of room for all four of us. No response to my presence yet. There's no light, and there doesn't seem to be another doorway. But then, I can't see any mechanism for the hatch I came through, so maybe I just can't recognize the exit."

"Watch your assumptions," said a new voice— Bijo Hammax. "Just because you came out through a double-hatch airlock doesn't mean that's what you've entered."

"Hey, Bijo! I thought you'd be sore at me for stealing your date."

"I decided to wait and see what happened," said Hammax. "If she kills you, I plan to forgive you."

"Thanks, buddy," said Lando, turning. "Wait, here's something—that's odd—"

Looking back toward the outer hull, Lando thought he could see the attachment ring through the wall of the chamber, encircling the opening as a faint gray shadow. He turned off his suit lights, and the ring became more distinct.

"Why have you turned your lights off, General?"

"Can you see this?" Lando demanded. "I don't know why or how, but I can see the attachment ring through the bulkhead. There's a gray ring, a shadow, exactly that size, visible on the inside."

"Not visible on the relay. Are you saying that the hull is translucent, Lando?" asked Lobot.

"Well—yes. Where're the ship's spots? Can you sweep them across the outside?"

"Coming up."

With *Lady Luck*'s brilliant spotlights trained on the hull, there was no mistaking the sight—the whole bulkhead glowed faintly, and the ring darkened to a sharp-edged black shadow. When Lando brushed his gloved fingertips across the surface, he could feel that the shadow was slightly raised.

"It's almost like a bruise," he said. "Like the hull is swelling where those thousands of tiny grapples have grabbed on to it. Artoo, come in here. I want you to scan and record this."

"That could be a self-repair function at work," said Hammax. "Mechanical One *does* do some microscopic damage to the attach point. As for the translucent hull—General, you may have discovered why the ship has so few surface features. We're not seeing the true hull, just an outer membrane, probably differentially transparent to radiation. All the sensors are concealed underneath."

By the time Hammax finished his speculations, Artoo appeared at the portal. He chirped at Lando, then entered when Lando waved him in. The lack of handholds in the chamber was not the problem for the droid that it was for the general. Thanks to the array of small gas thrusters built into all astromech droids, Artoo's motions were far more controlled than Lando's—who found he kept drifting into one bulkhead or another, slowly twisting from side to side and turning end over end.

"You getting a better image now?" Lando called.

"Much clearer," said Lobot. "Are you ready for the rest of us?"

"There's nothing else to see," said Lando, switching his suit's floodlamps back on. "The bulkheads are completely bare."

"Does it appear to be the same material as the outer hull?" asked Hammax. "If so, there could be any kind or number of sensors or weapons concealed underneath it. They could use that material the way we use one-way mirrors. For all we know, they could be as close to you as the nearest bulkhead, watching and listening."

"Thank you for that thought," said Lando. "But if this is a Qella ship, it's a dead ship. It's been in space too long. And, Colonel, this is starting to look like a dead end. We may have to make our own entrance."

"Lando, remember what we talked about yesterday," said Lobot. "Any obvious path, any unlocked passageway, may be a trap. If there was a big red switch in the middle of one of those walls, I wouldn't want you to touch it. Access must require more than observation—it requires knowledge. The perfect lock is invisible to you and self-evident to the Qella."

"Maybe there's something about the mottling on these walls," said Lando, craning his head. "It's the only thing in here I can see that could carry information. Lobot, Threepio, why don't you come on over and see what you can make of it. Bring the equipment sled with you, too. Artoo's making out like a fish in water, but the rest of us can use something to hang on to."

Lando sighed and touched a suit control to blow a jet of cool air across his face. "I haven't a clue," he said finally. "Colonel? Anything there?"

It was Bijo Hammax who replied, "No. We're stumped here, Lando."

"Being stumped was my best strategy," Lando said forlornly. "I was hoping that if we showed ourselves to be slow learners again, they'd give us another hint."

Bijo laughed.

"Maybe if we touch the right pattern of spots," Lobot suggested.

"I touched about thirty spots already before you got here, with my head, my elbows, my bottom, my knees—"

"I said the *right* pattern, not a random pattern."

"So tell me what the right pattern is," Lando said sharply. "Light or dark? Fast or slow? Left to right or top to bottom?"

"I don't know," Lobot said. "I'm sorry."

"Aw—it's not your fault. What we need right now is a Qella brain, and we're fresh out of them. I knew I'd forget to pack something."

"Lando—"

"What?"

"Have you ever seen Donadi stain-painting?"

"What? Lobot, you've picked a strange time to start practicing idle conversation."

"Answer my question," Lobot said shortly.

"All right—no, I haven't. What's that got to do with anything?"

"To human perception, stain-painting consists of huge canvases covered with random splotches of color. The Donadi sit and stare at a painting for ten minutes or more at a time. If they stare long enough, and practice what they call 'looking past,' something happens in their brain that turns the splotches into a three-dimensional image."

"*I've* seen it," said Hammax. "Strangest thing. The Donadi go into this meditation thing and end up in a state of high rapture over something that might as well be a hallucination."

"But it isn't a hallucination," said Lobot. "A Donadi painting isn't an image—it's a stimulus to the perception of an image. The image isn't real, but it's contained in the painting all the same. It's a perceptual trick, and it only works for their species."

"You think maybe if a Qella came in here, he'd see the answer right away?"

"I'm saying that these markings may have been made not just for Qella eyes, but for Qella minds."

Lando frowned and shook his head. "Even if you're right, that doesn't get us any closer."

"Artoo is the only one of us capable of seeing the entire chamber at once. I can send him alternate sets of perceptual parameters, which I am retrieving now from the Institute for Sentient Studies on Baraboo. They have the most comprehensive collection of neurocognitive models that exists. Artoo can reprocess the image according to the parameters I provide, and project it for *us* to see."

"Sounds a lot like trying to fill out a sabacc on a draw of four cards to me."

"Luck is chance informed by applied knowledge," said Lobot. "You said so yourself."

"I did?"

"You did. Stand by."

It is said on Gaios that a seed does not know the flower that produced it. What is true of seeds and flowers is true of civilizations and worlds. In the long history of the galaxy, many a family tree has grown too tangled to be clearly remembered by either ancestor or descendant.

On a thousand thousand worlds and more, life erupted from creation's crucible of energy and time—and vanished into extinction in an eyeblink.

On a hundred thousand worlds and more, life erupted from the crucible and would not be dislodged, brandishing cleverness and fecundity as its weapons against entropy and change.

On ten thousand worlds and more, life erupted from the crucible and then transcended it, learning to bridge the unbridgeable distances, venturing forth as explorer, and settler, and conqueror to worlds far from that which gave it birth.

And some of those worlds touched with the gift of life in time passed it on to their own children, until the gift had been passed across the eons to a million worlds, flower begetting seed begetting flower until the galaxy itself sang of it. But in all the history of all that is, no species anywhere has ever known its whole heritage, for memories are shorter than forever, and the only witness to those hard first births is the Force itself.

The people who called themselves the Qella had no children of their own. No colony worlds owed them allegiance. No free worlds owed them honor. The

Qella had possessed the tools to leave their homeworld, but they had lacked a sufficient reason.

But the Qella had parents, parents they scarcely remembered, but to whom much of what they were and knew could be traced. The parents of the Qella had called themselves the Qonet, and they had had many offspring, as had *their* parents, who called themselves the Ahra Naffi. So although the Qella had no children, they had siblings in some number, and cousins close and distant in numbers beyond counting.

It was with the hope of finding such kin as the Qella might have that Lobot sifted the archives of the Institute for Sentient Studies. Lobot knew no more about the family history of the Qella than did the Qella themselves, but he knew the patterns and principles that applied. His hope depended not on luck but on a well-chosen search algorithm, the thoroughness of the archivists, and the fruitfulness and resilience of the Ahra Naffi line.

Or, at least, so Lobot would forever claim. Luck was Lando's game, and Lobot preferred to distance himself from anything so ephemeral and unpredictable. It was a silent rivalry, and Lobot took unvoiced pleasure from the times when Lando's way failed him and Lobot's own succeeded. He prided himself on playing a more precise and controlled line, where competence counted for more than chance and diligence was rewarded more often than daring.

This time the reward was the mind-prints of the Khotta, of Kho Nai.

The image Artoo was projecting covered only part of one wall, but incorporated the patterns of the entire chamber as they would have been perceived by a Khotta. Compressed, processed, and translated, they needed no explanation. The entire image had but one focal point and one possible meaning.

"There," said Lando. "In that corner. There's your big red switch."

"I don't see anything," Threepio declared. "Artoo, you must be making a mistake."

"You're not supposed to see it," said Lando. "Not unless you have the right eyes. But it's there." Pushing off from the equipment sled, he floated toward the corner.

"General Calrissian? Hammax here. Suggest you have your R2 unit make the initial contact with its claw arm."

"Where's the colonel?"

"Colonel Pakkpekatt is monitoring."

"Tell him I wish he was here," said Lando. "Okay, Artoo. You have the spot zeroed in?"

Artoo chittered enthusiastically.

"Okay—let's ring the bell."

Artoo rose from the equipment sled where he had been clinging and jetted across the open space. The droid's left equipment door snapped open, and the telescoping claw arm extended toward a spot along the curved corner where the two bulkheads merged.

The claw yawned open to its fullest and a moment later touched the bulkhead.

Nothing happened.

"More pressure, Artoo," said Lando.

The droid's thrusters spat plumes of vapor into the chamber, until its silver body was visibly vibrating.

"That's enough, Artoo," Lando said. "Let me in there."

"What are you thinking, General?" asked Hammax.

"That maybe this ship knows it wasn't built by droids," said Lando, extending his gloved hand to touch the same spot Artoo had tried.

Again there was no response, even when Lando's suit thrusters exerted themselves.

"We must have misread the instructions," said Threepio. "Artoo, could you possibly have turned everything upside down?"

The little droid's response was indignantly terse.

"I can't get any real pressure on it," Lando fumed.

"Maybe these Qella were stronger than we are, at least under these conditions."

"Strength hasn't opened any Qella doors yet," said Lobot.

Lando twisted around to look at Lobot. "No, it hasn't, has it?" Grasping his right wrist joint, Lando squeezed the release and twisted.

"What are you doing?" Hammax protested.

"A spacesuit and a droid probably register about the same, wouldn't you say?" With a sharp yank, Lando tugged the glove off his right hand.

The air in the chamber was bitterly cold, and his hand begun to ache almost at once. Tucking the glove under his left elbow, Lando spun back to face the corner and reached out to touch the bulkhead.

It retreated under his touch, the surface folding back on all sides until there was a hole in the corner almost as large as a bubble helmet and deep enough that Lando was uncertain whether he could reach the farthest recesses.

"He did it!" Threepio exulted.

"There's some sort of handle back here," Lando said, peering into the opening. "At least, that's what it looks like to me. Artoo, get over here and get a picture for the folks at home."

"General, suggest you reglove," Hammax said while Artoo attended to that duty. "The handle might be keyed to Qellan biology."

"I guess we'll find out, won't we?" Lando said. "That's enough, Artoo. Anyone want to retreat back into *Lady Luck* before I knock on the door? Counting one, two, three—"

"We're ready here, Lando," said Lobot.

"Okay, then." Drawing a deep breath, Lando reached with his bare hand for the handle deep inside the hole. His shoulder was pressed against the opening before his fingertips brushed it. He had to slip his shoulder inside the hole and press his helmet against the bulkhead to close his fingers around the handle.

"Got it," he said. "What do you think, Lobot? Push, pull, twist, lift—"

But Lobot never had a chance to answer. There was a flash of brilliant blue light outside the portal, and when it was gone, so was the tunnel to *Lady Luck*'s airlock. In the next instant the atmosphere in the chamber began boiling out into space, sweeping everything and everyone toward the open portal.

Lando clung desperately to the handle inside the hole, though he lost his grip on the glove and watched it being whisked away beyond his reach. But both Artoo and Lobot were being swept toward the opening, their thrusters unequal to the sudden windstorm. The equipment sled, with Threepio perched atop it, spun crazily toward the opening as well.

The glove, far lighter and moving faster than any of the party, struck the outer bulkhead, rebounded, and tumbled out into space. But bare moments before Artoo reached the opening, there suddenly was no opening. As neatly as the smaller hole had opened under Lando's touch, the portal knitted itself closed from edge to center.

Artoo, Threepio, Lobot, and the sled all struck an unbroken chamber wall—and then began sliding aft along it.

"The ship's moving!" Lando cried, feeling the acceleration pressing him more firmly against the aft bulkhead. "Hammax! Colonel! What's going on?" There was no answer—not even static. "Anyone on the *Glorious,* respond!"

"Lando!" Lobot called. "All of my links are gone. We're not just moving. This ship just jumped into hyperspace."

It all happened so quickly that no one witness was certain of all the details.

Without warning, one of the Qella's beam weapons sliced *Lady Luck* free from the vagabond. Another pierced the hull of the interdiction picket *Kauri* and left it in flames.

As the interdiction field collapsed, the vagabond swung about with surprising swiftness and accelerated away from its previous course.

The captain of the *Marauder* screamed for permission to fire—just as the Qella vessel seemed to suddenly stretch to twice its true length and then vanish into a blinding white pinch of spacetime.

Lady Luck was left drifting, the remnants of the cofferdam trailing from its airlock.

"Do we have a good track?" Pakkpekatt demanded.

"Yes, sir."

"That's something to work with," he said.

"Sir, she jumped toward the Core."

Pakkpekatt's expression did not change. "Dispatch a crew to recover the yacht. Bring *Lightning* around to the target's last heading and jump her out ten. We'll go out twenty, *Marauder* thirty, and then walk it out at intervals of one light-year till we get to the border. She's got to be out there somewhere."

"Yes, sir—but how far? She could have jumped all the way to Byss, for all we know."

The mere mention of the former Emperor's throne world, deep in the Core, darkened the mood on the bridge still further.

"Let's hope not, sailor," said Pakkpekatt. "Let us earnestly hope not."

Chapter 12

♦

Long before they reached Lucazec, Luke Skywalker settled on *Mud Sloth* as the name for Akanah's previously unnamed Verpine Adventurer.

He realized he had been spoiled by years in high-performance military spacecraft, operating under wartime conditions or a military waiver. But realizing that didn't make it any easier to adjust to civilian navigation restrictions. Not only was *Mud Sloth* a dawdler in realspace, but its hyperspace motivator simply refused to enter or leave hyperspace within a planetary Flight Control Zone.

Luke didn't object in principle to FCZ regulations. They helped ensure that less experienced pilots in less capable ships made slow approaches to populated worlds and busy spacelanes. But he had never been subjected to a four-day realspace crawl just to leave Coruscant. He was accustomed to reaching for the hyperdrive moments after his ship cleared the atmosphere. *Mud Sloth* insisted on waiting until it had cleared the star system.

But there was nothing to be done about it. The Adventurer wouldn't accept his military waiver, and didn't even have a System Configuration option on its cockpit displays. It was designed to prevent such meddling.

Driven by impatience, Luke briefly considered powering down the hyperdrive and opening up the service access to see what he could do with it. But he soon talked himself out of it, realizing that reprogramming a motivator was beyond his talents as a tinkerer. Even a starship as simple as the *Adventurer* was far more complex than the Incom T-16s and landspeeders he'd spent so many days hopping and rebuilding back on Tatooine.

No, when it came to hyperspace, it was too easy for a small oversight to become a final, fatal error. Anyone who'd flown for long had heard the stories and respected the danger. Of all the risks inherent in traveling unimaginable distances at incalculable speeds, the one that entered most pilots' nightmares was the one-way jump—never coming out of hyperspace. Even Han and Chewie left the exacting business of rebalancing a motivator to professionals, and never begrudged them their hefty fees.

But that had left Luke trapped in cramped quarters with Akanah for just over eleven days on the way to Lucazec—something he had not been prepared for. After months in isolation, he had not been prepared for that much close contact with anyone. Luke wondered how he would have borne it if Akanah had not been so willing to make allowances.

She did not force conversation on him, either idle or earnest. Nor did she make him feel as though he was being watched, that she was waiting for him to do something. Without his ever asking, she granted him the only kind of privacy available under the circumstances—the privacy of the mind and heart. She did not intrude there without his invitation, hiding her own needs and curiosity so perfectly that they seemed more like comfortable old friends than strangers.

At her suggestion, they adopted a watch schedule that had them sleeping at opposite ends of the day, spaced so that neither of them had to climb into a hot bunk. She seemed to welcome the reassurance that someone was awake while she rested, and did not seem to mind that the schedule reduced their time together to a few hours twice a day.

Luke thought Akanah must be accustomed to being alone, for she seemed to have mastered the art of keeping time moving without restless motion. She read from a battered old datapad, meditated in the copilot's couch, and intently studied the Adventurer's owner, pilot, and system helps.

At times she even sought privacy for herself. Akanah practiced her Fallanassi craft in silence behind the drawn curtain of the sleeper, and stripped to a body-hugging monoskin to exercise only when it was Luke's turn in the zippered bunkbag. She even politely ignored him when he made both discoveries, making it unnecessary for him to apologize, or for her to explain.

They did take meals together, dipping twice a day into Akanah's modest cache of stabilized foodstores—many of them long-expired Imperial expedition packs, a telltale sign of desperately tight finances. But even meals did not become an occasion for substantive conversation until near the end, with Lucazec visible through the viewport and the reason for their journey too much in their thoughts to be ignored.

"Sixteen more hours," Luke said, tearing open a pouch of Noryath brown meatbread. "I hate the waiting. I want to crawl back in the bunk and sleep until the autopilot starts asking whether we want to orbit or land."

"If I thought this was the end of our journey, rather than just the end of the beginning, I might feel the same way," said Akanah, and sipped at her flask of tart *pawei* juice.

"Do you think there's any chance the Fallanassi may have come back, after the war?"

"No," said Akanah. "You see, the Empire feared us as well as coveted our power. They didn't come down with weapons drawn to round us up, as they did with so many other populations they enslaved—"

"Yeah, I've seen how they work. But how did they even know you existed? I thought you were a secret sect. Or am I the only one who never heard of the Fallanassi?"

"You are right, there is a contradiction," said Akanah. "The explanation is simple, but an embarrassment. We were divided among ourselves about the coming war and what our moral duty was. One of our community, for reasons of her own, went to the Imperial governor and revealed herself."

"You were betrayed."

"No—no, that's too strong a word. Even though her name is no longer spoken, she had a high purpose in what she did. She believed that by allying ourselves with the Empire, we could be the water that would quench the flame." Akanah's eyes were touched by wistfulness. "But she was wrong. It was too late for that—the fire was already beyond control."

"Well—I don't know why you called it an embarrassment," said Luke. "The only communities that think with one mind are those that only have one mind. And I haven't met anyone yet who hasn't ever been passionately wrong about *something,* sometime."

"You are generous," said Akanah, "more generous than the circle was able to be."

"It's easier for me," he said. "I wasn't the one betrayed."

She acknowledged him with a nod. "The Empire sent General Tagge to Wialu—who held the wand of privilege then—to offer us the protection of the Emperor. He said it was important for us to show our loyalty—that that was the only way we could escape the fate of the Jedi. We knew what that meant. The Jedi were being hunted down as traitors and sorcerers, and no one dared openly favor or befriend them."

"Forgive me—I don't mean to sound suspicious. But how do you know all this?" Luke asked. "You said you were just a child, and offplanet at the time."

"No, I was still on Lucazec when General Tagge came there," said Akanah. "My mother—her name was Isela—was one of the women who met with Wialu in circle afterward, to decide what to do. And children are not protected from adult concerns in our community, as they are in so many places. Isela told me of the Empire's invitation, and what it might mean to refuse it."

"I guess I don't understand, then," said Luke, trying to remember where he had heard the general's name before. "How did you become separated from the others? I assume the Fallanassi left Lucazec rather than either refuse or accept."

"No, that was months later," explained Akanah. "Wialu *did* refuse General Tagge. She told him that the loyalty of the Fallanassi was to the Light, and that we would not let ourselves be used to further the ambition of generals, kings, or emperors."

"Tagge—I remember now," said Luke. "He was on the first Death Star when Leia was a prisoner." He paused, then added, "He was probably still on board when my proton torpedo blew it to bits."

Luke didn't know what possessed him to make that claim before Akanah, and her response made him feel even more foolish for having done so. She stiffened as he spoke, and he could feel her withdrawing from him, though she barely moved.

"Do you seek honor from me for this? In time you will understand that the Fallanassi honor no heroes for killing, not even killing one who has been our tormentor," said Akanah.

"I'm sorry," Luke said, and wondered at his own words. Everything suddenly seemed upside down. It was strange and unsettling that the deed for which he had been so lionized now became touched with regret—regret over the killing of an enemy who had been his own sister's tormentor. That moment had decided both his future and the galaxy's, and he had never, in all the years since, questioned the rightness of what he had done.

Akanah nodded, and her face seemed to soften. "I will not speak of it again."

Luke was happy to leave behind his ill-considered words, and the jumbled thoughts and alarming feelings that had followed them. "How did the Empire respond to Wialu?" he asked. "Is that when you left Lucazec?"

"No, not until later," said Akanah. "Tagge tried to force us to come to him by destroying our relationship with our neighbors. Lucazec was an open-immigration world then, and tolerant—or so we thought. We shopped in villages nearest to ours and hired workers from them. Tagge placed agents in those villages, to kill house animals, and set fires, and turn the waters bitter, and make other strange things happen."

"And then blame the Fallanassi," Luke guessed.

"Yes. The Empire's agents whispered against us, until those who'd been our friends feared us. The workers stopped coming to our village, and three of our circle were attacked when they went to Jisasu for food and to sell our medicines.

"That was when my mother sent me away—not to protect me, because she and the others could protect the children well enough. But she didn't want to expose me to the hate that surrounded us then. I was one of five who were sent away, to friends on Paig, to schools on Teyr or Carratos."

"How many of you went to Carratos?"

"Only me," Akanah said. She smiled sadly, her eyes bright with tears. "They were to send for us when Lucazec was peaceful again, or come for us when they headed for a new home."

"But they never did."

"No. I never heard from any of the body again." She shook her head. "I don't know why."

"And you still don't know what happened?"

"All I was ever able to learn is that they left Lucazec, that our village was abandoned and in ruins. I couldn't even find the other children, on Teyr and Paig. I think the circle came for them. I think I was the only one left behind." She tried to say it matter-of-factly, but the hurt still showed.

"Or maybe you're the only one the Empire didn't find. Have you considered that?"

"I have tried not to think about that," Akanah said, looking past him to the pale brown disk of Lucazec. "I would rather be the only one left behind than the only one left alive."

The region of Lucazec that Akanah called the North Plateau had no true spaceport. Luke was directed to set the *Mud Sloth* down at a quiet little airfield identified only by its latitude and longitude. There he and Akanah were met by three men wearing drab brown clothing so similar one to the next that it might as well have been a uniform.

They identified themselves as the airfield marshal, the district censor, and the port magistrate. The censor had a small recorder, into which he both spoke and repeated their answers. "Point of origin."

"Coruscant," said Luke.

"Registry of your vessel."

"Carratos," Akanah supplied.

"Do you affirm that you are both citizens of the New Republic?"

"We are," said Luke.

"Purpose of your visit."

"Research," said Akanah. "Archaeological research."

"No digging is permitted without a license from the proctor of history," the magistrate warned them. "All artifacts must be submitted to the Office of the Proctor so that the appropriate taxes can be determined. Evasion of antiquities taxes is a state crime punishable by—"

Luke made a small gesture, slicing the air with his fingertips. "We are aware of the regulations, Magistrate."

"What? Yes, of course," the magistrate said, and lapsed into silence.

Luke turned to the shortest of the three men. "Marshal, I would like to arrange for my ship to be hangared. I wouldn't want any curious children to accidently injure themselves."

"I'm afraid there are no—"

"I'm prepared to pay the reasonable and customary fees, of course."

"How long do you think you'll be on Lucazec?"

"I couldn't say," Luke said. "Is that a problem?"

"No, no. I believe some space recently became available in Hangar Kaa, our newest and most secure. I'll have your ship towed in. A Verpine Adventurer, isn't it? I hear that's a fine vessel. I don't think we've ever had one of those in here before—"

"Thank you," Luke said. His gaze settled on the censor. "Was there anything else?"

"I must see your identity cards, of course," the censor said, puffing up his chest.

"We've already shown them to you," Luke said, intensifying his focus on the man.

"Of course," said the censor, his eyes suddenly blank. "Your destination was—"

"Jisasu," said Akanah.

"Yes, of course. You'll want to hire a cart. Go by the East District Trail—the bridge at Crown Pass Road has been out since the last rain, and the river can't be forded on account of the debris."

Luke nodded. "Very kind of you," he said, smiling pleasantly. "I'll be sure to mention your helpfulness in my report." He hoisted both their bags and slung them over one shoulder. "Come, Lady Anna. I'd like to see if we can't get there before dark."

"Lady Anna!" Akanah said when they enjoyed the privacy of the road, jolting along in one of the big-wheeled, two-seated utility vehicles common on Lucazec. "I like that. And what shall I call you? The Duke of Skye?"

"I'd prefer not to give any name at all," said Luke. "I'd rather anyone we meet not quite be able to recall my face, or remember my name, as though they were too distracted by you to pay attention."

"I'd like that, too," she said with a smile.

There had been a few structures near the airfield that might have been houses, but East District Trail had quickly turned into a road through a brown and hilly nowhere. "Is anything familiar yet? Do you know this part of the district?"

"It's all familiar, after a fashion. I knew Crown Pass Road better—that was the short way to Jisasu and Big Hill. But I hardly recognized the airfield, it's so built up now."

Luke shot her a surprised look. "Built up?"

"Oh, yes. When I left here, the airfield was nothing more than a flat spot everyone had agreed not to farm or fence, and a few marks on the ground to guide the pilots in. There weren't any hangars, because there weren't any flyers kept there."

"Or perhaps the other way around," said Luke. "I'm glad we didn't need a docking bay on this stop—we would've had to put down five hundred kilometers from here."

"Yes, at The Towers. It's a long trip. But then, I remember this being a long trip—and look, there's the river ahead, you can mark it by the trees. See beyond, where it gets more hilly? That's Hastings Watershed. The haze is from cookfires—there are villages all through the Hastings, anywhere there's a permanent supply of water."

"Any impressions of our welcoming committee?"

"Cold," said Akanah. "No one ever carried or asked for an identity card back then. People didn't automatically look at you with suspicion."

"They *were* bureaucrats," Luke reminded her.

"There weren't any officials in charge of suspicion back then."

"Well—this was occupied territory. Strike even a friendly animal often enough— Whoops, hang on."

The cart pitched sharply down and jerked to a stop as the front wheel dropped into a deep rut. Both Luke and Akanah were thrown forward, nearly catapulted from their seats. Akanah grabbed for the sideboard and seat back, while Luke clutched the steering arm in one hand and braced himself with a foot against the splashboards.

For a long moment the constant-speed motors driving the rear wheels whined in complaint, until the front wheel popped free of the rut and the cart lurched forward.

"Oh, something else," said Akanah. "The roads are a lot smoother now."

"You're kidding."

"No. We used to have to hang on with both hands the whole way to Jisasu." She smiled to herself at the memory. "The kids made a game of it, standing up in the cargo box, holding on to the back of the seats—or not—trying to keep from falling down or falling out. I did both." Just then a rock under the left wheel sent a hard jolt up both Luke's and Akanah's spines. "But that was a long time ago. I suppose a little levitation is out of the question—"

"Are you asking, or offering?"

"Either. Both."

Another cart appeared over the rise ahead of them, coming toward them. "I think we'd better keep the wheels on the ground," Luke said. "It's a little late to start disguising us as a whirldust."

Akanah nodded, raising her cupped hands in greeting to the wiry old farmer and clean-faced young woman in the approaching cart.

"And I still think concealing ourselves would be a mistake," she said. "We may still have to talk to the neighbors to find out what we need to." She paused as the other cart passed by at close range, neither occupant answering her greeting or offering more than a quick stony-eyed sidewise glance. "If anyone will talk to us, that is."

They missed the turnoff for Ialtra, because it no longer existed.

The common market that had stood at the intersection of Crown Pass Road and Ialtra Trail was gone, its location marked only by the stump of its centerpost.

And there was no longer a road to the village of the Fallanassi, not even by the modest standards of Lucazec—which, Luke had decided, required only a three-rut path from which the largest rocks had been removed. The old ruts could still be seen, but it seemed as though the trail had been deliberately strewn with large rocks, especially where it had once joined the main road.

"Are you sure this is the right place?"

"Yes," Akanah said. "Completely sure."

"I've got a bad feeling about this," Luke said, shaking his head.

"So do I, Luke," she said timorously, reaching for his hand. "So do I."

In its heyday Ialtra had had more than thirty buildings, and all but a few had transcended the simple, pragmatic architecture of the region.

The circle house had stood three stories high, with a great open archway that divided the lower floors in half, and tiled facings in complex abstract designs. Its rooftop gardens, fed by pipe and solar pump, offered not only lush grass and flowers in profusion, but a view over the surrounding hills.

Medicinals and food crops once grew under three translucent domes nested between pairs of small workhouses. Ring dwellings had been scattered everywhere, each with half a dozen wedge-roofed sleeping cottages surrounding the common rooms.

Ialtra had enjoyed two wells and a walled pond, and a long wandering meditation trail with more than a dozen hillside shelters. One slope facing north had been carved away into an open-air amphitheater large enough to seat the entire community, with a focus that could accommodate either a performing stage or a ceremonial fire.

None of it remained untouched, and it was clear

to both Luke and Akanah that weather and time alone had not done the damage.

The circle house had been collapsed into rubble, its supporting walls knocked out from under it. The growing domes had been exploded from within—fragments of the clear crystalline material littered the ground everywhere, crunching underfoot as the visitors walked slowly among the ruins. The amphitheater was buried under a landslide.

The walled pond had been breached and now was bone dry. The large well had been filled and heaped over with masonry from a wrecked ring dwelling. The small well appeared to have been poisoned with whatever solvents and reagents could be found—a small mound of empty, dust-covered containers of assorted shapes and sizes standing nearby gave testimony to that.

A few of the ring dwellings stood nearly intact, but even those had been defaced. Their tiled facings had been smashed, and a symbol—two lines slashed across a circle—had been crudely burned onto the walls with blaster fire. Akanah stood by one of these, biting her lower lip, saying nothing. Anguish and sadness radiated from her with such intensity that Luke found it necessary to shield himself from most of it.

"This was our home," Akanah said at last. "Isela and I lived here—Toma and Ji and Norika next to us on this side. Nori was my best friend." Closing her eyes, she bowed her head for a moment, as though steeling herself. Then she ducked through an entry arch, walking across the door that had once sealed it.

The door had had no lock, but its hinges were blaster-scorched and melted all the same.

Luke waited outside, granting Akanah privacy in the ruins of her memories. She rejoined him a few minutes later, standing taller and seeming stronger.

"They weren't here when this happened," she said. "Whether they were taken or escaped, none of them died here."

"Why do you say that?"

"Because of the way it feels here," Akanah said. "I don't know quite how to describe it, except that I'm sure that I'd be able to feel it if even one of us had been killed here. This was—an empty gesture. It didn't touch the Current."

"It feels that way to me, too," Luke said. "And I'd vote for 'escaped.' I've been thinking as I look around that this was all done out of frustration. They desecrated your home because that was all they could do. Something else—they didn't use anything bigger than a personal blaster for this. Nothing military grade. This isn't the Empire's work."

"Our friends in Big Hill and Jisasu," Akanah said stiffly.

"They were lied to," said Luke. "None of us are immune to fear."

"Please—don't try to stop me from being angry at them," Akanah said. "We do not pretend to emotional purity. This was my home. I have the right."

"Of course," Luke said. "Akanah—which was my mother's house?"

Akanah closed her eyes in thought for a moment. "Ahred," she said, opening her eyes and pointing across the compound. "Number Four." She smiled faintly. "I understand. Go on—I'm all right."

Nodding his appreciation, Luke turned and started across the open ground toward the ruined ring dwelling at the foot of the highest of the enclosing hills. But he was not even halfway there when a scream froze him. He whirled, his cape sweeping outward, and a blaster bolt burned past him so close that he could smell the heat.

He rolled away from the heat, came out of the roll with a forward flip that carried him five meters away from where he had stood, and ended the flip searching for his attacker, his lightsaber in his right hand. There were two men near Akanah, who was huddled on her knees with an arm raised as though she had just fended off a blow.

"Akanah!" he cried, and charged toward them.

The next blaster bolt was dead on target, but Luke deflected it neatly skyward with his lightsaber. In the next moment he drew deeply on the Force and reached out to crush the blaster with a thought as powerful as a vise. His next thought yanked the disabled weapon from the man's hand and hurled it far out of reach.

Akanah had raised her head when he called her name. "No, Luke, don't—" she cried.

But Luke's focus was the second man, who was now showing a weapon, too—pointed at Akanah. "Keep your distance!" the man shouted at Luke. He did not sound afraid.

Luke's answer was a thought-blow that tore the blaster from the man's hand and smashed it against the wall of the dwelling behind him. It exploded into a shower of sparks and shattered into a dozen fragments.

Then he was on them, the lightsaber held for attack, not defense. The first man he had disarmed projected a personal shield, which blunted Luke's initial stroke. But the blow took the man to his knees all the same. The next stroke, with the power of the lightsaber married to the will of a Jedi Master, sliced through the shield and deep into the assailant's chest. He gasped once as blood erupted, then crumpled backward onto the hard ground.

Turning quickly, Luke found the second man closing on Akanah again, reaching for her, as though meaning to use her as his shield. Instantly Luke threw his lightsaber, spinning the weapon end over end with a sharp snap of his wrist. It scythed through the air, severing the attacker's left arm above the elbow. The man screamed and collapsed as Luke brought the lightsaber back to his hand.

"Who are you?" Luke demanded, standing over the fallen attacker.

The stump of his arm scarcely bled. "Commander Paffen reporting—Skywalker," the man said. Then he closed his eyes, and his entire body shuddered. A moment later his eyes flew open again. "Skywalker is here."

With a flick of the tip of his lightsaber, Luke disabled the comlink on the man's equipment belt. "Who are you?" he demanded again. "Why are you here?"

"Not fair—waited so long," the man said, and moaned. "We only expected the witch."

"Why were you waiting? What did you want?"

The man grimaced. "They said the poison wouldn't hurt," the man whispered, and died, still staring at the sky.

Wearing a mask of worry, Luke crouched beside Akanah, who was still huddled on the ground, shaking from head to toe and sobbing. "Akanah—are you hurt?" he asked, touching her arm.

Recoiling violently from his touch, she turned away from him.

"I'm sorry—I must have been distracted," he said, shifting to where he could see her face. "I should have known they were here. But it's over. They can't hurt you now."

Still trembling, Akanah turned away from him again. "They never could have hurt me."

"What are you talking about? You screamed—you were on the ground—"

"I wasn't hurt. I wasn't in danger. There was no reason for what you did—"

"What *I* did—"

With a will, she gathered her feet under her and staggered away from him, hugging herself fiercely. He followed, dimly beginning to grasp that the depth of her distress came from the second assault, not the first—his acts, not the acts of the dead men.

"I thought you were in trouble," he said.

"Couldn't you have protected us without harming them?" she demanded, whirling to face him. "They startled me—nothing more."

Luke extended his awareness, searching the ruins, the hills. "We'll have to talk about this later," he said.

"These were Imperial agents. There's no telling how close or how far away their friends are. We have to leave. We have to get back to the ship, now."

"No—no, not yet—"

"Akanah, no matter what you think, we *can* be harmed—"

"Is the river harmed by the rock a child throws?"

"We don't have time to debate this now," Luke said impatiently. "The *Mud Sloth* may not be much, but I don't want to lose her. This planet isn't what I had in mind for my retirement, and I'd rather not have to play hide-and-seek with an Imperial gunship to get out of here."

"Where do you suggest we go?" Akanah asked.

"It doesn't matter. Away from Lucazec, as fast as we can. We're not going to find the Fallanassi here— the only explanation for all this that makes sense is that your people escaped both the Empire and the mob. The Empire doesn't know where they are, and we don't want to be the ones who show them. It's time to go."

Akanah shook her head slowly. "There's something I have to show you first," she said. "Come."

Backing away, she led him through the arch into what had once been her home. Light streamed in through the windows and broken roof of the common room, but the sleeping cottages were cool and dim beyond the light trap.

"This was my mother's space," Akanah said. "There—can you see it?" Her sweeping gesture took in the full width of the back wall.

"See what?"

"Listen for the sound," she said. "Like water slipping through sand. Drop all your shields."

Luke tried to concentrate on the wall, but confusion was the enemy of concentration. "What is it—is there something written there? Am I supposed to see it, or hear it?"

"Yes," she said, her one answer covering all his questions.

"You're a lot of help," he said, squinting.

"Let go of the Force," she said. "It can't help you in this. You've trained yourself to see the shadows. Let yourself see the light."

Drawing a deep breath, Luke tried to focus on the wall—to open his awareness to every aspect of its existence as a material object traveling through time, every immanent quality perceivable on any plane. Color and texture, mass and temperature, the feeble tug of gravity, the faint glow of radiation, its solidity deflecting the currents of air, its opacity blocking the light, its contribution to the scent and flavor of the air, and a hundred more subtle measures that defined its reality.

"Let me help," she said, taking his hand. "Do you perceive the wall?"

"Yes—"

"Take it away. Stop perceiving the substance. Make it disappear from your thoughts, and look inside it. Stay open—let me guide your eyes."

Then he saw it—not written on the wall, but written within it, the pale white shapes of symbols drawn not with matter, but with some elemental essence swirling within it.

"Is that it?" he asked, as though she could not only guide his eyes but see through them.

She smiled and tightened her grip on his hand. "The way home is always marked. That is the promise made to us."

"Can you read it? What does it say?"

"I know where we have to go," Akanah said, and released his hand. "Can you still see it now, without my help?"

The symbols had been brightening, but they vanished abruptly when the contact was broken. "No—it's completely gone. I can remember the shapes, but I can't see them now."

Nodding, she said, "It doesn't matter. If you can see Current scribing with guidance, I can teach you to see it on your own. It's how children learn."

"Is there more—in the other cottages, or outside, on the other buildings?"

"No. Just here. This was meant for me."

"The attack—it came *after* you'd been in the house," Luke said with sudden understanding. "They *knew* there was something there. That's why the Empire still had agents here. They were just waiting for someone who could read it to show up."

"But would the Empire risk sending a ship this deep into New Republic territory?"

"That depends on how badly someone still wants the Fallanassi," Luke said. "I don't think we should wait around to see."

Akanah frowned. "No."

"And we can't be followed."

"No," she agreed. "Can you cloak us?"

"I can disguise our appearance. But we have to do more than that," Luke said. "You need to erase the message."

Even without looking at her, he felt her reluctance and resistance. "It's the only way to be sure this trap has been disarmed," he added. "Can you erase it? Can it be done at all?"

"Scribing opens a tiny breach between the real and the unreal," Akanah said with a slow nod. "It's easier to collapse it than create it." She hesitated, then sighed. "Wait for me outside."

She did not keep him waiting long.

"It's done," she said, taking his arm as she joined him. "But, just to be certain no one can undo it, please knock it down."

"Are you sure?"

"Please," she said. "I'm never coming back here. Bring all of it down."

Without moving from where they stood, Luke complied. A twist of a corner, a push in the middle of a long wall, opened a spiderweb of cracks. The cracks widened in turn, until the stonework fell in and the roof collapsed atop it, kicking up a billow of yellow dust.

"We'd better hurry now," Luke said.

"There's one more thing," she said. "You need to go inside your mother's cottage."

He shook his head sadly. "There isn't time."

"Take the time," she said. "I'll hide us, so you can stay open while you're there."

"Akanah—"

"A few minutes won't matter to the outcome," she said. "The nearest friend of the men you killed is either very close already, or a very long way away. But those few minutes may matter a great deal to you. Go."

Luke sat in the middle of what had been the floor of the ruined cottage and whispered his mother's name, as if to ask the broken stones whether they remembered it.

"Nashira," he said, but the sound fled into the dark corners and vanished.

"Nashira," he called, but the echoes escaped out through the cracks and fissures in the walls.

He brushed the litter aside and pressed the palms of his hands to the floor, drew the dusty air deep into his nostrils and tasted it on his tongue, slowly scanned all around him for anything that might have belonged to the last person to make a home of that space.

"Mother," he said, and the reality of the moment welled up inside him. It was a point of contact, after so many years without one. She had been where he was now.

It did not matter that he could not find her touch lingering on the rude substance surrounding him. The knowledge alone was enough. Where before he could only pretend, now he could imagine, and imagination overleaped the time that separated them.

She had slept here, laughed here, retreated here for sanctuary, cried and sought peace here, perhaps loved and grieved here, moving through this space as real as life and as human as the rush of longing Luke felt in that moment.

He could not see her face or hear her voice, but, even so, she was more real to him in that moment than she had ever been before.

It was not enough, not by half, but it was a beginning.

The village was in shadow by the time Luke emerged from Nashira's cottage and rejoined Akanah. The sun had dropped below the hills, and the breeze had a softer edge.

"How long was I in there?"

"It doesn't matter," she said. "Are you ready?"

Luke nodded. "You were right," he said. "Thank you."

"I knew it was important. But we'd better hurry now. It'll be dark before we reach the airfield."

Neither had anything more to say as they returned to the cart and climbed atop it for the return trip. Luke checked it closely for any sign of a tracker or tampering, then raised the vehicle a meter off the ground. "No bumps this trip," he said with a small smile. "But I'd still hold on. What do they call those carrion birds here?"

"Nackhawns."

"That's what we are, then. A big, ugly nackhawn." Luke swung the cart in a wide circle over the hills enclosing Ialtra, scanning for any other vehicles. He found none, and wondered how the Imperial agents had followed them there.

But Luke shook off the thought, and sent the cart arrowing toward the southeast and the airfield. Their passage was silent but for the air tearing past the contours of a vehicle that was never meant to fly.

Not long after, back in the ruins of the village of Ialtra, the bodies of two dead Imperial agents merged with the shadows that had enveloped them, and vanished as though they had never been.

Chapter 13

◆

Near a brown dwarf star on the edge of the Koornacht Cluster, the New Republic astrographic probe *Astrolabe* dropped out of hyperspace.

The broad flat underside of the small unarmed ship was heavily studded with scanners. Four scan platforms carried everything from stereo imagers and neutron dippers to quark detectors and wide-band photometricons. Many of the instruments were duplicated as a hedge against malfunctions. The combination of the thin, wide profile and the scanner configuration had given the *Astrogator*-class probes the nickname "flatfish," which in turn had given rise to an unofficial logo popular with the crews.

"Your tour operators, the Astrographic Survey Institute, welcome you to Doornik-1142," the pilot called back to his survey team. "Be sure to take in all the recreational opportunities of this undiscovered gem of Farlax Sector—look out the viewports! Then later, you can look out the viewports! And whatever else you do during your nineteen-hour stay, make sure you take the time to look out the viewports!"

It was an old, familiar joke, and drew no more than ritual chuckles from the survey team. ASI vessels were the restless, peripatetic travelers of the stars—

professional tourists on breathless sightseeing expeditions through the galaxy. Capable of exceptionally high speeds in realspace, a flatfish rarely took more than a day to complete a mapping and survey pass across the top of an entire star system.

Most planets were overflown at close to maximum speed. Only if the approach data showed signs of life would a probe slow to quarter-speed. Only the markers of technological habitation could make them linger as long as a single orbit. Only the most extraordinary anomalies in the scans could make a flatfish pilot turn back and make a second pass. And landings were so rare as to be nearly unheard of.

Astrolabe had been diverted from work in Torranix Sector to fill a gap in the standard star charts—a gap left by the fallen Empire's obsessive secrecy, which treated ordinary astrographic data about the territory it controlled as classified military data.

The pilot, an eighteen-year veteran known to his crew as Gabby, had overflown more than a thousand planets in his career—but had set foot on only three. His senior surveyor, Tanea, had nearly three thousand overflights on her jacket, yet had ground-level memories of only half a dozen. The junior surveyor, Rulffe, expected to pass the five hundred mark on this tour, but had never drawn a breath on any world but his homeworld.

This mission began like all the others. The first hour was the busiest—while Tanea and Rulffe checked out the scanners, Gabby calibrated the probe's autonav for the shortest-path mapping pass over the system's quartet of cold, gaseous planets. They had every reason to think that their visit to Doornik-1142 would be short and uneventful, ending with a compressed data dump to Coruscant and the jump to the next gravitational well.

But it would end early, and hard.

Gabby and Tanea were playing a word game over the ship's comm system as *Astrolabe* approached the second planet.

"Hemostat," said Gabby.

"Oh, easy. Statistics."

"Eh—experience."

Tanea laughed. "That's not legal, but I'm going to give it to you anyway, because I'm such a kind and loving soul. Encephalitis."

"Tissue."

Tanea frowned. "I take it back. I think you've got *me* now—"

Without warning the ship began to shake violently. The cabin was filled with a roaring sound like an animal wind, a deep growly rumble, and crackling like fire.

"What the hell!" Rulffe exclaimed.

"Something's wrong with the engines!" Gabby cried as the roar became a screaming whistle.

In the next moment, the air was ripped from his lungs in a frosty plume, and silence reigned.

Moments later, with the temperature plunging, the cabin lights failed. The trouble board, now a mass of blinking red and yellow squares, provided the only illumination.

In the last excruciating seconds of consciousness, with the gases boiling in his blood vessels, the pilot tried to reach the switches to manually fire the emergency buoy and transmit the log. But his limbs, bound up by agony, would not obey him. He was already dead, and consciousness soon gratefully followed volition into the abyss.

Vol Noorr, primate of the battle cruiser *Purity*, watched approvingly as a fierce salvo of high-energy laser pulses blindsided the intruding vessel.

The accuracy and discipline of his gun crews pleased him, and he made a note to commend the weapons master. The firing ceased with the vessel holed and ravaged but not destroyed. A cloud of white fire and metal dust would have had little to tell them. But there would be wreckage enough to examine, and

Vol Noorr's follow-up report could be as complete and useful as possible.

"Send out the salvors," he ordered. "Make certain they maintain hygienic protocols on all material recovered."

Then Vol Noorr locked himself in the secure communications booth. A few minutes later he transmitted what would be the only alert concerning the destruction of the *Astrolabe* to be sent from Doornik-1142—a short burst of code aimed not at the Astrographic Survey Institute on Coruscant but at the viceroy's flagship *Aramadia,* ground-moored at Imperial City's Eastport.

"Three days in a row now," Princess Leia said to those gathered in the staff conference room. "Does *anyone* have any hint why Nil Spaar has been canceling our sessions? Is he ill? Do we know anything about what he's been doing?"

"He's only left the ship once," said General Carlist Rieekan. "He went to the diplomatic hostel and stayed two hours and thirteen minutes—"

"Never mind that. Who did he go there to see?" asked Ackbar.

"We weren't able to develop that information," Rieekan admitted. "You know what the hostel is like— hot and cold running privacy. The diplomatic missions expect that. I can tell you that the hostel host has been keeping a chalet reserved for the Yevetha since before they arrived, and this is the first time any of them have turned up there."

"So he could have met with any or all of the legates staying at the hostel," said Leia.

"That's correct."

"I want to see a list," Ackbar demanded.

"We've prepared one, and transmitted it to everyone on the clearance sheet for this meeting," said Rieekan. "I do have some additional information, which was given to me just before I left the office to come over here. The viceroy received visitors today on board the *Aramadia*—"

"What?" exclaimed Nanaod Engh. "They haven't allowed anyone but their own past the portal since that ship arrived. Who was it?"

"Senator Peramis, Senator Hodidiji, and Senator Marook," said Rieekan. "They arrived together, and all stayed more than two hours. Senator Marook left before the others."

"Do we know if they were invited or they invited themselves?" asked Leia.

"I made a discreet inquiry to Senator Marook's staff. It seems they were invited."

"Have they been in contact with the Yevetha all along?"

"Princess Organa, I can't answer that."

"Let's get them all in here, and we'll get some answers," Admiral Ackbar said testily. "Let Senator Peramis answer."

"Easy, my friend. Let's try to keep this in perspective," said Leia. "The viceroy has every right to meet with whomever he chooses. He doesn't need our permission to hold a tea party."

"Princess, forgive me—if you were not ready to hear the answers, why did you ask the question?"

Leia turned to Rieekan and frowned. "What are you talking about?"

"You asked if anyone had any notion why the viceroy was canceling his sessions with you. Now you learn that he's met privately with some of the candidate legations, and publicly with some of the Senate's most iconoclastic members. He's not only broken all precedent, but pointedly extended courtesies to others that he's never extended to you—and you refuse to draw the obvious conclusion."

"Which is—"

"That something fundamental has changed. That your negotiations with Nil Spaar are over."

"But what could have caused the change?" Leia protested. "There were no problems at our last meeting. I can't believe that he would throw all our work away without so much as a word—"

Admiral Ackbar, who was standing, was the first to notice the viewpanes of the conference room beginning to hum. The broad expanses of transparisteel had been darkened against the morning sun and prying eyes, so he could not immediately see the cause of the tremor when he turned.

"Princess—a moment—"

"What is it?"

"I know that sound—" Engh was saying.

"Something big over at Eastport," Rieekan said. "Can't you hear it?"

By that time, Ackbar had strode to the controls for the viewpanes, and the room was abruptly flooded with light. As one, they turned their faces toward it and squinted into the glare.

They saw the bright spherical shape of *Aramadia* slowly ascending from the spaceport, with its three tiny escorts circling it like planets around a star. Ripples of atmospheric distortion rolled out of scalloped depressions in its hull.

"I guess we'll have to believe it now," said Engh.

"I have the port commander online," Rieekan said.

"Let all of us hear it," said Leia.

"Yes, sir. Go ahead, Commander—what's happening out there?"

The roar of the Yevethan vessel's pulse-lifters was louder over the comm line than it was in the conference room. "We're still sorting things out. I can tell you *Aramadia* did *not* request a launch window from the tower. Our first warning she was gonna lift was when she started to launch escorts. That wasn't enough warning to get everyone clear of the downblast. There are six port sentries and at least three ground personnel injured, and the ship in the nearest bay, *Mother's Valkyrie*, looks like it took some substantial damage. Those pulse-lifters are nasty— we've got reports of ships being bounced as far away as the commuter docks."

"Thank you, Commander. Stand by," Rieekan

said, and closed the link. "Princess, I recommend we immediately place the Home Fleet on high alert."

"We must do more than that," said Ackbar. "I have ordered the *Brilliant* to move into position to fire on the *Aramadia* if necessary."

"What? Why would that be necessary?"

"Princess, *Aramadia* is inside our planetary shield," said Rieekan. "A ship that size could carry enough munitions to make quite a mess down here—at least the equivalent of a couple of Imperial assault frigates. We can't wait until we know what she means to do to respond."

"This is insane," Leia protested. "It's a diplomatic vessel. We have no evidence that it's even armed. Why would Nil Spaar *do* such a thing?" She looked back over her shoulder at Alole. "Any response?"

Her aide shook her head. "No, sir. No answer at all to your earlier messages, or to my red-line page."

"Princess," Ackbar said, "with respect, the question we need to be asking right now is not why he might do it, but what we can do to prevent it. We can't afford the luxury of thinking we have friends on that ship."

"I agree," said Rieekan. "The casualties at Eastport testify to Nil Spaar's priorities. They had to know what the consequences of a full-power lift with no advance warning would be. They've demonstrated that their convenience was more important to them than the lives of our people on the ground."

"Not convenience," Ackbar said. "This was no coincidence. This was calculated. He must have known that we were meeting. This was meant to embarrass you, just like the invitation to the senators."

"No—I can't believe that," said Leia. But her face wore a defeated expression. "Nevertheless—" She sighed. "Alert the fleet and the ground defenses. Instruct the captain of the *Brilliant* to take up position and stand by for further orders. But we will *not* be the first to fire—I want that understood by everyone. This has to be a misunderstanding. Let's not do anything to make it worse."

Aramadia went into orbit forty klicks below the lower limit of Coruscant's planetary shield, with *Brilliant* shadowing it astern.

There it remained for the next two hours, as mute and inscrutable as ever—in General Rieekan's words, "running the yard like a dog who knows exactly where the fence is." Ackbar and Leia watched the orbital traces of both ships on a monitor in her office, with Leia growing more and more impatient.

"What is he *waiting* for?" she demanded of no one in particular, pacing the room. "He was in such a hurry to raise ship, and now he just sits there. It doesn't make any sense. If he's planning to leave, he'll have to ask for clearance to transit the shield, won't he?"

"So far as we know," said Ackbar, "it's not possible to jump through or over our planetary shield."

"That's what I thought. But if he has something else in mind, he's squandered his moment of surprise, and then some. So what could this be about?"

"Maybe he's giving us a chance to apologize."

"Apologize? For what? Am I supposed to guess? It's hard enough dealing with all the ones who won't say what they mean, or tell you what they think you want to hear—what am I supposed to do when they won't talk at all? They come here and expect me to dance at their protocol ball without ever showing me the steps—"

As she spoke, Ackbar recoiled at the bitterness of her words and the harshness of her tone. Belatedly Leia noticed his reaction. "I'm sorry," she said, and sighed deeply. "It isn't you. I just don't understand why this is happening, and it's making me a little crazy."

"Princess," said Ackbar, "that may be exactly why it's happening."

At the rostrum of the huge Senate chamber, Behn-kihl-nahm gaveled the body into order. He wondered at the unusual number of senators present for the opening—more than half the number seated, if his eyes did not deceive him.

There had been much talk in the corridor and the cloakrooms about the sudden departure of the Yevetha that morning, but that could not account for the turnout. The first hour or more of each daily session was usually lost to self-serving speeches intended more for the homeworlds than for the senators' peers. It was common to find the chamber empty except for those waiting to speak. Behn-kihl-nahm glanced at the list and could find no name that could explain the high attendance or the speed with which the senators were moving to their seats.

There is something here, he thought worriedly. "The chair recognizes Senator Hodidiji."

"I rise to speak on a point of privilege."

"Senator Hodidiji is recognized on a point of personal privilege."

Hodidiji rose at his seat and addressed the rostrum without benefit of the microphone available to him, his voice booming out across the rows of planetary representatives. "Chairman, a matter of substantial urgency has arisen since I first requested my time. Due to the seriousness of this matter, I elect to yield my time to Senator Peramis of Walalla, and I ask that this body attend carefully to his presentation."

There was a stir in the chamber, but less of one than Behn-kihl-nahm would have expected. Apparently Peramis was the reason for the turnout. Just as apparently, Behn-kihl-nahm had not heard all of the morning's gossip and rumors, a prospect that brought a frown to his face. "Senator Peramis," he said with a nod, then stepped back from the podium.

"Thank you, Chairman. And I thank Senator Hodidiji for his indulgence," said Peramis. "Most of you know by now that the Yevethan consular ship *Aramadia* made an unscheduled liftoff from Eastport this morning. I have been informed that three port employees are dead and more than a score injured—"

This time the stir had an angry edge to it.

Behn-kihl-nahm reached out and dragged an aide closer by means of a fistful of fabric. "Call the princess," he whispered harshly. "Tell her she'd better get herself down here, now—and bring her firesuit."

"—Three ships were also damaged, including a consular ship belonging to the autonomous territory of Paqwepori.

"However, it's not the collapse of negotiations with the Yevetha, or the damage to property, or even the loss of life which should make this a matter of great import to us," said Peramis. "It is the reason *why* these things happened which must concern us.

"So far, there's been no information forthcoming from the president's office about these events—not a word of explanation, or regret, or indignation. The princess has been unavailable, and there's been only silence from her staff.

"I'm not surprised by that. When you've heard what you're about to hear, you won't be surprised, either. There isn't much they can say without lying, because the truth shames them."

Senator Tolik Yar shot to his feet. "A point of privilege is not a license to slander and defame, sir!"

"Chairman, I ask for order in the chamber," Peramis said, not even looking in Senator Yar's direction.

"The chamber will be in order," Behn-kihl-nahm said without enthusiasm.

"I warn you, recant your words, before you flirt with treason—"

Peramis shot the round-bodied Oolid a look of contempt. "Sit down and listen, Senator, and you will learn something about treason, and about this woman you call your friend. Chairman, I ask that the Senate recorder activate the chamber's display screens and set them to Channel Eighty-one, the diplomatic frequency."

"For what purpose, Senator?"

"For the purpose of allowing Viceroy Nil Spaar of

the Yevetha to add~ess this body from aboard *Aramadia,* which is presently orbiting Coruscant."

Behn-kihl-nahm turned away from the podium just long enough to send a second aide on a hasty mission. "This is most irregular, Senator Peramis."

"So are the events in dispute, Chairman. And I consider the information the viceroy can provide this body not merely relevant, but essential to understanding those events."

"Am I to understand that you already have knowledge of what the viceroy will say?"

"I was contacted by the viceroy and asked if I would help bring the truth to light. When I learned what the truth was, it seemed unlikely to me that we would hear it from any other source, and I agreed."

There was a growing restlessness in the chamber. "Let's hear what the viceroy has to say!" cried a voice from the high rows.

"It's a point of privilege—he can introduce whatever he likes," shouted another.

"If you don't want to hear it, leave!"

"Senator Noimm made us look at recordings of her last brood-birth, and you allowed *that* irregularity."

There was a ripple of laughter at that reminder, though Senator Noimm glared unhappily.

"Turn 'em on!" someone called, and it became a chorus. "Turn 'em on! Let's hear from the viceroy."

Behn-kihl-nahm pounded his gavel. "The chamber will be in order. Sergeant, you are to eject the next member I identify who speaks out of turn. There *will* be order, or I will suspend this session."

The sergeant-at-arms, a hulking Gamorrean, moved forward from his usual post to the center of the well, from which he glowered up at the front benches. With Behn-kihl-nahm alternately pounding the gavel and pointing it at the worst offenders, the chamber slowly settled into something resembling civility.

"That's better," Behn-kihl-nahm said scoldingly. "Remember who you are! This is the Senate of the

New Republic. We are not a rabble." He peered down to his left. "Senator Peramis."

"Yes, Chairman."

"Do you accept responsibility for your speaker's remarks as though they were your own, including any and all sanctions which would fall on any member of this body for transgressions against the Senate's code of conduct?"

"I do."

"Then proceed with your presentation."

When Behn-kihl-nahm's first warning reached Princess Leia in her office, she headed not for the door but for the darkened display on which she was able to monitor the Senate's hypercomm feed on Channel 11.

"I'm not rushing down there to put out a fire until I know what's burning," she told Ackbar.

Moments later they were joined by First Administrator Engh, who had been routinely monitoring the Senate on his own and came running to alert Leia.

"Did you hear him? No information forthcoming!" Engh raged. "The situation's still developing—what is there to say? *Aramadia* is still sitting up there ignoring us. Bless Tolik Yar, anyway. Peramis hasn't even called here—he didn't *try* to get our side of it."

"Shhh," Leia said. "I can't hear what he's saying."

They did not have to watch long for Leia to conclude there was little she could accomplish by going to the Senate chamber.

"They know me," she said. "They know him. Let him make whatever intimations he wants. The Senate won't rush to judgment. I'll get my turn to be heard—but not today, in a shouting match with Peramis. He can have the floor to himself this morning."

But when Peramis announced his intention to have Nil Spaar address the Senate, Ackbar became livid. "This is absurd. Benny can't let Peramis do that."

"He can't stop him," Leia said. "He has to allow it."

"The Duskhan League is not a member of the Republic," Ackbar said. "Nil Spaar has no right to use the diplomatic channels."

"A technicality," said Leia. "The chairman doesn't dare hold such a feeble reed up in the wind that's blowing down there."

"If the viceroy addresses the Senate on Channel Eighty-one, it's going to go out on the repeaters to every New Republic homeworld," Engh said. "Let me call someone I know over at Network Operations. He'd be willing to stop this from going offplanet on my word."

"No," said Leia. "I'm not afraid of what he might say. Besides, the newsgrids are sure to have it by now. No, if the viceroy won't speak to me, let him speak to whomever he wants. At least we'll find out what this is all about."

"Then proceed with your presentation," Behn-kihl-nahm was saying.

"I told you he'd have to allow it," said Leia. "Quiet, both of you, until he's done. I don't want to miss any of this."

Both the Coruscant Global Newsgrid and the independent New Republic Prime Newsgrid, tipped off by staffers from the offices of Senators Hodidiji and Peramis, had been following the contretemps in the Senate since Peramis had taken the floor.

Port officials hadn't released any of the images captured by the official visual logs, but Global had an amateur recording of the liftoff of *Aramadia,* made by a Belovian envoy who was seeing family off at the Eastport terminal.

That such a recording existed was almost inevitable, given how many lenses had been pointed in the direction of the Yevethan consular ship since its arrival. But it was just chance that the first moments of the recording included a blurry glimpse of one of the sentries being tumbled along the ground by the downblast like a rag doll.

Prime's recording of the liftoff had been made

from much farther away, by a space hobbyist who kept a bank of automated recorders on the balcony of his dormitory, and included no such graphic detail. But Prime had somehow gotten close-ups of the damage on the ground, including shots of bodies draped in deathrobes lying on the ground and being loaded onto emergency speeders.

Nil Spaar studied both the Global and Prime broadcasts intently as he awaited the outcome of the wrangling between the two vermin. As had been the case ever since the Yevetha mission had begun, what he saw on the grids was instructive. He had been obliged to learn how to think like the vermin in order to exploit their weaknesses, and the grids had brought him all the lessons and opportunities he could have asked for.

But the viceroy could still hardly believe the mad absurdities he had witnessed, not least of all the scene playing out before him.

The idea that the vermin were allowed to speak against their supreme leader, without fear that they would be slain on the spot and their blood used to drown their children—the idea that an anointed body of elders would even listen to an outsider, much less give credence to an outsider's insults—these were notions no Yevetha could easily accept.

If Nil Spaar had not seen for himself the weak hand that now ruled over the vermin, he could not have credited such reports.

The body and the spirit of the vermin were fatally polluted by impurities of blood and honor. Their thousands of species had the same quality of unity as a handful of pebbles—each still separate, and its separate identity preventing it from merging into a greater whole. The vermin were contentiously divided, selfishly predatory, foolishly trusting, relentlessly arational, fatally idealistic. Not a one of them had earned his respect. And none had earned more of his contempt than Tig Peramis, the traitor whose face now filled both displays.

"I do," Peramis was saying.

They will kill you slowly when they learn what you have done, thought Nil Spaar, *and you will well deserve it.*

"Then proceed with your presentation," said Behn-kihl-nahm.

A signal light appeared before Nil Spaar, and he muted the grid displays.

"Yes, Senator," he said. "I am here."

His long fingers steepled with gentle precision, Hiram Drayson leaned back in his chair and watched as the face on the Senate monitor changed from that of Tig Peramis to that of Nil Spaar.

Drayson had hoped for—though not expected—a glimpse inside the *Aramadia,* but the Yevetha had avoided that bit of carelessness. Wherever Nil Spaar was transmitting from, the space behind him appeared as empty and unenlightening as a blank bulkhead. Given the universal propensity of starship designers to fill every available space, Drayson suspected the use of a screen, either physical or electronic.

"Before I begin, I want to share my deep regret over the unfortunate casualties resulting from our ascent from Eastport," the viceroy said. "It was with great sorrow that I learned that our warnings had not been honored and the thrust radius of the *Aramadia* had not been cleared. We had no thought or intention of injuring anyone. We left Eastport to avoid a confrontation, not to cause one."

"Oh, very good," Drayson said to himself, nodding. "Well done."

"I regret the casualties," Nil Spaar went on, "but I cannot take responsibility for them. For more than three days we requested clearance to leave Coruscant. Three members of your Senate witnessed two such attempts and can testify that we received only silence in reply.

"We warned the tower at Eastport and the president that we would raise ship without clearance if they left us no other choice. Their only response was to surround our ship with more soldiers and replace the ground crews with agents of the Intelligence Service."

Ah! Drayson thought. *Very interesting. Now, is it that you think they'll believe any accusation against the Service, or do you have an honest card to play to help sell the lies?*

Allowing his fingers to lace together, Drayson rocked slowly in his chair as he listened for the answer.

"Stars on fire," Engh breathed. "Is it possible that any of this is true? Could there have been some sort of misunderstanding, and we didn't *hear* them asking for clearance?"

"Shut up," Leia said.

Nearly every seat in the Senate chamber was full now. Those not occupied by their owners had been commandeered by curious interlopers. Dozens more staffers lingered in the aisles, along the back wall, and in the open areas near the entrance doors. The six-meter-tall image of Nil Spaar on the display boards commanded their attention more powerfully than anyone at the podium or in the well was accustomed to.

"It became clear that the government of Leia Organa intended to hold us here against our will," Nil Spaar said. "It became clear to me that we could not wait any longer. We risked losing not only the right of free navigation we had been promised, but the capacity to exercise it. *Aramadia* is a consular ship. It is ill equipped to repel an armed assault.

"I am sure that those of you who think you know Princess Leia Organa may doubt that she is capable of ordering soldiers to attack diplomats. After spending so many hours with her, I thought *I* knew her, and *I* would have trouble believing it, if there were not other evidence of her bad faith."

The screen flickered, and Nil Spaar's face was replaced by images of burned and twisted metal laid out on bronze decking. "What you see now is the wreckage of a New Republic spy ship which violated the territorial hegemony of the Duskhan League four days ago. It self-destructed when spotted by a local patrol vessel, but we were able to recover enough of it to identify its purpose and origin."

At that moment, the audience in the Senate, in offices all over Imperial City, and on worlds throughout the New Republic saw Yevethan hands turn over a large fragment to reveal a recognizable portion of the New Republic seal—the blue crest, the ring of stars, and the gold circle.

Drayson leaned forward, staring, then slowly rose to his feet. "Bloody bilge—that's no prowler. That's a flatfish, or used to be." He stabbed at his communication computer with a finger. "Verify."

"Verified—Drayson, Hiram."

"Call Kiles L'toth. Scramble."

"Calling Kiles L'toth. Waiting. Verifying. Ready."

"Kiles—this is Drayson. Is that one of your ships being splashed all over the grids by the Yevethan ambassador?"

The associate director's voice was shaky. "We, uh—yes, we think so. It could be the *Astrolabe*. She's four hours overdue for her logout from Doornik-1142."

"Four *hours*. The viceroy said this happened four *days* ago. How is it you didn't know you'd lost a bird?"

"Admiral, you know there's not usually much traffic while they're in-system. Look, what he's saying—it's not true. *Astrolabe* wasn't on a spy mission. This was routine survey work—"

"I didn't ask," said Drayson. "But others will. Better work on your answers."

Princess Leia's face paled when three red body bags appeared briefly on the monitor.

"I regret to report that there were no survivors," Nil Spaar was saying. "We *were* able to recover three bodies, which we are prepared to make arrangements to return."

The viceroy's face reappeared. "But we cannot and will not negotiate this or any other matter with President Princess Leia Organa Solo. Everything she has said to us has been revealed by her actions as a lie. She claims to negotiate in good faith, while she sends spies to our homelands. She claims to respect our independence, and yet she sends a New Republic fleet toward our territory. She claims to want a treaty between equals, and yet she seeks to weaken our position with espionage and threats.

"I do not know that any act is beyond her, if she thinks it will help secure her power. I am gravely disappointed to learn that she falls so short of the ideals to which the New Republic aspires.

"At this very moment, I, my staff, and my crew are imprisoned within the planetary shield of Coruscant. We are being hounded by a battle cruiser of the Coruscant Home Fleet. We want nothing but to return to our homeworld—but Princess Leia stands in our way, denying us the freedoms to which she so glibly gives lip service.

"I ask the chairmen of the Senate and each member world represented there to use whatever influence you can to persuade the princess to abandon her needlessly reckless and aggressive course. Open the shield. Allow us to go home."

The Senate erupted in angry voices and harsh words as Nil Spaar's face vanished from the displays. "Turn it off," Leia said, and slumped into a chair. "Turn it off!" she repeated sharply when Engh and Ackbar were slow to move.

Engh finally complied, and the monitor dimmed to the color and brightness of the wall on which it hung. For a moment there was silence in the room.

Ackbar turned away to the viewpane, embarrassed for his friend. "This is a disaster," he said simply.

"He's misinterpreted everything," Leia said disbelievingly. "How could this have happened? We played right into their strongest fears. How could it have gone so wrong?"

"Leia—we must do *something*—" Engh pleaded with his eyes.

She nodded, and it seemed a great effort. "Contact General Baintorf. Have him open the shield. Tell the *Brilliant* to break off. Let them go. Ask Benny if he'll appoint a representative of the Senate to arrange retrieval of the bodies."

"Yes, Princess. Right away." Engh excused himself as though glad to escape.

"Flawlessly played," said Hiram Drayson. He stood with crossed arms before the monitor, watching as Senator Peramis and Senator Hodidiji submitted Articles of Withdrawal for their respective worlds. Three other small worlds, all represented in the Senate by their hereditary rulers, followed suit before Behn-kihl-nahm succeeded in suspending the session.

As the grids broke away from live coverage to analysis, Drayson called up a recording of Nil Spaar's address. "Utterly flawless," he said after watching the replay, affirming his original judgment. There was more than a touch of admiration in his voice.

"But there's one missing piece, Viceroy," he added, stroking his face with one large hand, a thoughtful expression in his intent black eyes. "What did it gain you? What's the payoff for weakening Leia's hand and stirring up the Senate? There's something not seen here—"

Turning back to his desk, Drayson spun his computer toward him. "Verify."

"Verified—Drayson, Hiram."

"Call Etahn A'baht. Scramble and blind-route."

"Calling Etahn A'baht. Working. Waiting, Verifying—"

"Admiral Ackbar."

The big Calamari turned away from the viewpane

to find the princess standing near the door. "Yes, Leia."

"Why was one of our ships anywhere near Koornacht? Did you know anything about this?"

"I do not have any answers," Ackbar said uncomfortably.

"Try to find some for me," she said, and turned away.

"Where are you going?"

Leia looked back over her shoulder. "Home, to think about resigning."

"Leia—"

"Don't try to argue with me," she said. "Not now. Maybe tomorrow."

The Battle Operations Center of the fleet carrier *Intrepid* was deserted except for two generals carrying unhappy burdens. General Etahn A'baht carried the burden of knowing what he had done, while General Han Solo carried the burden of knowing what must come.

For more than two hours A'baht had been signaling Coruscant, attempting to speak directly with Princess Leia. All his attempts, using every direct and indirect route available to him, had failed.

He had reached Fleet Operations, the administrative message center, an apologetic first administrator, an uncharacteristically taciturn Admiral Ackbar, the president's communications and protocol droid, and message boxes for half a dozen offices and their highly placed occupants. But Leia herself seemed to have disappeared from the command and communications structure of Imperial City, and no one A'baht spoke to seemed overly eager to look for her.

Finally Ackbar had agreed to carry a message for A'baht to the president's residence, asking Leia to contact him on board the *Intrepid*. That was when the waiting began—an excruciatingly tedious exercise in clock-watching and uncomfortable silence. The sprawling BOC, which easily absorbed dozens of officers and ratings when staffed, seemed as claustrophobic as a cell in *Intrepid*'s brig.

When the hypercomm finally lit up and squawked a Red Line alert, both men started. When the holodisplay brightened to show Leia from the shoulders up, Han was startled and dismayed by how pallid her face was, how dark and lifeless her eyes.

"General A'baht," she said with a nod. Her voice was husky, and she cleared her throat after she spoke.

"Princess Leia," said A'baht. "Thank you for responding to my request."

"I understand from Admiral Ackbar that you have some information for me."

"Yes, Princess." He straightened his back and sat tall in his chair. "I am the person responsible for the astrographic probes being sent into Farlax. Before the Fifth sailed, I requested an updated survey of that sector, including Koornacht Cluster. I did this with the full knowledge that this was in violation of your orders. I offer no excuse, and accept full responsibility for my actions."

There was hardly a flicker of reaction on Leia's face. "Thank you, General. You are relieved of command, effective immediately. The next person to sit here will decide the rest." Her eyes sought Han. "General Solo."

"Yes, Leia," Han said, stepping forward.

"I'm placing you in command in General A'baht's stead. Your orders are to bring the Fifth Fleet back to Coruscant as soon as possible."

"Uh—Leia—"

Her pain shone momentarily through the mask of numbness. "Just come home, Han—please." The holodisplay went dark.

A'baht turned away from the hypercomm. "I'm sorry," he said, standing. "You will need to recall the patrols before turning the formation."

"What? Sure. Now forget excuses, and tell me why you did it." When A'baht hesitated, Han added, "That's an order."

"Very well," said A'baht. "I believed I had been denied the information I needed to do my job properly—both parts of my job, protecting my command and protecting the New Republic's interests. Princess Leia made a military decision for political reasons, and it left me in an untenable position. I attempted to make an end run around her objections by going outside the Fleet, to the Astrographic Survey Institute. You already know the results."

"I think I do. Do you?"

"What do you mean?"

"That flatfish was no spy ship."

"No."

"And it didn't blow itself up, did it?"

"No."

"Then maybe it found what you wanted it to find—what you were worried is out here."

"Perhaps so," said A'baht. "But it doesn't matter. The probe made no report, and there'll be no more probes sent into that area. Whatever secrets the Yevetha have, they'll keep." He saluted diffidently. "Request permission to return to my quarters, sir."

Han frowned. "Granted," he said, and A'baht headed for the hatchway. "General—"

A'baht paused and turned back.

"How many prowlers are assigned to the Fifth Fleet?"

"One squadron—eight. There are also two squadrons of reconnaissance drones."

Han gestured broadly at the bank of empty stations. "You want to tell me which one of these buttons calls in your tactical staff?"

"What are you saying?" A'baht's face wore an uncertain expression.

"Well—we know someone or something out here's unfriendly to the New Republic," Han said grimly. "Right?"

"I'd say so."

"Seems as though we'd better do something to

cover our withdrawal, then. That seem reasonable to you?"

"You are in command of the Fleet, General Solo."

"So I am," Han said. "And I *never* turn my back to a dark corner when I know someone's after me. Which button?"

A'baht pointed. "There."

Chapter 14

◆

"Koornacht Cluster" was always an outsider's name—an astronomer's name, hundreds of years old, but barely more meaningful than a cataloger's letters and numbers.

Aitro Koornacht had done a favor involving a woman and an Imperial coach for the First Observer at the Court of Emperor Preedu III, on Tamban. That next night, the astronomer spotted a bright, fuzzy disk in the eyepiece of his newest telescope. That grateful First Observer had repaid his benefactor by naming the newly discovered star cluster after the night commander of the palace guard.

But that same gathering of stars had other names. To the Fia of Galantos, in whose skies it appeared as a great oval of light, it was known as The Multitude. The Wehttam, another galactic neighbor, revered it as God's Temple. The Ka'aa, a wandering species old enough to have seen the youngest stars in the Cluster wink on, remembered it as *no'aat padu'll*—the Little Nursery.

The Yevetha knew it by a word that meant Home.

Two thousand suns and twenty thousand worlds, all born together from the same great cloud of dust and gas that still filled the spaces between them. They were young suns and hard worlds, and there were few eyes on hand to know either. The faces of fewer than a hundred planets had been brightened with the colors of life, and only a single species spawned in the Cluster had made the leap from its home soil to the stars.

Two thousand suns keeping company in space, burning so brightly in the skies over N'zoth and its daughter worlds that they blinded the eye to the dimmer lights, the wider galaxy beyond. It was not until visitors came from beyond the Cluster to mine its riches that the Yevetha learned they were not alone.

It was a difficult lesson. A young species with a hard ethic, the Yevetha were accustomed to their place as the center of their universe. The relentless *otherness* of the outsiders was a profound challenge to the Yevetha's conception of themselves. In the end, the answer to that challenge was a new vision built on purity of line, sanctity of territory, and hate.

The occupation by the Empire had been an education for the Yevetha, in more ways than one.

When the Empire came to Koornacht, it belonged to the Yevetha alone. Traveling through realspace in their immaculate spherical thrustships, they had spread from the spawnworld of N'zoth to eleven daughter worlds.

In all the recorded history of the galaxy, no species had established more interstellar colonies without the benefit of hyperdrive technology. To the Yevetha, the stars of N'zoth's bright night sky seemed to hover just above their heads, beckoning. Their will was strong enough to leap the distances between the stars.

After the Empire retreated from Koornacht, that will was wedded to a technology that could leap the distances between the stars. Vastly faster ships made the other Yevethan worlds seem no farther away from N'zoth than the other side of the globe, and Imperial comm units could carry the viceroy's voice throughout the Cluster in a matter of minutes.

N'zoth and its daughter worlds were bound together as one in a way never before possible, and the

Second Birth began. The Yevetha scouted and settled a dozen more prime worlds in a spasm of expansion that satisfied the frustrated ambition of the occupation years.

But the greater vision guiding the Yevetha required a longer period of preparation and consideration. In that time, Yevethan engineers worked to adapt thrustship designs to Imperial technologies, while the metal artisans labored to complete and repair the captured warships.

Claiming and protecting all of the Yevethan birthright would require that and more, an unparalleled marshaling of effort—not only ships and crews, but whole communities, an entire generation ready to leave their birthworld for a home in the sky of stars.

And it would also require that someone go before and prepare the way.

For during its time as trustee of Koornacht Cluster, the Empire had allowed some immigrant colonies, encouraged others, and created still others for its own purposes. When the Empire left Koornacht, the Yevetha were no longer alone.

The transfer between *Aramadia* and the eight-kilometer-long Star Destroyer *Pride of Yevetha* took place at a rendezvous point deep in the heart of the Koornacht Cluster, far from any prying eyes.

Three trips by the thrustship's ferry were required to complete the transfer of the viceroy. In the first trip his *darna* and breeding mates came across. The second brought his personal staff, including first attaché Eri Palle. The final run delivered the honor guard, Nil Spaar himself, and Vor Duull, *Aramadia*'s proctor of information science. Vor Duull's inclusion was a reward for his work during the successful Coruscant mission.

They were met by Dar Bille, who had been Nil Spaar's loyal second since long before the day of retribution. Now primate of *Pride of Yevetha*, he had directed the training of the other primates as each former Imperial warship had joined the growing Black Fleet.

"*Etaias*," Dar Bille said, adding the salute of obeisance to the honorific. It was more than was called for by the difference in their standing, and drove the lower-ranking officers behind him to a similar excess; each dropped to one knee and bowed his head.

"*Noreti*," Nil Spaar said warmly. "This was unnecessary, but it pleases me. Eri, see that everyone finds his quarters. Dar, lead me to the bridge. Is the fleet ready?"

"This way, Viceroy. The fleet is well ready. But *Glory* could not be launched in time to join us," Dar Bille said, knowing that Nil Spaar would not be surprised by that news. *Glory* was the vessel the Imperials had called *EX-F,* and its curious propulsion system, unlike that in any other starship, had been an ongoing vexation.

As he followed Dar Bille into the corridor, Nil Spaar let his fingertips graze across the bare necks of the kneeling officers as he passed them. The touch symbolized his acceptance of the offer of their lives, and freed them to rise. "And the others?" he asked.

"After the last combat trial, I made the decision that the crew of *Blessings* was not ready. But that will not hinder us on this mission."

"I presume the primate earned the expected reward for his failure."

"He did, at my hand, and his second as well."

"Excellent," said Nil Spaar. "It doesn't do for those who serve in the lesser posts to think that the knife will cut only the throat of authority."

"The new primate of *Blessings* expects another combat trial when we return. Perhaps you would like to witness it."

"Perhaps," Nil Spaar said as they reached the bridge. "For now, my mind is full of the work ahead of us. And of memories. It seems a right thing to me that you should be the primate of my flagship today. Do you remember the *Beauty,* and the day we discovered the first nest of the vermin?"

The little starship *Beauty,* a former Imperial corvette, had carried Nil Spaar to the far reaches of the Cluster and beyond. That long scouting mission had opened his eyes to the true challenge ahead and had given purpose to everything he had done since. He had taken the measure of the All and understood its meaning, taken the measure of their enemies and understood their threat, and had come home to N'zoth to make himself viceroy.

"Of course, *etaias*. And here we are again, together on the bridge of a fine ship. Soon we will again look down undetected on the nests of the vermin—but this time they will know that we were there." He looked past Nil Spaar to the proctor of information. "*Lifath*—what news do you have of the New Republic's Fifth Fleet?"

"Primate, our shadow reports the fleet has disappeared from Hatawa. Our contacts on Coruscant tell us that it has been recalled."

Nil Spaar bowed his head and breathed relief. "Then it will be done. I am vindicated."

Dar Bille turned a proud and joyful face toward Nil Spaar. "On your orders, Viceroy."

"I wish to speak to all our vessels."

Turning quickly toward the proctor of communications, Dar Bille arranged the necessary connections and announced the viceroy to the crews of the twenty-five warships secreted in twos and threes across the Cluster.

"Remember that we are the blessed, born of the light of the All," Nil Spaar told them. "All beauty belongs to us. All that we see in our skies was meant for our children. It was not meant for the creatures that creep in from the darkness beyond. Their presence alone fouls the light and defaces the beauty of the All.

"Today we will remove them, as the steward of a granary must remove the vermin to keep the stocks pure. And when next you stand on N'zoth and look to the sky, you will know that none but the children of N'zoth stand above you."

Then Nil Spaar stepped away from the hyper-comm and looked back to Dar Bille. "You may give the order," he said generously.

Dar Bille's crests swelled with pride and gratitude. "All vessels of the Black Fleet—this is the primate of the flagship *Pride of Yevetha*," he said in a strong clear voice. "On the word of the viceroy, I direct you to commence your attacks. May each of us honor the name of the Yevetha today."

Wearing an approving look on his dirty, deep-lined face, Negus Nigekus slammed the check hatch shut and threw the locking bolt home. The ore sheds were more than two-thirds full, and there was still a month to go before the gypsy freighter returned to New Brigia. Perhaps this time there would finally be enough profit over the cost of their supplies to clear the last of their passage debt.

Nigekus would never have dreamed that after eighteen years working the chromite digs in the hills above the village, the little colony would still owe a debt to the captain of the freighter that had brought them there. In the beginning the land had been generous. And with the Cluster under the Empire's protection and their claim to New Brigia accepted by Coruscant, there had been more than enough buyers for the blue-white metal to ensure good prices. War—so long as it stayed at a safe distance—was good for business.

In the first four years there wasn't a quarter when the community failed to pare its debt. Even with the extra costs as families left the longhouses for cottage shelters, even feeding new mouths too young to contribute, and the mothers who gave their labor share in the nursery rather than the mines, even the summer when the crops withered and the winter when the processing dome burned, there was always something offered against their obligations.

But then the land had grown stingy, and, not long after, the Empire was gone. With the spacelanes from Koornacht to Galantos and Wehttam no longer secure, the colony's best buyers lowered their offers or stopped bidding at all, pointing to the risk of piracy.

In time only Captain Stanz and the *Freebird* came calling, and his price was the lowest of all—an insult to the sweat and labor of the two hundred who each morning hiked up from the village to the diggings and each evening returned bowed by their labors. But Stanz was a pirate in heart if not in fact, and had no sympathy for them.

"This is droid work yer doing," he said, "picking rocks from the ground. You can't expect a living wage for droid work. Even at these prices, it's hardly worth my trouble to come here."

Nigekus doubted the truth of that, but there was no point in arguing. He had no choice but to stand there and listen to Stanz's poor-mouthing as he figured the load and calculated the overage, using whatever prices the old Bothan's whim dictated. And for years the overage had hovered around the figure for a quarter's interest, sometimes a little more, more often a little less, with the shortfall added to their debt.

If the community had had its own hauler, even a worn-out Corellian freighter or a battered space barge—but that was a dream beyond reason.

Still, the land had suddenly turned kind again, with two new diggings bringing up rich ore that reminded the surviving elders of the promise that had coaxed them there from Brigia. If they earned no more for this load than the price Stanz had paid on his last visit, the overage should cover not only the interest but the balance.

To guarantee that, Nigekus had decided that this time he would hold back a third of the ore until Stanz set the price. It was a tactic not without risk, or it might have been tried long before. If the Bothan took offense, the community could lose its lifeline—and the offender might lose his life.

But Nigekus was determined to see New Brigia escape Captain Stanz's thrall before the dust-cough that now plagued him at night rendered him fit only to sweeten the dirt of the gardens. If Stanz snapped his neck in a fury at being caught as a cheat, Nigekus would lose little.

"He will only spare me the last weeks of the coughing death," he had said to the other elders in winning their approval. "And you can then kill him without shame, and claim his ship as honor payment to my family."

Negus Nigekus walked slowly but proudly across the common toward the processing dome, his thin body warmed by the knowledge that a turning was coming.

It had been hard for him to admit that he could no longer make the climb to the diggings and do more than take up space in the pit. The aches of hard labor were easier to bear than the deep ache of feeling useless, of standing with the children and feeling that he had become one of them, a mouth that could not earn its table share. He was grateful to have found a way of escaping that feeling.

Before Nigekus reached the dome, a shadow flashed across the common. But by the time he looked skyward, there was nothing to be seen. The whine and clatter of the machinery had covered the sound of the approaching dropships until very near the end, and the landing sites were downriver around the bend, safely out of view. Shaking his head, Nigekus entered the dome, ignorant of the threat already moving up the valley toward the village.

When he left the dome just a few minutes later, his inspection complete, everything had changed. Tall creatures in green and brown body armor were advancing through the village in a wide line, their weapons turning the cottages into burned and broken shells. A child's screaming pierced the din of the machinery behind him, then ended with ominous abruptness.

Nigekus was ignored or overlooked long enough

to take half a dozen uncertain steps out into the common, long enough to realize in horror that some of the blackened objects littering the ground were carcasses, long enough to feel a wild rush of indignation over the fact that he did not even know the species of the invaders.

Then he found his voice and cried out his rage, raised both fists in defiance and started across the common toward the nearest of the soldiers. A silver-barreled weapon turned his way, and Nigekus fell in agony, his last breath full of fire.

Two of the diggers at Pit 4 had seen the descending ships, making that crew the first to start back down to the village. The pall of black smoke rising over the ridgelines drew the other crews away from their work and onto the well-trod trails. Some had shouldered their tools as weapons, but most were armed only with fear for their families. They had had no enemies on New Brigia, and energy weapons were a luxury the colony could not afford.

The Yevethan troops, masked against the smoke and the stench of the vermin, waited patiently in the village for the diggers to return. There was no need to do anything more. As Nil Spaar had predicted, the sight of the ravaged village gave the diggers the final spur to a reckless charge.

It was a methodical slaughter. Standing back to back in a circle on the common, the soldiers allowed the diggers to reach the valley floor, then cut them down.

The last few deaths were suicides in all but name. With both the carnage and the futility before them, the remaining Brigians dropped their inadequate weapons, gave up their cover, and walked down the slopes to the village, offering themselves as targets rather than be left alive to remember.

When it was over, and the breeze falling through the valley had blown all but the last tendrils of smoke away, only the Yevethan troops, the ore sheds, and the processing dome were left standing.

It was no accident that those buildings had survived. As the troops returned downriver to their dropships, a fat-bodied cargo transport landed on the common. Within an hour its empty belly easily swallowed both the contents of the ore sheds and the machinery from the processing dome.

Once the cargo transport was safely clear of the target zone, *Star Dream* completed its sterilization of the valley with a long salvo from the cruiser's heavy batteries.

The bodies turned to vapor and vanished, and the blood was scorched from the rocks. The ground turned to black glass, and the river exploded into steam. When the barrage was over, nothing was left of the vermin but the holes they had carved in the ground with their hands and the trails they had beaten into the hills with their footsteps.

Star Dream returned to N'zoth triumphant in her glorious victory, carrying a passage price in chromite in her hold.

In a garden city on J't'p'tan, a world gentled by patient hands, a woman awoke from a dream to a nightmare. A falling star became a starship, the starship a warship, and the warship a fountain of death raining on the face of the world. In the dream, or the nightmare, the Current ran wild with the thrashings of murdered souls, and ran dark with the stain of blood.

"Rouse everyone, at once," Wialu said, shaking her daughter. "Hurry—something terrible has begun."

New Brigia was the smallest of the thirteen alien settlements visited by the ships of the Black Fleet in the first hour of the Great Purge.

Polneye was the largest, and the only one to fight back.

Orbiting a star on the far side of the Cluster from Coruscant, Polneye was an orphan child of the Empire.

It had been established to serve as a secret military transshipment port for Farlax Sector. Cloaked in high-altitude clouds whose rains rarely reached the ground, arid Polneye became home to a vast open-air armory and supply depot.

Bustling hub-and-spoke landing and holding zones sprawled across the dusky-brown flats. Eventually, even the largest vessels capable of grounding could be accommodated, with cargoes unloaded, assembled, and transferred by small armies of droids.

As the traffic through Polneye grew, so did the population. At first it was a purely military billet, staffed by the Supply Command on a normal rotation. The planet was chosen to satisfy certain strategic criteria, not for its suitability for habitation. But over time, as more and more jobs were bid out to civilians, the center of each landing zone had grown into a small city largely comprised of semipermanent residents.

When the beaten remnants of the Imperial Fleet abandoned Farlax and retreated into the Core, the military staff fled in whatever ships were available on the ground. But the civilian population, which by then numbered nearly a quarter-million scattered across fifty sites, was left behind to fend for itself.

And though, suddenly, transports no longer dropped through the clouds with thrusters roaring to land on Polneye, the droids and cargoes that had been waiting for them proved a rich enough treasure to ease the shock of abandonment. Virtually everything a great army and a fleet of starships required to function could be found somewhere in the cargo containers left scattered on holding pads across the face of Polneye.

There were few missteps, and little was wasted or discarded. Polneye was blessed by strong leadership at the outset, and the cargoes became the raw material for a transformation—from client to self-sustaining settlement to a unified state of eight consolidated cities.

So it was that the Yevethan warships *Honor, Liberty,* and *Devotion* arrived over a planet boasting a healthy population of nearly three hundred thousand sentients, seventy thousand droids—and six operational TIE interceptors.

"Weapons master! Attend me! Why has the attack not begun?"

The weapons master of the Star Destroyer *Devotion* bowed deeply to Jip Toorr before speaking.

"Primate, there is an ionization inversion above the clouds over this planet. Together, the two are interfering with the targeting computers on all our ships. I am not confident that the accuracy of our firing will satisfy your expectations."

"The viceroy has expectations as well, which we both must fulfill," said Jip Toorr. "How do you propose that we do so?"

"Sir—there are scout fighters waiting in their bays to confirm the success of our attack. I ask that three of them be launched now and sent below the clouds to direct the fire of our batteries."

"Will this provide the accuracy needed to ensure the success of our mission?"

"Without fail, Primate."

"Then I so order it. Tactics master, launch three scout fighters. The weapons master will direct them."

The last of the navigation satellites on which Polneye's traffic control system had depended had failed nearly a year earlier, or the arrival of the Yevethan task force would have been detected as soon as the ships exited hyperspace.

But the ground components of the traffic control system were still operational. Alarms began to sound the moment the Yevethan scout fighters cleared the ionization boundary, calling technicians to rarely tended stations. Many other Polneyi ran outside to look up and see what sort of visitors had come calling.

Those whose eyes were sharp enough saw three tiny black ships circling just below the clouds. One was over the city called Nine South, a second over Eleven North, and the third over the ghost city of

Fourteen North, which was still being cannibalized for its structures and equipment.

Then fire poured down from the sky. Fierce turbolaser pulses tore holes in the clouds and split the air, and all three cities vanished under acrid mushroom clouds of golden dust and black smoke. Even after the firing stopped, thunder rumbled across the open reaches of Polneye like death drums.

On what had been one of the wide, flat landing pads of Ten South, those who had come out to watch the visitors land were evenly divided between the stunned and the screaming. A man near Plat Mallar went to his knees and vomited. Turning away from the sight, Mallar found a woman clawing madly at her allsuit with such force that she was bleeding profusely from beneath what was left of her nails. The sight galvanized Mallar out of his paralysis, and he began edging his way toward the east edge of the pad.

Then a cry went up, as someone in the gathering saw that the tiny ship that had been circling over Nine South was moving to a new position over Nine North. In a matter of moments, the crowd broke and ran, some for the feeble but comforting shelter of the terminal buildings, some for the open spaces beyond the city, as far from the city as their legs would carry them. Mallar fought free of the sudden stampede, then turned and ran as well.

Twelve students in Mallar's second-form engineering classes had been granted the privilege of learning to maintain and fly the TIE interceptor berthed in 10S Technical Institute's docking bay and equipment garage. The bay was halfway around the terminal hub from where he had stood with the crowd, and though he ran as hard as he could, he didn't expect to be the first of the twelve to arrive.

But he was. The bay doors were standing open, and members of the junior form were hastily clearing away the droids and vehicles blocking the entrance, but the cockpit of the interceptor was still unoccupied.

Mallar did not hesitate. Grabbing a helmet and rebreather from the equipment lockers, he clambered up on the interceptor's right-side wing brace and popped the access hatch release. "You!" he shouted, pointing at the nearest student. "I need a power droid over here, *now*!"

By the time Mallar settled in the cockpit and started the power-up sequence, two other would-be pilots had arrived. With a cool and purposeful efficiency that would have done a carrier deck crew credit, they helped hasten the dull gray power droid into position beside the fighter.

The moment the power coupling clicked in the starting port, Mallar ran up the capacitors for both ion engines, then dropped them back to a neutral idle. There was no point in completing the rest of the system checks. There was no time for repairs, and crashing was no more fearful a prospect than the next attack from beyond the clouds.

"That's got it," Mallar called over the microphone. "Uncouple me, and then clear the bay—I'm flying her out."

Ordinarily, the TIE would have been towed out of the bay and onto the landing pad on her skids by a tug droid. But that would take precious time, and Mallar was already afraid he was far too late. The moment the last of the other students fled out the bay doorway, he shoved the throttle forward.

The interceptor jerked forward as the engine back-blast lifted loose debris and rained it on the fighter's combat-hardened solar panels. Picking up speed rapidly, the ship began to lift just as it passed through the bay doorway, and the upper edge of the left panel dragged against the durasteel frame with a screech that shivered everyone in earshot, including Mallar.

Then, with a bump and a lurch, the ship cleared the bay, bursting out into the bright, diffuse light of a Polneye midday. Pointing the twin booms of the wing-mounted cannon skyward, Mallar threw the interceptor into a full-power climb.

The tiny black ships were still circling high in the

air like carrion birds. Activating his targeting system, Mallar was heartened to see that three more of the settlement's TIE interceptors were in the air. Selecting the nearest target and steering toward it, Mallar then did something no instructor had ever authorized—powered up the four Seinar laser cannon.

With an insistent beeping, the targeting system informed Mallar that it had identified the primary target as a TIE/rc reconnaissance fighter. But to Mallar's surprise, there was no safety interlock preventing him from firing on what the interceptor took to be a friendly target. Moments after the target was identified, the attack computer locked on.

TARGET IN RANGE, said the cockpit display as the indicators changed from red to green.

He squeezed both triggers, and the ship quivered around him as the quad cannon spoke.

No one was more surprised than Mallar when the target stayed in his sights and then exploded in a yellow-white gout of flame. Whether it was the interceptor's superior speed, Mallar's crude headlong rush up from the surface, or simple surprise, the TIE/rc never responded to the approaching ship's presence.

As he blew past the falling debris, Mallar heard voices over the interceptor's combat comm, exulting. But he himself felt neither joy nor relief. He was shaking and covered in clammy sweat, the reckless momentum dissipated, the awful reality sinking in.

The interceptor entered the clouds, and in the next moment Mallar was suddenly blinded by light pouring in through the viewports. The interceptor was shoved roughly sideways as though by a great hand, and shuddered violently in the aftermath. For a long moment he was certain his ship had been hit and he was about to die.

But the moment stretched out, and he did not die. The afterimage of the flash began to fade from his eyes, and his ship, still climbing, emerged intact into the space between the clouds and the stars.

Immediately the targeting system again beeped urgently at him, and Mallar squinted, first to read the display, then to peer out the viewport. What he finally saw nearly overwhelmed him with fear. Riding above him in orbit was the largest ship he had ever seen, a great triangular shape bristling with gun ports and launching fighters from bays on either side.

"Identify."

PRIMARY TARGET: *VICTORY*-CLASS STAR DESTROYER, the computer informed him.

And he was still climbing toward it.

SECONDARY TARGETS:

"I don't want to know," Mallar said nervously. Hauling the interceptor over on its back, he dove away from the starship at a flat angle and all possible speed, seeking the cover of the clouds.

The weapons master of the *Devotion* lay cowering on the bridge catwalk. The ship's primate, whose back-hand blow had sent the master sprawling, loomed over him.

"Your incompetence sacrificed the life of a Yevethan pilot!" the primate bellowed. "How will you repay his family for this dishonor?"

"Sir! I wasn't told that this infestation was capable of resistance—"

"The scout fighter was under your direction. You did not free him to pursue or evade when the vermin fighter appeared. *That* is your offense."

"We were preparing to fire—"

"You are relieved. And there will be a price in blood, I promise. Get out of here. Report to the stockade." The primate turned to the tactics master. "Launch your fighters. I want the skies of Polneye cleared of vermin."

The fight for Polneye did not last long.

One of the three TIE interceptors that followed Mallar into the air was piloted by a first-form student who had never been aloft. That he got the ship off the ground under control was a credit to the simplicity of

Imperial cockpit design. But the first-former's target melted into the clouds while he was still calling for help unlocking the laser cannon. Not long after, a squadron of Yevethan fighters, tracking his comm signal, fell on him from the clouds. His flight ended in a fiery flat spin and an explosion on the plains east of Twelve North.

The interceptor launched from Eleven South was piloted by the engineering instructor. Like Mallar, he climbed through the cloud layer to the edge of space and found the cruiser *Liberty* orbiting above. Unlike Mallar, he did not escape after his discovery. An antifighter turbolaser battery on the cruiser tracked the interceptor and blew it into a thousand pieces, which returned to the surface as a rain of metal.

A veteran combat pilot was at the controls of the interceptor from Nine North, but he barely escaped the destruction of the city, and one of the fighter's engines was damaged by shrapnel. It faltered as he was swept into a dogfight with three Yevethan fighters, and he and his ship vanished in a brilliant ball of flame.

The fourth interceptor was destroyed on the ground by strafing TIE fighters as a frantic volunteer crew tried to ready it for launch.

The fifth was lost in the first moments of the attack, as Eleven North came under *Liberty*'s savage cannonade.

Plat Mallar's success against the TIE/rc was the only victory of the day, and no one was more aware than he how meaningless it was. Because he was afraid to die, he fled to the far side of the planet, hiding in the clouds under the ionization shield the Empire had created for Polneye. Because he was afraid to face the guilt of not dying, he lingered there, circling.

Before long, though, both of those fears paled against the fear that no one would ever know what had happened to his parents and lovers and friends. After reviewing the images captured by his combat recorder, he realized that he had to have more, and turned back.

Approaching the cities of Polneye, Mallar brought the interceptor up above the clouds just long enough to record the three marauding warships, now orbiting together. If his little fighter appeared on their defense screens at all, it was as a momentary blip among the static caused by the inversion.

Then he dipped below the clouds, and found the sky free of fighters. His holocam scanned across the ruins of seven cities, captured seven thin plumes of smoke spaced across the plains. But only seven, for Ten South was still standing, and a giant transport was ground-docked beside it.

The sight brought the first hope to Mallar's heart since Nine South had disappeared under blaster fire. There was a chance for more than mere justice—there was a chance he could bring help in time to matter. Ducking back between the veils, he pushed both the interceptor and his ability to control it to the limit, racing for the receding horizon.

Half an hour later, on the far side of Polneye, a tiny single-seat fighter with a determined young student at the controls flung itself up from the clouds and out toward the stars.

Aboard the flagship *Pride of Yevetha,* Viceroy Nil Spaar personally supervised the extermination of the Kubaz colony—a particularly repulsive variety of vermin, he thought, with faces so hideously mutated that he actively took pleasure in their destruction.

Then, as *Pride* continued on to seize the Imperial factory farm at Pirol-5, the viceroy retired to his quarters to receive the attentions of his *darna* and the reports from the other elements of the fleet.

The news was uniformly good. There had been an unfortunate accident at Polneye that had left a pilot dead and the weapons master a suicide, but that was of no consequence. Everywhere the ships of the Yevetha appeared, the vermin were swept off the faces of the worlds they had soiled.

Calmly, ruthless, efficiently, the Black Fleet drew a

curtain of death across the Cluster. One after another the vermin settlements fell beneath it—the Kubaz, the Brigia, the Polneye, the Morath, the Corasgh, the H'kig. The targets included colonies and species whose names and histories were unknown to those who plotted their eradication.

Full sterilizations were carried out on the two worlds to be reclaimed for the Yevetha. The colonists meant for those planets were already outbound from The Twelve in the new thrustships, which were faster than light itself. Others would soon follow.

It was the realization of a great destiny. At the end of one long day of glory, the All again belonged to the Yevetha alone.

When the last report was in hand, Nil Spaar called his broodmates to join him and his *darna* in celebration.

Afterward, the viceroy slept long, deep, and well.

Leia Organa Solo waited hopefully, eagerly, behind the gate for the Fleet shuttle to land at Eastport 18. The moment the shuttle's engines were cut, she brushed past the gate supervisor's earnest cautions and ran out onto the landing pad. When the hatch hissed open and the boarding stairs unfolded, she was already waiting at the bottom.

Han was the first to appear on the top step, wearing his lopsided grin and carrying his flight bag over one shoulder. Taking the stairs in three long strides, he tossed the flight bag down and gathered Leia up in a hug so deep and warm that it almost began to drive away the icy chill that had invaded her spirit since the collapse of the Yevethan negotiations and her humiliation by Peramis and Nil Spaar. She hid her tears against his chest.

"It's gonna be all right," Han murmured into her hair. "You should hear about some of the bad days *I've* had."

Leia laughed despite herself and hugged him fiercely. "Let's go home."

"Can't think of one good reason not to," Han said, bending to pluck his flight bag from the ground. "Don't make too much of it, hon, but I kinda missed you."

Twenty-three hours out from Polneye, Plat Mallar turned on the cockpit recorder of the TIE interceptor. His face was pale and slick with perspiration. His voice was weak, and his eyes wandered as he tried to force his blurred vision to clear.

Designed without hyperdrive, the interceptor had never been intended for the kind of journey Mallar had attempted—across realspace from one star to another. He had fled Polneye, eluded the Yevetha, and left Koornacht Cluster behind, but he could not escape the cold equations of time, energy, and distance.

Mallar had run the fighter wide open for as long as the solar panels and the capacitors had allowed, accelerating the little ship to a straight-line speed well above that any pilot could use in combat. He had even persuaded the autopilot, designed for simple in-system navigation problems, to accept Galantos as a destination.

But the engines had been cold for hours now, and only emptiness surrounded his hurtling craft. The nose of the fighter was pointed directly at Galantos, but it would not reach that system for—he calculated—nearly three years. And Mallar did not expect to live another three hours.

The ship's small oxygen reserve was gone. His rebreather could no longer cleanse the breaths he drew well enough to end the agonizing headaches. The recirculators were keeping the air dry, but he was slowly suffocating on his own waste gases.

Memory had deceived him. The images from his childhood, of Polneye as a bustling port, as the hub of the region's spacelanes, were too strong to be shaken by facts. Those images offered what had proved a false promise—that he would find another ship to offer help or transport.

Dirtbound his whole life, he found it was beyond him to imagine how empty space was, or to believe how deserted that region had become. In twenty-three hours, not a single vessel of any size had been detected by the interceptor's targeting system. He knew he was going to die, and he was going to die alone.

He cleared his throat, an uglier sound than his rasping breaths. "My name is Plat Mallar," he said. "I was born in the city of Three North, on the planet Polneye. My mother was Fall Topas. She was a plant biologist, and quite beautiful. My father was Plat Hovath, a droid mechanic. I was their only son. We lived in Ten South, on blue level, near the algae pool.

"Yesterday was the fortieth day of Mofat. Yesterday warships attacked Polneye without any warning—without any cause. Unidentified ships. Imperial designs. They destroyed most of Polneye—killed my parents—killed most of us. I think the survivors are hostages now—there was a transport—"

He paused, heart pounding, to try to catch his breath. His voice had become frail and wheezy.

When he could continue, Mallar said, "The combat recorders of my ship contain evidence of this attack—of the destruction of my home. They *murdered* my people, thousands and thousands and thousands. Please help us. Please—if any are still alive—try to save them. Whoever sees this—you must find these monsters and punish them. It's wrong. It's terribly wrong. I beg—I beg for justice for the dead. For my parents. For my friends. For me."

Mallar sagged back into his seat, exhausted by the effort of speaking. But the recorder kept running—he could not manage to raise an arm to stop it. It kept on, faithfully capturing Mallar's image, for as long as he moved or made a sound at turns.

But it stopped when at last he slipped into unconsciousness.

He was still unconscious, barely clinging to life, when the crew of the Fifth Fleet prowler *5P8* stumbled on his hurtling ship.

Chapter 15

◆

The first early-morning rays from Coruscant's sun were throwing long shadows down the east-west streets of Imperial City when Admiral Ackbar reached the family entrance to the presidential residence.

"Good morning," said the security droid. "This entrance is closed. The family is not receiving visitors at this time. Please come back anther time, or call the scheduling center for further information."

Ackbar cocked his head and blinked in surprise. "I am Admiral Ackbar."

"Good morning, Admiral Ackbar. This entrance is closed. Please move back to the sidewalk."

"It's all right," Ackbar said. "I have a key." He squeezed his eyes shut while he concentrated. "*Aleph—lamed—zayin—shin*. Yes, I think that's it."

"Good morning, Admiral Ackbar," the droid said. "You may enter."

The grounds were quiet, except for the tiny cowlpups grazing on the lawns. When Ackbar passed too close to one, it growled at him with a ferociousness all out of proportion to its size.

"Go back to your breakfast," Ackbar said, amused. "I'm not here for you."

None of the early rays reached the well-shaded

main house, and there were no lights on inside, except in the kitchen, where a butler droid was completing its nightly maintenance. There was no sound from the direction of the children's rooms, which was a relief—he was not ready to deal with their eager energy. Ackbar supposed that, with Han's return, the whole family had been up late.

Sleep in as long as you like, children, he thought with a melancholy tenderness. *Sleep in while you can.*

Ackbar followed memory and the floorboard glow strips through the darkened halls to Leia and Han's bedroom. Out of consideration for the children, the door was closed but not secured. He hoped his friends were not busy mating.

"Open," Ackbar told the housecomm. "Lights."

When the bedroom was suddenly flooded with light, Han reflexively spun over on his back and sat bolt upright. Squinting, he sighed away the rush of adrenaline when he recognized Ackbar. "You," Han said gruffly. "It's a lucky thing for you I don't sleep with a blaster anymore."

"Not luck," the Calamari said. "You told me, after the time you and Jaina scared each other half to death."

Han's sudden movements had shaken the bed enough to bring Leia up from her deeper sleep. Now she rose on her elbows.

"Admiral Ackbar," she said, a quizzical expression on her face. "When I invited you to come talk me out of resigning, I thought you might at least wait until I was awake."

"Good morning, Princess."

"Don't try to disarm me with politeness," Leia said. "What are you doing here at this hour?"

"Getting you out of bed," Ackbar said. "I'll wait outside while you get dressed."

"Oh, you will? Then what?"

"Then there's somewhere we have to go. I have a speeder waiting."

"Slow down a second. I'm not on call," said Leia. "Not for state business. Especially not at this hour—what time is it, anyway?" She glanced sideways at the bedroom chrono. "Oh, heaven—I'm sorry I looked."

"I understand how you feel," said Ackbar. "I would rather have stayed in the water myself. Still, there's somewhere we have to go."

"Why don't you tell me a little more and let *me* make that decision?"

"I'm afraid I can't do that," said Ackbar, holding out her robe. "Your head isn't clear yet. You'll have to trust me—if you *do* trust me."

Leia frowned as she studied him. Finally she sat up and took the robe from his hand.

"Thank you, Princess." His gaze moved to Han. "General Solo, I think you should come, too."

"What is this, divide and conquer?"

"Please. This involves you as well."

"Let me find my pants," Han said resignedly. "Leia, tell me again why we gave the fishhead a key to the front door—"

Leia peered through the viewpane of the Fleet infirmary's Intensive Care Unit Number 5 at the pale-faced young man who had just been transferred from a medical cocoon to the bacta tank. A Fleet doctor and two MD-7 medical droids hovered over the biomonitors.

"Who is he?"

"He is Grannan by stock, Polneye by allegiance," Ackbar said. "His name is Plat Mallar. He's suffering from severe metabolic disruption due to breathing his own wastes. He may not live. I thought you should see him now, just in case."

"Why?" asked Leia. "I'm sorry for him, of course, but . . ." She left the sentence unfinished.

"Polneye? I never heard of it," Han said. "What happened to him?"

"According to the prowler that found him, he was

trying to make an interstellar run in a TIE interceptor—"

"Why would anyone do a fool thing like that?"
Han asked dismissively. "It's suicide."

"Or self-sacrifice," said Ackbar. "Sometimes they
are hard to tell apart."

"What are you talking about?"

"It appears that Plat Mallar was trying to get a
message out of Koornacht Cluster—apparently the
only way he could."

Leia's eyes flashed. "What message?"

"I will show you," Ackbar said. "But let us stay
here awhile longer. I do not know why it is, but the
Fleet casualty officer tells me that patients with family
and friends to wish them health are strengthened by it.
And I am afraid this young pilot needs every edge right
now."

In the privacy of Admiral Ackbar's offices at Fleet
Headquarters, in grim silence, Han and Leia watched
the holorecordings taken from Plat Mallar's TIE interceptor.

It was unsettling to see the familiar, forbidding
shapes of warships once again at the business of dealing out destruction, and profoundly dismaying to see
the cities of Polneye reduced to smoking scorch marks
on the planet's barren plains. But Mallar's deathly ill
face gave the greatest power to his words.

"—Please help us. Please—if any are still alive—
try to save them. Whoever sees this—you must find
these monsters and punish them. It's wrong. It's terribly wrong. I beg—I beg for justice for the dead. For
my parents. For my friends. For me."

When it was over, Leia pushed back from the table without a word, turning her back on Han and the
admiral. Hugging herself, she stood before the galactic
holomap that covered nearly one whole wall of
Ackbar's office, staring up into it with haunted eyes.

"Did you orchestrate all this to humiliate me,
Ackbar?" she said finally, still facing the map.

"No, Leia," Ackbar protested, surprised. "I do not understand."

"That makes two of us," Han said, standing. "What are you talking about, hon? This doesn't have anything to do with you."

She whirled around to face them. "Doesn't it? Look at him—he's just sitting there waiting for me to draw the same conclusion he has. If you wanted to convince me to resign, Admiral, you couldn't have picked any better way."

"I'm missing something here," Han said, looking to Ackbar for help.

"Princess, you are wrong," said Ackbar. "You could not be more wrong. You are the Chief of State of the New Republic. I would not have anyone else sit in that chair. We need your strength and dedication—and more now than we did yesterday, to answer this challenge."

Ackbar's praise deflected off Leia's defensiveness, leaving her untouched. "Whose ships were those?" she asked, pointing at the monitor.

"You know as well as I."

"Imperial design. Imperial fighters. What does that prove?"

"Plat Mallar got close enough to the first ship to interrogate it with his targeting system. It answered as the Imperial Star Destroyer *Valorous*."

"Are you arguing with me?"

"*Valorous* was one of the Black Sword ships on Nylykerka's list."

"I know that," she said. "And if it was at Polneye under Yevethan command, then you're looking at the biggest fool in the whole Republic. But we don't know that, do we?"

"Does it matter?"

"Isn't that why you brought me in here? Your subtle way of telling me I was wrong?"

Ackbar shook his head slowly. "I thought that before you made your decision about giving up your work, you needed to know that there's still more for us to do. Whoever sent those ships to Polneye is the enemy of the peace you've tried so hard to build."

"Isn't there something in the apocrypha about wisdom beginning with knowing your limitations? Peace was a goal, not a guarantee. Besides—I was naive. Which would make a fine summation of my short career," she added acerbically.

"Admiral Ackbar's right," Han said, shaking his head. "All this other stuff—who burned the toast, who borrowed whose shirt, who left the light on—none of that matters. What matters is, what are we going to do now?"

"What *can* I do?" Leia asked plaintively. "Nothing. Polneye wasn't a member of the New Republic. They weren't even applicants."

"You're talking about obligations," said Han. "I'm talking about the right thing to do."

"But that's the trick, isn't it? You can't get three people to agree on the right thing to do," Leia said. "Peace is impossible. No matter what, it seems like there's always someone who wants to kill someone else. You can't give them enough reasons not to. At least, I can't."

"Leia—"

"I'm sorry about the Polneye, I truly am. But it's too late to help them. Besides, if I were to send forces anywhere near Koornacht, I wouldn't have to resign— the Senate would hang me first and impeach me later." Leia shook her head. "I hope Mallar lives—though I'm not sure that's not being cruel, if it turns out he's the only survivor. Who else knows about him? Who else has seen the recording?"

"A very short list," Ackbar said.

"See that it stays that way," she said, and moved toward the door. "I'm going home, Han. Are you coming?"

Han was looking at her as though she were a stranger. "I think I'll stay awhile," he said.

Leia shrugged. "Suit yourself."

As soon as the door closed behind her, Han

cocked his head to one side and shot Ackbar a quizzical look. "I have just one question—who was that person, and what have you done with Leia?"

"She is hurting," said Ackbar. "She is questioning herself, and her ideals."

"Tell me something I don't know," Han said. "What in the world *happened* while I was away?"

"I will tell you what I can," said Ackbar. "But I am afraid some of the answers will have to come from her."

A stranger was sitting cross-legged in the street outside the family entrance, facing the house, when Leia reached it in a borrowed Fleet skimmer. He was dressed in a long robe the color of saffron, which spilled out around him in a circle on the pavement. She recognized neither his profile nor his species, and slowed only so that she could hop the fence at a speed that wouldn't alarm the house defenses.

But after she had disembarked and sent the speeder heading back, curiosity got the better of her. She walked out to the fence and, with the security droid hovering protectively nearby, called out to him.

"You—who are you?"

"Jobath, the councillor of the Fia, of Galantos," he said, and then his face brightened. "But I know you. You are Princess Leia, the warrior queen who rallied the oppressed to rise up against the Emperor. You saved my people from slavery."

"Well—you're welcome. But that was a long time ago," she said. "And I don't know whose version of history you've been listening to, anyway. I don't remember ever being a queen or a warrior."

"Oh, yes, I know all the stories. You are a great woman. It is an honor to meet you."

"What are you doing out there?"

"I am waiting for you," the Fian said. "Your metal servant said that you were not receiving visitors, but my need is urgent. And now I see you have returned. May I rise and approach without alarming your loyal protector?"

"What? Oh, the droid. No, he doesn't like people loitering around the entrances. What was your name again?"

"Jobath, of the Fia."

"Did we have an appointment, Jobath of the Fia?"

"No, Princess."

"All right. I was afraid for a moment I'd forgotten," she said. "Here's the way it is, Jobath of the Fia—I intend to go inside and sleep for about three days. If I'm still president when I get up, you can make an appointment with the scheduling center, in the protocol office." She turned away from the fence and started toward the house.

"Princess! Please, wait! I've come about what's happening in The Multitude. You must talk to me now!"

"Must I?" said Leia, looking back. "The Multitude—what's that?"

"The Great Multitude of the Circle of the Heavens," Jobath said earnestly. "There is another name, an ugly name—"

"Are you talking about Koornacht?"

"Yes!" Jobath said brightly. "Koornacht."

Leia scowled. "This is too much. You tell Ackbar that I'm tired of being manipulated."

"Admiral Ackbar?"

"Right. Tell him he can have this job anytime he wants it. All he has to do is say the word."

"Oh, yes, Ackbar, I know this name, too. He, too, was a great warrior in the Rebellion. But you are mistaken. I have not had the honor of the counsel of the Ackbar," said Jobath.

"No?"

"I have come here directly from your Eastport, and before that from Galantos, to speak with you in a matter of great urgency. A terrible evil prowls The Multitude. Many have died already. My people fear for their future."

As he was speaking, Leia was slowly drawn back to the fence. She curled her fingers around the wrought work and closed them into fists. "How do you know what's happened?"

"There was a warning sent to us from a ship which came out of The Multitude," said Jobath. "A freighter bound for Woqua intercepted the beam of this signal, or we would not have heard the warning for a very long time—if ever. We sent our own vessel out to find this ship. It, too, found the signal, but the ship itself has vanished."

Leia realized that Plat Mallar, facing unconsciousness, must have used the interceptor's combat comm to transmit his recordings toward his destination. Doing so would make him, and even his ship, expendable, since no force in the galaxy could gather up or destroy his comm signal.

"We have the ship," she said, resting her forehead against the fence. "And the pilot."

"I am glad to know this. I would like to offer him refuge on Galantos, and, if he wishes it, citizenship in the Fia."

"That will have to wait, I'm afraid," said Leia. "What do you want from me?"

"I've come to ask the protection of the New Republic and the great Princess Leia for my planet and my people," said Jobath, clasping the fence with long-fingered hands just below where Leia clung to it. "I beseech you to accept a petition for membership, and fortify us against these murderers."

Leia pulled her hands back as though fearing contact with Jobath. "I'll consider your petition," she said uncomfortably, and started to back away.

"Please hurry," said Jobath. "There is little time. If they who fell on Polneye choose to leave The Multitude, we could be the next to suffer their predation. Our entire navy has only two patrol corvettes, and the cutter which brought me here. Half a million lives are at risk on Galantos alone."

"I understand that," Leia said. "Go to the diplomatic hostel. They'll provide you with quarters. I'll send word to you there."

Then she turned and fled into the house. But the walls did not offer the same sanctuary they had recently promised, and sleep was no longer possible.

Within an hour of Jobath's arrival at the diplomatic hostel, three other worlds with legations quartered there submitted emergency petitions for membership. Two of the three were located in sectors far from Koornacht, the third in Hatawa, but still many light-years from the trouble.

All three, along with the Fia, received only silence in reply.

For the moment there was silence, too, on the newsgrids. So far the Polneye tragedy had escaped their attention. Coruscant Global Newsgrid was still dissecting the fallout from the explosive Senate session earlier in the week.

But in its midday refresh, Global added a new item to the feature queue—a speculative report that Princess Leia had already resigned as president. According to the rumor (treated as fact), an announcement would be made as soon as the top military leaders and the Senate agreed on a replacement.

Sitting in his Fleet office, Admiral Ackbar viewed that news with mixed contempt and bemusement. Even if Leia had resigned, the idea that the Fleet would have any part in selecting a new Chief of State was absurd. The idea that any such negotiations would take place without him was equally absurd.

But Ackbar pondered long and hard whether he should pick up his comlink and start a rumor of his own. "We ought to get out in front this time," he said aloud to himself. "Put Plat Mallar's face and story on the grids. Show everyone what happened on Polneye, and bring them over to Leia's side. That's what I would do. If she could just bring herself to admit that the viceroy never was a friend—"

He shook his head. It wasn't time yet. He would

watch the news from Farlax, where the Fifth Fleet's
prowlers were now all on station outside Koornacht
Cluster, sweeping hyperspace with their sensitive ripple
filters, and the news from the Senate and administrative complex, where every analyst and commentator in
Imperial City was on duty, sifting the corridor gossip
with their hypersensitive news antennae. And he would
wait to see which situation changed first.

Absurd or not, the Global report on Leia's resignation ran through the diplomatic hostel like a virulent
infection. It puzzled many, and worried Jobath, who
began to fear he had brought his appeal to the wrong
ears. That fear carried him, in the company of the sen-
eschal of the Marais, to the office of Chairman Behn-
kihl-nahm.

Half an hour later they left the office reassured
that Leia still held executive power for the New Republic and that their petitions were being acted on
with all possible dispatch. The moment they were
gone, Behn-kihl-nahm tried one more time to reach
Princess Leia. But he had no more success than with
any of his many previous attempts that morning.

Behn-kihl-nahm was fast losing patience with
her—Leia had closed everyone out at exactly the worst
time, when they should be planning their strategy and
response together. He disliked having to make tactical
decisions unilaterally.

Would Leia approve of his tying the withdrawals
of the Walalla and the others up in procedural knots,
as he had successfully done that morning? Or would
she have preferred he simply let them go? Should he
offer Peramis and Hodidiji the appointment to negotiate the return of the bodies? He thought it might give
both a way to justify a change of heart, but would they
conduct themselves with dignity, or simply become an
embarrassment?

Even more than making decisions, Behn-kihl-
nahm disliked being caught out uninformed. The business with the Polneye, the pilot in the hospital—why

should he have had to hear about that from a couple of ambassadors-without-portfolio? How had one of them been able to meet with Leia while his calls were still going begging? *Was* she going to resign? If not, what was she going to do about the petitions for protection?

When his usual sources were unable to satisfy his curiosity, Behn-kihl-nahm called Hiram Drayson. The machinery of governance was frozen, paralyzed in the face of crises that would only grow worse if not attended to. Did Drayson know what had gotten stuck in its gears?

"I couldn't say, Chairman," Drayson said.

"You can't say, or you don't know?"

"Chairman, my suggestion to you would be to put up the best pretense you can that everything's under control. And that includes letting whoever wants to huff and puff in the well of the Senate do so to his or her heart's content."

"Admiral," said Behn-kihl-nahm gravely, "that advice worries me more than any other development of the last week."

"Admiral Ackbar."

The man in the doorway wore casual civilian clothing, but he still had the posture of a soldier in uniform. "Mr. Drayson. Come in."

"I'm not here to visit this time. Can you get me in to see Leia?"

"I'm afraid I cannot," said Ackbar. "My key was deactivated this morning."

"I have to talk to her," Drayson said simply. "Do you have any suggestions?"

Ackbar grunted. "I'm a little surprised to learn that the Old Ghost of Coruscant has no secret passages or secret passwords available to him."

"Getting in isn't the problem," said Drayson. "Getting listened to is. I'm afraid that none of the means at my disposal would be likely to earn me a reasoned hearing."

"There are many people who want to talk to her," said Ackbar. "She does not seem to want to talk to us."

"I'm afraid I can't permit her the luxury of refusing," said Drayson.

"She is tired of being pushed and poked at," said Ackbar. "If we give her some time—"

Drayson shook his head so slightly it was almost imperceptible. "There's no more time," he said.

Blinking slowly, Ackbar sat back in his chair. "Do you know her husband?"

"Not professionally," Drayson said. "But his loyalty to her is well known."

Ackbar nodded thoughtfully. "He was here with me for three hours today," he said. "He was the one who ordered the prowlers to Koornacht—not General A'baht."

"Interesting."

"There is more. He brought the Fifth Fleet back, as she ordered—but only as far as the outer marshaling point, and he kept it at combat readiness, with full crews aboard. He understands the stakes. He may be more sympathetic than you expect. But I cannot promise that she will even listen to him."

"Thank you, Admiral," said Drayson. "That's useful. If you'll excuse me—"

"Admiral—"

"Yes?"

"I was wondering—could the viceroy have done this to Leia? All those hours he spent alone with her—we know so little about the Yevetha," said Ackbar. "Is it possible that something happened in that room? Is it possible that he has done something to her mind?"

"No," said Drayson. "No, I can tell you that nothing happened in that room."

The answer did not seem to please Ackbar. "Thank you," he said all the same.

*　　*　　*

The sounds of splashing and gleeful childish laughter covered any sounds of footsteps on the walk. But Leia, with her wariness magnified by powerful feelings of isolation, was aware of Admiral Drayson's approach before he had even emerged from the trees.

Jaina, in turn, quickly sensed her mother's dark mood. "Mommy, who's that? Do you want me to make him go away?"

"No—no," Leia said with a quick smile, and tousled her daughter's wet, stringy hair. "Jacen, Jaina, take Anakin inside. I want you all dry and dressed when I come in."

For once the children obeyed without argument. Leia thought it a telling sign that the stress and chaos of the last weeks, of the last few days, was affecting them as well.

Drayson stopped a polite distance away, hands laced together behind his back. "Princess."

"You know, if security is supposed to keep unwanted people out, the security around the president's residence leaves a great deal to be desired."

"Your husband admitted me, Princess Leia."

"Did he," she said. "Well, my husband leaves a bit to be desired himself lately. What do you want?"

"Five minutes," said Drayson. He brought his right hand forward and showed her the datacard he had cradled in the palm. "I think this will be useful to you in regard to the decision you're facing."

"Which one is that?"

"The only one that matters."

"Five minutes?"

"And then I'll be gone."

"All right," she said with a sigh. "Five minutes."

The datacard contained a brief recording, timestamped less than two hours earlier. The recording showed a pair of Yevethan thrustships unloading on a hilly, brush-covered landscape. The kind and volume of material being unloaded and the shape and size of the clearing being made for it dictated one conclusion—it was the first phase of a colonization landing.

"Where is this?"

"The astrographic office knows it as Doornik-319," Drayson said. "It's part of a system inside the Koornacht Cluster. The Kubaz who lived there till yesterday called it Morning's Bell."

"What happened yesterday?"

"The same thing that happened to Polneye," said Drayson. "And it doesn't stop there. The evidence I've seen suggests that every non-Yevethan settlement in Koornacht received the same sort of treatment."

"What evidence? Where did you get this recording?"

"I'd rather you not ask me that, Princess."

"I *am* asking you."

Drayson nodded. "Princess, is it absolutely necessary that you know the source for you to credit the evidence? If so, then I'll answer. But if you don't need that knowledge to accept what that recording means, then I'd rather not risk those assets any more than I already have by revealing what they've discovered. The information is what matters."

Leia stared at him.

"I think my five minutes are up," he said, with a little bow. "Thank you for seeing me."

"Stop!" she said sharply. "Who *are* you, really?"

Drayson turned and looked back at her. "I do what I do under the authority of an executive order issued by Mon Mothma," he said. "You'll find it in your personal library files as D9020616."

"Mon Mothma! She never said a word about this—"

"She found the machinery of the New Republic unwieldy when it came to certain aspects of statecraft—getting information into the right hands, projecting policy into ambiguous situations. I try to address those shortcomings."

"Who do you answer to?"

"The same as you do, Princess—the same as anyone at our level does," Drayson said. "I answer to my conscience and my sense of duty. And yes, if either ever fails us, we can do a great deal of harm—and probably hide most of it, too. But that's all there is, isn't it? Conscience or obedience. Leader or follower. Whose orders do you obey?" He pointed at the datacard. "Who will tell you what to do about that? You see? Conscience and duty." He bowed again. "Good evening, Princess."

She let him go.

Turning back to her datapad, Leia watched the recording a second time and then a third. The images were sharp and unambiguous. The design of the ships was distinctive and incriminating. Yevethan colonists were setting up housekeeping on a world which one day earlier had belonged to the Kubaz.

Leia dug her comlink out of the drawer where she had thrown it the night before and selected a familiar channel. "Han," she said. "You can stop hiding from me now. Where are you? Please—come talk to me."

"Murderers," Han muttered as he watched the recording from Doornik-319. He shook his head disbelievingly. "I've been around enough to see some cold moves pulled, but killing a family one day and moving into their house the next is right up there with anything our old buddy Palpatine ever thought up."

Leia nodded. "I'm beginning to wonder if the greatest indignity that the Empire subjected the Yevetha to wasn't holding them to a higher standard of behavior," she said.

"Now, that's a picture, isn't it? The Emperor's stormtroopers setting the example for good manners," Han said. "Like arming protocol droids with blasters."

He tried to win a smile from her, but she had looked away to gaze at the map of Koornacht Cluster displayed on the main screen, and he turned his attention there as well. "Look at what they've done—it makes no sense at all," he said. "It's not like any of these settlements were crowding the League worlds. Or that real estate is getting scarce in there."

"I'm afraid it makes perfect sense," said Leia, propping her chin on folded hands. "So much of what he said sounds different to me now—almost as though he lied to me with the truth. 'What we want more than anything is to be left alone.' I remember that clearly, from the first time we met. He mentioned how strange it was to see so many different species. He told me the Yevetha didn't need our protection."

"No," said Han. "It was the Kubaz who needed protection."

"He as much as told me that, too," said Leia. "He said it was his mission to protect his people—and he did. He kept them inside that ship, safely away from us. He controlled his own exposure to us—as though he were afraid of contamination. That's why those settlements were destroyed, Han. This wasn't a boundary war, or a matter of competing territorial claims. It was an act of revulsion."

Han looked dubious. "Maybe so. But there's something else, too. Look at the results. Doornik-319 sits nearly on a line between Coruscant and N'zoth, just where you'd want a forward base. These other targets—it's like they burned a firebreak between themselves and all of us."

She reached out and touched the point of light that was Doornik-319. "Or dug a moat. Complete with gate and drawbridge, maybe."

"Yeah," said Han. "So what are you going to do?"

Withdrawing her finger, Leia shook her head slowly. "It seems as though it's already all over. All I can see to do now is try to make sure Nil Spaar stays on his side of the moat. Protect the settlements that haven't been torched—Galatos, Wehttam, The Marais." She looked up at Han. "I'm going to have to send the Fifth Fleet back to Farlax."

"I thought that might happen," Han said. "I left the Fleet at readiness high—no shore leaves, no major maintenance. They should be able to sail on a half hour's notice."

She touched his hand. "I'm sorry. I know you don't want this."

"Hold on just a moment," Han said, pulling back from her. "I'm not going anywhere."

"I can't change commanders on them again, not twice in a week, not under these circumstances. You've been out there with them for two months now. That gives some continuity, at least."

"Right idea, wrong man," said Han. "If it were me, the first thing I'd do is hand the Fifth back to General A'baht."

"How can I do that? He was disloyal to me."

"Was he? He disobeyed your orders, but is that the same thing as being disloyal? Did he do what he did for personal gain? Did he do it to enhance his career, or aid the enemy? No. He was trying to protect all those people out there with him, and all the people back here, too. And hell, Leia—he was right. He ought to get some points for that."

"You said it yourself," she said stiffly. "He disobeyed my orders."

"He disobeyed an order you never should have given," Han said. "And if that's your reason, you're going to have to disqualify me, too. That prowler that picked up Plat Mallar—what do you think it was doing out there?"

She realized she had never asked herself that question. "I guess I assumed it was Admiral Drayson's handiwork."

"You weren't paying close enough attention," Han said. "That's a Fifth Fleet prowler. I sent it there."

"You?" Leia said, and her eyes flashed anger. "I don't understand. Is it because I'm a woman? Is that why lately everyone seems to treat my orders like suggestions?"

"Aw—blast, no, Leia. I keep telling you the uniform doesn't fit me very well," he said. "I'm just as bad at following orders from men. I always have been—you know that. Look, I was there. You weren't. I did it on a hunch."

"How do you explain General A'baht?"

"Why don't you ask him?" Han parried. "But remember this—before he came to Coruscant, General A'baht was the senior military commander of the Dornea. He was accustomed to a greater degree of autonomy than we grant our Fleet commanders. He answered to his own conscience. I happen to think he was tremendously loyal to you—not least in the way he accepted his demotion. You could do a lot worse than to ask him to come back."

"How can I? I humiliated him in front of his crew, his command."

"If you think what you did changed how they felt about him, you've forgotten the rules of the game," Han said. "What you did changed how they felt about *you*. Give them back their commander. They won't have anything worse to say about you than they're already saying. You might even win back a couple of points."

"What should I say?"

"You don't have to say anything, not to them. Send the Fifth Fleet back to Farlax under General A'baht's command, and they'll get the message," Han said. "Leia, only weak leaders never admit to mistakes. Strong leaders don't need to pretend to be infallible. Just fix this. There are bigger problems to chew on."

She glanced up at the map of Koornacht, then studied the backs of her hands. "I have Bail Organa's stubborn pride," she said quietly. "It's hard for me to admit when someone else was more right than I was."

"If you weren't headstrong, you wouldn't be my Leia," Han said with a crooked, affectionate grin. "You're staying on, then? No resignation."

"I can't leave this mess for someone else," Leia said. "I'm going to have to take the responsibility for it. Nil Spaar wouldn't have done this if he hadn't been sure that we would let him. That I would let him."

"You're not responsible for his miscalculation."

"What do you mean?"

"We're not going to let him."

"Oh," Leia said. "Do you know where General A'baht is?"

"He came back with me in the skiff. He's probably over in the Fleet dormitories, expecting to be court-martialed. The Fleet Office will know."

"I'd better go see him," she said, gathering her feet under her. "I'll call on the way over."

"You're doing the right thing," Han said. "I'll hang out with the kids till you get back."

"Thanks." She kissed him quickly and started to leave, then stopped and turned back. "Han—"

"What?"

"How could I have been so wrong about Nil Spaar? How could I have sat there for so long, being lied to with smiles, and never have known? I'm a Jedi—I'm supposed to be more perceptive than that."

"You don't lean on that talent very hard," he said. "From what I can see, you don't really want to."

"I guess there's some truth in that," she admitted. "Still, I can't stop thinking I should have known what he was."

"I think maybe you saw what you wanted to see," Han said gently. "You still believe in the basic goodness and rationality of the people you meet. Not everyone has that handicap."

Though he likely could have had for the asking one of the suites held for senior officers and guests, General A'baht was billeted in a double in one of the enlisted dormitories. And though he had more than enough right to have it closed, the door to his room was standing open, respecting a tradition that redrew the boundaries of privacy from the first day of training.

A'baht himself was prone on the floor, turned half away from the door, going through a strenuous series of body lifts without so much as a grunt.

"General," Leia said. "May I come in?"

The Dornean officer came to his feet smoothly

and saluted smartly. "Princess," he said. "I am—surprised—to see you."

Leia closed the door behind her. "I think we need to talk. I received your apology, and offer to resign, on the way over here—"

"Princess, I hope you understand that I am not bargaining to escape the consequences of my actions," A'baht said. "I'm willing to stand for court-martial, or resign, or accept demotion to whatever grade you deem fit—whatever you think would be best for the Fleet and the Republic. I do not want to be the cause of any further embarrassment for you, or the Fleet, or Chandrila."

Leia pulled a straight-backed chair out from under the small desk and sat down. "You know, General, I've been thinking a lot about resigning myself. I've made several—mistakes—lately that I've had trouble accepting.

"A little while ago, after talking things over with my best friend in the world, I decided that the hardest thing for me to do would be to stay where I am—and so that was what I was going to do. And it's going to be hard enough that I think I'd better have your help. Your offer to resign is rejected."

"I understand, Princess. If I may—has a date been selected for my trial?"

"Trial?" She shook her head. "You don't have time for a trial, General. You and I both still have work to do."

"Sir?"

She sighed. "General—I was wrong. I can't put it any more plainly. Will you accept *my* apology, and return to the *Intrepid* as commander of the Fifth Fleet?"

Surprise sat uncomfortably on the Dornean's features. "Princess, can I possibly have your confidence after what's happened?"

"What happened shouldn't have happened. But the blame is mine, not yours," Leia said. "Your conduct—and your judgment—were both faultless. You will have my confidence for as long as your service to the New Republic remains on such a high plane."

A'baht was visibly embarrassed. "Then—Princess, I thank you for your apology, which you did not owe me. And I am at your disposal, to serve in whatever capacity you feel I can be useful."

"Good," she said, standing and gesturing at their surroundings. "Because you really don't belong here. Can I give you a ride to Eastport, General?"

The loyalty of small men can be bought cheaply, because greed has no pride.

Within minutes of General Etahn A'baht's return to the Fifth Fleet, the armada jumped into hyperspace, heading for Farlax and Koornacht Cluster. Within minutes of that event, Belezaboth Ourn, extraordinary consul of the Paqwepori, had reported it to Viceroy Nil Spaar by hyperspace comm.

"I don't know what orders the general has been given, of course," Ourn said. "But the princess herself was seen delivering him to his shuttle, and the entire fleet is gone, as quickly as it returned, and with as little explanation."

"Thank you, Consul," Nil Spaar said gravely. "Your assistance will not be forgotten by the Yevetha. I urge you to be on guard for more lies from the princess and those who serve her."

"Oh, we will watch her, we will watch her," said Ourn. "Viceroy—a small question."

"Of course."

"When can we expect delivery of the thrustship you promised, in payment for the damage to *Mother's Valkyrie* which we agreed to allow? Should I decide to leave Coruscant, my only options are to charter a vessel, at considerable expense, or take a commercial flight, at considerable inconvenience."

Nil Spaar smiled ingratiatingly. "Soon, Consul, soon. The newest vessel from our best shipyard is being altered to your specifications as we speak. Have patience. You will not be disappointed."

*   *   *

In an empty room of a deserted lodge on the grounds of the diplomatic hostel in Imperial City, a hypercomm repeater answered a coded call from light-years away.

The repeater in turn activated a delicate and elegant transmitter, which bounced a curious signal into the heart of a bland-faced building filled with the machinery of the New Republic government's official information net.

Moments later, second-shift supervisor Turat Il Feen sat in open-mouthed amazement at his master controller station as the Channel 1 homeworld notification system awakened of its own accord.

Only three offices could originate the rare Channel 1 dispatches—the Ruling Council, the President, and the Fleet High Command. But the background blue screen that appeared on Channel 1 carried none of their identifying insignia. All that appeared were the words TRANSMISSION BEGINS IN:, followed by a counter.

Even so, Channel 1 went active. The tickle went out, alerting the net that a priority message was imminent. Almost immediately, hypercomm receivers on every homeworld and in every administrative center began to respond, signaling their readiness.

"We're being hacked," Turat raged at his technicians. "Find out where the signal is getting in. If we can't lock it out, I want to take the system down."

But there was little they could do. "Not enough time," a technician muttered. "C-Ones are supposed to get out no matter what. That's the way we built the system."

At Turat's station, the acknowledgment counter had climbed to ninety-five percent. "Do something," he pleaded. "If we let a pirate broadcast out on C-One, we'll all be lucky to get jobs as grid installers."

But they had run out of time. The counter reached 00:00 and stopped. The blue background began to fade.

Turat looked at the acknowledgment counter and thought about the audience it represented—not only the countless thousands of receivers and recorders, but the officials charged with attending them. Cabinet ministers and diplomatic liaisons, senior advisers and planetary rulers, roused from sleep, called away from other duties, torn away from their private business to gather in front of monitors on every planet from Bespin to Byss.

Turat Il Feen could not sit quietly with that audience and watch his career ending. As the broadcast began, he stood up from his station, turned away, and walked out.

"Citizens of the New Republic—"

The door slid closed behind him. He heard no more. In that, he was one of the few.

At the moment the broadcast began, a late meeting was under way in the office wing of the president's residence. Behn-kihl-nahm, Admiral Ackbar, Admiral Drayson, Leia, and Han were painstakingly crafting an announcement about the Yevethan massacres, and a strategy to guide them after its release in the morning.

They had just broken a deadlock over how to handle Plat Mallar's involvement—Leia was determined not to exploit him, and carried the argument—when all four datapads on the table began to chirp warning signals.

"Channel One," Leia said, silencing her alarm. "Did any of you—"

"No," said Ackbar.

"Absolutely not," said Behn-kihl-nahm.

"Then who?" asked Drayson.

"I've got a bad feeling about this," Han said darkly.

The holomonitor on the end wall came on by itself for a Channel 1 dispatch. "Citizens of the New Republic," said the image of Nil Spaar. "I beg your indulgence for this intrusion, and I apologize for the unhappy news I must bring you."

Behn-kihl-nahm flushed in an angry red. "If any member of the Senate has had any part in this—"

"Quiet," Drayson said sharply.

"I am the viceroy of the Duskhan League, a free federation of Yevetha worlds in what you call the Koornacht Cluster," said Nil Spaar. "I have come to you a second time to tell you of events far from your homeworlds, and warn you of a danger very close at hand.

"Two days ago, the forces of the Yevethan Protectorate successfully thwarted a deadly plot against our people and our way of life. The plot involved inhabitants of three planets—"

"Three?" said Behn-kihl-nahm. "They can't count *or* tell the truth."

"—located near the boundaries of our territory. These outsiders, whom we had generously allowed to settle on Yevethan soil, betrayed our trust and hospitality. All were discovered to be secretly assisting our enemies prepare for an invasion.

"We have escaped the immediate danger. We acted swiftly and forcefully in our defense, and we make no apology for doing so. All those responsible have been executed for their crimes—"

"Great stars," said Ackbar. "He's claiming *credit* for the massacres."

"—but you, the homeworlds, remain in danger. Because the plot against us was hatched on Coruscant, by a new generation of warlords. *They* are our enemies—not because we wish it, but because they have chosen it.

"They are your enemies as well. They hide their faces and their evils behind a cloak of open government. Do not underestimate their perfidy. A New Empire is being born, led by a child of the old Empire. Your dream has been betrayed. You have placed your trust in immoral and deceitful leaders.

"I accuse President Princess Leia Organa Solo of high crimes against her office, and against my people.

"Even now, after her conspiracy has been revealed, she threatens us. Warships of the New Empire are in Farlax at this very moment, seeking to compel my silence and our submission. She covets our wealth, and fears our independence.

"But know this—the Yevetha will never bow our necks to this woman and her hired killers. We will resist her predations to the fullest measure. Her spies and conspirators know that now. Her generals will know it soon. We will resist, and we will prevail.

"We regret the deaths which have already transpired. But they are on *her* hands, and the hands of those who serve her without question. We have the right to protect ourselves. We will never accept the authority of the Coruscant warlords over our dominion. And we will not tolerate the daughter of Vader meddling in our affairs.

"If you do not renounce her, and you will not restrain her, then be prepared for war."

ABOUT THE AUTHOR

MICHAEL P. KUBE-MCDOWELL* is the pen name of Philadelphia-born novelist Michael Paul McDowell. His highly praised works include the star-spanning 1985 Philip K. Dick Award finalist *Emprise* and the evocative 1991 Hugo Award nominee *The Quiet Pools*.

In addition to his eight previous novels, Michael has contributed more than two dozen short stories to leading magazines and anthologies, including *Analog, The Magazine of Fantasy & Science Fiction, After the Flames,* and *Alternate Warriors*. Three of his stories have been adapted as episodes of the horror-fantasy television series *Tales from the Darkside*. He is the author of more than five hundred nonfiction articles on subjects ranging from "scientific creationism" to the U.S. space program.

A popular guest at SF conventions, Michael is also a member of the cheerfully amateur folk-rock group The Black Book Band, in which he plays guitar, keyboards, and viola. A live album, *First Contact,* was released in 1995 by Dodeka Records.

Michael resides in central Michigan with artist and modelmaker Gwen Zak, children Matt and Amanda, cats Doc and Captain, and "entirely too many books." At various times he has called Fairview Village (Camden), New Jersey; East Lansing, Sturgis, and Lansing, Michigan; and Goshen, Indiana, home.

*"Kube" is pronounced "CUE-bee."

The World of STAR WARS Novels

In May 1991, STAR WARS caused a sensation with the Bantam release of Timothy Zahn's novel *Heir to the Empire*. For the first time, Lucasfilm Ltd. had authorized new novels that *continued* the famous story told in George Lucas's three blockbuster motion pictures *Star Wars, The Empire Strikes Back,* and *Return of the Jedi.* Reader reaction was immediate and tumultuous. Since then, each Bantam STAR WARS novel has been an instant national bestseller.

Lucasfilm and Bantam decided that future novels in the series would be interconnected: that is, events in one novel would have consequences in the others. You might say that each Bantam STAR WARS novel, enjoyable on its own, is also part of a much larger tale.

THE TRUCE AT BAKURA by Kathy Tyers
Setting: Immediately after *Return of the Jedi*

The day after his climactic battle with Emperor Palpatine and the sacrifice of his father, Darth Vader, who died saving his life, Luke Skywalker helps recover an Imperial drone ship bearing a startling message intended for the Emperor. It is a distress signal from the far-off Imperial outpost of Bakura, which is under attack by an alien invasion force, the Ssi-ruuk. Leia sees a rescue mission as an opportunity to achieve a diplomatic victory for the Rebel Alliance, even if it means fighting alongside former Imperials. But Luke receives a vision from Obi-Wan Kenobi revealing that the stakes are even higher: the invasion at Bakura threatens everything the Rebels have won at such great cost.

Here is a scene showing the extent of the alien menace:

On an outer deck of a vast battle cruiser called the *Shriwirr,* Dev Sibwarra rested his slim brown hand on a prisoner's left shoulder. "It'll be all right," he said softly. The other human's fear beat at his mind like a three-tailed lash. "There's no pain. You have a wonderful surprise ahead of you." Wonderful indeed, a life without hunger, cold, or selfish desire.

The prisoner, an Imperial of much lighter complexion than Dev, slumped in the entechment chair. He'd given up protesting, and his breath came in gasps. Pliable bands secured his forelimbs, neck, and knees—but only for balance. With his nervous system deionized at the shoulders, he couldn't struggle. A slender intravenous tube dripped pale blue magnetizing solution into each of his carotid arteries while tiny servopumps hummed. It only took a few mils of magsol to attune the tiny, fluctuating electromagnetic fields of human brain waves to the Ssi-ruuvi entenchment apparatus.

Behind Dev, Master Firwirrung trilled a question in Ssi-ruuvi. "Is it calmed yet?"

Dev sketched a bow to his master and switched from human speech to Ssi-ruuvi. "Calm enough," he sang back. "He's almost ready."

Sleek, russet scales protected Firwirrung's two-meter length from beaked muzzle to muscular tail tip, and a prominent black V crest marked his forehead. Not large for a Ssi-ruu, he was still growing, with only a few age-scores where scales had begun to separate on his handsome chest. Firwirrung swung a broad, glowing white metal catchment arc down to cover the prisoner from midchest to nose. Dev could just peer over it and watch the man's pupils dilate. At any moment . . .

"Now," Dev announced.

Firwirrung touched a control. His muscular tail twitched with pleasure. The fleet's capture had been good today. Alongside his master, Dev would work far into the night. Before entenchment, prisoners were noisy and dangerous. Afterward, their life energies powered droids of Ssi-ruuvi choosing.

The catchment arc hummed up to pitch. Dev backed away. Inside that round human skull, a magsol-drugged brain was losing control. Though Master Firwirrung assured him that the transfer of incorporeal energy was painless, every prisoner screamed.

As did this one, when Firwirrung threw the catchment arc switch. The arc boomed out a sympathetic vibration, as brain energy leaped to an electromagnet perfectly attuned to magsol. Through the Force rippled an ululation of indescribable anguish.

Dev staggered and clung to the knowledge his masters had given him: The prisoners only thought they felt pain. *He* only thought he sensed their pain. By the time the body screamed, all of a subject's energies had jumped to the catchment arc. The screaming body already was dead.

STAR WARS: X-WING by Michael A. Stackpole
ROGUE SQUADRON [and more coming soon!]
Setting: two and a half years after *Return of the Jedi*

Inspired by X-wing, the bestselling computer game from LucasArts Entertainment Co., this exciting series chronicles the further adventures of the most feared and fearless fighting force in the galaxy. A new generation of X-wing pilots, led by Commander Wedge Antilles, is combating the remnants of the Empire still left after the events of the STAR

WARS movies. Here are novels full of explosive space action, nonstop adventure, and the special brand of wonder known as STAR WARS.

In this very early scene, young Corellian pilot Corran Horn faces a tough challenge fast enough to get his heart pounding—and this is only a simulation! [P.S.: "Whistler" is Corran's R2 astromech droid]:

The Corellian brought his proton torpedo targeting program up and locked on to the TIE. It tried to break the lock, but turbolaser fire from the *Korolev* boxed it in. Corran's heads-up display went red and he triggered the torpedo. "Scratch one eyeball."

The missile shot straight in at the fighter, but the pilot broke hard to port and away, causing the missile to overshoot the target. *Nice flying!* Corran brought his X-wing over and started down to loop in behind the TIE, but as he did so, the TIE vanished from his forward screen and reappeared in his aft arc. Yanking the stick hard to the right and pulling it back, Corran wrestled the X-wing up and to starboard, then inverted and rolled out to the left.

A laser shot jolted a tremor through the simulator's couch. *Lucky thing I had all shields aft!* Corran reinforced them with energy from his lasers, then evened them out fore and aft. Jinking the fighter right and left, he avoided laser shots coming in from behind, but they all came in far closer than he liked.

He knew Jace had been in the bomber, and Jace was the only pilot in the unit who could have stayed with him. *Except for our leader.* Corran smiled broadly. *Coming to see how good I really am, Commander Antilles? Let me give you a clinic.* "Make sure you're in there solid, Whistler, because we're going for a little ride."

Corran refused to let the R2's moan slow him down. A snap-roll brought the X-wing up on its port wing. Pulling back on the stick yanked the fighter's nose up away from the original line of flight. The TIE stayed with him, then tightened up on the arc to close distance. Corran then rolled another ninety degrees and continued the turn into a dive. Throttling back, Corran hung in the dive for three seconds, then hauled back hard on the stick and cruised up into the TIE fighter's aft.

The X-wing's laser fire missed wide to the right as the TIE cut to the left. Corran kicked his speed up to full and broke with the TIE. He let the X-wing rise above the plane of the break, then put the fighter through a twisting roll that ate up enough time to bring him again into the TIE's rear. The TIE snapped to the right and Corran looped out left.

He watched the tracking display as the distance between them grew to be a kilometer and a half, then slowed. *Fine, you want to go nose to nose? I've got shields and you don't.* If Commander Antilles wanted to commit virtual suicide, Corran was happy to oblige him. He tugged the stick back to his sternum and rolled out in an inversion loop. *Coming at you!*

The two starfighters closed swiftly. Corran centered his foe in the crosshairs and waited for a dead shot. Without shields the TIE fighter would die with one burst, and Corran wanted the kill to be clean. His HUD flicked green as the TIE juked in and out of the center, then locked green as they closed.

The TIE started firing at maximum range and scored hits. At that distance the lasers did no real damage against the shields, prompting Corran to wonder why Wedge was wasting the energy. Then, as the HUD's green color started to flicker, realization dawned. *The bright bursts on the shields are a distraction to my targeting! I better kill him* now!

Corran tightened down on the trigger button, sending red laser needles stabbing out at the closing TIE fighter. He couldn't tell if he had hit anything. Lights flashed in the cockpit and Whistler started screeching furiously. Corran's main monitor went black, his shields were down, and his weapons controls were dead.

The pilot looked left and right. "Where is he, Whistler?"

The monitor in front of him flickered to life and a diagnostic report began to scroll by. Bloodred bordered the damage reports. "Scanners, out; lasers, out; shields, out; engine, out! I'm a wallowing Hutt just hanging here in space."

THE COURTSHIP OF PRINCESS LEIA
by Dave Wolverton
Setting: Four years after *Return of the Jedi*

One of the most interesting developments in Bantam's Star Wars novels is that in their storyline, Han Solo and Princess Leia start a family. This tale reveals how the couple originally got together. Wishing to strengthen the fledgling New Republic by bringing in powerful allies, Leia opens talks with the Hapes consortium of more than sixty worlds. But the consortium is ruled by the Queen Mother, who, to Han's dismay, wants Leia to marry her son, Prince Isolder. Before this action-packed story is over, Luke will join forces with Isolder against a group of Force-trained "witches" and face a deadly foe.

In this scene, Luke is searching for Jedi lore and finds more than he bargained for:

Luke popped the cylinder into Artoo, and almost immediately Artoo caught a signal. Images flashed in the air before the droid: an ancient throne room where, one by one, Jedi came before their high master to give reports. Yet the holo was fragmented, so thoroughly erased that Luke got only bits and pieces—a blue-skinned man describing details of a grueling space battle against pirateers; a yellow-eyed Twi'lek with lashing headtails who told of discovering a plot to kill an ambassador. A date and time flashed on the holo vid before each report. The report was nearly four hundred standard years old.

Then Yoda appeared on the video, gazing up at the throne. His color was more vibrantly green than Luke remembered, and he did not use his walking stick. At middle age, Yoda had looked almost perky, carefree—not the bent, troubled old Jedi Luke had known. Most of the audio was erased, but through the background hiss Yoda clearly said, "We tried to free the Chu'unthor from Dathomir, but were repulsed by the witches ... skirmish, with Masters Gra'aton and Vulatan. ... Fourteen acolytes killed ... go back to retrieve ..." The audio hissed away, and soon the holo image dissolved to blue static with popping lights.

They went up topside, found that night had fallen while they worked underground. Their Whiphid guide soon returned, dragging the body of a gutted snow demon. The demon's white talons curled in the air, and its long purple tongue snaked out from between its massive fangs. Luke was amazed that the Whiphid could haul such a monster, yet the Whiphid held the demon's long hairy tail in one hand and managed to pull it back to camp.

There, Luke stayed the night with the Whiphids in a huge shelter made from the rib cage of a motmot, covered over with hides to keep out the wind. The Whiphids built a bonfire and roasted the snow demon, and the young danced while the elders played their claw harps. As Luke sat, watching the writhing flames and listening to the twang of harps, he meditated. "The future you will see, and the past. Old friends long forgotten ..." Those were the words Yoda had said long ago while training Luke to peer beyond the mists of time.

Luke looked up at the rib bones of the motmot. The Whiphids had carved stick letters into the bone, ten and twelve meters in the air, giving the lineage of their ancestors. Luke could not read the letters, but they seemed to dance in the firelight, as if they were sticks and stones falling from the sky. The rib bones curved toward him, and Luke followed the curve of bones with his eyes. The tumbling sticks and boulders seemed to gyrate, all of them falling toward him as if they would crush him. He could see boulders hurtling through the air, too, smashing toward him. Luke's nostrils flared, and even Toola's chill could not keep a thin film of perspiration from dotting his forehead. A vision came to Luke then.

Luke stood in a mountain fortress of stone, looking over a plain with a sea of dark forested hills beyond, and a storm rose—a magnificent wind that brought with it towering walls of black clouds and dust, trees hurtling toward him and twisting through the sky. The clouds thundered overhead, filled with purple flames, obliterating all sunlight, and Luke could feel a malevolence hidden in those clouds and knew that they had been raised through the power of the dark side of the Force.

Dust and stones whistled through the air like autumn leaves. Luke tried to hold on to the stone parapet overlooking the plain to keep from being swept from the fortress walls. Winds pounded in his ears like the roar of an ocean, howling.

It was as if a storm of pure dark Force raged over the countryside, and suddenly, amid the towering clouds of darkness that thundered toward him, Luke could hear laughing, the sweet sound of women laughing. He looked above into the dark clouds, and saw the women borne through the air along with the rocks and debris, like motes of dust, laughing. A voice seemed to whisper, "the witches of Dathomir."

HEIR TO THE EMPIRE
DARK FORCE RISING
THE LAST COMMAND
by Timothy Zahn
Setting: Five years after *Return of the Jedi*

This #1 bestselling trilogy introduces two legendary forces of evil into the Star Wars *literary pantheon. Grand Admiral Thrawn has taken control of the Imperial fleet in the years since the destruction of the Death Star, and the mysterious Joruus C'baoth is a fearsome Jedi Master who has been seduced by the dark side. Han and Leia have now been married for about a year, and as the story begins, she is pregnant with twins. Thrawn's plan is to crush the Rebellion and resurrect the Empire's New Order with C'baoth's help—and in return, the Dark Master will get Han and Leia's Jedi children to mold as he wishes. For as readers of this magnificent trilogy will see, Luke Skywalker is not the last of the old Jedi. He is the first of the new.*

In this scene from Heir to the Empire, *Thrawn and C'baoth meet for the first time:*

For a long moment the old man continued to stare at Thrawn, a dozen strange expressions flicking in quick succession across his face. "Come. We will talk."

"Thank you," Thrawn said, inclining his head slightly. "May I ask who we have the honor of addressing?"

"Of course." The old man's face was abruptly regal again, and when he spoke his voice rang out in the silence of the crypt. "I am the Jedi Master Joruus C'baoth."

Pellaeon inhaled sharply, a cold shiver running up his back. "Joruus C'baoth?" he breathed. "But—"

He broke off. C'baoth looked at him, much as Pellaeon himself might look at a junior officer who has spoken out of turn. "Come," he repeated, turning back to Thrawn. "We will talk."

He led the way out of the crypt and back into the sunshine. Several small knots of people had gathered in the square in their absence, huddling well back from both the crypt and the shuttle as they whispered nervously together.

With one exception. Standing directly in their path a few meters away was one of the two guards C'baoth had ordered out of the crypt. On his face was an expression of barely controlled fury; in his hands, cocked and ready, was his crossbow. "You destroyed his home," C'baoth said, almost conversationally. "Doubtless he would like to exact vengeance."

The words were barely out of his mouth when the guard suddenly snapped the crossbow up and fired. Instinctively, Pellaeon ducked, raising his blaster—

And three meters from the Imperials the bolt came to an abrupt halt in midair.

Pellaeon stared at the hovering piece of wood and metal, his brain only slowly catching up with what had just happened. "They are our guests," C'baoth told the guard in a voice clearly intended to reach everyone in the square. "They will be treated accordingly."

With a crackle of splintering wood, the crossbow bolt shattered, the pieces dropping to the ground. Slowly, reluctantly, the guard lowered his crossbow, his eyes still burning with a now impotent rage. Thrawn let him stand there another second like that, then gestured to Rukh. The Noghri raised his blaster and fired—

And in a blur of motion almost too fast to see, a flat stone detached itself from the ground and hurled itself directly into the path of the shot, shattering spectacularly as the blast hit it.

Thrawn spun to face C'baoth, his face a mirror of surprise and anger. "C'baoth—!"

"These are *my* people, Grand Admiral Thrawn," the other cut him off, his voice forged from quiet steel. "Not yours; mine. If there is punishment to be dealt out, *I* will do it."

For a long moment the two men again locked eyes. Then, with an obvious effort, Thrawn regained his composure. "Of course, Master C'baoth," he said. "Forgive me."

C'baoth nodded. "Better. Much better." He looked past Thrawn, dismissed the guard with a nod. "Come," he said, looking back at the Grand Admiral. "We will talk."

The Jedi Academy Trilogy:
JEDI SEARCH
DARK APPRENTICE
CHAMPIONS OF THE FORCE
by Kevin J. Anderson
Setting: Seven years after *Return of the Jedi*

In order to assure the continuation of the Jedi Knights, Luke Skywalker has decided to start a training facility: a Jedi Academy. He will gather Force-sensitive students who show potential as prospective Jedi and serve as their mentor, as Jedi Masters Obi-Wan Kenobi and Yoda did for him. Han and Leia's twins are now toddlers, and there is a third Jedi child: the infant Anakin, named after Luke and Leia's father. In this trilogy, we discover the existence of a powerful Imperial doomsday weapon, the horrifying Sun Crusher—which will soon become the centerpiece of a titanic struggle between Luke Skywalker and his most brilliant Jedi Academy student, who is delving dangerously into the dark side.

In this scene from the first novel, Jedi Search, *Luke vocalizes his concept of a new Jedi order to a distinguished assembly of New Republic leaders:*

As he descended the long ramp, Luke felt all eyes turn toward him. A hush fell over the assembly. Luke Skywalker, the lone remaining Jedi Master, almost never took part in governmental proceedings.

"I have an important matter to address," he said.

Mon Mothma gave him a soft, mysterious smile and gestured for him to take a central position. "The words of a Jedi Knight are always welcome to the New Republic," she said.

Luke tried not to look pleased. She had provided the perfect opening for him. "In the Old Republic," he said, "Jedi Knights were the protectors and guardians of all. For a thousand generations the Jedi used the powers of the Force to guide, defend, and provide support for the rightful government of worlds—before the dark days of the Empire came, and the Jedi Knights were killed."

He let his words hang, then took another breath. "Now we have a New Republic. The Empire appears to be defeated. We have founded a new government based upon the old, but let us hope we learn from our mistakes. Before, an entire order of Jedi watched over the Republic, offering strength. Now I am the only Jedi Master who remains.

"Without that order of protectors to provide a backbone of strength for the New Republic, can we survive? Will we be able to weather the storms and the difficulties of forging a new union? Until now we have suffered severe struggles—but in the future they will be seen as nothing more than birth pangs."

Before the other senators could disagree with that, Luke continued. "Our people had a common foe in the Empire, and we must not let our defenses lapse just because we have internal problems. More to the point, what will happen when we begin squabbling among ourselves over petty matters? The old Jedi helped to mediate many types of disputes. What if there are no Jedi Knights to protect us in the difficult times ahead?

"My sister is undergoing Jedi training. She has a great deal of skill in the Force. Her three children are also likely candidates to be trained as young Jedi. In recent years I have come to know a woman named Mara Jade, who is now unifying the smugglers—the former smugglers," he amended, "into an organization that can support the needs of the New Republic. She also has a talent for the Force. I have encountered others in my travels."

Another pause. The audience was listening so far. "But are these the only ones? We already know that the ability to use the Force is passed from generation to generation. Most of the Jedi were killed in the Emperor's purge—but could he possibly have eradicated all of the descendants of those Knights? I myself was unaware of the potential power within me until Obi-Wan Kenobi taught me how to use it. My sister Leia was similarly unaware.

"How many people are abroad in this galaxy who have a comparable strength in the Force, who are potential members of a new order of Jedi Knights, but are unaware of who they are?"

Luke looked at them again. "In my brief search I have already discovered that there are indeed some descendants of former Jedi. I have come here to ask"—he turned to gesture toward Mon Mothma, swept his hands across the people gathered there in the chamber— "for two things.

"First, that the New Republic officially sanction my search for those with a hidden talent for the Force, to seek them out and try to bring them to our service. For this I will need some help."

"And what will you yourself be doing?" Mon Mothma asked, shifting in her robes.

"I've already found several candidates I wish to investigate. All

I ask right now is that you agree this is something we should pursue, that the search for Jedi be conducted by others and not just myself."

Mon Mothma sat up straighter in her central seat. "I think we can agree to that without further discussion." She looked around to the other senators, seeing them now in agreement. "Tell us your second request."

Luke stood taller. This was most important to him. He saw Leia stiffen.

"If sufficient candidates are found who have potential for using the Force, I wish to be allowed—with the New Republic's blessing—to establish in some appropriate place an intensive training center, a Jedi academy, if you will. Under my direction we can help these students discover their abilities, to focus and strengthen their power. Ultimately, this academy would provide a core group that could allow us to restore the Jedi Knights as protectors of the New Republic."

CHILDREN OF THE JEDI by Barbara Hambly
Setting: Eight years after *Return of the Jedi*

The Star Wars *characters face a menace from the glory days of the Empire when a thirty-year-old automated Imperial Dreadnaught comes to life and begins its grim mission: to gather forces and annihilate a long-forgotten stronghold of Jedi children. When Luke is whisked onboard, he begins to communicate with the brave Jedi Knight who paralyzed the ship decades ago, and gave her life in the process. Now she is part of the vessel, existing in its artificial intelligence core, and guiding Luke through one of the most unusual adventures he has ever had.*

In this scene, Luke discovers that an evil presence is gathering, one that will force him to join the battle:

Like See-Threepio, Nichos Marr sat in the outer room of the suite to which Cray had been assigned, in the power-down mode that was the droid equivalent of rest. Like Threepio, at the sound of Luke's almost noiseless tread he turned his head, aware of his presence.

"Luke?" Cray had equipped him with the most sensitive vocal modulators, and the word was calibrated to a whisper no louder than the rustle of the blueleaves massed outside the windows. He rose, and crossed to where Luke stood, the dull silver of his arms and shoulders a phantom gleam in the stray flickers of light. "What is it?"

"I don't know." They retreated to the small dining area where Luke had earlier probed his mind, and Luke stretched up to pin back a corner of the lamp-sheath, letting a slim triangle of butter-colored light fall on the purple of the vulwood tabletop. "A dream. A premonition, maybe." It was on his lips to ask, *Do you dream?* but he remembered the ghastly, imageless darkness in Nichos's mind, and didn't. He wasn't sure if his pupil was aware of the difference from his human perception and knowledge, aware of just exactly what he'd lost when his consciousness, his self, had been transferred.

In the morning Luke excused himself from the expedition Tomla El had organized with Nichos and Cray to the Falls of Dessiar, one of the places on Ithor most renowned for its beauty and peace. When they left he sought out Umwaw Moolis, and the tall herd leader listened gravely to his less than logical request and promised to put matters in train to fulfill it. Then Luke descended to the House of the Healers, where Drub McKumb lay, sedated far beyond pain but with all the perceptions of agony and nightmare still howling in his mind.

"Kill you!" He heaved himself at the restraints, blue eyes glaring furiously as he groped and scrabbled at Luke with his clawed hands. "It's all poison! I see you! I see the dark light all around you! You're him! You're him!" His back bent like a bow; the sound of his shrieking was like something being ground out of him by an infernal mangle.

Luke had been through the darkest places of the universe and of his own mind, had done and experienced greater evil than perhaps any man had known on the road the Force had dragged him . . . Still, it was hard not to turn away.

"We even tried yarrock on him last night," explained the Healer in charge, a slightly built Ithorian beautifully tabby-striped green and yellow under her simple tabard of purple linen. "But apparently the earlier doses that brought him enough lucidity to reach here from his point of origin oversensitized his system. We'll try again in four or five days."

Luke gazed down into the contorted, grimacing face.

"As you can see," the Healer said, "the internal perception of pain and fear is slowly lessening. It's down to ninety-three percent of what it was when he was first brought in. Not much, I know, but something."

"Him! *Him! HIM!*" Foam spattered the old man's stained gray beard.

Who?

"I wouldn't advise attempting any kind of mindlink until it's at least down to fifty percent, Master Skywalker."

"No," said Luke softly.

Kill you all. And, *They are gathering . . .*

"Do you have recordings of everything he's said?"

"Oh, yes." The big coppery eyes blinked assent. "The transcript is available through the monitor cubicle down the hall. We could make nothing of them. Perhaps they will mean something to you."

They didn't. Luke listened to them all, the incoherent groans and screams, the chewed fragments of words that could be only guessed at, and now and again the clear disjointed cries: "Solo! Solo! Can you hear me? Children . . . Evil . . . Gathering here . . . Kill you all!"

DARKSABER by Kevin J. Anderson
Setting: Immediately thereafter

Not long after Children of the Jedi, *Luke and Han learn that evil Hutts are building a reconstruction of the original Death Star—and that the Empire is still alive, in the form of Daala, who has joined forces with Pellaeon, former second in command to the feared Grand Admiral Thrawn. In this early scene, Luke has returned to the home of Obi-Wan Kenobi on Tatooine to try and consult a long-gone mentor:*

He stood anxious and alone, feeling like a prodigal son outside the ramshackle, collapsed hut that had once been the home of Obi-Wan Kenobi.

Luke swallowed and stepped forward, his footsteps crunching in the silence. He had not been here in many years. The door had fallen off its hinges; part of the clay front wall had fallen in. Boulders and crumbled adobe jammed the entrance. A pair of small, screeching desert rodents snapped at him and fled for cover; Luke ignored them.

Gingerly, he ducked low and stepped into the home of his first mentor.

Luke stood in the middle of the room breathing deeply, turning around, trying to sense the presence he desperately needed to see. This was the place where Obi-Wan Kenobi had told Luke of the Force. Here, the old man had first given Luke his lightsaber and hinted at the truth about his father, "from a certain point of view," dispelling the diversionary story that Uncle Owen had told, at the same time planting seeds of his own deceptions.

"Ben," he said and closed his eyes, calling out with his mind as well as his voice. He tried to penetrate the invisible walls of the Force and reach to the luminous being of Obi-Wan Kenobi who had visited him numerous times, before saying he could never speak with Luke again.

"Ben, I need you," Luke said. Circumstances had changed. He could think of no other way past the obstacles he faced. Obi-Wan had to answer. It wouldn't take long, but it could give him the key he needed with all his heart.

Luke paused and listened and sensed—

But felt nothing. If he could not summon Obi-Wan's spirit here in the empty dwelling where the old man had lived in exile for so many years, Luke didn't believe he could find his former teacher ever again.

He echoed the words Leia had used more than a decade earlier, beseeching him, "Help me, Obi-Wan Kenobi," Luke whispered, "you're my only hope."

THE CRYSTAL STAR by Vonda N. McIntyre
Setting: Ten years after *Return of the Jedi*

Leia's three children have been kidnapped. That horrible fact is made worse by Leia's realization that she can no longer sense her children through the Force! While she, Artoo-Detoo, and Chewbacca trail the kidnappers, Luke and Han discover a planet that is suffering strange quantum effects from a nearby star. Slowly freezing into a perfect crystal and disrupting the Force, the star is blunting Luke's power and crippling the Millennium Falcon. *These strands converge in an apocalyptic threat not only to the fate of the New Republic, but to the universe itself.*

Here is Luke and Han's initial approach to the crystal star:

Han piloted the *Millennium Falcon* through the strangest star system he had ever approached. An ancient, dying, crystallizing white dwarf star orbited a black hole in a wildly eccentric elliptical path.

Eons ago, in this place, a small and ordinary yellow star peacefully orbited an immense blue-white supergiant. The blue star aged, and collapsed.

The blue star went supernova, blasting light and radiation and debris out into space.

Its light still traveled through the universe, a furious explosion visible from distant galaxies.

Over time, the remains of the supergiant's core collapsed under the force of its own gravity. The result was degenerate mass: a black hole.

The violence of the supernova disrupted the orbit of the nova's companion, the yellow star. Over time, the yellow star's orbit decayed.

The yellow star fell toward the unimaginably dense body of the black hole. The black hole sucked up anything, even light, that came within its grasp. And when it captured matter—even an entire yellow star—it ripped the atoms apart into a glowing accretion disk. Subatomic particles imploded downward into the singularity's equator, emitting great bursts of radiation. The accretion disk spun at a fantastic speed, glowing with fantastic heat, creating a funeral pyre for the destroyed yellow companion.

The plasma spiraled in a raging pinwheel, circling so fast and heating so intensely that it blasted X rays out into space. Then, finally, the glowing gas fell toward the invisible black hole, approaching it closer and closer, appearing to fall more and more slowly as relativity influenced it.

It was lost forever to this universe.

That was the fate of the small yellow star.

The system contained a third star: the dying white dwarf, which shone with ancient heat even as it froze into a quantum crystal. Now, as the *Millennium Falcon* entered the system, the white dwarf was falling toward the black hole, on the inward curve of its eccentric elliptical orbit.

"Will you look at that," Han said. "Quite a show."

"Indeed it is, Master Han," Threepio said, "but it is merely a shadow of what will occur when the black hole captures the crystal star."

Luke gazed silently into the maelstrom of the black hole.

Han waited.

"Hey, kid! Snap out of it."

Luke started. "What?"

"I don't know where you were, but you weren't here."

"Just thinking about the Jedi Academy. I hate to leave my students, even for a few days. But if I *do* find other trained Jedi, it'll make a big difference. To the Academy. To the New Republic . . ."

"I think we're getting along pretty well already," Han said, irked. He had spent years maintaining the peace with ordinary people. In his opinion, Jedi Knights could cause more trouble than they were worth. "And what if these are all using the dark side?"

Luke did not reply.

Han seldom admitted his nightmares, but he had nightmares about what could happen to his children if they were tempted to the dark side.

Solar prominences flared from the white dwarf's surface. The *Falcon* passed it, heading toward the more perilous region of the black hole.

The Corellian Trilogy:
AMBUSH AT CORELLIA
ASSAULT AT SELONIA

SHOWDOWN AT CENTERPOINT
by Roger MacBride Allen
Setting: Fourteen years after *Return of the Jedi*

This trilogy takes us to Corellia, Han Solo's homeworld, which Han has not visited in quite some time. A trade summit brings Han, Leia, and the children—now developing their own clear personalities and instinctively learning more about their innate skills in the Force—into the middle of a situation that most closely resembles a burning fuse. The Corellian system is on the brink of civil war, there are New Republic intelligence agents on a mysterious mission which even Han does not understand, and worst of all, a fanatical rebel leader has his hands on a superweapon of unimaginable power—and just wait until you find out who that leader is!

Here is an early scene from Ambush *that gives you a wonderful look at the growing Solo children (the twins are Jacen and Jaina, and their little brother is Anakin):*

Anakin plugged the board into the innards of the droid and pressed a button. The droid's black, boxy body shuddered awake, it drew in its wheels to stand up a bit taller, its status lights lit, and it made a sort of triple beep. "That's good," he said, and pushed the button again. The droid's status lights went out, and its body slumped down again. Anakin picked up the next piece, a motivation actuator. He frowned at it as he turned it over in his hands. He shook his head. "That's *not* good," he announced.

"What's not good?" Jaina asked.

"This thing," Anakin said, handing her the actuator. "Can't you *tell*? The insides part is all melty."

Jaina and Jacen exchanged a look. "The outside looks okay," Jaina said, giving the part to her brother. "How can he tell what the *inside* of it looks like? It's sealed shut when they make it."

Anakin, still sitting on the floor, took the device from his brother and frowned at it again. He turned it over and over in his hands, and then held it over his head and looked at it as if he were holding it up to the light. "There," he said, pointing a chubby finger at one point on the unmarked surface. "In there is the bad part." He rearranged himself to sit cross-legged, put the actuator in his lap, and put his right index finger over the "bad" part. "Fix," he said. "Fix." The dark brown outer case of the actuator seemed to glow for a second with an odd blue-red light, but then the glow sputtered out and Anakin pulled his finger away quickly and stuck it in his mouth, as if he had burned it on something.

"Better now?" Jaina asked.

"*Some* better," Anakin said, pulling his finger out of his mouth. "Not *all* better." He took the actuator in his hand and stood up. He opened the access panel on the broken droid and plugged in the actuator. He closed the door and looked expectantly at his older brother and sister.

"Done?" Jaina asked.

"Done," Anakin agreed. "But *I'm* not going to push the button." He backed well away from the droid, sat down on the floor, and folded his arms.

Jacen looked at his sister.

"Not me," she said. "This was your idea."

Jacen stepped forward to the droid, reached out to push the power button from as far away as he could, and then stepped hurriedly back.

Once again, the droid shuddered awake, rattling a bit this time as it did so. It pulled its wheels in, lit its panel lights, and made the same triple beep. But then its holocam eye viewlens wobbled back and forth, and its panel lights dimmed and flared. It rolled backward just a bit, and then recovered itself.

"Good morning, young mistress and masters," it said. "How may I surge you?"

Well, one word wrong, but so what? Jacen grinned and clapped his hands and rubbed them together eagerly. "Good day, droid," he said. They had done it! But what to ask for first? "First tidy up this room," he said. A simple task, and one that ought to serve as a good test of what this droid could do.

Suddenly the droid's overhead access door blew off and there was a flash of light from its interior. A thin plume of smoke drifted out of the droid. Its panel lights flared again, and then the work arm sagged downward. The droid's body, softened by heat, sagged in on itself and drooped to the floor. The floor and walls and ceilings of the playroom were supposed to be fireproof, but nonetheless the floor under the droid darkened a bit, and the ceiling turned black. The ventilators kicked on high automatically, and drew the smoke out of the room. After a moment they shut themselves off, and the room was silent.

The three children stood, every bit as frozen to the spot as the droid was, absolutely stunned. It was Anakin who recovered first. He walked cautiously toward the droid and looked at it carefully, being sure not to get too close or touch it. "*Really* melty now," he announced, and then wandered off to the other side of the room to play with his blocks.

The twins looked at the droid, and then at each other.

"We're dead," Jacen announced, surveying the wreckage.